TIGERS
IN BLUE

Also by Richard Buxton

Whirligig (Book 1 of Shire's Union)
The Copper Road (Book 2 of Shire's Union)

TIGERS IN BLUE

THE CONSTANT PROMISE

RICHARD BUXTON

OCOEE PUBLISHING

First published 2023 by Ocoee Publishing
www.richardbuxton.net

ISBN Paperback 978-0-9957693-7-3
eBook 978-0-9957693-8-0

British Library Cataloguing in Publication Data
A CIP catalogue record for this book is available from the British
Library.

Cover art by Phil Williams
Typesetting by Phil Williams

For Major Jeff Houston

Richard lives with his family in the South Downs, Sussex, England. He completed an MA in Creative Writing at Chichester University in 2014. He has an abiding relationship with America, having studied at Syracuse University, New York State, in the late eighties. His short stories have won the Exeter Story Prize, the Bedford International Writing Competition and the Nivalis Short Story Award.

Richard's first novel, *Whirligig*, was published in 2017 and shortlisted for the Rubery International Book Award. His second novel, *The Copper Road*, was a finalist in the 2020 Wishing Shelf Book Award. To learn more about Richard's writing visit www.richardbuxton.net.

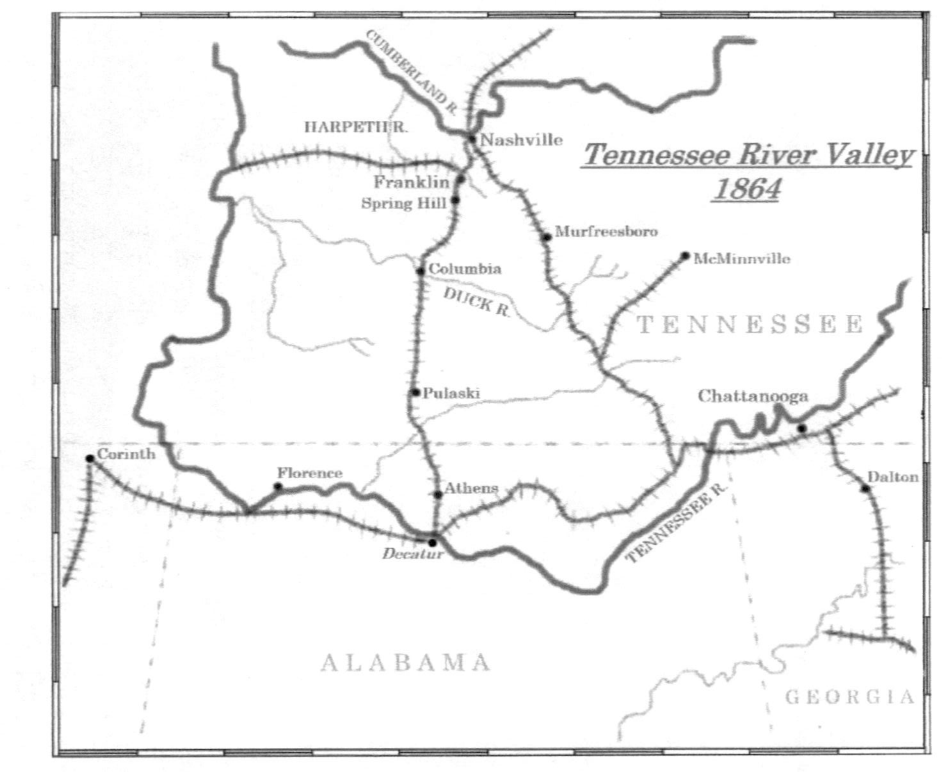

CUMBERLAND R.
HARPETH R.
Nashville
Tennessee River Valley
1864
Franklin
Spring Hill
Murfreesboro
McMinnville
Columbia
DUCK R.
TENNESSEE
Pulaski
Chattanooga
Corinth
Florence
Athens
Dalton
TENNESSEE R.
Decatur
ALABAMA
GEORGIA

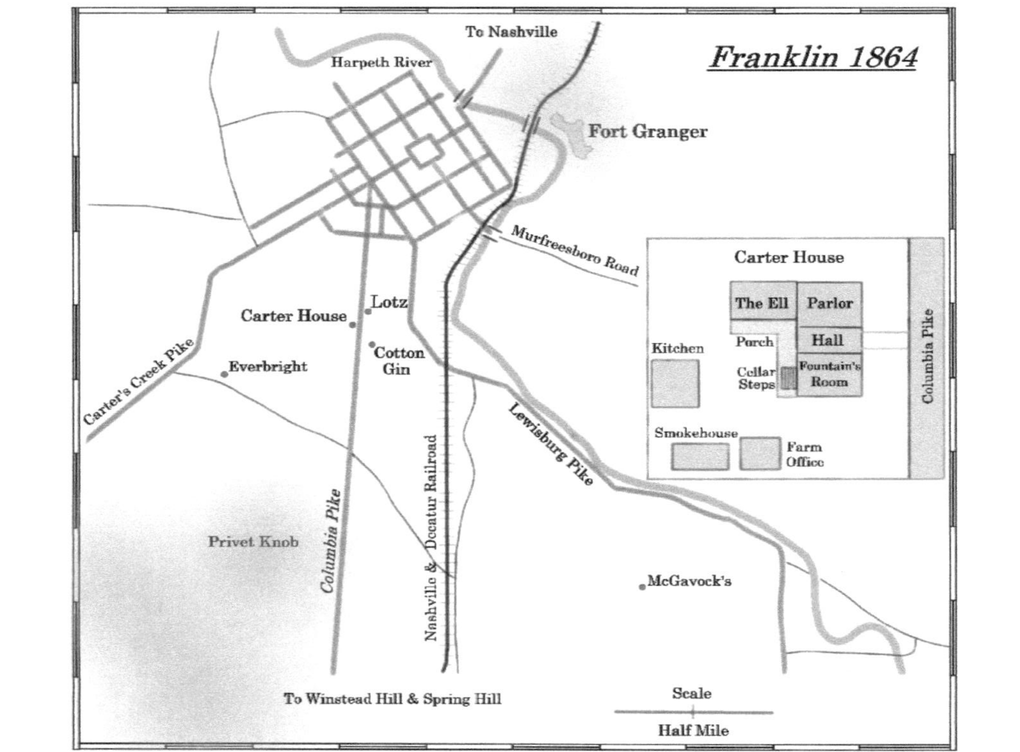

Franklin 1864
To Nashville
Harpeth River
Fort Granger
Murfreesboro Road
Carter House
Lotz
Cotton Gin
Everbright
Carter's Creek Pike
Columbia Pike
Privet Knob
Nashville & Decatur Railroad
Lewisburg Pike
McGavock's
To Winstead Hill & Spring Hill
Scale
Half Mile
Carter House
Columbia Pike
The Ell
Parlor
Hall
Fountain's Room
Porch
Cellar Steps
Kitchen
Smokehouse
Farm Office

PART I

Chickamauga, Georgia – October, 1864

The single dry snap beneath Shire's foot was at odds with the softer crack and splinter of twigs. Like breaking chalk. He froze and looked down. His muddy army shoe lay square across what looked like a shinbone. His mind started to form an apology, but it failed to reach his lips.

Ocks would grin to see him standing here, suddenly too nervous to go forward. Last night around the campfire with the squad, the big sergeant had joked that Shire should take a walk in the woods and look for, 'that ramrod you fired with your eyes closed and your knees knocking last year. You might find it in a Rebel skeleton pinned to a tree.'

Shire had laughed with his friends; it wasn't a true story, and these days his reputation could wear a little ridicule. But he'd woken early and on edge, unsure as to why. The idea of a walk had taken root; perhaps it would help. Leaving Tuck asleep in their worn tent, he'd sat on the dewy grass to pull on his shoes, then quietly moved away from the regiment's waking coughs and smoldering campfires. Ocks, his fellow Englishman, might make fun of him, but Shire wasn't fresh to the world or this war, and certainly not to this small square of Georgia.

Chickamauga. This ground mattered to him.

The bone break, its sudden irreverence, echoed inside him and did nothing to help the disquiet he'd woken with. He stepped off the shin and looked back the way he had come. Should he retreat out of the woods and back to his army for fear of nothing but an old bone? He'd seen plenty worse in countless battles this last year; seen flesh blasted from bone, or both bloodily sawn through. So why these jitters today?

He'd fought his first battle on this ground. A full year ago. He'd lost two good friends here. The trees were scarred by bullets, the ground littered with lifeless boughs amputated by shellfire. He'd press on. He'd found the courage to do that a year ago and there was no lead flying today, no thick sulfurous smoke between the trees. He began forward again, no destination in mind, just this nameless dread for company.

His regiment was resting half a mile away down beside the creek that had gifted its name to the battle. They'd camped in the exact same spot the night before last year's fight. Coming away alone, maybe he might gain some insight, some fresh perspective on the intervening year. Perhaps that was what was bothering him, that it all seemed one big circle, whether looked at geographically, cosmologically, or through the lesser lens of his rudderless life. This summer just ended, he'd fought his way down toward Atlanta with Sherman's Army, only to be captured. A jocular fate had drawn him deep into the hills of Tennessee and back to Comrie and Clara. Comrie was now no more than ashes, and here he was, back with the 125th Ohio. Back at Chickamauga.

Clara was still alive and so was he; that was about the sum of it. It was hard to tell if anything had truly changed between them. Tuck said, how could it not have? Shire couldn't see it. But then his own feelings were the constant; nothing had changed for him. He shook his head. He didn't want to spend another long day only thinking of Clara.

He thought about his first fight here instead, struggled to reach back across the battles since to rediscover the ocean depth of fear that had all but drowned him last September. He remembered walking into the half-light of the forest, friends beside him, his rifle before him. It seemed a memory he'd borrowed from someone else, someone he barely knew.

Beneath the leaf litter, he crunched another bone but this time hurried on. That day contained a deep well of guilt to draw from, if he cared to lower the bucket. He tripped on a tree root and fell. Lifting his head from the mulch, he stared into at the wide empty sockets of a yellowing skull, so close his urgent breath disturbed a last tuft of hair. The skull, angled upward and nested in the orange and red decay of fall, stared back, a lightning-rod to his terror a year ago. The door to his memory flew wide. Shells screamed above the trees. He heard again the pitiful cries of the wounded as fire burned through the night-woods, saw wild pigs root in a day-old corpse, watched the pell-mell rout of the Union Army. He scrambled to his feet and raced away, wildly fending off low branches and undergrowth, until he broke free of the forest as if from a burning barn and stumbled out into the bright low sunlight.

'Hold up there. What you runnin' from?'

Shire stopped, put up a hand to shield himself from the sun. He saw the rifle first, the barrel at his gut. Holding it level was a soldier dressed in green.

'It's alright,' the soldier said, 'I'm Union.' He nodded toward the woods. 'What spooked you?' A moment longer, then he lifted the gun away.

Short of breath, Shire told him what he'd seen and blurted out his memories of last year.

'I'm Gideon.' The soldier said he'd fought here himself, and that certainly it was a hard memory to live with, but that defeat was way at the end of last summer and they'd won most every scrap since. 'Too many battles ahead to keep fighting those behind. You can help me hunt.' Gideon declared he needed to find a large spider's web. 'By which I mean, one put together by a large spider. The two don't always go together. I need as thick a thread as we can get.'

The curious request was enough to slow Shire's pumping heart. 'Why do you need a spider thread?'

'Crosshairs.' Gideon held up his rifle as if this was self-evident.

Shire, still half in this year and half in the last, noted the overlong barrel with almost as long a metal sight mounted above. A sharpshooter. He considered that maybe Gideon was soft in the head. There were plenty cut to less than a full shilling in this war, and Tuck had told him sharpshooters were a strange breed. Gideon wasn't waiting on an answer so together they began to quarter the bushes and the tired October grass. Looking for nothing more than cobwebs, while trying to put behind him the aftershock of the skull, Shire began to fancy he was a boy again. It wasn't an easy hunt, not this far into fall – autumn in Shire's old life – but the dew helped, strung-out as sunlit beaded treasure on what webs there were. A few birds started to sing; he couldn't recall hearing them inside the forest.

Gideon was particular, dismissing Shire's early finds. They moved on and climbed a small hill. On top was the burned-out square of a home beside a large round pond. Shire gazed out over the red and orange forest in every direction. The familiar shape of Lookout Mountain was to the north. An eagle, heavy winged and too hungry to wait on the thermals later in the day, worked hard to earn some height. Chattanooga was out of sight somewhere beyond and below.

'No spider webs in the sky.'

Shire hadn't meant to come so far from his regiment. At last, close to the pond, he found an acceptable specimen at waist height spun between two dried out thistle heads. Gideon lightly tapped off the dew, talking all the while. 'You have to possess the pinkie and skinny thumb of a pixie, or at the very least a small girlchild. Both hard to press into service out here in the wild. I'd hazard that the pixie is the more common beast.' He put his open palm against the web and delicately cut it free so it clung to his hand. They walked over to the destroyed house and found a ruined wall to sit on. Gideon worked delicately at the web with a pocket knife.

'It's impossible,' Shire said. 'No one can work with a spider's web.'

'It's like most things,' Gideon said, laying a first thread across the felt of his canteen, 'a young colt, a bloodhound pup or your last dollar. If you ain't the master of it, it'll be the master of you.'

He laid a second thread in parallel then rubbed the web from his hand. Detaching his rifle sight, he unscrewed it into two parts and gave one piece to Shire. Shire had never held one before. He closed an eye and looked down inside.

'Time for a turn later. Hold it up to me now.'

Collecting a strand from his canteen, Gideon approached slowly with his head to one side. He set the first thread across the open join of the sight. 'You have a steady hand, Private Shire. Very steady. My compliments on that.'

Shire considered that a short while ago he'd near lost his mind, yet here he was as calm as the pond. He wasn't sure it was healthy that his mood should prove so malleable. 'Will it stay attached?'

'It's a spider's web. Attachin' is what it does.' Gideon retrieved the second strand. 'Give the scope a quarter turn. That's it.' He moved in close again with his tongue out, one eye closed as if that was his most comfortable outlook on the world. 'There now. A perfect silk crosshair. It's 'propriate use for a web, don't you think?' He took the scope back. 'Spider spins it with death in mind and I just use it for bigger game.' He fitted the two halves of the sight and lightly twisted them together.

'Won't that break the thread?'

'Never seems to. Can't never figure that myself.' He looked down the sight, well satisfied. 'Last one stayed fixed for months. The silk endures whether it's a hot Georgia summer, a cold Tennessee winter or anything in-between.' He fixed the scope back onto the barrel.

'I should get back to my regiment,' Shire said.

'Are you near by the mill?'

'Yes.'

'I'll walk with you.'

Shire started down the hill but right away Gideon urgently called him back, gripped him by his arm and dragged him roughly behind the wall where they'd been sitting.

'What is it?'

'Keep your blue-self down low. Somethin' caught my eye. There. See that. Field glasses. Gotta be.'

Shire couldn't see anything. 'Probably just someone out like us.'

'Could be. But if I was checking on your brigade, that spot is where I'd put myself.' He placed his hat on top of the wall and slowly rested the rifle barrel in the hat's soft felt cradle. 'Let's take a looky.' He put his eye to the scope. 'There. He's got his horse tucked in the bushes but its ears are showing. Kinda funny. Hard to tell the color of his hat.'

Shire could still see nothing. He followed the line of Gideon's rifle to where it might intersect the ground. It had to be more than half a mile away. 'He's too far.'

'Aw no, he's in my orbit alright. Chance to try out Mister Spider's handiwork.' Gideon adjusted the scope then drew the gun back down behind the wall and then quickly loaded through the breach.

'What if he's one of ours?'

'Well, if he's a Johnny, sooner or later he'll back up out of the bush and come off the hill on the west side. He'll likely mount up first though. When I see him head to toe, I'll know if he's a Reb.' Once more he set the barrel to rest on his hat atop the wall.

Shire's gut tightened. The web hunt had been a lark of sorts; he hadn't expected death to be the product. He saw again the yellow skull. 'Let him go.'

'What?'

'There's been enough death in this place.'

Gideon turned his head to look at Shire, as if sizing him up afresh. 'It's your people he's going to report on.' He put his eye back to the scope.

'The whole brigade's hiding in plain sight. The Rebels aren't going to pick a fight.'

'You sure about that? Maybe they've got a battery nearby and will take a pop at your friends. You hush down and let me do my work.'

A light breeze fed up the slope and Gideon adjusted the sight. The seconds drew out. Perhaps nothing would happen. Then a movement, a distant figure leading his horse out from behind the bush as Gideon had predicted. The sharpshooter was as still as the stone wall but for his lips that pursed and blew out a slow gentle breath. Shire fought the impulse to push Gideon off balance. He couldn't bear it. He didn't want any part of adding to last year's tally of dead. He reached out.

A wet slap and he closed his eyes against a sudden sting.

Then a distant shot. He pulled his hand back and across his face and fought to open his eyes. His hand came away with flecks of red. Beside him Gideon's head was slumped over his rifle stock, a raw and bloody hole in the back of his neck. Shire spun and looked up to the higher ground. The shot must have come from there. He couldn't see anyone. Scarcely in time, he threw himself flat as a second bullet smacked into the wall above. The soldier in Shire jumped up to wrestle the precious rifle from Gideon's dead grip and let him fall to the ground. Carrying the heavy rifle, he ran as fast as he could down the hill. If they shot at him again, he never heard it. He ducked in under the trees and raced on, running away for a second time in the young day, not caring how many bones snapped beneath his feet. He'd gained his new perspective: that he'd been keeping company with death for a whole year and wasn't free of it yet.

Spring Hill, Tennessee – October, 1864

The crack in the white china plate angled through the glazed pink rose at its center. Clara placed it on the discard pile, which was competing for size with the surviving stacked pieces. It had been her mother-in-law's wedding set. Emmeline used to mourn over a single lost plate. Now there would be no more than a half set. Clara should have packed more carefully, but who knew how the boxes were mishandled on their train journey between Comrie and her new home halfway across Tennessee. There was no call for a full set anyway. She couldn't imagine dinner parties in her near future. There wasn't a large enough table. There wasn't a suitable room. And there was no one at all to invite.

The loss was more financial than personal. She'd seen enough wealthy farms and homes from the train ride into Spring Hill to know she could easily have found a buyer for quality china. That might have paid a hand for a month, or replaced some of the tack that had been lost in the Comrie fire and that Moses said they were in need of, despite her pointing out the absence of horses to wear it.

Cele raced into the parlor, circled the boxes and raced out again, further decimating a broken saucer. *There* was something that could have been left behind. Just the energy of the little black girl was enough to set Clara on edge. Mitilde, bulky and breathless, stepped inside as Cele ran out, but gave up the chase and collapsed onto the chaise longue. 'I's too old, Miss Clara. You gonna have to find a girl to bring that one to heel or do it yerself. I spend more time runnin' after her than settin' this place to rights. Lord save me.'

'What's Moses doing?' Clara asked. 'Cele could help him.'

'Ha. He knows better 'n that. He's away over your new fields and dreamin' what crops to sow. No matter we got no seed and no hands. It's fine land though. Says so ev'ry time he walks through the door.'

'Roaming the fields might tire Cele out.' Anything to get her out of the house.

'Marchin' with the Union Army ain't gonna tire that child out.'

Clara searched for a softer heart. If any of them deserved a home it was Cele, the product of Taylor's forced attentions on Hany, a former slave at Comrie. Rape would be the less genteel description. That was long before Clara came across from England to marry him; there was no blame attached to her. Taylor was dead now anyway, but so was Hany, murdered by bushwhackers in front of Cele's five-year-old eyes. Small wonder she chose to run. Like it or not, there was a debt of care owed to that child and it fell to Clara, if she could only find some Christian spirit.

After Comrie burned, her friend Julius Raht had let her use his old house in Cleveland, Tennessee. Shire had stayed on with her while his parole held, until the war tugged him away again. They'd tried to find Cele's grandmother; the child belonged to her by right, but she was gone. Like half of America, she'd been thrown to the four winds by the war, the black with considerably less shelter from the storm than the white. Clara wasn't exempt from the contagion, but at least she'd had somewhere to go. She still harbored a desire to track down Cele's grandmother, but where would she start? No. All the family Cele had left lived under this new roof: Clara,

Mitilde and Moses. The sad thought occurred that it was possible neither of her old friends would outlive Cele's childhood. There'd be no one left but herself to protect the child then.

Mitilde struggled up and exasperated herself out of the room. Clara followed her onto the veranda, tired of unpacking broken china. Cele was running away down the arrow straight drive that ended at the Columbia Pike. Moses sat on the porch step in the cold sun trying to fashion a tired rope into a working halter, his old fingers shaky. She resisted the temptation to reach out and pat his woolly gray head. He was right about the land. Sixty acres, a neat square parcel with the road for a boundary on the east side.

It had come as a shock while in Cleveland to discover that Matlock, who her father had sent across the Atlantic to meddle in her finances, had removed most of her money from the bank. She'd expected to have to buy out her tenants, the Tolivers, at Spring Hill. It was their home after all. Raht said he'd be happy to advance her money against the sale of the Comrie land, which he was managing. It might take a while, he said. Any buyer would have to take on Comrie's own tenant farms and the daunting prospect of building a new home on steep land that was far from town. She'd sold her share in the Copper Road Turnpike Company to Raht as well. It was a bad time to sell. She suspected Raht had inflated the price with kindness. There would be no toll income for her, after the war, if the road became busy again. She looked beyond Cele to the pike. Shame she didn't have shares in that road; there was a busy toll-house in the village.

She'd written to the Tolivers and waited, but grew impatient and arranged for an agent to visit the farm. He'd written that the place was empty. There had been a raid a few months back. The house was intact but the neighbors said the Tolivers had lost their livestock and given up the ghost.

She looked up to see that Old George, who'd been grazing the front field beside the drive, had gathered up enough energy to plod over for a friendly visit with Cele at the fence. The little girl shouted and shooed at him. He put his ears back and turned away, not overly concerned. It irked Clara though.

With the Tolivers gone, there was no reason not to move right away. She'd paid up the few Comrie people that remained and they'd scattered. Moses could list where each family or couple or lone soul had headed, but couldn't tell you if a single one of them had got there. Then there was the cost of shipping what was left to here. That wasn't so much. Most of the farm equipment burned with the stables. Comrie's treasures, those which had survived with her in the mine, had arrived the day after her in a pair of wagons from the depot. Apart from the chaise longue, they remained for the most part where they were unloaded in the barn. Perhaps she could sell some of those. Two of the Comrie farm hands were due to come on with Mitilde and Moses but her old friends arrived with only Cele. The men had had a change of heart, Moses said. It was a blow, but who could blame them? Most of Tennessee saw slavery as God's intent. Further north was the better prospect. She would need help though, and soon if they were to set the fields for winter and begin to establish some livestock. Shire would have been useful if he hadn't returned to the army. A wagon and a team were the priority. She'd reasoned it made more sense to buy a new wagon than to bring her old one. She'd paid for Old George to come along despite his being as worn-out as the wagon he used to pull. He was an indulgence, past moving anything other than himself. A less sentimental farmer would have made an end to him back at Comrie and saved the expense.

Mitilde knelt down in front of Moses. She slapped his feet out of the way, setting him back in his work on the halter, and started to pull at the seeded spears of grass that had sprouted from under the lowest porch step. 'It ain't as much fuss as cleaning the grand steps before Comrie, but it's low work for an old lady.'

Clara had learned not to respond to Mitilde's constant references to Comrie. They usually included something akin to regret, though it was hard to understand why that might be. Long ago, Mitilde had been bought and brought to Comrie as a wedding present to Clara's mother-in-law, stolen from her own loves to be no more than a token of someone else's. But then even in bondage, Mitilde had risen to hold some station, a matriarch to the array of Comire's slaves more than Clara ever was. Watching her work on the steps, Clara realized before her was her only female friend. Perhaps it was easier not to discuss Comrie because at that place Clara was once counted with the slaveowners.

'Tolivers should never have up and left without tellin' us. Place wouldn't need so much work. Shame you couldn't bring your bo' with you.'

'Bo' was a provocation too. Clara no longer corrected her to say Shire.

She had rechristened the farm as Eversholt, the previous name of New Farm being too prosaic. Measured by English time, all the farms here were new. Eversholt was a village close to her own home in England and a pretty one. The country north of Spring Hill wasn't so different to Bedfordshire if you thought beyond the landscaped grounds of Ridgmont. Low rolling hills, a mix of forest and cleared land put to crops and pasture. Better soil here though, if she was any judge. She remembered caroling with Shire in Eversholt one Christmas Eve. That seemed like someone else's life. She'd given little thought to the new name. It had simply come to her. She'd not yet told Mitilde and Moses, so it was christened in her mind only, but now she was having second thoughts, suspicious of the need to commemorate her old home.

During September a slew of letters had arrived at the Raht house from her parents and there'd been one waiting for her here. Rather than begin early this morning with the unpacking, she'd read them all again. It was notable how the tone moved steadily from sympathy to stridency. Initially, after learning Comrie had been burnt to the ground with their steward and envoy, Matlock, trapped inside, their concern was for her only. Come home, they said. America was lost in chaos and violence, England and her father's Dukedom the better place for her future. When she wrote to explain that Matlock had tried to have her killed and, what's more, had removed six thousand dollars from her bank using her father's authority, they became more insistent. Comrie had a debt to Ridgmont that might never be repaid if Clara used what funds were left to establish herself elsewhere. Matlock had been embezzling Father's money in England as well, they told her. She *must* come back. There were not-so-subtle hints that if she didn't, they would come to get her or take steps to recover what they were owed. It had settled her mind to transplant herself to here, a few hundred miles further away, convinced that she could make a fresh start. Another one. Now she'd arrived, she wasn't so sure.

Shire had been skeptical too. 'Where do you *want* to be?' he'd asked.

That still grated. *Where* wasn't the right question. *How* would have been better and *not alone* would have been the answer. Maybe even, *with you*. Did she truly mean that? She missed him. She wished he was here to help. He'd be able to do more for the place than pull up spears of grass. If he was here, calling it Eversholt might make more sense. He had the harder path though, back in the Union Army. And where would Shire go if he saw out the war?

She watched Cele stand on the bottom rail and tug at the top one with all her weight until she fell and tumbled to the drive. She didn't cry. That child never did.

Saw out the war. That was a weaselly term. Not get killed by the war is what it meant. The thought stabbed at her. Shire was only in America because of her.

She'd travelled a day ahead of Mitilde and Moses to avoid a long journey with Cele. The trains were a lottery with the war still rumbling on down in Georgia and there were tiresome stops in Chattanooga and then in Nashville while she waited for the train south to Spring Hill. Once aboard the final leg, she'd started to breathe more easily. Williamson was a far wealthier county than Polk. There were rich farmlands and grand houses beyond the sooty window. The train stopped at Franklin: Tod's home. She'd allowed herself to think of him. She'd kept a tight lid on that until now. She'd no way to find out where he might be or which Rebel army he was a part of. There had been copies of the *New York Daily Tribune* at the station in Nashville if she wanted news of the war, but she hadn't bought one. It was time to leave that behind. Tod wouldn't have been home to Franklin. She knew that much at least. He was the wrong side of the lines with Tennessee safely back in the Union.

She should leave Tod behind too. It had been a dalliance, that's all, albeit a passionate one. She'd never told Tod that she had been with child and she hadn't been for long. That short pregnancy had ended in the copper mines of Ducktown. At least he'd given her back one hope, that she wasn't as barren as her marriage had been. It was a tie, though, carrying Tod's child if only for a short while. He was the only man she'd ever truly made love to. She called the memory to mind often enough. Taylor had been worse than harsh and with Shire… well, she'd probably never know.

When she'd alighted from the train on the outskirts of Spring Hill, there'd been no buggies. The best she could do was to leave her valise to be delivered later, ask the way and walk. The day was warm and she was overdressed, but it was pleasant enough. She found her way to the Columbia Pike, a smart road of tamped-down white gravel, and followed it north.

When she found her property and walked up the drive, weeds surrounding every fencepost, the farmhouse had struck her as smaller than she remembered from her brief visit in the spring. Gray, rustic beams stretched either side of a simple porch, its white paint flaking. Above was a modest covered veranda with room for no more than two rockers. She'd only need the one. There were two tall windows downstairs and two more upstairs, chimneys both ends, an orange tiled roof that looked sound enough and tall white oak timbers as a frame. Like the porch, the windows needed a coat or two of paint if she could afford any. It was a smiling house. An aspiring house for a proud family hoping to better themselves. It hadn't ended that way for the Tolivers. What did she aspire to here?

She looked out from the porch and down the fenced drive. Cele was again climbing the rails on one side and then the other. Her mind bent back again to caroling that Christmas Eve in Eversholt. She closed her eyes to see it the better. She'd been so young. It had come on to snow and Shire had to hurry her home. The snow had become so heavy they'd had to take shelter in the gatehouse. Shire had stoked the fire and she'd flirted with him, shameless, until they'd almost gone too far. He had a lover's hands, though calloused from his work on the farm.

Mitilde's hollered threats brought her back to herself. Cele was out the far end of the drive, on the pike.

'I'll fetch her,' said Clara. She half-walked and half-ran, fearful of the frequent horses and carriages on the road. When she got close, Cele dodged beneath her outstretched arms and ran giggling back to the house. Clara stayed where she was, content to have shooed Cele away. Nobody was in sight on the road. She looked south toward Spring Hill and the few houses that were outliers of the village proper, nearly a mile away. After that it was Maury County. Columbia lay some way beyond. She didn't know how far. She turned to the north. That way was Franklin and then Nashville. Ten miles or more to Tod's home. Not exactly neighbors, but the war had to end one day, and then Tod would return.

She paced determinedly back to the house and stole the slate and chalk from Cele's room that she'd been using to teach the girl her letters. There would be another slate somewhere in the unpacked boxes for Cele. She marched back to the roadside, rested the slate on her fence and scratched 'Eversholt' in capital letters. It didn't look a lot better than if Cele had written it. It would do until she could fashion something better. There. That was done. Tod could live up the road but Shire could live in the name. She laid the crude sign at the foot of the gatepost and walked back to her new home.

Franklin, Tennessee – October, 1864

Moscow stepped down from the back porch and pointed himself beyond the farm office and the smokehouse. The hubbub could not be entirely left behind: the Carter house was too populous for that. But he needed to get away, if only for a short while. The competing cries of children and the voices of his sisters, elevated just now, escaped the redbrick walls of his childhood home. He blew out his cheeks. If he didn't enjoy the random melodies of children, he shouldn't have moved back to live with his father and his sisters. His four additions had brought the count in children up to nine.

He moved past the smokehouse and relaxed with his arms on top of the rail fence, looking to the south. He needed to breathe before supper. Otherwise, he wouldn't be able to eat. The air was cool, the light beginning to fail. The view beyond the half-acre vegetable garden, out across the fall fields that stretched to the forested hills, never failed to help. He drank it in, tried to shut out the rival shouts of the children, the knock of crockery from the detached kitchen and the distant strokes of an axe. Instead, he favored the whistles of the waxwings in the cedar trees beside the house and the raucous crows mustering in the locust grove away to his right.

The house *was* crowded. No denying that. All the same, he should have moved home sooner, after the Lord took Callie. Four years as a widower was a long time. He should start to cast his eye. Maybe after the war. The whole family could breathe again then. Here and now, at least he could count on his sisters. Combative they might be, but they were a blessing for him and for the children.

He turned from the view and set his back to the fence, spread his arms wide along the top rail. It would be a hard thing to admit to poor lost Callie, but this felt more like home than their farm north of Franklin ever truly did. Perhaps that would have come in time. Right here, if someone had spun him around blindfolded, he would need only a moment to point to where the mint grew wild down the fence a way, to the salty tang of the smokehouse, to the azaleas opposite which Father kept tended. Mother had always liked those. Memories both tender and sad were preserved below those stepped gables and the red-tiled roof. Sometimes he imagined adventures elsewhere might wait beyond the war, but his cares were planted too deeply in Franklin. Four of them were running around that house right now.

As he watched, his father, Fountain, exited the house as he had and took the same route toward the rail. His gray beard was freshly trimmed square and there was only the hint of a bend to his gait. Moscow knew his strength. They shared a strange bond for a father and son. Both widowers, both with more of a care for children than they'd ever imagined. Father would never remarry, but Moscow didn't care for that lonely future. He'd find someone when the time was right. He'd be an attractive prospect with the wealth of land they all shared. Though love wasn't conjured up so easily. Perhaps he should remove it as a requirement, on his part at least. How would that be? A practical marriage. He couldn't imagine.

Fountain came closer and shared a broad smile. 'You too?' He took station beside Moscow at the fence, looking out to the fields while Moscow stayed facing the other way.

'How is it,' Fountain said, 'that you and I can both work a long day on the land and feel nothing but comfortably tired, but an hour among that brood and I'm fit for my bed?'

Moscow laughed. 'I apologize for adding to your burden.' He sighed. 'It was a sad necessity which filled your house again with children, but now they're all collected, I doubt you'd want them to leave.'

'Build me another annex then, or a summer house. Grandchildren are easier to enjoy from a distance.'

'They'd only seek you out.'

John, one of the few blacks who'd chosen to stay after the Union arrived last year, dipped his head while heading toward the root cellar with a barrowload of turnips. Moscow raised a hand in return.

'Maybe so,' Father said. 'A few more years and they'll prove useful about the farm. God knows we need all the help we can get.'

Most of the blacks had left. How could Moscow blame them for that? He recalled sitting down with Father last fall to rethink their crops. Cattle and hogs were less work but there was always the risk if an army happened this way that you'd be left with no more than a docket.

'It can't be long now,' said Moscow, meaning the war. 'Georgia's lost as well as Tennessee, Lee pinned down in the east. If it weren't for the South's honor, we'd have sued for peace already.'

'Is it honor or pride? At my age both those so-called virtues seem poor stock. You and I can at least be honest that we never thought the war would bring a good return, and it's done a lot worse than that.'

Moscow turned again to share the view with his father. Out on the Columbia Pike a single mule wagon, monotone in the creeping dusk, ambled north, seemingly in no rush to reach Franklin. 'What choice did we have once the thing was underway?'

'The choices came earlier. Other people's choices, long before we ever put our cross on the ballot.'

'Let's hope it ends soon. Lincoln will get back in. We know his stripes so best face up to it. Then Tod and Francis can come home and help get the farm in full order again.'

His younger brothers had signed up at the start of the war as he had.

'Maybe,' said Father. 'Francis has to mend first.' They'd got word Francis had been captured fighting for the Texas cavalry and was in a hospital in Union-held New Orleans. 'And he's not a homebird, you know that. I doubt his future is here.'

'Tod then. I wonder where he is, where my old regiment is.'

Moscow had been the colonel for the 20th Tennessee early in the war, until he was captured in Kentucky. He'd been seven months in prison before his exchange and by then his term was up. He'd never rejoin, no matter what. He'd made an oath of allegiance to the Union to gain his parole. When he'd signed, he'd thought of no allegiance except to his children and to his dead wife.

'Wherever the 20th Tennessee is, I'm glad you're here.' Father patted Moscow's shoulder.

Sometimes Moscow wondered if he should have gone to fight at all. It had never felt right ordering men to fire on a flag he used to fight for. Something inside jangled all the same, a mixture of guilty pride and his own faded need for adventure. He'd had his time in another war, in Mexico, and was lucky to make it home from there. 'My duties are all here and they're about to sit down at your dinner table.'

'*Our* dinner table. We should get back. Put our own little

company in order.'

'Company C?' joked Moscow. He always enjoyed drawing a smile from Father. 'I'd sure like to know where Tod is though. If he's still with the 20th.'

'We've not heard any different. He'll likely be with General Hood somewhere. At least we can follow him in the Union papers. Sooner or later a letter will make it through. If not from Tod, from someone in the 20th. Then the whole town will know where they are.'

In point of fact, there had been two letters, both curious. The first arrived last Christmas from a Union soldier to tell them Tod had been captured at Missionary Ridge. The soldier, an Englishman, had been billeted here with the 125th Ohio in the spring of sixty-three. His company had helped Moscow gin some cotton. The boy had even waited on table at the farm when they'd entertained Union officers. The letter was a kindness. Afterwards Moscow had discovered Tod was likely imprisoned on Johnson's Island in Ohio but had been unable to contact him there.

The second letter was hand-delivered in the spring. A young lady, a beautiful one according to his daughter Lena who'd taken the letter from her at the door and not thought to invite her in. It was written by Tod. He'd escaped and was making his way back to Georgia and his regiment. They'd heard since that he'd made it, but no more than that.

'Shall we brave the enemy?' asked Fountain.

'Why not?' said Moscow, ready to eat. He took his weight from the fence. 'If we charge in together, perhaps we'll win the day.'

They walked back to the house, but were made to wait while children of every size rushed onto the porch and down the steps to the dining room.

Decatur, Alabama – October, 1864

Tod Carter steered Rosencrantz between the soldier traffic that was busy behind the main front. A small company was ordered into line by an overzealous second lieutenant. Every man looked twice the officer's age and bore his directions with thinly disguised contempt.

'Lieutenant,' called Tod from his saddle. 'Is this Brown's Division?'

The boy turned and looked up at Tod. Behind him his men quickly shuffled into better alignment. 'It is,' he said. 'Maney's Brigade.' He eyed the captain stripes on Tod's collar. 'Who are you looking for, sir?'

'Gist's Brigade. Are they next in line?'

'No. Strahl's on our right. Beyond him I couldn't say, but most likely it'll be Gist.'

'Much obliged.' Tod touched his hat and got a stiff-armed salute in return. A bit too stiff. He nudged Rosencrantz into a walk. General Hood commanded a veteran army and Tod was surprised they could still find young men in the South to bring in as lieutenants. He was on his way to find another. Fresh meat.

He paused again to let a pair of soldiers pass in front bearing an ammunition chest. At least he was spared those sorts of duties now. No longer a quartermaster, he was aide-de-camp to Brigadier General Thomas Benton Smith. His not-so-glorified fetching and carrying days were over. He much preferred his new duties, closer aligned as they were to the direction of the men and to the fighting.

His horse spooked as yet more soldiers passed behind. Now he knew where to go, it would be easier to drop back further from the front. He angled away and took Rosencrantz up a gentle rise, let him set his own slow pace along the crest. As a quartermaster captain he'd managed to get along fine without his own horse; there was always a spare one he could commandeer or a wagon to ride. That wouldn't do for an aide-de-camp. His pay was better, but gray Rosencrantz had cost him every penny he had plus an advance from the paymaster. He had no money for a second horse.

To his left the fog that had been all pervasive at dawn was in retreat. Below him was Hood's army, a long, curved line of men and guns, an arc facing in toward the formidable Union works that surrounded the ruined town of Decatur. A busy mix of shouts, drums and bugles lifted up to him: the army talking to itself, orders rippling out from Hood's headquarters. Between the line and the Union defenses was over half a mile of flat, cleared land. A killing field should the army attack. Surely even Hood wasn't that rash. Tod had seen fortifications aplenty after three years in the army and this wasn't one to charge. He knew it and this tired army knew it. There was only a Union garrison in there, a fraction of Hood's army outside, but they'd had time to prepare. Hood's first moves yesterday had been rebuffed. Tempted though Hood might be, it wasn't worth the price.

The temptation itself was out of sight at present, but Tod knew it was there: a pontoon bridge that stretched from inside the fort across to the north bank of the Tennessee River. If Hood's army could win that fort and get quickly across, they could march on Nashville and maybe on into Kentucky before the Union could muster a large enough army to stop them.

Small hope. They'd lose too many men. Even if they took the fort, the Union would break up or burn the pontoon before allowing a single Confederate boot across the river.

He stopped and turned Rosencrantz to fully face the scene. The fog bank peeled back to the west, revealing first the river and then the ruin of Decatur. Most of the houses had been pulled down to provide materials for the fortifications. His home was over that river. A long way once over, but if he was ever going to get there, they'd have to cross the Tennessee somewhere. It wasn't going to be here, so Hood should move on. What miracle was he waiting for? Their own pontoon bridge was disassembled in a long wagon train some way behind, no doubt weighed down in the mud the army had churned up on its way. Hardly Hood's most impressive piece of planning when getting over the river mattered so much.

As Tod watched, a Union gunboat ghosted out of the fog bank. Three quick flashes followed seconds later by matching detonations; a broadside aimed at Confederate cannon west of the fort. More Union guns fired from across the river. A caisson exploded in a Rebel battery. Tod and Rosencrantz winced in unison. The subsiding blast was trailed by shouts and screams as a mushroom of smoke boiled up into the morning sky. Hood should either stir the pot or get the hell out of the kitchen. His show of force wasn't working. Rebel cannon sought the gunboat but it would have to be a lucky shot. Hood had no gunboats to help his army, and the Union had the better cannoneers. These days, that was a fact of life.

Tod's unit – Smith's Brigade – was well back of the line, otherwise he'd not have asked to come away. As it was, Smith had him on a long leash. Secretary Trenholm had seen to that. Tod had suggested to Smith that he ride out and report on the wider position. It wasn't easy to understand the picture with the partial information that came down from division H.Q. Tod could track down his quarry at the same time; namely Frank – Trenholm Junior. With the army concentrated, he didn't think Frank should be too hard to find. Tod wanted to make sure he wasn't planning to do anything foolish, or worse, heroic.

Tod had met with George Trenholm when the army was camped back in Palmetto, Georgia, in late September, when the air was still warm and the ground still dry. President Davis had been visiting, long before any of them knew Hood would try and lead them back into Tennessee. A note had arrived along with a guide who escorted Tod to a guarded three-car train at rest in a siding. He was directed to the middle car. His boots left dusty prints on the washed metal steps as he climbed aboard. Inside brought to mind the plush City Hotel in Nashville that Moscow had once sheepishly hurried him in and out of, as if they were truant schoolboys. Most of the carriage was given over to high leather chairs and bureaus. Fine art hung between the windows. Silver-haired George Trenholm hailed him from the far end. They had the carriage to themselves. Trenholm sauntered toward him and collected a pair of charged glasses en route. 'Captain Carter. Welcome.'

Tod took off his hat. 'Mr Trenholm. It must be you, sir. We've not yet met without you extending a glass of whiskey in my direction.'

Trenholm laughed. 'Actually, today it's brandy. Imported whiskey is in short supply, even in the presidential car. Can we make do?'

Tod took the glass and Trenholm showed him to a seat in the shade, the white leather a soft and cool luxury. Through the window and away from the siding, the hot business of the army went on under the Georgia sun. His quartermaster's eye followed an unsteady wagon, the head of a slaughtered bullock lolling from the tailboard.

The first time Trenholm had summoned him, soon after midsummer, resulted in a two-month foray into the Tennessee mountains, an unlikely and unhappy reunion with Clara, and the violent loss of many good friends and many more mules. Small wonder he had his guard up. He took a wary sip of brandy. It was shockingly excellent. 'Our President's car you say?' He leaned out of his chair and looked both ways along the carriage. 'High ground for a lowly captain.'

'Oh, the President won't be joining us. At least I don't think so. He's with Hood. He's probably trying to fit a collar on him. This is my car and my brandy.' Trenholm raised his glass. 'I've loaned it to Jeff for the visit. He needs to look the part more than I do. How's life as a staff officer?'

Aide-de-camp, thought Tod, but decided against correcting Trenholm. 'Preferable to that of a quartermaster. It's a fine brigade, my old outfit the 20th Tennessee the best part of it, though I may be biased. Should I be thanking you for the change?' His promotion had come out of the blue. Not that it wasn't deserved. He'd wondered at the time if Trenholm had a hand in it.

'I'm sure your qualities were plain for all to see.'

Hardly a denial. 'Why are you here, sir? Is our economy in such rude health that the Financial Secretary of the Confederacy is free to visit the army? Why am *I* here?'

Trenholm straightened his smile and stared out of the window. 'That's a fistful of questions. As to the last, I don't know so many captains in the Army of the Tennessee. Plenty of generals, but they're not always in touch with the common soldier and they're inclined to tell me what they think I want to hear.'

'I'm glad my rank is lowly enough for you.'

Trenholm laughed. 'How old are you?'

'Twenty-four.'

'And already a captain.'

'There's plenty younger than me.'

'No doubt, but if you were a year or two older, I'd have you down for a major, maybe your own regiment. I respect you, sir. I know I dealt you a tough hand to get to Ducktown and back. It was no fault of yours it failed.'

Befriending Shire. That was the only fault, thought Tod. That Englishman had blown up the mule train and half of Tod's men.

'I should offer you a cigar,' said Trenholm. 'We're drinking brandy after all.'

'I'm fine as I am.'

There was a quiet moment while Trenholm lit one for himself and drew into it. The thought of Shire tarried with Tod, Clara not far behind. He had to ask. 'Did you ever hear news of that Englishman? Shire. And Clara.'

Trenholm wore a half-smile. 'She leaves a mark that one, doesn't she?'

'I'm curious, is all.'

'A letter did get through.' Trenholm spoke around his cigar. 'From Raht. You'll remember Raht. He told me they made it back to Comrie, Clara's home, but it was burned out before they got there. By our side, he said.'

'That's harsh.' *Poor Clara.* 'But I guess there's a war on.'

'Shire was with her, but he's back in the army now. He exchanged his parole.'

'That boy just can't stay out of the fight.'

'Clara has moved west. Spring Hill, Tennessee, I think Raht said.'

That jolted Tod. 'May I have another brandy, sir? I might never encounter one this good again.' Clara had once told him of her tenant farm in Spring Hill. The Tolivers. He knew them well enough. Up and over Winstead Hill from Franklin and an hour more. Fancy that, Clara so close to his home.

'So, what's the mood?'

'Sir?'

'Will the men trust Hood? If the President leaves him in command?'

Tod dragged himself back from warm memories, and suddenly warm hopes. 'They trust him to fight, maybe not to keep them alive,' he said. 'Johnston did a good job at the latter, but only by giving ground. Hood doesn't have his finesse. Johnston was a chess player. Hood keeps it simple. Head down and charge.'

'And it isn't always simple, is it?'

'Hardly ever. Do you think Jeff Davis will stick or twist with Hood?'

'He'll stick. Hood plays him well. He's buttered up the President over the months, knows he responds to flattery and that Jeff sticks by his friends, even to a fault.'

'And Hood is a fault?'

'I have my concerns. All shared with Jeff of course, but he's never been one for changing his mind. My opinion carries small weight in military matters.' He looked Tod in the eye. 'I have a further care.'

Tod waited.

'My youngest, Frank. He's been busting to get into the fight and I couldn't rightly stop him, not now he's eighteen. General Gist has taken him on to his staff, in Brown's Division. The truth is, on my son's account, I'd prefer almost anyone other than Hood to be at the head of this army. While

I had you chasing copper up in the hills, Hood spent a lot of men around Atlanta, and not that wisely by all accounts. I don't expect his casualty rate is about to drop.'

'Doesn't seem likely.'

'Will you keep an eye on Frank for me?'

Tod hadn't known what to expect but nonetheless was surprised. 'That would have to be some eye, sir. I'm in the same corps but in Bate's Division. Unless the army is encamped or concentrated, we won't be close.'

'I understand. You're not the only one sharing the presidential brandy. General Gist will have a care for him, of course. And I've advised your own general, Benton Smith. He'll let you go find Frank when you can. You and Frank are both staff officers after all. You're used to roaming far and wide, am I right? You could show him the ropes.'

Trenholm appeared to have had it all lined up before Tod stepped into the carriage. What it must be like to be so well connected. 'The ropes are pretty new to me too, sir.'

'The war isn't.' An added intensity crept into Trenholm's voice. 'Staying alive isn't.' Trenholm dropped Tod's gaze and looked out of the window again. 'I've been luckier than most in this war, Captain Carter. I confess I helped bring it on. Many in my circle did, all of us indignant, boastful. None of us believed the Yankees would have the stomach for it. Now look at us. But I've not fought. And my children and family are all alive. My businesses have profited, at least until this year. And I still have a home. I'm worried I'm in debt to the Lord, and that the settling payment might be Frank.'

Tod set down his near empty glass and leaned forward. 'Sir,' he said. 'I'll do what I can. There are some easy lessons, mistakes to avoid. But when the shells scream home and regiments are firing toe to toe, well, prayer is all any of us have.

And sometimes, sir, we don't even have time for that.'

Soon after, Frank was shown in and Trenholm made the introductions. Frank hadn't been best pleased. 'Another nursemaid for me?' were his exact words. Frank was as handsome and as imposing as his father. Tall too, in his polished buttons and unblemished gray jacket. Tod had seen plenty of fresh-faced recruits over the years. They never lasted long unless they said a rapid farewell to childhood. They left Trenholm Senior and walked out to where President Davis and General Hood were conducting a review in the Georgia dusk. Afterwards the 20th Louisiana band – scarecrows each one, but tuneful scarecrows – serenaded the President, playing 'Dixie' and 'The Yellow Rose of Texas' in the torchlight. Hood, leaning heavily on his crutch, followed on with a few words. When he finished, the crowd pressed closer to the flag-laden stage to hear the President. His was a sound speech and the men cheered in the right places, but if Tod was any judge, the mood was uneasy and bordering on suspicious. They'd all heard rabble-rousing speeches over the years, but they weren't a rabble even if they looked like one, and it would take more than crafted presidential rhetoric to rouse them.

*

A further burst from the Union cannon over the Tennessee River summoned Tod back to the here and now. That side of the river was also the state of Alabama, but those guns stood between him and his Tennessee home. His meeting with the Trenholms at Palmetto was over a month ago. The mood of the army was different now. There was an expectation. They'd spent the first half of October tearing up the rail line between

Atlanta and Chattanooga; captured or bypassed all the Union garrisons. Then they'd struck west into Alabama and the news came that Sherman had given up the chase. Seemingly he had his own plans to attend to and wasn't inclined to play cat with John Bell Hood as the mouse. It wasn't clear to Tod who would oppose them with Sherman's Army beating its own path. As things stood, if they could get over the river, there was little to stop them before Nashville. A good portion of this army were Tennessee born and bred as he was. Now they had the prospect of home. That did much more for them than a presidential speech; it gave them a portion of hope, however small. Wasn't it home they'd been fighting for in the first place? They might be wary of Hood, but their step had quickened once he'd pointed the way.

Two-thirds round the arc he found General Gist's command and with him Frank Trenholm. They were doing nothing more than watching on like most of the army and Frank, much to his chagrin, was excused to come away and talk with Tod. 'Could you pick a better moment, Carter? It's mortifying in front of my general. Like I'm being taken out of class.'

'You'll call me captain or sir, Lieutenant,' Tod said sharply. 'Either will do.'

Now he was here, it was hard to know what to say to the boy. Their brigades being on different parts of the field, they swapped dispositions. At least that was useful. Frank appeared to have a good grasp on those. Other than that, Tod just asked Frank to keep his wits handy. 'I don't think Hood will throw the army in here. But if he chooses to start a sideshow, it's not a place to get yourself killed if you want to make it to the main event. Do you understand?'

'It's not like I have a choice,' Frank said. 'I go where

General Gist goes.'

'Alright, but don't go volunteering to lead a reconnaissance or pick up any fallen flags. We got a ways to go yet.'

Frank sullenly took his leave to return to Gist's staff. Tod's return journey was largely uneventful. Behind him some rifle fire broke out down to the right of the fort and near to the river, but he couldn't see enough to gather who got the better of it. Most likely it was the Union, as that night Hood pulled out and started them heading further west, still held below the river. Tod got precious little sleep. He was cold when he woke, unsure if he was excited or merely fretful that his army might not find anywhere to cross, and that he might never get closer to home.

Memphis and Charleston Railroad, Alabama –
November, 1864

The train jolted forward. Shire stopped himself from grabbing hold of Mason. The big man's tempting anchor weight was close beside him. It wouldn't do to appear anxious and invite mockery from Cleves, just now playing dice with Corry. It also wouldn't do to tumble from the roof as they picked up speed. Tuck seemed to have no such concern. He sat with his legs dangling over the edge and his back hunched, like an overlong question mark. He played his fiddle, a wordless serenade to autumnal Alabama. The brisk November air watered Shire's eyes as their boxcar rumbled and rocked along the Memphis and Charleston Railroad, headed west. Shire edged his rifle in next to his thigh and leaned back on both arms to affect a relaxed look while feeling more secure. He'd had to hand in Gideon's sniper rifle. It would have been too heavy to march with in any case.

Cold though he was, he should take in the scene; enjoy this. Train rides had not been a scarcity in his army life. There was the regiment's first trip out of barracks to Cincinnati, then as a prisoner on a hot night through Atlanta, and most recently on his own down into Georgia to rejoin the 125th. But until now, they had all been perpetrated *inside* a boxcar. The plain fact was that Opdycke's whole brigade could not fit within the train. No matter that it was thirty-six cars long. Shire had stood to count when they boarded before noon, next to the Tennessee River and tight under Lookout Mountain. They'd been outside Chattanooga. The 125th Ohio was the last in line so had been directed to the rear and *upstairs*, despite there being no stairs to speak of. The 88th Illinois had already taken the tops of the forward cars. There were two extra engines spaced at intervals along the train. The three roofs immediately ahead of Shire's squad, up as far as the third engine, were uninhabited on account of the smoke hazard. Even this far back, if they got up a lick of speed and the wind was just so, they caught a dose of smoke and hot coal dust. It all added to the fun.

It *was* fun. Shire couldn't deny it, despite the fact they were shadowing Hood's Rebel army and there was the prospect of another fight this late in the year. The regiment was in a buoyant mood after the pay began to be handed out yesterday. There had been a long queue at the paymaster to receive the money, and a second one at the postmaster for those who hadn't before now arranged allotments to go to their dependents at home. Shire hadn't cause to join the second queue, with no family in the world to send money to. Tuck shared a similar circumstance and they'd sat together. Shire had read a copy of Harper's Weekly – acquired with his new funds – while Tuck worked a less than joyful melody from his fiddle.

Today, against the backdrop of the red and yellow plumage of the high mountains that rose up either side of them, Tuck had moved onto a jig to match the happier disposition of the regiment. Or maybe Tuck was easier in his own mind now they were on the move. Shire couldn't tell of late. Tuck had been first up onto the roof when they got the order, as if he had a ticket to some distant contentment that only he was aware of. Shire had got into the habit of gauging the color of Tuck's day over his dawn sip of coffee. Would it be old Tuck or new Tuck? It didn't usually vary after that. The change in Tuck had been obvious when Shire had rejoined the regiment.

When he'd come away from the burned-out ruin of Comrie and announced his return from the other side of the lines to the Union garrison down in Cleveland, Tennessee, Shire had expected to be put back in uniform and shipped off there and then, but it hadn't been that simple. This was irregular, said the major, a man out of uniform arriving down from the hills with parole papers. *Exchanging* a parole, one Rebel for one Union, wasn't straightforward this deep into the war. Special permission had to be sought. It dragged on for weeks, which had allowed him plenty of time with Clara. Not that it had got them anywhere.

The frigid air atop the speeding train lent a certain clarity to Shire's perspective. He'd been a coward; dropped back into the lopsided relationship he and Clara had always had rather than trying to stake an even claim. The junior partner, the minority shareholder. He'd told himself that because both their lives were so up in the air that it wasn't the time to settle anything. In all likelihood, it had been the perfect time. Clara had been surprisingly sanguine concerning her circumstances, given her home had been burned to the ground, all except the splendid columns at the top of the high flight of porch steps. Maybe it wasn't so surprising. Comrie had never been good to her. Bodies buried up and down the hillside could testify to that, just not in this world.

Time and again he thought to write to Tuck but, expecting day by day to get his exchange, he'd reasoned he'd likely reach the regiment before a letter would. Besides, they must have checked the prisoner lists. Tuck would know by then that Shire had survived at Kennesaw.

He was more interested in what Clara would decide. He'd become a tentative sounding board, not brave enough to let what was in his heart see the light of day. The opportunity was there for Clara to draw a line under her American experiment, to call it a poor lot and sail home to England and leave him behind with the war. She could return to a life of privilege, tarnished but somewhat exotic: a widow back from the great American war. Instead, she'd doubled down, with no intent to go home. Even then she could have set herself up in New York or in Cincinnati near Raht. He was sure there was at least enough money for that. Instead, she planned to move to Spring Hill, further west, a small farm by all accounts. Why had he been surprised? She'd always been bloody-minded. In the days before he'd left, there'd been an unspoken tension between them that he couldn't fathom beyond the fact he'd done something wrong, or maybe hadn't done something right. He shouldn't think about her so much. It was nothing but wishing in circles. She wasn't here. She was gone to Spring Hill and he was sat atop a long, cold train to who knew where.

After his exchange, he'd been ordered back to the regiment around Atlanta, the city captured in his absence. When he'd arrived unannounced, Tuck had grabbed him so tightly and held on for so long that Shire had to slap him on the back so he could be let out to breathe. His miraculous return had been roundly celebrated by Mason, Ocks and the rest of the company, but once he and Tuck were alone around the fire after sundown, Tuck had plain broken down and wept. After that, old Tuck came and went. Some days he'd be his former lanky, buoyant self, trading up, orchestrating card games, telling long-eared tales to entertain the squad. Other days it was hard to get a happy word out of him. Once they'd come back north to Chattanooga, Tuck had spent more time with his fiddle than talking to Shire. Clara had gifted it to him last year. That fiddle was Tuck's new best friend.

Shire believed that if he waited long enough something would surface; Tuck had long been in the habit of thinking out loud so everyone could hear, especially Shire. But there was nothing. Instead, Tuck would play that fiddle, the only thing that seemed to soothe him. Other times he would pace around the camp or endlessly tidy through his knapsack as if there was something he'd misplaced. When Shire had asked out of frustration what the trouble was, Tuck had looked at him in dumb confusion, as if that was the very thing he'd like to know himself.

The wheels and axles rattled all the louder as the train crossed over a creek on a high trestle. Shire stretched his neck to look at the drop. Tuck's fiddle took on an exaggerated and bouncy cadence to match the clackity-clack of the crossing. He looked more content than Shire had seen him all autumn. Perhaps the train ride, simply going somewhere new and unfamiliar, might itself be a consolation. Shire could understand the joy in that.

Out of nowhere, he saw again the fresh wide wound in Gideon's neck. The dead sharpshooter supplanted his view of the forest for a long second. He had to gather himself, suck in a steadying breath. This wasn't Gideon's first visit. It was only a few days ago, he told himself; this memory would eventually get in line with all his others. He lifted his gaze just the same, as if death was watching them from the hills.

Cleves picked up the dice, ready to roll them into the safety of Corry's cooking pot; the deepest they had. 'Tuck. How come the first time you play a reel that might get us jiggin' is when we're in no place fit to dance?'

Mason answered in Tuck's stead. That happened a lot.

'We'd all be happy to clear a space for you to dance up here, Cleves. It'd be entertainin' if you stayed on and more so if you didn't.'

'Fine talk from my corporal. Your job is to preserve me, not encourage my demise.'

'You're still alive, ain't you? I can't be doing so bad.'

'I'd say that's more down to Providence than the stripe on your arm. The good Lord must have a life in mind for me beyond the war.'

'Careful now,' said Corry, his meaty fingers husbanding an ever-smaller pile of coins. 'Don't draw fate's eye. Best to keep your head down.'

'Cleves keeps everything down,' said Mason. 'Has done all year. Why, I saw him duck behind a chipmunk that day the scrap got fierce at Peachtree Creek.'

Cleves bent a toothless smile into his pockmarked face. Shire had never trusted the man, they'd had too many run-ins for that, but they'd both survived going on two years in the 125th along with Mason and Tuck. Mason had conceded on the quiet that Cleves had done his share of fighting in the final battles for Atlanta. At that time, they'd all believed Shire to be dead. Instead, he was prosecuting his private war with Tod in the Tennessee hills. It left Cleves with more battle-honors than Shire, a point that Cleves was happy to remind him of most days of the week and twice on Sundays.

Late in the day, the rail line swept back to the banks of the Tennessee River, broad and wide here well into Alabama. Acre after acre of sculptured white-water raced across the shallows in the early-evening light. The cold air off the water mixed with the breeze fashioned by the train. Shire wrapped his coat as tight as he could. They'd stopped and been allowed down only the once, and then not long enough to cook or brew coffee. He had no idea how far there was to go, but was scared to take out his dog-eared map for fear he'd lose it to the elements. The long forward line of the train drove toward dark clouds. He was glad when they finally came away from the river and back into the fractional shelter of the trees. Night came on quickly and still the train ran on hour after hour, Tuck playing all the while. The fun departed from the day. Then it started to rain. The squad huddled together, coats and blankets used as best they could to make a single outer-skin, only blue fingers exposed to the wet and the cold.

'Tuck. Get in here,' Shire called, but Tuck played on, barely visible, the rain dampening the vibration of the strings such that the liveliest of tunes became no more than a pacey dirge; happiness gone bad.

*

The next afternoon, the brigade marched north in the fall sunshine. Tuck was beside Shire, as ever. The regiment had shrugged off the cold and the wet of the night before and were in fine spirits, singing 'Hail Columbia' as they marched through the mud. The talk was that if they needed to whip Hood again, they would. No matter that he had the jump on them. It could only be the pay, thought Shire. By rights they should all be dead of pneumonia. The station clock had been showing one in the misty lamplight when they'd reached Athens and stiffly climbed from the cars to find what shelter they could. He preferred this sunny march in the mud to a cold, wet ride atop a train. Evidently the regiment felt much the same.

Colonel Opdycke trotted by on Ben, his back as upright as a church door. The 125th gave him their usual ragged cheer, but there was no hint of acknowledgement in his eyes or below that perfectly trimmed moustache. Opdycke might now command a brigade, but to Shire, the squad and the 125th, he was still *their* colonel, *their* unsmiling tiger-in-chief.

Opdycke had brought the paymaster with them from Chattanooga – kidnapped him almost – to finish paying the rest of the brigade. Whenever there was a stop on the march, the fat, bespeckled man set up with his green safe and a small army of clerks and called the men in by companies. The brigade was getting richer by the mile but presented a somewhat preposterous appearance. Their wagons were to follow overland from Chattanooga. That would take some days and, in the meantime, the brigade was left with no transport for what baggage they'd managed to bring along. Opdycke had sent them out and about in Athens this morning to see what they could *acquire*. They'd been only partially successful. The 125th boasted a polished open buggy with a mixed team hauling crates of ammunition, three somnolent roped mules saddled with provisions, and a near skeletal ox loaded down with pots and pans.

Mid-afternoon they were moving again. Shire and Tuck lagged behind Cleves and Corry to their front. For once, Sergeant Ocks was relaxed about closing up the column. It was old Tuck today, having to dawdle with his long legs to keep to the lesser pace of everyone else. 'You know,' he said, edging closer but only marginally lowering his voice, 'young Corry fills out that uniform pretty good. You think he gets parcels from home we don't know of?'

It was true enough, Shire thought. Most everyone else, himself included, was bone, muscle and cloth. An ounce of fat laid down overnight was marched off before sunrise most days, yet Corry had a roundhouse gait to his march that hinted at not-so-hidden reserves. 'It's still his first year,' said Shire.

Tuck stooped slightly and nudged Shire with a sharp elbow. 'It's down to you he's seen the second half of it.'

Shire looked behind to see if there was as much of a gap behind them as there was in front. 'We don't need to talk of that.'

Tuck ignored him except to speak a little quieter. 'Surely you must think on it? I know I would, if'n I'd saved a man's life. I'd watch him like he was a young colt or a prize onion or such, thinking that the fact he has any girth at all is down to me.'

'It's not like I'm his maker,' said Shire. 'There was a price.'

'You'd pay it again, though. Don't tell me you'd rather be looking on Lieutenant Wick's sick self rather than Corry's fat behind, 'cos I won't believe it. That was the best shot you ever fired.'

'Hush.'

Tuck did as he was told, but it left Shire to weigh it one more time. He'd killed Wick at Kennesaw Mountain when the lieutenant was getting ready to proffer up Corry, as he had others, as some warped sacrifice to an angry God. It was Wick or Corry, plain and simple, but that didn't make it an easy burden to carry. Only Tuck had seen the shot. Corry had no idea. Everyone else took it for a Rebel bullet. Corry was just about the full shilling but not a ha'penny more. He made a habit of stating the painfully self-evident on a regular basis. There were times it irked Shire more than its due. The unkind thought arose that he'd committed a capital crime wholly to preserve a well-fed Ohio farm boy. He recalled unburdening himself to Tod Carter. Tod had absolved him more deftly than any Bishop of Rome might have done. *Doesn't sound like murder. Sounds like justice.* It had helped. And how had he repaid Tod for that?

'Feels right *and* wrong to be headed north, don't it?' said

Tuck.

'What's that?'

'Well, we've moved south for most of the war, pushing the Johnnies back. It feels good to be headed north, but truly we're backing up on account of Hood. At least we're on the move.'

'You like that?' asked Shire, content for Tuck to bounce him out of thinking of Corry and Wick not a minute after bouncing him into it. 'Even though you've no idea where we're heading?'

'I can't say I like dancin' to someone else's tune, but there's a certain freedom in moving along. We might not be steering the wagon, if we had one that is, but the view is everyone's to share.'

As far as Shire knew, Tuck was the only man in the 125th Ohio from Kentucky, an outsider like himself, though Kentucky was a deal closer to Ohio than England. But then most men could see themselves as an outsider for one reason or another. It was better to work on belonging.

'What bothers me,' Shire said, 'is we seem to be one brigade shadowing a whole Confederate army. I hope we keep our distance. Maybe we'll get backed up right across Tennessee and into Kentucky. Perhaps that's where we're headed. Toward your home.'

Tuck slowed almost to a halt and bent as if he'd taken on a weight. Shire wished he could take back his thought. Tuck's parents had burned to death on their farm while Kentucky violently made up its mind which side to fight for. Eventually, the grief and the anger had told and determined Tuck to sign up, but for Ohio, a state he saw as being of 'sounder mind'.

'I gotta go find Wilkins.' Tuck swung his knapsack off and reached in for something. 'I heard he found some whiskey in

Athens.' He stepped out of column holding something in his hand. Shire couldn't see what.

'Buy some for me,' Shire called after.

Mason caught up and took Tuck's place. 'He alright?'

'Tuck? He was. I started to talk about Kentucky. I guess he didn't want to.'

'He oughta be dead after playing the fiddle in the rain last night. Half the company think he's touched. Lieutenant Rice asked after him.'

'He's been up and down ever since I came back.'

'It began before then. Best I can figure it was after Kennesaw, though the fights came so thick and fast after that it's hard to be sure.'

'It was a rough fight for us all at Kennesaw,' said Shire.

'If you think about it, maybe rougher on him than you as things turned out.'

Shire *didn't* like to think about it, but not a day passed when it didn't come unbidden. Kennesaw was constantly there. After killing Wick, Shire got tangled in a thorny abatis, pinned by the sharpened branches and the piled undergrowth. It was set afire. Tuck couldn't reach him. He could still see Tuck's despairing face as the flames cut between them. He'd thought it would be his last sight on this earth. Tod had saved him at the last moment from the Confederate side. 'Tuck wasn't the one nearly burned alive,' Shire said.

The column stopped, a blockage up ahead. Mason turned to him. 'You're his pard,' he said, 'his best friend since we joined. And he thought he'd left you to the fire, the same way his parents perished. And then two months later you show up back from the dead.'

It wasn't Shire's fault that the prisoner lists hadn't made it through. How could he have known that?

'He ain't right in the head,' Mason said. 'You see enough people killed or near killed and, well, death becomes so familiar you might see it plain and close all the time, as if through a damp and stretched cheesecloth.'

Franklin, Tennessee – November, 1864

Clara stepped outside the small train depot and let the handful of other alighted passengers move past her and up the street. She could have asked Moses to drive her to Franklin in the new wagon, or looked to drive here herself, but she'd yet to try the two-horse team for anything like this far.

The train had been the easier option and allowed for a later start. It also meant she was alone and could do as she pleased. Ostensibly, that was to see if they had any salt in Franklin as it was lacking in Spring Hill yesterday. It was a mere side benefit that she might get to see more of Tod's hometown. Where was the harm in that? She'd have come here sooner or later.

Mitilde had complained that there was more to worry about on the farm and that they had nothing to salt anyway. Clara felt she'd done her bit yesterday by finding and buying a wagon and a two-horse team. It hadn't been an easy negotiation. She'd been uncertain whether to introduce herself as the widow of a Confederate officer and use the Spencer part of her cousin's name. She didn't want to be a Spencer-Ridgmont anymore. In point of fact, she believed she never legally had been, given Taylor's bigamous deceit. She'd helped put the horses into their traces, checked how each was shod and picked out their hooves. Then she'd run the wagon up and down the pike, thinking on the way how useful it would have been to have Shire's horse knowledge to add to hers. When she returned, the sellers, an older couple, bluntly asked how it was an Englishwoman was taking on a farm alone. In the end a dead Confederate husband had played well enough. It hadn't swayed the price though. She'd used up most of her cash to hand. Before leaving early this morning, she'd asked Moses to turn the horses out into the fields to settle.

Her fellow passengers were disappearing up the road. To the right of the Franklin depot, looking over the track as it headed north, the land cut away into the Harpeth River. A steep bluff on the far side was capped with a fort. She couldn't see any cannon, just a single sentry lazily pacing the walls. She put her arm through the loop of her empty basket and began down the street a polite distance from the other passengers, supposing some might also be on a shopping errand and lead her in the right direction. Two blocks along and one to the left, the house fronts gave way to the town square and a handsome county courthouse. There were a pair of grocery stores to choose between and Clara visited both before buying the cheaper salt, some cheese and a wrinkled apple. There was a bench in the square and for a while she sat and ate, watching the people of Franklin share their pavements with a handful of Union soldiers. There was no obvious enmity, but then the Union had been here a long while. She'd asked for the way to the Columbia Pike when paying for her food but after she stood and brushed cheese crumbs from her dress and started along Main Street, a sudden stab of guilt was almost enough to stop her.

Two boys raced past, one chasing the other; the second knocked her basket and nearly dislodged the bag of salt.

She'd always intended to walk out to the Carter house before heading back for the train. There was little else to do. So why did every step feel so leaden? It was as if Shire was standing to the side and slightly behind her, a habit that irritated her: as if he still thought he was some lackey despite all he'd done. Out of nowhere she became angry and quickened her step. The pike arrived soon, angling to the south off Main Street. Two more blocks and the town proper abruptly ended with the pike rising straight and steep through cleared pasture toward a pair of houses visible atop the hill. She found herself inventing increasingly elaborate and far-fetched circumstances which might allow her to talk to Tod's family, presently no more than a quarter-mile away. She felt suddenly exposed, a lady walking alone. The first house was on the left of the pike and was somewhat grand compared with those back down in the town. Two stories, it was as deep as it was wide. High square columns faced the road. The house was pristine white and bordered by a smart fence. As she passed, Clara felt a sudden affinity: this house was as out of place as she was.

Ahead on the crest of the rise, close and to the right of the road, was the distinctive stepped gable and red-tiled roof of the Carter house. She recognized it from her visit in the spring. She'd come back then to deliver a letter from Tod given to her during his escape, much of that spent secreted in her cabin and bed as they steamed down the Ohio River. The letter had been snatched from her hand by a gaggle of children at the door. She'd seen no one else.

She came level with the garden fence and a low gate, planning to slowly pass by. That way she'd be doing nothing more than walking to the rise to look out over the fields and open country beyond. Instead, she stopped and stared at the house. They might want news of Tod. Almost certainly she'd seen him more recently than they had. She'd be doing a kindness if she talked with them.

'Can I help you, young lady?'

She turned. A gray-haired man, old but upright, approached her from across the road, a heart-shaped spade in his hand. She was taken aback. He had the same strong forehead as Tod, the same deep-set intelligent eyes.

He stopped a polite distance away. 'Are you looking for someone?'

'Yes… I am… Do you live here?'

'I do. Are you a friend to one of my daughters, perhaps?'

'You must be Moscow.'

'Ha. He wouldn't thank you for that. I'm his father, Fountain.'

'I'm sorry.' Clara took a step toward him. 'I wasn't sure if I should impose.'

'I'm not averse to young Englishwomen imposing, though I'm not sure one ever has before.'

'I know your son. Tod. I delivered a letter from him, in the spring.'

The smile dropped from Fountain's face. 'You have news of him?'

'Some. It's a little dated.' She saw the fear in Fountain's eyes. 'He was well when last I saw him. That was in July.'

Fountain stepped around Clara and opened the gate with his free hand. 'Glory be. I feared you might be an angel of death. My heart can start beating again. The family will want to hear what you can tell us.' He led her to the front door. 'We heard he was back with his regiment. Some news gets through, but that's all. Come inside.' He propped the spade against the wall and opened the door.

Stepping in from November, the house was warm. Clara removed her gloves and took in Tod's home. The hall was more spacious than her new one: wide, high and light, with cream tiled walls. A carpeted staircase switched up, across and back. The woodwork around the paneled internal doors was a happy bright blue.

'Please,' said Fountain, 'wait in here.' He opened the door on the right and let her show herself into the parlor. It was well appointed. Somewhat bold floral wallpaper for her taste, but a stylish low settee. What had she expected of Tod's home? He'd spoken more about the land than the house. There were shouts from inside and out, running footsteps above, doors opened and closed. Soon a stream of children entered the room and bunched together. Most stared doe-eyed at her, the smallest one climbed on the settee. She counted nine. Five women formed up behind them and tried to keep them settled and facing forward. Fountain returned, trailed by a younger and taller version of himself who was wiping his hands on a cloth. *That* must be Moscow. Everyone looked at her expectantly. There was a dearth of husbands. The war, no doubt.

Fountain came to stand beside her. Clara was glad of the company, her audience somewhat daunting in her otherwise lonely day.

'I apologize, ma'am,' said Fountain. 'Here we are with the whole household gathered and I haven't yet asked who it is I'm introducing.'

'My name is Clara. Clara Ridgmont.' She might still have to play the Confederate widow, but it felt like the right time to stop being Mrs Spencer-Ridgmont.

*

From his spot at the back of the parlor, Moscow Carter listened as attentively as everyone else to the news the young Englishwoman delivered concerning Tod. It began to seem that it wouldn't add a huge amount to what they already knew, dated to July as it was, and he found he was listening more to her exotic English accent and admiring her dark brown eyes. He didn't object to being whistled in from the fall fields for this.

The mention of the mines at Ducktown and Tod leading a doomed mission to collect copper for the fight around Atlanta got his attention again, especially Tod's narrow escape from the landslide on the return trip. He shared in the collective relief of his sisters. Hands touched mouths; children's shoulders were squeezed. He had his misgivings about this war, but it didn't stop him being proud of his brother.

Clara hadn't said what she was doing in Ducktown that had allowed her to meet Tod for a second time. It seemed a heavy coincidence. Questions started to rain in, first from Fountain and then from Moscow's sisters. How had Tod come to be on the riverboat? Had she come all the way from East Tennessee just to deliver this news? All things he was curious to understand too, but the poor lady hadn't even been offered a seat. She appeared in command of herself though, almost enjoying this.

He let it run a few minutes more but then stepped in front of the children and suggested they could catch up on any more news later and should return to their chores. It was only early afternoon, but maybe Miss Ridgmont would care to stay for dinner? With perfect English politeness she explained she had the farm in Spring Hill to get back to. In the end, after Father pressed in a last question or two, Mary, as the ranking sister, suggested she, Sarah, Sallie and Annie 'take coffee' with Clara if Frances would care to keep an eye on the children. Predictably, Frances did not care to and left in an undisguised huff. Moscow, not being listed, reasoned he too was surplus to requirements. Before leaving the room, he offered to drive Clara to the depot when she'd finished 'taking coffee', which seemed to be Mary's new and anglicized way of describing an American pastime. It was two hours before he was summoned. By that time he had his best gelding, General Scott, ready in the traces and had wiped over the leather seat of the covered buggy more than once. He helped Clara up, passed up her basket and climbed in beside her. The reassembled family waved from on and around the front steps as if he and Clara were heading for a new life together, or maybe that was just how he imagined it. 'You seem to have made quite an impression,' he said, as they moved away back down the pike.

Clara was leaning out and waving back. 'That's quite some collection of children, sir.'

'Moscow, please. And yes, a collection is largely what it is. It's what you do in hard times. Gather everyone together.'

'Which of the ladies is your wife?'

'Good Lord. You mean to say my sisters kept you hostage the best part of the afternoon but didn't sketch out the family?'

'Not entirely. Some of the children found their way back into the room, so I did get to know a few names.'

'Well then, all the women in the house are my sisters, direct or by marriage. The children I lay claim to are Lena, Walter, Annie and Hugh. I lost my wife. Four years since.'

'I'm sorry.'

'It's a long time ago. The war makes it seem more so. Mary is married but her husband Daniel stayed on in Texas while she came home for her health. Three of the children are hers. Sallie is widow to my brother James who died in fifty-nine.

She accounts for two more. Annie is widowed without children. Sarah and Frances are unmarried.' He glanced sideways at Clara who stared back at him wide-eyed, her mouth attractively ajar. He laughed. 'Let me simplify things. We're all widows, widowers or unmarried but for Mary. Everyone takes a part share in the children.'

Clara laughed with him. 'The house doesn't appear large enough.'

'There are rooms below ground and an annex out the back. We make do. It'll settle out again after the war.'

He slowed General Scott to a walk. The trains were largely random in their timings anyway so there was no sense in rushing. 'Are you warm enough? There's a blanket in the tail-box.'

'I'm fine. Thank you.'

It had been a while since he'd ridden in a buggy with anyone other than his sisters. He kept quiet down the hill until they reached town. A brace of Union soldiers stepped aside to let them overtake. Moscow nodded his thanks. 'Your farm in Spring Hill, that would be the Tolivers' old place?'

'That's right. They were my tenants. Did you know them?'

'It's not so far away and we take an interest in all the land hereabouts. They were good people. Union I think, but I don't disqualify people on that account. They worked their farm well until the raid.'

'I only found out they'd left when I sent to ask if they would vacate the tenancy,' said Clara. 'I didn't know they'd gone.'

'It hit them hard, I guess.'

'I'd have let them stay on, if they'd wanted to.'

'Where would you have gone?'

'I don't know.'

'Do you still have family in England?'

'Yes, but I chose to make a life in America.'

'Sounds as if it's gone awry.'

'It's America that's gone awry. I'm simply another widow, trying to outlast the war like everyone else.'

'I'm sorry. I don't mean to pry.'

They rode around the square. He could have cut toward the depot earlier but thought he'd stay on the wider roads. There was no easy way to ask Clara if she had some romantic attachment with Tod, but it felt like a solid bet. She'd come out of her way to visit. Young as he was before the war, Tod always had a way with the ladies.

General Scott broke into a trot of his own accord. The rail depot lay ahead. There was no train visible and Moscow slowed them to a walk again. 'Have you got help on the farm?'

'Two friends from my old home. A couple. Both a little old, but strong. I'll need to hire some hands.'

'I could come down if it's useful? I know the soils in Williamson County as well as anyone. We could walk the fields.'

'That would be very helpful.'

'Alright then. It's hard to find crops that the armies won't carry away. You have to harvest early and sell fast.'

'Surely we're safe from the war here?'

'I don't think the Tolivers would agree, and this week the news is that General Hood is scuttling along south of the Tennessee River. If he gets over, he'll most likely make a play for Nashville. Lots of ways to get there but, the same as my home, your property fronts one of the best roads. Here we are. I can wait if you'd like?'

'I'll be fine.'

He hurried around but Clara was out of the buggy with

her basket and looking up toward Fort Granger.

'I shouldn't have worried you over Hood,' he said. 'If the Union don't stop him the winter will. He has to get across the Tennessee. And that's a wide river.'

Colonel Emerson Opdycke sawed Ben back and forth on the sodden ground before the three small dams. He could feel his horse was getting jumpy so slackened his grip on the rein and tried to ease his own mood. It was early afternoon and his pioneers were finishing their constructions for the second time. In truth this was the fourth attempt, General Grose's 2nd Brigade having failed twice before Wood summoned Opdycke to make a better job of it. That was the story of his war, Opdycke thought: a colonel sent in to do a general's work.

Yesterday, he'd given one hundred and twenty of his own pioneers precise directions. He'd not stayed to oversee; he'd had brigade business to attend to. They'd made a complete hash of it, the dams breached as soon as modest pressure built up from the converging springs behind. So today he'd stayed to watch over them.

Army life was all water of late. There was the damp train ride to Athens and the mud-march that followed. On route to here at Pulaski, where parts of the 23rd Corps had consolidated, they'd waded the waist-deep Elk River, his men undressing to spare their uniforms. They'd gone in white and come out red, poor devils. And now this dam in case the Rebels took a liking for Pulaski. Wood said the small lake created would impede the enemy's approach. He supposed Wood was right. It was best to be prepared. Though if the news was accurate and Hood had begun crossing at Florence, then Pulaski wasn't on the direct route to Nashville.

The men working at the dam made a small show of standing to attention, prompting Opdycke to look behind. Here came Wood, mounted as well, though with more necessity given the foot wound he was carrying.

'Colonel Opdycke.'

'Sir.'

'How are you getting along? Will we hold back the Red Sea this time?' Wood was no longer in Opdycke's chain of command, but had been made the general director of the defenses for Pulaski.

'God will have to decide that, sir.' Opdycke chose not to join Wood's jovial mood. 'I wasn't at West Point. I'm not schooled as an engineer.'

'And yet I know you'll do the best job, Emerson. You're long past being a civilian soldier.'

Not where rank is concerned, thought Opdycke. 'I've had them construct smaller gabions this time. We can pack them better. So far, we have four feet of water and it's holding.'

'And your other project? Your lunette?' Wood twisted in his saddle to look up the nearest hill on the edge of town, where a small host of soldiers were at work.

Not for the first time, Opdycke wished his brigade was in Wood's Division and not under Wagner. It was Wood who had christened the 125th as the Tigers for their strong showing at Chickamauga last year and Wood who had made sure Opdycke got some credit. He could talk to Wood. Wagner was such a cold fish, lately. 'Two more days, sir, and it'll be done.' The fortification was being thrown up around a female seminary, much to the indignation of the locals.

Wood smiled. 'It's an honor, General Stanley naming it for you.'

Opdycke tried to avoid a sour look but suspected he'd failed. 'Lunette Opdycke doesn't exactly trip off the tongue. Sounds more like a distant cousin.'

'Opdycke's Lunette, surely?' laughed Wood.

Opdycke encouraged Ben forward to lead Wood away from the men. 'I'd prefer Stanley secured my promotion rather than named breastworks after me.' If he was made a general, he might get a proper fort christened in his honor. As yet he merely rated this lunette, a demi-fort that only faced the expected line of attack. He wasn't sure if it was half a compliment or half an insult.

'The election news is all good.' Wood was still trying to buoy him up. 'Lincoln will be in fine spirits when his new term is confirmed. That'll be his time for signing promotions. Stanley is sure of it. You know Sherman's recommended you as well. And you already have your fine brigade.'

He'd waited so long for a promotion. If it arrived now, it would resemble an afterthought. It didn't do to dwell on it. 'Do you think my handiwork will get tested? Hood's further to the west.' He'd lost count of the forts and field-defenses he'd built in this war that had never been used in anger.

'Not so far west that he couldn't send a corps this way,' said Wood, 'or Forrest's cavalry. It seems Hood's got the numbers on us this time. At Florence, he can supply himself using the railroad to Corinth. My bet would be he'll head straight north. He strikes me as a man who aims straight at the target, but while we're ordered to stay, we might as well use the time.'

Wood remained with him an hour more until he was satisfied the dams would do the job, then rode away. Opdycke left a detail to watch over things but sent the bulk of his men back to camp. He followed on, Ben walking slowly. He missed old Barney – who he'd buried outside Atlanta – and had vowed never to get so attached to another horse, but how could you do that when sharing the trials of war every day? Ben was a dependable fellow. Two weeks back, his brigade had moved through Dug Gap not so far from Chattanooga and had charge of more than a thousand head of cattle for the whole corps. The men on foot driving them had lost control. The hungry herd had started to beat its own path until Opdycke, aboard Ben, had ridden around them in a wide arc, waving his hat and corralling them back. It had raised a few smiles with the men; their colonel cowboy to the rescue.

He patted Ben's neck, steered him into town and toward his brigade headquarters. Pulaski was a smart enough place, so far unspoiled by the war. It would be a shame if Hood chose to come this way. Opdycke's H.Q. was in the home of one Mr Gordon, a solid Union man at odds with most of his neighbors. Smiling John jumped up to take Ben's bridle. Opdycke had found the black boy by the roadside in LaFayette south of Chickamauga three weeks ago. He was a good boy, happy to be smartened up and have a way north with the army. What a strange world it was when you could find whole human beings like you might a lost penny.

Orders from Wagner and brigade paperwork were pressed on Opdycke as soon as he stepped through the door. He took it into the parlor. That was his space, doubling as bedroom and office. He hadn't so much as sat down when his host, Mr Gordon, knocked and entered without waiting. It was his parlor after all. As had become the norm, he set down a healthy plate of apple pie and a jug of coffee on Opdycke's desk. Judging from his girth, Gordon hadn't suffered many hungry days of late. He was good company and Opdycke always thought it advisable to take the temperature of a town.

Gordon didn't ask if he had the time for a visit, just leaned back in his rocker which had been holidayed from the porch for Opdycke's benefit. 'I wanted your advice, as a businessman, not a soldier.'

Opdycke poured two coffees, handed one to Gordon and sat down on his cot. 'Sounds like I'd best remove my hat.'

'There's a property north of town, five hundred acres. Good land for cotton but fallow these last two years. It's available to rent. With the price as it is, I reckon I could bring in a hundred and twenty-five thousand dollars next summer.'

Opdycke didn't react to the big number, at least not outwardly. He simply said, 'There's a reason it's fallow. Farming requires peace as well as good soil.'

'War helps the price some, though. And maybe they'll be peace next year.'

'Strange confidence from a man whose town I'm busy fortifying.'

'You think you'll still be in uniform come next summer?'

'No way of telling,' said Opdycke. 'If you'd have asked me after we fought our way out of Chattanooga this time last year, I'd have said we'd have won the war by now. The truth is we've all been wrong more than once and, I have to tell you, sir, Hood has the advantage this time. Thomas is scrambling for men enough to stop him. It's not easy with Sherman away on his jaunt in Georgia. This isn't a good time for making business plans.'

'I estimate the cost at fifteen thousand to raise the crop.'

That widened Opdycke's eyes. Such a profit. 'Well now, that does put a different spin on things.' He'd shared with Wood that he was starting to think of options outside the army. It had needed to be said even if he wasn't sure he meant it. Why see out the war given his lack of promotion? Soldiering ı't ever going to mend his finances. 'I need to come up with a venture at some point.'

Gordon rocked plumply forward. 'We could go in together. Spread the risk. Five hundred acres is a lot for one man.'

Opdycke barely knew Gordon, but it was an opportunity nonetheless. 'I'm flattered, but there's Hood to deal with. And frankly, you'd be a brave man to invest in

a secession state, Union as you are.'

'Maybe it's not as secesh as you think, Colonel. There are plenty in Pulaski wishing the war away. The world's gonna have to right itself one day.' Gordon sat back and the conversation moved on. How did this man survive here? That took a particular kind of bravery. Where Opdycke had so recently been in Georgia and Alabama, Gordon would have been run out of town or murdered.

After he left, Opdycke had time to write to Lucy and despite himself found he was telling her about Gordon and his offer. It was pleasant to consider a future, any future, where he was together with her and little Tine. That evening he and a few other officers were invited to dine with General Cox and celebrate the mounting good news of Lincoln's re-election. Cox commanded the 23rd Corps. Opdycke knew him well from the general's days as a lawyer in their hometown of Warren. Cox was a volunteer soldier too, only two years older than Opdycke. So he could hardly blame Cox's high station on professional army favoritism. Politics was the other route up the ranks if you hadn't been to West Point, and Cox's name was on the rise in Ohio before the war. All Opdycke had was his fighting record.

Over cigars, Cox took him aside and quietly said he understood Opdycke's frustration on having to wait for advancement. Wood must have had a word in his ear. Opdycke took a chance and said there were opportunities starting to present themselves that he had his duty to his family to consider.

Cox wasn't buying that. 'Come now, Emerson. Your prospects for promotion are better than any other colonel in this army. I'll do all I can, but I need you to stay in any case. Even if we see off Hood, who knows how things will settle out? If there's to be peace beyond the war, we have to win the argument as well as the fight. But the fight comes first and we need soldiers.' His voice dropped lower still. 'Thomas is drawing reinforcements to Nashville from across the Mississippi, but they're weeks away at best. We're asking every brigade to send a few good men up to Nashville to fetch out the shirkers and those mended and fit to fight. I've no idea of the numbers, but Thomas says it's worth the effort. The orders will come along, but I want you to get moving on it.'

Opdycke walked back to the Gordon house alone, thinking about a life beyond the army. He had a choice at least. As an officer he could up and resign his commission and barely a word would be said, but his soldiers would have to see out their terms. If they chose to head for home, it was his job to have them found and shot. The solitude and the cold, dark streets of Pulaski fostered some inner honesty. There had been a calling from God to enter this fight, but if they saw off Hood, and if he could square it with the Lord, perhaps he could stand to leave the army and maybe his brigade, but he'd be damned if he was ever going to walk away from the 125th and leave them to fight on without him.

In his room, Julia was there – another 'find' – leaving folded and ironed underclothes on his cot. She washed for the whole staff, not just him. How old was she? Thirty? He made a point of telling her about the election, but it was evident she knew as much as he did and was rightfully happier to boot. It was more pertinent for her future than for his. What sort of life was this for her, a handsome black woman travelling alone with a brigade of soldiers? She closed the door on her way out. He supposed that if she decided to up and leave in the morning, no one would have the right to stop her. That had become the point of the whole enterprise. Not what people like Julia did, but that they could *choose* to do it or not. He smiled at the simplicity of it. Promotion or no promotion, he was still on the right side of the argument.

Franklin, Tennessee – November, 1864

The Carter house parlor was oversized for a class of two. Alice and Lena sat at makeshift desks that Moscow had conjured from somewhere. Both were attentive students, although at eight and *I'm nearly twelve*, they were on different pages. Clara had to use her imagination to find common ground. She had greatly underestimated their standard in the first lesson. Above the diminutive piano and between two pastoral paintings hung Moscow's sister Annie's framed certificate from the Franklin Female Institute. Williamson County was a step up from Polk, it appeared. Both Lena and Alice had been schooled in French and Lena even possessed some rudimentary Greek. Clara was using the fables both by way of entertainment and to introduce a few more French nouns. She'd chosen *The Lion and the Mouse*, partly for her own amusement: little Alice seemed more akin to the lion and older Lena the mouse.

'When did you last do me a good turn, Lena?' Alice asked her cousin.

Lena twisted to face her. 'I asked you to call me Orlena in class,' she said, through a tight mouth. 'It's more 'propriate.'

'*A*-ppropriate,' encouraged Clara.

'Well, what's my favor if I do?' complained Alice. 'I don't need chewin' out o' no net.'

Clara chose to correct Alice's sentiment rather than her speech. 'The point is not that we should look for something in return, rather that we are all dependent on each other, no matter what size we are or how fierce we might be. Sit up straight, dear.'

'I keep lots of Lena's secrets. Seems to me she'd do best to keep me happy.'

Lena stared wide-eyed at her slate.

'I think you should be pleased that your cousin trusts you enough to share her secrets.' Clara's assumption that the pecking order among the children was defined by age had been wide of the mark. She tried to focus them back on the nouns: *lionne, souris, filets, pitié.* Moscow hadn't been specific about his expectations. She should discuss that with him and Alice's mother, Mary, after the lesson. There was no train to catch today. She wondered where she would best fit in this fable. Lion or mouse?

Moscow had waited only a few days before he rode to Eversholt as promised. Clara had any number of decisions to make on the farm, so had been thankful to receive her first guest and to invite him in from the porch, where he'd stood squeezing the shape from his hat. Mitilde had thrown up her arms. 'This place ain't fit for vis'ters yet. I needs to be told if folk are gonna present themselves before the breakfast dishes is cleared.'

'Will I make the coffee then?' asked Clara. That had been enough to encourage Mitilde to the kitchen, although she could be heard complaining from there. Moscow apologized for the early hour but it had allowed them to spend the morning walking her farm with Moses. The Tolivers had left a logbook for the last several years. It detailed which crop had been in which field: corn, oats, sweet potatoes. No cotton. Moses and Moscow consulted, heads together. On occasion, Moscow would squat to collect a handful of soil and rub it between his fingers. He pointed out where he thought the drainage could be improved or fields that needed a fallow year. From behind them, struggling to pull herself from the mud, Clara heard Moses outline ideas to Moscow that he'd yet to share with her.

'He's a fine old boy,' said Moscow, when they were back at the house. Mitilde had laid out lunch and left them to it, ignoring Moscow's contention that he should start the ride back. 'Where does he stay?' he asked Clara.

'I'm sorry?'

'Moses. You have no slave huts.'

'I have no slaves.'

'Of course. None of us really do anymore.' He didn't appear the least affronted and held her gaze a little longer than was comfortable. 'Although it remains legal in Tennessee. No state statute passed as yet. In reality things have changed, though. Most of our blacks up and left when the Union arrived. Weren't a thing we could do about it.'

Moscow said it so wistfully that it seemed to Clara he felt let down. 'This is Moses' and Mitilde's home too,' was all she said.

'The few who've stayed on with us still use the huts. We have no room in the house anyway, but some folks round here would see it as unseemly to share.'

'We've been through a lot together. They've become family.'

'I understand. It must be hard on your own.'

'Sometimes.'

Moscow pushed his empty plate aside, leaned forward and put his hands on the table. 'Moses is too old for some of the heavy work that's going to be needed. And it'll be hard to hire hands with the war on. I could help, up to a point. Put the word out. Let you know who you can trust. If they hadn't mostly left, you could have rented our people. It used to be no more than a few cents a day per hand.'

Clara inwardly debated whether renting a soul from someone was any better than owning that soul.

'There's time to get some barley in the ground if you had a mind to, though it might be better to just subsist for now. It's hard to be ambitious while the war lasts. We've let our stock in hogs and beef run down. Confederate cavalry raids have been mostly south and west of here, excepting the one that did for the Tolivers.'

'My neighbors' farms look fine.'

'Maybe your neighbors weren't for the Union. People talk. The soldiers might as well be locusts if your crops are up. One bad day will ruin you. Longer term, I'd be happy to help you build up the place for a share in the crop.'

'Am I not too far from Franklin?'

'It's tolerable. We could work something out.'

No final answer seemed called for. Clara quietly finished her meal.

'I have one other thought.' Moscow dropped his gaze. 'If you'll oblige me? It's only a suggestion.' He sipped some water. 'It's been hard, with the war on, looking out for the children, even with my sisters.'

Clara struggled to swallow.

'The boys' school, the Harpeth Academy, is destroyed and the girls' schools have been mostly closed during the war. So many teachers are away in the armies. We make do, at the churches and at home, but my Lena in particular, she needs bringing along and, with you being, well, clearly a lady of refinement...' The color rose in Moscow's cheeks. He sat back. 'She's a bright girl. Some extra lessons would be good for her.'

'Are you asking me to be her governess?'

'That sounds a mite grand for the Carter home, but we can call it that if you like. Alice could sit with her. I know it's a long way, but the Lotz family, across the road from us, they have a room you could overnight in. Then you could spread lessons over two days each week. I'd pay, of course. I hope you're not offended.'

*

Now here she was with the two girls before her. She stared at the silver-faced clock on the wall while she waited for them to finish and got lost in the flower motif and the Roman numerals. Governess or teacher, she wasn't really sure. Certainly, an impostor either way. She should at least be honest with herself. If only they knew about Tod, about the child that never was. Moscow might not think of her as a *lady of refinement* then.

Alice laid her slate flat. Lena was still scratching away, tongue out, head on one side. Clara had never seriously considered turning Moscow down. This was something in her life other than the farm and perhaps a way into Williamson County society, although a fair distance from her new home. She would do better to find friends in Spring Hill. And the Carters weren't exactly gentry. Having spent more time in the house, she'd spotted that the 'tiled' hallway was artfully achieved by a brush or a pencil, and that the marble skirting was no more than painted wood. The sugar-safe tucked next to the stairs in the hall was real enough, but there for show all the same.

They were good people. That was plain. Yet here she was, a daughter to British nobility aspiring to gentry, if that term meant anything in Tennessee. What would Shire say as to her new position? Something acidic about her presence in Tod's house, no doubt. Or he might laugh. A teacher once himself, he knew how much she'd detested her own governesses, how she'd machinated to have them dismissed, one after the other. Part of the appeal of escaping to America was that she could cut her own path. She'd no intention of mentioning her new station in letters back to England. Perhaps that was a measure of how well her escape was going. It would shock her parents to know their daughter was *employed*. While as a governess she might impart ladylike qualities, it was generally accepted that, in teaching them, she forfeited any pretense to be a true lady herself. She was left with the sense of how far she'd fallen, her move from Comrie the latest in a downward spiral. She tried to measure how much any of this truly mattered but couldn't find a yardstick.

She'd waited for the right moment to tell Matilde that not only was she going to teach, but she'd be away one night a week. The moment was slow in coming so she'd taken the cowardly route and told Moses instead. Money would have been useful but she preferred to keep it as an informal credit against future help at Eversholt. Moscow said he would square the cost of her lodging at the Lotz house.

She wasn't blind to the fact that this idea of Moscow's might presage a romantic approach, but chose not to tell him about Tod. Not yet. She cast forward to the day when Tod might return home, fresh from the blessed end of the war, to find Clara schooling his nieces in his front parlor.

Lena finished and Clara stood between them to see the results. No mistakes on either slate. Lena's writing was noticeably neater. 'Alice, you can fetch the others.'

Such was the dismay among the younger girls that they

were to be excluded from lessons, Clara suggested to Mary that the little ones could join them at the end of the morning for a few deportment exercises and perhaps a further story.

Annie and Ruth, and Matilda from the Lotz house, all of them five or six or thereabouts, were bundled into the parlor by Frances, who stayed to watch. Matilda seemed almost resident here. Clara lined them up, had them grip their hands behind their backs and push down. The exercise was meant for girls older than Lena, but backs straightened and chins lifted. Ruth, up on her toes, asked if this was 'how people growed?' After a minute or so, excitement descended to complaints. Annie, losing her balance, threw herself on the sofa in a strop. Frances joined the line, chest raised and presented. Clara truly had become a governess.

Giles County, Tennessee – November, 1864

'Shire, Tuck! With me.' Lieutenant Rice surprised them as they were making ready to move camp. 'Knapsacks and haversacks. The whole caboodle. We'll be gone a number of days.'

Shire hurriedly rolled his blanket and strapped it to his pack. It was all he had left to do. 'Gone where, sir?' As they were otherwise already prepared for the day, he and Tuck simply followed their company commander.

'Lieutenant,' Mason called after them.

Rice walked at a fair lick.

'Lieutenant, where are you taking them? Does Sergeant Ocks know? Sir?'

'Nashville,' Rice yelled back. 'Special assignment. Straight from Schofield. Tell Ocks we've gone hunting.'

Shire struggled to keep up as Rice led them away from the regiment. General Schofield was in charge of the Army of the Ohio; what could he possibly want with them? Being old hands, Shire and Tuck were on friendly terms with Lieutenant Rice, but he was closed to Shire's questions, saying he'd just now got the orders himself and wanted to hurry to the rail track. They struck it soon enough and ambled north until a whistle sounded from behind. Rice stood square across the track and waved his rifle in the air. He had to jump aside when the driver merely slowed, preferring to get a look at them, his stoker beside him doing the same above the barrel of a shotgun. Rice waved a paper at them. 'We have orders to go to Nashville. Can we board?'

The gun was withdrawn. Brakes squealed and the train stopped. 'Climb on. The third car has some space. Last stop told us there's a bridge out halfway to Columbia, so you won't be in Nashville today.'

The space in the third car turned out to be what was left over once a half-dozen equine recruits were taken into account. Shire moved among them, soothing them whether they needed it or not as the train struggled up to speed again. He found one sweating and shivering, picked up some straw and rubbed it down. Tuck's fiddle came out but was ordered sheathed by Rice. 'I'd hate for these horses to stampede in confined quarters.'

Not an hour later the train stopped again. The three of them disembarked and walked beyond the engine. It had pulled up a handful of crossties before a fire-blackened and wounded trestle bridge that spanned a deep and wide ravine. There must have been three hundred men or more working on the repairs. They swarmed over the bridge, a busy blue infestation, some out along the incomplete top span, others either end of a crane carried on a flatbed railcar, many more perilously among the posts and cross-struts. Men struggled to shout instructions over a chorus of hammer and saw. Way down in the ravine and across a swift creek stood a clump of engineer officers. One held a sheet of paper so big he looked in danger of being lifted into the air. Others pointed and gestured up at the bridge. As Shire watched, a steam winch puffed into action on the crane-car and a thick trestle rose and swayed up from below like a miracle, before being claimed by many hands and dragged into the great puzzle of wood. Despite their industry, the nearer half of the bridge was missing the top forty feet.

The engine driver came and stood beside them, wiping

sooty hands on a dirty rag. Rice, greasy hair pushed back off his forehead, asked, 'If you knew the bridge was broke, why did you set out? We'll be stuck for days.'

The driver took his time surveying the works. 'Well,' he said, 'you're welcome to climb down and up the other side, but any trains that happen along from Nashville will only queue up to go south. Watch a while.' He turned to walk back to his engine. 'These people will have us over before nightfall.'

With nothing to do but wait, Shire and Tuck left Rice at the engine and worked their way along the top of the ravine to a spot where they could watch the repair. The ground fell steeply away before them. Predictably, Tuck dropped his pack, took up his fiddle and sat. He hadn't said a word today. A stiff breeze struck up under a gray sky. At least they had the car to retreat to if it came on to rain. Shire got out his dog-eared map of Tennessee and Kentucky and unfolded it carefully so as not to bring on further dishevelment. He found Pulaski and traced the rail line to Nashville via Columbia. Short of Franklin he found Spring Hill. They would pass right by. Clara had been full of dubious enthusiasm for her move when he'd left her. What would have changed since? He wouldn't need the train to stop again to be certain how he felt. That question had always been for her, though he wondered if she'd answered it quietly to herself a long time ago. Maybe Tod had answered it for her.

He folded his map away and got busy with a fire. In the army it paid to eat when the opportunity presented itself. 'I'll cook your pork. We ate mine yesterday,' he said. They often shared rations. That way if one of them got a runt portion the hardship was shared too.

There was no response from Tuck. Sometimes it was like living with an elderly relative whose mind had been misplaced.

In his own time, Tuck bowed into a slow waltz, utterly at odds with the exertions of the bridge builders. Evidently, it carried on the wind into the ravine and on to those high on the bridge, as not a few faces turned their way. There was a moment's lull in the hammering before it stuttered up again. Two men on the flatbed end of the crane-car moved elegantly into closed hold and took a turn or two before their corporal beat them apart with his hat. Shire smiled but saw Tuck was too far inside his tune to take it in.

Once he had the fire going, he dug in Tuck's pack for the salt belly-pork they'd been doled out back in Athens. It was a mess in there. An apple long past saving, percussion caps loose that should have been in a box, a lone dollar bill left to its own devices. The string hadn't been tied properly on the pork paper. The exposed meat had picked up a covering of cotton threads and other miniature detritus. Shire reasoned it would cook off in his small skillet. Tuck's ration was more than ample, so he cut off two-thirds and put it to cook slowly, not too close to the heat so that the fat would stay aboard. He wrapped the remains with care and was finding a safe corner back in Tuck's pack when he happened on something round and hard. He drew out an enamel doorknob.

He recognized it. Tuck kept it as a grim reminder of his parents who were burned alive in their farmhouse, Tuck's home. The enamel was scorched on one side, a smooth, mute witness to their murders. He'd been about to look for some wild onion or anything that might flavor the meat, but instead he took the doorknob and went to sit next to Tuck.

He didn't expect to be acknowledged, but the lack irked Shire all the same. The waltz looped around and around. Shire could have sworn some of the hammering was striking out *one*, two, three… *one*, two, three. 'I think you're slowing down their industry,' he said.

Tuck played on and Shire felt a bubble of anger pop inside. It wasn't like Tuck was fighting this war on his own. Shire had been an open book when it came to his own problems. Tuck was the only person he'd told about Clara's romance with Tod, of how the two of them had kept it from Shire like he was some lovesick youth. Tuck had had precious little to say on it. And he'd barely passed comment when Shire had told him how he'd gone after Tod in the hills, blown up his mule train, his men and his copper. Why, in different circumstances he'd have got a medal for that. Not that he wanted one. Recollection mixed with the here and now and he imagined the far side of the ravine jolting then sliding away to bury the officer engineers below. He shook his head to dismiss the memory and fumbled with the doorknob where he thought Tuck might see. When he still got no joy, he tossed it into Tuck's lap, so Tuck had to drop his bow to stop his keepsake from bouncing away and down the slope.

Tuck looked wounded. 'Ain't no call for that.'

'How else will I get you to talk to me?'

'I wasn't aware there was an answer owing.'

'Not an answer. Just…'

'Just what?'

'Companionship. Discourse. The time of day. We're off on a jaunt to Nashville. Have you nothing to say on that?'

Laughter and excitement at the bridge drew Shire's gaze. A coffee pot was being precariously hoisted on the winch to the amusement of the men.

Tuck said, 'Well, in my reckonin', Nashville ain't a lick of paint compared to Louisville.'

It might have been sardonic, but Shire judged that Tuck

was making what effort he could. 'That so?'

A gentle cheer greeted the pot's recovery by a team on a high trestle.

'Surely. The Cumberland don't square up to the Ohio as rivers go, feeding into the Ohio as it does. Why, you might reason that Nashville is no more than a tributary city.'

Strange as the conversation was, Shire didn't feel in a position to complain. 'The same would have to be said of Louisville then, with the Ohio flowing into the Mississippi.'

'It's a fair point,' said Tuck, 'but one that accepts that Louisville still ranks Nashville.'

'I'm not disputing it.'

Silence followed the agreement, but for the orchestra of hammers and the slow sizzle of pork. Tuck collected up his bow.

'Can we talk a while first?' Shire asked.

'Alright.' When Tuck lowered his bow again, it looked as if the sacrifice caused him considerable pain. 'I was thinking on what you said.'

'About Louisville?'

'About their industry.' He waved his bow out into the ravine to indicate the repair regiment. 'Look what we can do when we put our mind to it. Our engine driver was right. They're gonna fix that bridge quicker than a house-proud beaver after a spring flood. We've been industrious, haven't we? You and me, the squad, all the armies, Union and Confederate.'

'If you're not busy in a war, you're liable to lose it.'

'All that energy.' He said it like he was feeling for it. 'All to one intent, which, at the end of the day, is to kill other people.'

'I remember you once told me that in this war, if a man

wanted to fight slavery, he could point a gun right at it.'

'I recall.' Tuck looked down at the burnt doorknob. He spoke more quietly. 'A man has a right to get tired though. I'd like to put what industry I have left into something else. Imagine what those men could do if they was directed someplace different. What food they could grow, what homes they could build.'

'It's a rightful army we're in. Not so many armies get busy for their fellow man.'

'But *I am* tired. I want my home back. As it was. Whole.' He looked up at Shire. 'I thought I'd lost you as well, to fire and violence. I get so angry somedays.' He nodded at the fiddle. 'The music helps sometimes. It draws out the poison.'

'I'm sorry.'

'Weren't hardly your fault...' He turned over the doorknob in his hand. 'Maybe it's best that I let some of that anger go.' Before Shire could say anything more, Tuck tossed it away like it was no more than a worked-over chicken bone.

Shire watched it tumble down the steep slope until it disappeared.

Tuck stood and walked away back toward the train. Shire sat and watched him go, slowly registering the aroma of burnt meat.

*

It was as the engine driver had prophesized. By late afternoon, the bridge was completed and rails carried from the north to lay across the mended section. Their train was unhitched from its cars and edged over and back with nothing but its tender in tow and a large number of weary soldiers watching on. Shire wondered if there was a place where this test had ever failed.

The cars were hooked on again. They climbed aboard and passed over themselves. Rice considered how long it might be, 'before Forrest happens by with his cavalry and burns it again.'

Rice had been tightlipped on why they were going to Nashville, but Shire pressed him once more. Rice scratched his brush beard. 'Bates took me to see Colonel Opdycke.'

Shire saw less of the colonel now he headed up a whole brigade rather than just the 125th, but Captain Bates was a good replacement.

'Opdycke had papers ready for me. "We need men," he says. "The 4th and 23rd Corps together are no more than twenty thousand and that's not enough to face up to Hood. There are men in Nashville, men who belong in my brigade who were injured. Many are now hearty but have contrived to stay on and draw rations and pay. They pass themselves off as sick. Others might be working in the hospitals, but they're my men." The colonel didn't look too friendly, neither. "You understand me, Lieutenant Rice? Dig them out. If they don't respond to the need, they will have to be cajoled. There's no necessity to go easy on them. I need as many men as you can find. These papers will get you a hearing with the people that matter in Nashville." He told me that other brigades will likely be sending their own officers to do the same.'

'Just the three of us?' said Shire. 'And you picked Tuck and me to do the cajoling? We're not going to scare anybody.'

'I'm guessing you haven't had the chance to look in a mirror lately, Private Shire. All I need you to do is to lay a scowl over those scars you've collected. That oughta hurry them along.'

The journey remained stop-start while the north and south traffic sorted itself out. There was nothing to see after the light faded. Shire tried to sleep but turned over with every halt and restart. One such time, deep into the night, he heard a station-guard call out 'Spring Hill'. That brought him wide awake. Clara was close by. He couldn't avoid thinking about her now. It was cold in the car, the November wind burrowing any number of ways into the carriage. He wrapped himself tightly in his blanket, but sleep had abandoned him. When the train pulled forward again, he stood and wobbled his way in among the horses, fruitlessly searching dark Tennessee through the small, barred window.

He'd parted from Clara so many times; his heart couldn't grow any fonder. How hers might be apportioned he hadn't ever truly known. The word love had been slipped into their conversation here and there but not as a point of emphasis, rather in passing like it was a given that didn't need to be dwelt upon. You could argue that was reassuring: a bedrock of love, enduring, everlasting; love as a constant promise as he'd framed it once long ago. But presented in that form you couldn't corral it and work it up to a crescendo. How could you bring passion into a friendship as old as theirs? There had been opportunities in the past. They'd taken shelter from the snow back in England when walking home from Eversholt, then warmed by the fire. At Comrie, Clara had crept into his bed to escape the ghost of her husband, Taylor, but Shire had left her there alone. Both jumping off points for a different life, he supposed, but both impossible in their own way. He doubted they would have survived the landing.

The stars above Tennessee were suddenly wiped away as the train cut between unseen hills.

He might have fashioned a further moment after Comrie had burned down. They'd slept beside each other under the stars that first night and for several more before they'd salvaged all they could and moved down into town. He'd never asked the question. It wouldn't have taken much: a roll to his side and a stroke of her hair. But he'd still been able to smell the ashes of her life surrounding them, and then there was Tod. He'd had an easier route to passion. The excitement of new eyes, on the run, pushed together on a paddle-steamer. He turned his mind from that. Besides, Tod was in the wrong army. Clara must see that.

It had been a timid parting. He'd kissed her on the cheek, shouldered his pack and marched off to war again, both of them set for new horizons before they might come together once more. He didn't doubt that fate would conspire to do just that, if the war spared him long enough. Even now he was passing by her new home in the night, though he might as well have been a thousand miles away. What could he say to Clara that she didn't already know? He was tired of waiting. Somehow, he was going to have to find a return to life after this war. Music that wasn't a marching band. Dances that weren't two engineers on a trestle bridge.

Until the train started forward again, he didn't realize it had stopped. He pressed to the bars. There was a lantern ahead. As the train sped up, he could just make out a sign on the edge of the light that read *Franklin*. Spring Hill was already far down the track. His latest visit to Clara, such as it was, was over.

Franklin, Tennessee – November, 1864

The square-framed grand piano at the Lotz house was
polished to within an inch of its life. Clara felt the cool walnut,
stroked the rich grain that followed perfectly rounded corners.
Each solid leg was topped with a carved lion-head, with every
foot a wide paw. She'd been invited to play the first night she'd
stayed and had since persuaded Mr Lotz – Albert – to allow
her to use his piano to teach Lena and Alice, who stood
waiting. The ivory was unblemished. Her fingers held the
memory of the perfectly balanced keys.

'It is here to be played,' Lotz said in his Germanic accent,
tailing off into a nervous laugh. He'd made it himself. It was
superior in every way to Clara's Comrie piano that had been
dashed to pieces at the bottom of the mineshaft in Ducktown.
The thought conjured a sudden memory of exploding wood
and wire whipping along the tunnel where she'd crouched.
That crashing chord had announced the start of many weeks
trapped underground. She'd miscarried in that mine, squatting
alone in the dark. A child that would have been one more
cousin for Lena and Alice.

She made a conscious effort to banish the thought and
asked the girls to show their hands, palms up. Lena's were
passable. Alice kept hers hidden behind her back and looked
sideways at her host. Lotz, wavy haired and sharp-bearded, his
attire tending toward the formal – as if he had missed a
vocation as a composer – smiled thinly and somewhat
painfully before turning away. 'I will leave you to it.' The

Carters had an instrument of their own but it had suffered too many little fingers over the years. Also, the first time they used it for a lesson, various mothers or aunts had come to stand over them and offer advice. If part of her role was to inspire these children, Mr Lotz would have to pay the price. Frances took Alice to wash her hands while Lena took her place at the piano as if it were an altar.

Staying at the Lotz house brought to mind Clara's good friend Julius Raht. She wondered how long it would be before he could come to visit. It wasn't only the Germanic accents of her hosts – naturalized in fifty-nine, as Margaretha had proudly told her several times – but the furnishings. Each piece in the house that Lotz had built was in keeping with the piano: ornate, heavy, spotless. Her bedroom, for the one night a week she now spent in Franklin, might not have been out of place in Ridgmont, such was the indulgence. After she blew out her candle, she could still feel the close weight of the dark wood wardrobe and over-patterned wallpaper. The house was much bigger than the Carters' and yet the children from both houses tended to congregate at the farm. Perhaps because there was a 'look, but don't touch' feel to the Lotz house.

Mr Lotz had a plentiful supply of sheet music and Clara had picked out Bach's Prelude No. 1 in C. It was a rewarding piece for a learner and Lena's hands would just about have the reach. Clara placed the music on the rest and started to introduce it.

'Oh, I seen this one,' said Lena, positioning her hands.

'*I've* seen this one.'

Lena didn't wait for instruction. Her pedal work would require some help – not that much was needed for this piece – but she played quite beautifully. Clara needed only to turn the pages. Frances and Alice returned quietly before the end and Mr Lotz put his head around the door and closed his eyes to listen. Clara took in a stuttered breath and turned the last page. She hadn't heard enough music lately. She kissed the top of Lena's head.

After the piano lesson, she walked with Frances back up the pike to the Carter house. The girls raced on ahead. Meals at the Lotz house were as heavyweight as the furniture and Clara was grateful for Moscow's suggestion that she dine with the Carters on her stayover nights. It meant she only had to survive Margaretha's breakfast of assorted sausage meat and dark, tough bread. It was hardly any distance between the houses so they took their time. It was so rare to be alone with only one other person while among the Carters and the chance would be gone as soon as they arrived.

She'd come to know Frances a little better than the other women partly because, as the youngest of the sisterhood, Frances was frequently called to arms if the children needed handling or herding. It was something she clearly resented but used as an excuse to stay close to Clara. Frances complained repeatedly that the others took advantage of her younger age, though she was twenty. If so many men weren't away at the war, she said, she'd already likely be married and away herself.

Clara glanced sideways at her. She imagined Frances wouldn't have to wait long beyond the war's end, shapely and fair as she was. A certain childlike quality persisted, but perhaps that was the company she kept. 'Is that all you want? To marry?'

'How else will I leave home?'

Clara felt there should be a good answer to that, but the truth was she'd used marriage to flee home herself. She'd been so hopeful of her prospects at the time. Maybe Frances would do better.

'Were there no children in your marriage?' Frances asked.

Clara swallowed the directness she'd come to expect in America. 'We weren't married very long. For much of it, my husband was fighting. Are you and Tod close?'

'He's four years older than me. My brother Francis, my namesake you might say, he's nearer in age to me. I was closer to him. He was injured. We think he's in New Orleans.'

Clara tried to think of another way to work the subject back to Tod. Frances got there first. 'When you met Tod, on the river like you told us, were you a widow?'

'I was.'

'Were you in mourning?'

'Not really.'

'Only Tod is never slow to make himself known to a beautiful lady.'

Clara preferred to think that was said to elicit a response rather than true. 'It wasn't a large riverboat. We ate dinner with the captain. That's how we met.'

'I've never been on a riverboat. It sounds romantic.'

Frances' line of conversation wasn't particularly subtle. They stopped at the picket gate, left ajar by the girls. Maybe a hint would get back to Moscow through his sisters. 'It was certainly beautiful. And Tod was pleasant company. I'd like to do it again one day.'

'And your parents, have you written to them about Tod?'

Clara didn't rise to the assumption that there was something she was hiding about her and Tod. 'My parents are in England. They have their own concerns.' The thought of them took the edge off Clara's better mood after the lesson.

'England.' Frances giggled. 'It makes me imagine kings and queens and castles. I expect you lived in a castle, didn't you?'

It was a childish question, but not so far from the mark.

It disturbed some deeper loss. Walking up this foreign road, Clara suddenly missed her mother, missed her lost sister, wished she had a home and a family like the Carters who were noisy and combative but cared for each other all the same, so much so that they crowded into a house too small for half their number. She saw in Frances' face a concern that she'd somehow upset her. 'A little bigger than most castles,' Clara said. 'I'm the youngest daughter of the Duke of Ridgmont.'

Frances' eyes widened. She smiled as if she'd been given a gift.

*

With Clara having dined at the Lotz house the week she began teaching, this evening was the first time Moscow had cause to lead her to dinner. Who else had a subterranean dining room? He was embarrassed. He took Clara through Father's ground-floor bedroom – the accepted thoroughfare to the porch unless he had the door closed – and out onto the porch. The one hanging lantern was light enough given the white railings and the white beams and slats of the low roof.

'Take the rail. It's steep,' he said, going ahead down the steps that angled back directly beneath Father's room. Once inside, he stepped out of the way to allow Clara entry. He saw the room afresh, as through her eyes. A cold brick floor, rough whitewashed walls, a low ceiling. There were few furnishings to speak of apart from the long dining table surrounded by tightly packed chairs, plain and functional with woven reed seats. A fire on the south wall. Sarah and Annie were resetting the table, the children having just eaten.

Clara was wearing something halfway to an evening gown and looked aware that in this room she was overdressed. Like his sisters, Moscow was in his day clothes, although Frances had made an effort. He pulled out a seat for Clara and found himself apologizing in a roundabout sort of way. 'Father built down rather than up. It's the troll in him.' He took the seat opposite. 'Through that door we have the root cellar and a summer bedroom. It's cooler down here then.'

'And warm now,' Clara said.

'I know it's not a lick on the Lotz house.'

'You're farmers. It's a farmer's dining room.'

It wasn't delivered like an insult but it had the edges of one. Clara seemed to sense as much. 'I'm glad you invited me.'

Her smile bolstered him.

Sallie entered via the steps and excused herself as she lifted a large porcelain tureen onto the table. 'I wouldn't want to spill anything on that pretty dress.' It would contain the same vegetables as always for this time of year. Turnips and squash. The other women of the house arrived. Frances had eaten with the children but came to sit with the adults. She said she'd left Lena in charge. Father, entering to this news and taking a seat at the head of the table, said that was like leaving the chicken in charge of the wolfpack. Footsteps raced this way and that across the floor above. In answer to Clara's upward glance, Moscow said, 'Father's room is overspill for everyone, the children's bedrooms being so overpopulated.'

Moscow had picked out a good-looking ham but it tasted over salty and the gravy was on the thin side. Frances poured Clara a beaker of water and Moscow wished he'd thought to find some wine. Father begged Clara's indulgence while he talked farm business and set the tasks for tomorrow. After that, it was Clara who introduced talk of the war. 'Mr Lotz tells me that General Hood and his army are at Tuscumbia and looking to get over the Tennessee River. Should we be worried?'

Moscow let Father answer.

'It would be better if he was held south of the river. Tuscumbia is in Alabama. If he crosses there, he might head north and make a play for Nashville, but it's a long way in a wet autumn. We'll let you know if there's reason to worry.'

'I hope they *do* cross,' said Sarah. 'Why else are Tod and Francis away fighting if not to win back Tennessee?'

'You know my opinion.' Father cut into his ham. 'It was a fool's war to start with and they ain't run out of fools on either side yet.'

Annie, next to Clara, placed a hand on her arm. 'I apologize,' she said. 'You having lost your husband to a *fool's war*. The men left in this house are not overly patriotic.'

Fountain paused his eating and rested his hands either side of his plate, knife and fork pointing upward. 'That's hard on Moscow, don't you think, given he led a regiment and spent good time in a Yankee prison? I'm sorry for your loss, Mrs Ridgmont, truly I am, but patriotism, well, it's just which flag you choose, and I'd have more sons around this table if we could do away with flags altogether.'

'Was it busier on the railroad today?' Moscow asked Clara. 'I'd expect the Union to be moving men south.'

'Not so I noticed,' Clara said. 'Maybe it'll be busier going home tomorrow.'

Calfurnia, the older of the two black women who'd stayed on, brought in a heavy crusted pear pie. It would have been good enough for any other day but somehow, next to Clara, Moscow thought it looked rustic and rather plain. The noise, low above their heads, was becoming a distraction. Annie suggested Frances should go and rescue poor Lena. Instead, Frances, never one to take orders from Annie, said how well Lena played the Lotz piano today.

Moscow looked to Clara. 'Is that so?'

'It was quite wonderful,' Clara said. 'The Lotz piano drew the best out of her.'

'We know ours is tinny,' said Sallie, 'but it belonged to Mother.'

'Oh,' said Clara. 'Then you should –'

'How did Alice play?' Mary interrupted.

Moscow had seen Alice play Mother's instrument. Mostly she just attacked it.

'Very well also,' Clara said. 'A little more *forte* than her sister.'

Father laughed. 'That one's a *forte* sort of child.'

Mary looked crestfallen.

Clara said, 'Alice is very strong on her languages for one so young.'

That was adroit of her. It couldn't be easy for Clara to come into a house full of women. It was bound to raise the dust. It didn't help that they were all much the same age, but for Frances. Now he'd placed this English beauty among them and she was a favorite with the children already. It was as well that it was only two days a week.

He'd lost the thread. Annie was sniping at Frances again, saying how well dressed she was for dinner. The noise from upstairs was louder than ever. One of the children was crying. Mary asked Frances if she wouldn't mind attending to that. Frances stood up to go but answered Annie. 'Well, I think we should make an effort when we have a guest at the table.'

'Some of us have work to do,' said Annie. 'We don't have time to get our fancy frocks on like you. Besides, and beggin' your pardon, Mrs Ridgmont, we ain't entertainin' royalty.'

Frances walked to the door. 'Shows what you know,' she said, 'when you're sitting at the table with the Duchess of

Ridgmont.' Triumphant, she closed the door behind her.

Opposite as he was to Clara, Moscow didn't need to turn to look at her as most of the others did. She laid down her cutlery. 'My mother's the duchess,' she said, 'not me. And it hardly applies here.'

After a surprised pause, the questions rained in on Clara. Moscow's spirit sank. It shouldn't make a difference, but it did. She might be down on her luck, another widow lasting out the war, but she was beyond him. He hadn't realized how much hope had crept into his heart, until it was shot away.

Nashville, Tennessee – November, 1864

Shire helped Rice slide open the boxcar door and they sat down next to each other, facing east, their feet hanging outside as the train edged its way into the city. Nashville had been given over to the Union Army and the Union Army intended to keep it. That much was obvious. It was brighter today, but no less cold. Shire was hungry. He recalled sailing up the Cumberland and disembarking from a steamboat into Nashville early last year. The 125th had stayed only a couple of nights then quickly marched south to Franklin. The city he looked out on now appeared somewhere entirely new.

The train crawled along an embankment and the slight elevation afforded him a view of several imposing forts. Cannon bristled from their embrasures, their mute accusations pointing south. Each fort was attended by small tent-towns, canvas variously shaded from new white or cream to a stained and weatherworn gray. They were pitched well enough, but this long into the war the rows were far from ruler-straight and the canvas sagged a little, like an overworn shirt. He didn't doubt he'd have seen more forts if he could have looked out from the other side of the train. Ahead and to his left stood the Tennessee State Capitol, master of the city, fresh limestone atop a high hill. The narrow end, angled toward them, formed a huge portico with eight mammoth Grecian columns. Higher still rose a tall and somewhat skinny cupola surmounted by the biggest Union flag Shire had ever seen. Earth and cotton-bale barricades surrounded the edifice.

More cannon, more tents. A company of blue soldiers climbed up the hill. The Capitol and its defenses had the air of a commanding castle back in England, and not one at ease with the people: dominant rather than protective. There was no encircling Rebel army, not yet, but Nashville already wore the look of a city under siege.

Rice was quiet, enjoying his pipe while scratching deep inside his coat. He was probably the scruffiest lieutenant in the army, Shire thought. He remembered what Rice had said yesterday concerning Shire's own appearance. He didn't need a mirror to count his scars: a bullet through his calf from Dandridge, a dent in his breast from Missionary Ridge, a tear-shaped burn under his left eye from New York. And not all the deep scratches from Kennesaw Mountain had healed without leaving a mark. What would Father say – were he alive – if Shire could magically pitch up on his doorstep in Bedfordshire and present his new and grizzled self? How must he look to Clara? Perhaps that was the problem. Perhaps she wanted her untarnished Shire back. Fresh-faced, unspoiled, untested. It was hard to wholly remember that younger version of himself, and somewhat surprising that gentle fool had survived this far into the war. Maybe he hadn't. On the inside he wasn't so different to Nashville: fortified and barricaded against an uncertain future. He wondered if barricades came down as quickly as they went up.

At the station, Rice had to produce his papers before they were allowed out into the city. They asked for the best area to find lodgings and they were directed toward the riverfront. The streets were busier with soldiers than with citizenry. Men out of uniform were scarce. Women and children hurried about their errands. Shire couldn't confidently recall what day it was, but many businesses were locked up. He watched as an older belle, dressed in a full hooped-skirt and wide-brimmed hat as if on her way to a summer picnic, was forced to give up her carpetbag by two soldiers. It was deeply searched before being dropped in the mud for her to collect. She stood a while, cursing better than a sidewalk drunk at their retreating backs.

Rice worked them north beside the gray river which ran straight here, around a hundred and fifty yards wide. The lodgings he found were smart and well furnished, certainly compared to a damp forest floor. Rice took a room alone. Shire shunned the tall mirror in the room he shared with Tuck, who stood at the window for so long that Shire came to see what might be happening. Their room looked out over a fortified rail bridge that spanned the Cumberland; new thick wood latticed each side and above a single rail. Where the span started, two curious watchtowers perched on top, like oversized dovecots dotted with rifle-slots. A brace of steamers moved down the river. As they watched, a train slowed to walking speed to cross on the single rail. 'The line to Louisville,' was all Tuck said.

Rice left them long enough to wash but then had them out in the streets again, trudging up and down muddy city blocks between different army commands while he tried to get a grip on the mission. 'City ain't short of soldiers,' Rice said. 'Shame we can't commandeer the first bushel we see.' Armed as they were with fresh pay, Shire and Tuck frequently requested stops at a street vendor or a bakery. Rice was happy to oblige and partake. By late morning Shire was outside of a buttered corncob, a hunk of apple cake and a deep-fried pickle.

'Lieutenant,' Tuck said, with a rare hint of levity, 'I could become contented with this form of campaign.'

Around noon, Rice and his papers had sufficiently worked

their way up the city garrison chain of command that they found themselves climbing the hill to the Capitol itself, low gray clouds speeding by above the tall cupola. They were challenged at an outer circle of bales, again at an inner circle of earthworks and once more at the top of the steps. There stood two giant gas lamps, unlit at this hour, each closely defended by marble figures from antiquity and more effectively by two cannon aimed out over the city. War forged strange alliances, Shire thought. They were waved inside onto a polished stone floor under a long and low vaulted ceiling. The gas was lit in here, its yellow glow cradled by chandeliers painted in muddy-brown. They found a wooden bench and waited a good hour while doors opened and closed with officers hurriedly crisscrossing the marble. Conversations carried all the way from the other end but only in tone and energy, the words hopelessly blurred as they bounced and rolled from the cold stone. Someone dropped a book flat to the floor and the report made Tuck jump into a crouch.

'Easy, Tuck,' said Rice, gently enough. 'We don't want to lose you this far behind the lines.'

At last, they were collected and led upstairs and into a high library dominated by a gray metal spiral staircase, which the boy in Shire desperately wanted to climb. Heavy red curtains hung beside tall windows that looked out over the colorless cityscape. There were other small teams of men around the room, looking much like their own, captains or lieutenants with their lackeys. Five groups in all. Two officers entered and everyone came to attention.

'At ease,' said the taller man, moving behind a large desk and setting down some papers. He introduced himself as Colonel Beecham and, with the merest lift of his hand, the other officer as Colonel Truesdail. 'As you're all on the same errand from your respective brigades, it made sense to speak to you as one. General Schofield needs every man he can to help check Hood.'

Shire noted the word check rather than defeat.

'General Thomas wants to help. His idea is for you to root out some of your men that, shall we say, the army has forgotten.' He gave them permission to take with them those who would go. To Shire's mind that sounded a weak mandate; no one had given him a choice lately. Were these men in the army or not?

'But you'll have your work cut out. Men from your brigades are scattered across the city. Some remain convalescing in hospitals from wounds long healed. Others have found useful employ in those same hospitals while still drawing army rations and pay. Still more work in the prisons. It's a God-awful mess, but we have other priorities, so it's left to you.'

He indicated lists of hospitals on the desk, 'twenty-five at last count', as well as barracks and other places they might care to look. 'We can spare some of the provost guard to support you if things turn difficult, but choose men who you think will fight. A few of those are better than a crowd of malcontents. The hospitals are not full presently, but may not thank you for taking their nurses, porters and cooks. That's as it needs to be, but speak with the surgeons. In all likelihood these hospitals will be in full use again after you boys grapple with Hood.'

He gave way to Truesdail, telling them the colonel worked to police the city. Beecham's manner suggested to Shire he didn't care for the man. Truesdail, a head smaller and impeccably dressed, his hair side-parted as if by a hot bullet, stood with his hands resting on a chairback. 'Gentlemen.' He raised a weak smile. 'There's not a man, woman or child in this city that you can trust.' He said it slowly and almost with pleasure. 'It's as plain as that. Believe me. I've seen the worst of this place. We've labored to re-establish the Union here, but make no mistake, this city is for the Confederacy. If you're lucky you may encounter some loyalists among the citizenry, and there are some who work with us purely for gain and don't have a care as to who runs the place, but mostly they are plain sullen, brooding, hateful of all that is blue.'

Truesdail came out from behind his chair and walked slowly in front of them with his hands behind his back. Shire's early judgement, based on the slow malice of Truesdail's delivery, was that some of that hate had formed a reflection in the man.

'You're in a hurry. I understand. But trust no one, especially the women. They are as sold on this war as their men. Sometimes, I think more so. If they are not trying to smuggle goods or medicines to the Rebels, they will be spying, learning what they can about your units, our defenses, our intentions.'

'Sir,' said Rice. 'We're here only to recover our men. We have no need to converse outside of the army.'

Truesdail looked Rice up and down. 'I can see you have been a long time in the field, Lieutenant. Nashville must be a boon to you. How many vendors did you speak with this morning? Did they ask what unit you're from or how long you have been in Nashville?'

Rice looked at his shoes.

Truesdail moved on. 'And there are theaters and brothels where they'll be happy to pick your pockets and pick your mind at the same time. As to the men you hope to find, they are not so loyal as you. Otherwise, they wouldn't still be here, preferring to bathe in this city's vice.' He finished his lap and tapped the lists on the desk. 'Medicines that pass to the Confederates are stolen from these hospitals. I have in prison any number of Union soldiers we've caught. So have a care who you take. Rotten apples will smell some. When you have your names, come back to me. I have my own lists as to the troublemakers. They are better left for me to watch.'

After the meeting broke up, they climbed back down the grand stone steps outside. 'What now, Lieutenant?' Tuck asked. 'I'd call it a bum errand lookin' for men we can't trust.'

Rice halted and the three of them stood looking out over the city that was their hunting ground. It hadn't seemed that friendly before; now it looked more threatening still. 'Truesdail appears to own an ugly slant on the world. We have our warning. Let's get to it and take our own mind.'

Shire struggled to find the same generosity of spirit. Armed with Truesdail's words he turned each corner with suspicion, stepped into the mud from the boarded sidewalks rather than brush by the citizenry. Despite the tempting aromas, street vendors had lost their earlier appeal.

Working from Beecham's list and a gifted map of the city, Rice chose their first stop as the Nashville Female Academy on Church Street – ostensibly as it was near to the Capitol rather than from any allure in the name – a handsome two and three-storied school set in a few acres of pleasant gardens behind a high wall. It was a step into cleanliness. Shire couldn't help but look at his stained and war-worn uniform with embarrassment. His comrades looked no better. Nonetheless they gained entry, although the matron directed them to wash the mud from their boots. A Major Frederick Seymour was the surgeon-in-charge and he was forewarned. Rice was invited to his office. Shire and Tuck were permitted to walk the wards.

It was a sizeable place smelling of turpentine. There was constant cleaning in progress. The care was supervised by Catholic Sisters of Charity but the nursing staff was largely male, many of them soldiers who were themselves ex-patients, with black men and women servants also attending to the needy. At least half the beds were empty. The air of death that Shire had felt in so many field hospitals was absent. Maybe it was because there hadn't been a sizeable battle in recent weeks.

He and Tuck sought out soldiers belonging to the regiments in their brigade. Talking to them was like revisiting their own travels of recent years, towns and battles where they had fought: Chickamauga, Missionary Ridge, Dandridge, Resaca, Kennesaw. Some had been here so long that their stay predated the 125th coming into the war. Many fought at Stone's River, close by at Murfreesboro. That was nearly two years ago.

'Imagine,' said Tuck. 'All the marchin' air we've been sucking up and they've been laid out here, nothing to do but think.'

Those in bed were clearly not fit for service, but there were a number of nurses or porters, or clerks who had found a lodgment working for this or that surgeon, who said they had just become plain stuck in Nashville. Some openly welcomed the chance to return to a fighting army. They had written letters to their regiments, they said, even to their state governors, all to no effect.

'Why not simply go home?' Shire asked a Wisconsin orderly who was stripping sheets from a bed.

'I draw my corporal's pay here, my ration too. Seems like the army knows where I am.' The man was cleanshaven. No scars to speak of. He'd been out of war longer than Shire had been in it, and yet still outranked him. 'If I went home, I'd be a deserter. But I'll come with you. I know other boys who'll do the same.'

Others wouldn't talk with them or hurried away. Some were out and out hostile. 'You git, now and leave us be. The war goes on plenty well without me.'

'You're still in the army, aren't you?' challenged Shire.

'What of it? I weren't no volunteer to start with. Let 'em have their damn Confederacy for all I care.'

One of the sisters directed them to the academy's exercise hall where there was a sizeable number of men, mostly in old and faded uniforms. A baseball was tossed between a three-man triangle. Card games were on show, but the sister didn't object.

'Are these men patients?' Shire asked.

'Of a sort,' said the sister. 'They don't work, at least. Some may never be fit to leave. War foundlings. They have nowhere to go.'

Tuck wandered away to a two-man card game, pulled up a chair and sat close. Shire took his leave of the sister and went to stand beside him. One of the players wore a kepi with the cap-badge of the 44th Illinois, one of Opdycke's regiments.

'What's the game, boys?' asked Tuck.

'Poker.' The soldier shuffled a thin deck with a practiced hand. He and his friend each had a collection of small, washed stones before them. Shire saw they were of the same grade as the gravel beds in the garden.

'High stakes,' said Tuck. 'Can I join?'

The shuffling continued. 'Only if you got stones. Do you got stones?'

'Aw, I'm cleaned out,' said Tuck. 'I'll just watch a while. That alright?'

'It's your time to burn.'

The second player said nothing.

'You boys injured?' Tuck asked. 'Did you take a wound somewhere?'

'I was brung here after Chickamauga,' said the shuffler. 'I don't rightly know if I got wounded. No one said I did.'

The soldier shuffled a while longer but finally dealt out the whole deck – such as it was – face up. Some unseen calculation transpired and he took two stones from his partner's pile who whimpered in distress. The soldier collected the deck and began to shuffle again.

Tuck sat back, took off his hat and ran a hand through his hair. He closed his eyes. 'Yep,' he said. 'Sometimes it's hard to tell where you been hit.'

Shire looked away from his friend's aggrieved face and tried to sum all the hidden pain resident in the hall.

By the end of the day, they had visited four hospitals from the list of twenty-five. He'd not conceived of this sort of netherworld, a place that was neither home nor wholly the war. Many had never made it to the fight, getting sick on the way to the front, or their nerve had failed them and they'd found a side door to this in-between existence. It was both an escape and a trap. They'd avoided the fighting, but couldn't move beyond the war any more than Shire could. Some were making the best of it, some despised themselves, most just endured. How many other cities were there full of men like these?

Rice had arranged to meet with 'recruiters' from the other brigades by the riverfront at sundown. By pooling what they'd learned they were all able to get a better feel for where men from their particular brigades were clustered and Rice was able to build a target list of hospitals for the next day. Shire was beat, the same as everyone else. He was used to the marching miles but he'd had little or no sleep on the train up from Pulaski. Here was a real bed and the promise of a meal at their lodgings. They trudged back there, already familiar with the way. It was curious to sit round a table to eat. The food was fine. Nobody said much at all; the mood of the city had bled into the room and into them, their jaunt gone sour. Rice spoke with the proprietor and arranged for their uniforms to be collected and washed ready for the morning. Shire eased into his bed like a letter getting into an envelope, the temper of the day having drawn the last of his energy.

There was a web up high in the corner of the room, he only spotted it by the stretched shadow cast from his lamp. He tried to ward off another visit from Gideon but failed, saw the sharpshooter slumped again over his long rifle. He tried to think past it, to the happy half-hour before, where together they had boyishly hunted dewy cobwebs. This city was a web, he thought; spun in the backwoods of the war, it trapped the fearful, the damaged and the lost. He'd felt its viscid threads all day. How long would you have to be here before you gave up the struggle?

Across the room Tuck had his back turned. Shire knew his friend's night-breathing well enough to know he wasn't asleep. Tuck hadn't laid a hand on his fiddle this evening. Trying to shape a friendly question, Shire fell asleep.

Nashville, Tennessee – November, 1864

Shire started with more energy on his second day in Nashville. He stepped outside the lodgings beside Tuck and looked across a busy river. The sky was blue, the air crisp and cold. Rice joined them. They were all well fed. Tuck seemed to have escaped the slump he went to bed with and instead was on an up day, sniffing at the soap-scented collar of his uniform and saying that if they were going back to the Female Academy, he'd better find himself some stones for a game of twenty-six card poker.

The hospitals Rice led them to came in different shapes and sizes, every one of them adapted from an earlier purpose: a converted carriage factory, a masonic hall, churches of every denomination and even the former Western Military Academy. None were overcrowded, but those employed in them appeared grimly aware that their work was not yet done. There was no talk of any building being reset to its past use. Future business was expected.

The pattern was as yesterday. Rice would meet with the surgeon or the matron while Shire and Tuck ferreted out the men, but this time with the added purpose of putting names firmly to paper. They had to find a way into the under-mood of each hospital. Tuck was better at it than Shire, better at the bonhomie and better at laying it out plain to those who pushed back. Shire hammed up his English accent, let them make fun of him if it helped. *There's no necessity to go easy on them,* Opdycke had said. Once or twice, if Shire took a dislike to a man, he deployed what he thought might be a mean look. It didn't seem to make much difference. More often it was the other way around, and he harbored doubts about taking the over-enthusiastic or those weak of mind. Sometimes they were both: too keen to get back in the war and prove themselves. Despite what Truesdail had said, Shire didn't consider these men cowards, but that word hung in the air between themselves and their would-be recruits all day.

Despite the mixed response, the list grew readily enough. Rice said he'd been given no target as to numbers so didn't rightly know when they should stop. The long day and the repeating emotions slowly wore Shire down. Some men appeared fit, but collectively this was a damaged crowd. Although just how different were they to Tuck, or to himself?

They returned to the Female Academy late-afternoon but steered clear of the exercise hall. Shire found the cleanshaven corporal of the 24th Wisconsin, Corporal Cobb, who was still keen to come back with them. Shire put his name to the list.

Beyond that their last recruiting call was listed as the Zollicoffer Barracks, a square four-story building on the corner of Church and 4th where the land began to tilt more steeply toward the river. It was a prison for Confederate soldiers, put up before the war as a hotel but unfinished when the fighting broke out. While the hospitals had been mostly clean havens, this place was home to filthy, edgy resentment, hollow-eyed Rebels and jittery guards. Shire couldn't wait to get away. Evidently neither could the Union sentries, as they volunteered in droves. The commandant had to cull the numbers before they left. It was a sullen place to end the day. After that, Rice sent them back to the lodgings while he went to visit the city quartermaster to see about equipping the men.

That evening they'd agreed to meet with the other

recruiting teams to compare notes again, but in a more sociable setting at the New Nashville Theatre, a grand venue, mostly populated by soldiers. Showing was *The Married Rake*, bracketed before and after by the singing of patriotic songs. Shire couldn't tell if the actors and actresses obliged to sing were for the Union or the Confederacy, but they sang out well enough. Listening to the orchestra brought him close to tears, the swell and fall drawing out great gouts of emotions from where he'd kept them poorly shut away. Perhaps the lock had already been picked by Nashville and the encounters of the last two days. Tuck appeared to have shaken all that off and seemed ready for a good time, though it didn't stop him complaining more than once that the lead violin was off tempo. After the performance, the theatre bars were awash with soldiers and a sudden influx of women passing themselves off as performers in the show.

'If all these women had truly been singing on stage,' Shire said, 'we'd never have heard the orchestra.'

'Do you care?' asked Tuck, finishing up a beer. 'They can lie or act as much as they want so long as they're prepared to perform for me when the time comes.' A bottle of wine in one hand and a clutch of glasses in the other, he herded Shire in front of two women, both with unnaturally wide eyes and smiles. Shire discovered that two years of privation and fighting wasn't enough to cure him of a hot blush, which drew comment even amid the dim light and thick smoke of the bar. Rice joined them, nursing a whiskey. Despite the city being under martial rule, the bar stayed open and busy. Rice let slip they'd been to the quartermaster's office, Shire thought maybe deliberately. Soon they were everybody's best friends. Another self-proclaimed songbird latched onto Rice's arm. There were whispered promises of money or favors if they could procure coffee, boots or a few bottles of quinine. Shire pretended not to hear or politely demurred and his and Tuck's ladies were quick to edge away the competition. It seemed they had a more direct transaction in mind.

The wine began to tell. Shire's lady, Bridget, had a firm hold on him, her curves pressed close. He didn't realize he was talking about Clara until Tuck dragged him to the bar and told him to 'quit mooning over loves lost. It ain't the time.'

'She was interested enough,' said Shire. 'You think it is lost then?'

Tuck paid the barman and collected up the new bottle. 'I don't know, Shire, but seems to me you've checked most places twice over and ain't found nothin' yet. I'll help you start looking again tomorrow if you like, but not tonight.'

No one troubled them at their lodgings when after another bottle of wine – and none too quietly – they escorted the ladies up the stairs. Shire fleetingly thought of Clara again as he fumbled with the lock but a selfish part of him, suddenly to the fore, thought loud and clear that he was owed this comfort. Maybe Nashville had dragged them low as Truesdail had warned. Shire laid on the bed. Bridget partly disrobed, turned down the lamp then sat cooing above him in the thin light while he slowly drew the strings from her bodice.

*

He woke to a sore head and a blur of petticoats. The ladies dressed and departed with no more than a blown kiss from the doorway, money matters having been settled last night. He swung his legs out of bed and rubbed his eyes. A heavy weight of guilt sat in his otherwise empty stomach.

'Tuck. Are you awake?'

Tuck wasn't there. Neither was his greatcoat. Shire moved to the window and looked out onto a wet day, rain sheeting down over the river, obscuring the far side of the fortified bridge. On the near side, standing face to face with a guard, was Tuck. At least it appeared to be. Few other people were that tall. Shire dressed and hurried out into the cold. He followed a wet path that led along the bluff and up a low embankment onto the track, trying not to slip. Tuck and the guard were talking under the scant cover from one of the dovecot towers. Shire stepped up behind him.

'This a friend of yours?' asked the guard.

Tuck turned, bleary-eyed. 'What you doin' here?'

The guard lowered his voice. 'You only said…'

'It's alright,' said Tuck. 'He's with me.' He pushed Shire back a few steps.

Shire brushed Tuck's hands away. 'You seem to have a keen interest in this bridge.'

'I was seeing if he had anything to trade, that's all.' Tuck closed his eyes and let out a breath. 'You know this was a proper covered bridge when I used to come before the war. Smart it was. This fella tells me the Rebels burned it when they gave up the city in sixty-two.'

'Just yesterday you said Nashville was the poorer city compared to Louisville.'

Tuck opened a crow-eye on Shire. 'And I 'spect you feel Clara is a superior woman, but you seemed awful fond of Bridget last night. It used to be a good city for a visit is all. Now everybody's watching each other sideways and they have to build gun towers to get a train over a river.' He kicked at the wood. 'I really liked that bridge. Another thing gone to ashes.'

'Let's get some breakfast.' Shire turned and started to walk away.

Tuck stayed where he was. 'What if I don't want to come back?'

'It's raining hard, Tuck. Let's talk inside.'

Tuck pointed a long arm over the bridge. 'It's just there, Shire. Not far. Change at Louisville for Lexington and Paris. I can walk from there into Millersburg. Then I'm home.'

'Whatever home is, we won't find it until the end of the war. You know that.'

'Maybe I'm done with the war. What if I don't want to herd a bunch of lame ducks and muddle-minded men back to get shot?'

Shire took a step back up the slope. His hangover thinned his patience. 'What do you expect to find, Tuck? It's all ashes. Your old bridge. Clara's home. Your home. Same as a lot of places. Hell, my home might as well be too. Come on.' He gripped Tuck's coat sleeve.

Tuck stood his ground. 'What if that was a line I spun? I make up stories all the time.'

'Why would you do that?'

'And if I went back there, I'd find the farmhouse fresh painted, white as goose feathers. Ma and Pa would beat me for runnin' off to the war and then send me out to make a woodpile. Cousin Orville and Adam would be there.'

'Tuck.' Shire shook his arm. 'That's not what you'd find.' Maybe the burned doorknob had been the only thing holding Tuck to that harsh day. 'You have no pass to get out of the city and they'd shoot you for desertion. Now come on.' He led Tuck down the embankment. 'Rice will be up and looking for us.'

Tuck was subdued for the rest of the day. There were only two small hospitals to visit. After that, Rice made a copy of the lists and had Shire run them up to Truesdail's office.

They'd told all the men who'd signed to meet at the city quartermaster stores late in the afternoon, a huge, wooden, single-story warehouse half a mile south of the Capitol and beyond the rail depot. Shire had never seen such a place, the frontage an endless line of wide wooden doors, each guarded. Outside was an archipelago of stores between the mud: high piles of dried goods under oil-sheets, cask-pyramids of differing sizes. A never-ending line of wagons queued to load and unload.

The three of them found a barrel each to sit on. Rice, still seemingly hungover this far into the afternoon, got out his list.

'How many are there, Lieutenant?' asked Shire.

Rice blinked hard and rubbed his forehead. 'Two hundred and thirty-three.'

'That's more than two companies.'

'I doubt they'll be made into companies. Likely they'll be handed back to their old regiments, so the 125th won't see hardly any.'

'How many do you think will show?'

'Hell, if half of them show, Colonel Opdycke will give me a medal and cook us all a turkey dinner.'

It being the busiest of places, to make sure the men could find them Rice had Shire fetch some red paint from the stores and daub *Opdycke's Brigade, 2nd Division* on a large square of waste-wood with the regiments listed.

125th Ohio

24th Wisconsin

36th, 44th, 73rd, 74th and 88th Illinois

The church bell hit three and the first men began to arrive, early among them Corporal Cobb from the Female Academy. Shire slapped him on the shoulder and drew a wide smile. Rice checked men off the list while Shire and Tuck worked with the assistant quartermaster to find new uniforms and equipage. Most needed knapsacks, haversacks, cartridge and percussion boxes and canteens. A very few had their old weaponry but these were swapped out for newer models from the stores. Uncle Sam was in a generous mood. Shire was glad to be busy. It kept at bay memories of Bridget riding above him that surfaced as his own hangover retreated, though he struggled to recall the feel of her hair or the color of her eyes. In a waking dream, behind Bridget stood Clara, head held high, her deep brown eyes proud rather than hurt before she turned away.

Once outfitted, each man was dismissed and told to be waiting early at the rail depot for tomorrow's mail train. There was a swell in the numbers arriving. A long queue formed and Shire pressed Corporal Cobb and some other already equipped men to help. Despite the cold there was a jovial air, at least with everyone except Tuck. It was dark by the time they finished and began the walk back through the mud to their lodgings.

'How did we do, Lieutenant?' Shire asked.

Rice put an arm around Shire's shoulder. 'All but two, my favorite Englishman. All but two.'

*

It was wholly dark early next morning when they marshalled at the station for the mail train. Rice worked at the list under a hung lantern before he let each man along beside the train. Shire's job was to collect the men into boxcar-sized crowds, forty to a car. No one was to board until Rice gave the order. They were the only brigade heading back on this train. Tuck was somewhere at the station entrance directing the men in as they arrived. The train's steam was no more than a whisper. It wasn't due to leave until a quarter after five. Colonels Beecham and Truesdail were there, standing apart, Truesdail backed by a few provost guards.

From each gathered crowd of men, Shire picked one to be in charge. There were plenty of corporals, even a sergeant or two. Shire not having a single stripe, they outranked him but took his lead. While they waited, some practiced the art of stacking arms with their new rifles. There was only one soldier from the 125th; Opdycke hadn't ever been in the habit of losing track of men when he commanded the regiment. Overall, it was a fine late autumn harvest to take back to his brigade. There were fighting regiments with less men than they had collected.

Beyond the mail train a whistle blew as another engine drew slowly away on a second track, headed north out of the station.

Shire counted his groups. Five carloads. There should be one more if everyone showed. Mailbags were thrown into the first car. There was a hopeful burst of steam from the engine though the station clock still had half an hour to run. Rice beckoned and Shire hurried back to him. A hapless soldier was being dragged away by the provost guard; one of Truesdail's bad apples.

'Go see what in the hell Tuck's up to,' said Rice. 'These last men were headed for the wrong train.'

Shire hurried to the station entrance but there was no sign of Tuck. He cast about outside in the gloom. Maybe he was among the crowds at the train. He must have missed him. He stepped back inside, thinking how quiet Tuck had been on the walk from their lodgings. That wasn't so unusual these days. The tail lanterns of the second train were disappearing out of the shed. Tuck couldn't have boarded on his own without a pass. No one could.

Shire risked everything on one thought and raced out of the station and into Nashville's streets. It was a long half-mile back to the river and he had to beat that train. Dark though it was, he knew the way well by now. His gear was in the station. How long did he have? He raced up Lemore and once north of the Capitol cut east on Gay Street. He could hear the train somewhere to his left. It would have to slow for the bridge. He hoped to God it hadn't bothered to build up any speed in the first place. Nightguards stepped out from their sentry posts. Some raised a lantern but mercifully none challenged him to stop. His greatcoat was so heavy. He struck the river just south of the bridge and used all he had left to climb the embankment. A flash of steel. A bayonet was leveled at his gut. He backed up a step and doubled over, out of breath.

'Is he here?' he panted.

A train whistle sounded and he looked left down the track to see the engine approaching, barely at walking speed. He'd won that race at least. He stood straight again, brushed the rifle aside and stepped in close to the guard, still out of breath. 'I asked if he's here.'

Tuck stepped out of the deeper shadow across the track. 'Let him by.' The guard stood back. Shire stumbled over the rails, the train not twenty paces away.

'Deal's done,' shouted the guard over the rising engine noise.

'I know it,' Tuck called back before he grabbed hold of Shire and the engine interposed. They were alone.

'They'll shoot you, Tuck. You have no pass.'

'I got one alright. I just didn't want its finer detail checked at the station. Easier to climb on here.' The engine and the tender passed them by. Tuck moved Shire to one side and looked down the line of the slow train.

Shire moved himself back in the way. 'Fake pass or not, it's desertion.'

'This is a common spot for getting aboard if you pay the bridge guards. Turns out they have a small arrangement with the train crew. Everybody happy.'

'I'm not. You're my pard. We're supposed to see this out together.'

'Don't distract me. I gotta pick my moment if I don't wanna end up a grease slick the day before I'd get home.'

Shire repeated what he's said yesterday morning, only with more vigor. 'It's not there, Tuck. *They* are not there. You buried them together. Remember?' He shook him. 'In one big casket. Burned. Fused together by the fire.'

It was harsh medicine and Tuck looked wounded. He gathered himself and took a few steps along the track, ready to leap on at the next coupling. Shire caught up, pushed him off balance and the chance was gone.

'Quit it, Shire. You ain't got no right.'

Shire got in close, stuck his face in under Tuck's, shouted above the slow rattle of the train. 'The war is to the south. It's not finished yet. You've seen the city, how they're building it up ready for a fight. Hell, they aren't even expecting us to stop Hood, just give them enough time to get ready to stop him here. It's Nashville he's coming for.'

Half the train was by. Tuck wrestled with Shire. 'Let me go. I'll throw your damned English hide into the Cumberland if you don't.'

'But Hood won't stop if he wins here. Where d'you think he'll head? Louisville, I'll bet. Will you fight then? Or when they're in Lexington? When they're roping Adam to send him south and make him a slave again?' More cars slid by. Did this train ever end? 'Opdycke won't forgive this time, Tuck. Not again. He can't.'

Tuck wiped the sleeve of his greatcoat across his face. 'I didn't stop you. After Mission Ridge, when you had your reasons. If that wasn't desertion, why is this?'

Shire had no answer to that. 'No. You're right. You came with me, unasked.' He let go of Tuck and changed tack. 'Alright then… I'll come too.' He looked to his left. Only two more carriages. There would be steps up to the rear of the final car.

'You can't come. I got but one pass.'

'I get a choice too, don't I? If we aren't going south together, we'll go north together.'

'No Shire.' Tuck clenched his jaw and pushed Shire away so firmly that he stumbled back down the embankment. The end of the train drew level. Tuck reached for a hold and made to step on.

'Should I ask Clara to marry me?' shouted Shire.

'What?' The steps were right there. Tuck was walking beside the train and could easily climb up.

'I've been wondering if I should. It's the last place to look. What do you think?'

Tuck let go. 'Shit. Damn it all, Shire, that weren't fair.'

'It seemed like my last chance to ask you.'

The air went out of Tuck and he slumped over like a tall wet scarecrow lost in the night, beaten down to Shire's height. 'You swear to me when this fight's over, you'll come. You'll come *home* with me. See if it's burned or whole. You swear, now.'

'I swear, Tuck. I'll come with you. I swear.'

The train rattled on across the bridge and was gone.

PART II

Florence, Alabama – November, 1864

It was a fine day, a rarity of late, but colder for that. Frank Trenholm had to work to keep alongside Tod Carter who was setting a brisk pace. The two staff officers led their horses away from the path and through the bothersome scrub beneath a canopy of cottonwoods and black oaks. Behind Frank his bay gelding was at least a couple of hands taller than Tod's gray and was, if Frank was honest, something of an embarrassment.

When Father presented him with the horse, Frank had christened him Ashley, after their home in Charleston. It seemed appropriate enough at the time, but he'd since reflected that the name had no warlike aspect and that some revolutionary hero, Lafayette or Hamilton, might have served better. But the name had stuck, so there it was. His duty as a staff officer kept him close to General Gist and, atop Ashley, he would find himself looking down on the youthful general. Gist had lightly mentioned Frank's 'elevation' for one so young and the other staff officers repeated the joke at every opportunity. It made Frank wonder if they were aware Gist was watching over him. As a Trenholm, he was used to having the best of everything and naturally Father had provided the best of horses, superior saddle and tack. His second horse, Cooper, was only marginally smaller than Ashley. He doubted it made him popular with officers who struggled to fund their own mounts.

'Tod.' When no one else was around, Tod had softened

to allow Frank to address him as such. 'D'you think I should get a smaller mount?'

Tod glanced behind. 'Ashley's a fine horse.'

'He's just so big. General Gist passed comment on it. When I carry messages to General Brown at division or, on occasion, to General Cheatham, I'm like to find the officers and generals admiring my horse rather than listening to me.'

Single file was called for between two trees and Tod took the lead. 'There are other qualities in an army horse to concern yourself with,' he called back. 'He's fast I imagine. That's important for a staff officer. And if you get to fight a mounted Yankee, you'll have the height advantage. He's a bigger target of course, but then so are you. The flat truth of it is, you and that horse are built to scale.'

Frank had warmed to Tod. Sure, Tod joked with him as the other officers did but didn't make him feel the fool. Frank usually came away the wiser. They'd met a few times since two-thirds of the army had arrived and gone into camp at Tuscumbia to wait for orders to cross the Tennessee River. The other third had already passed over and waited in and around Florence. The weather and the lack of supplies had held them where they were since the start of the month. He'd noted Tod was more edgy each time they'd met, but today, the order having finally come to cross, Tod had a new energy about him. He'd come to find Frank early and hurried them up the steep bluff that bounded the south side of the river.

They struck a wide trail that had been hacked through the forest. 'Here we go,' said Tod and led them along until the track broke free of the trees and into a cleared semicircle, open to the sky. Two cannon, only a few feet from the cliff edge, aimed out high across the river. The crew sat off to the side playing cards. They stood, given Frank and Tod were officers, but Tod waved them down. They both tied their horses to a cannon wheel then went to the drop and sat down themselves, careless of the damp ground. Below, the Tennessee River ran straight and true, gray-blue in the November sun. Hood's pontoon bridge, down to Frank's left, stretched maybe four hundred yards three-quarters of the way across to touch the northern point of a thin island, before setting off again on the shorter leg to the far shore. There were more canvas boats than Frank could reasonably count aligned side by side, as if ready to start the boat race of all time. A plank road was laid across them to bear the long line of Cheatham's Corps.

Frank and Tod's brigades were late in the order of march and wouldn't cross for a while. It was Tod who eventually broke the silence. 'Quite a sight, don't you think?'

Frank considered it closer to a miracle, the combined weight of all those men low to the water. He'd waited so long to join the army. In his mind's eye he'd perfected images of cannon roaring, horses and men charging. But here below him was an unimagined aspect of war. Both ends of the pontoon were secured to the end-piers of what had once been a rail bridge before it had been burned. Out of site just now, a steep grade ran down to the pontoon proper on the near side and back up the gentler distant bank, into the partially burnt-out and largely abandoned town of Florence. In-between, the boats were so depressed, it was as if the men were walking on the rippled texture of the river itself.

Regiments that possessed a band had them march ahead. Competing fifes and drums, brass and strings. Their separate melodies passed over the water and rose to Frank and Tod high on the bluff. Barked orders to 'route step' mixed with the music.

'Why route step?' asked Frank.

'Regiments marching in time will stress the pontoon.'

'Even without boots? So many barefoot. I'd never expected that. I've no idea how they endure the cold.'

'They don't have a choice.'

Poor weather and high water had broken the bridge more than once in the preceding days, mercifully with no one aboard. Aside from the weather there were the attentions of the Union Army. The Confederates held the northern bank, S. D. Lee's Corps having crossed over when the pontoon went up at the start of the month. The Union gunboats that had shelled the army at Decatur couldn't operate here because of the shoals above and below Florence. Nonetheless, Yankee soldiers had canoed down under cover of night and cut through some of the anchors and lashings. A few pontoons were salvaged, but not enough to fill the resulting gap. Several more days were lost while new pontoons were brought up from Corinth.

When he spoke again, it seemed to Frank that Tod was addressing the distant horizon. 'I didn't believe, when we were beaten out of Atlanta, that I might find myself so close to Tennessee again. Not before the war's end.'

'How far? To your home, I mean. How far to Franklin?'

'Once across the river? If I was alone, I could ride to the Tennessee border in less than a day. Around a hundred miles more from there.'

'Why isn't the river the state border? Seems only natural.'

'Because men made the border rather than God. Perhaps if we'd been better aligned with the Almighty, we might have avoided this war. Who knows? But if Nashville is the prize, which it is, we're going to swing near to Franklin, unless the Yankees dig in ahead of us.'

Frank knew how long Tod had been away from home, but

Tod appeared to need to tell him again. 'It's been over three years since I signed up. My nieces and nephews will be a lot bigger. I can't remember a time when my home wasn't full to the brim with children. Father should put a bell on the roof and call it a school. The place might become more orderly if he did.'

Frank picked at the grass. 'I'd like to see it. If we get close, maybe our indulgent generals will give us a pass, a day's furlough to go and see your old folks.'

'Only Father's on the old side, and he wears it well. Or at least he did when I left. He's a strong man. Imagine. Ham from the smokehouse, hot buttered potatoes, turnips and beets. All tasting of Williamson County.'

'Why, we'd desert rather than go back to the army.'

'Desert? You've not been in the army more than five minutes? What would Secretary Trenholm say?'

Here was Father again, ever present. 'Oh, he'd like it well enough. He tried and tried to keep me out of the war, despite me being a fighting age, offered me any number of safe desk jobs in Richmond. I'd been begging to come away for more than a year.'

'Well, it was a good year to miss. Nothing but backing up. At least Hood has us going forward. You have to hand him that.'

'Maybe he'll get you home.'

'Even if we did come close to Franklin,' that distant voice again, 'by then the armies will be rucked up on Nashville, spoiling for a fight. That won't be the time to ask for a furlough, even if it was only for one day. If we *take* Nashville, that would be the time. No Yankees in Franklin then. Just buttered potatoes.'

Later in the day, when the sun was lower in the west and Tod was riding at the rear of his brigade toward the pontoon, Frank caught up to him again. Tod hoped Frank wasn't taking liberties with Gist and had at least asked to come away from his brigade. He supposed that Trenholms weren't used to seeking permission.

Maybe he was spending too much time with Frank, though no doubt Trenholm Snr would approve. Frank was likeable enough, even if he did reek of money and privilege as if he was wearing French perfume, but there were other places for him to learn away from Tod's coattails. If the armies did tangle in the weeks ahead, there would be nothing much Tod could do to look after the boy. General Benton Smith would need Tod to hand and Frank would have to attend to Gist. Decatur had been nothing. How would Frank cope in a full-scale battle? The noise, the confusion, the blood. He'd just have to get lucky. And there wasn't a way to train someone to that.

If he was honest, he'd rather have ridden alone across the pontoon. It meant something, this crossing. Before today he'd been away at war. Now he was accompanying the war home and the thought of it churned his gut.

Drums struck up beside the road and Tod jumped. Rosencrantz shied too, covering Tod's embarrassment. He settled him and alongside Frank they eased onto the steep grade that took them down toward the pontoon. Their horses stepped gingerly, keeping their weight to the rear. A long line of soldier heads, four abreast, stretched out ahead of them across the river. The pontoon wasn't straight at all. Occasionally lashed to a ruined bridge pier, it wiggled this way and that. Near at hand it bowed downstream toward the west, pushed out by the main current.

'I wish I could bottle this,' said Frank.

'What?'

'This moment. This sight.'

'I'd wager most men on this pontoon wish they could forget about the war.'

'You were lucky. You got in at the start.'

Frank clearly had a lot to learn about luck. Tod had a sizeable list of memories he'd like to strike off. Not all of them though. It was tempting to see his younger self in Frank. If he tried hard, he could remember his own excitement when he signed up with Moscow. Those were heady days. Unlike Frank, he'd had to work his way up the ranks to be a staff officer. He'd gotten here by hard work and survival. Frank had walked straight in at practically the same level on account of his father. After the war, it would be no different. Tod might hope for a little patronage from Trenholm, but Frank's future was already assured if Trenholm's wealth outlasted the war. There was an equality in battle though. Bullets passed through fine new cloth just as well as old. 'Why not write? It's the best way I know to preserve something.'

'Don't you get tired of it? General Gist has me penning orders all day.'

'That's not the same as writing for yourself.' He'd written a lot of late. Before Hood brought them first north and then west, Tod had filed a dispatch for a paper under his pen name of Mint Julep. He'd written less this year than he had before his capture in sixty-three, at least for the papers.

He wrote privately as a more truthful way of conversing with himself. A pencil seemed to draw out the honesty. He'd written to Clara too. Given George Trenholm had shared with him that her home in East Tennessee had been destroyed, the letters he'd sent there had probably been a waste. He had no idea if any passed through the lines these days. Maybe it was best if they hadn't reached her, poor wooden efforts that they were, with no real news and only hobbled feelings. And Trenholm said she'd moved to her tenant farm at Spring Hill. She'd told him of the place when they'd met on the Ohio. He knew it well enough, it being so close to the Columbia Pike. Privilege might be doing its best for Frank, but it hadn't protected Clara too well of late. She was become a farmer in middle Tennessee, more akin to his own station in life.

'Route step!' shouted a sergeant beside them as their horses leveled out onto the plank road above the water. A dog barked anxiously from the tailgate of a wagon ahead and was shouted quiet. Frank's tall horse was more nervous than Tod's. 'Why don't you lead him?' If that horse shied sideways, Tod might have to craft a few difficult sentences to Trenholm about how his youngest son came to drown.

'Nobody else is?' said Frank, sounding embarrassed. 'I got him.'

The dog started up again.

Tod looked across and a little up at Frank. To call him lanky might be unfair. Rangy might fit better. There was some filling out left to do but that wasn't so easy in an army on the march. It was a handsome Trenholm head on that long neck and he had his father's intelligent eyes. Tod hadn't enjoyed being embarrassed much when he was younger, but it was an emotion that withered with age if you weren't too proud to start with. At twenty-four, he was hardly an old-timer, he just felt that way sometimes, especially around Frank. The battles stacked up, each and every one brimful of so much death it was like to surviving a whole year. If you outlived enough people, saw them killed or their names on the casualty lists, then maybe it wasn't so different to becoming an old man. He gazed out over the water and caught himself wishing the war was over, that they'd surrendered at Atlanta and that he was riding home alone. What would his readers think, to know that their correspondent, Mint Julep, who'd written so patriotically in the early years of the war, secretly wanted nothing more than peace? It was hard to see the shape that might take beyond the word itself; easier to recall peace in the past than imagine it in the future.

Their horses couldn't quite settle, their eyes wide at the river that flowed so heavily under the pontoons. The men ahead began to sing 'Southern Soldier Boy'.

'Have you ever seen the army this spirited?' Frank said. 'The men are stepping out, don't you think?'

Tod twisted and looked behind. It was true enough. Men laughed or sang to the music. Their heads were up. They'd been waiting a long time to cross this river. The icy freshness of it, so sharp down on the water, got in behind his eyes. In his own brigade, four of the five regiments were from Tennessee, and mostly Middle Tennessee at that. Like him, they were veterans. Like him, they were headed home. It made him wonder why he didn't feel the urge to sing with them.

If it had been a more peaceful march they were about, he could have thought to pay Clara a visit. They'd almost be neighbors. There'd be no wildflowers this time of year though. Clara was hard to fit into his picture of home. She didn't really belong there. Rather she was part of his war. By far the best part of it. And it was hard to think of Clara without thinking of Shire, and then all sorts of feelings started to bubble up.

They moved well out onto the river. He looked behind and downstream to the south bank and the cliffs there, sheer and pinkish, were higher still than where he and Frank had sat in the morning. The breeze got up and the cold began to truly bite. The falling sun had little power out here on the water. He closed his cloak and hunkered down on Rosencrantz. He looked out at the row of taut anchor lines that angled steeply into the water, down at the knotted lashings that bound the boats and the road, and wondered on the physics of it all. Looking behind again, he could see Bledsoe's Missouri Battery descending onto the pontoon from the southern shore. Full teams of horses, cannon and caissons all added their weight to the equation. Ahead a line of wagons, canvas up, took the small angle at the island and wobbled on. He imagined the anchor lines popping one by one, the road snapping and shearing, tipping helplessly with Frank and the horses and the band, the song turned to wails, Hood's army swept away and under the dark water.

Frank stood in his stirrups and stretched his neck. 'Do you think we're halfway yet?'

Tod shook off his daydream. 'You're enjoying this, aren't you?'

'Why wouldn't I? They might tell tales of today. Like Washington crossing the Delaware. I want to remember this. Maybe I will write. Yeah. I'll write to Father.'

Frank's mood was infectious and Tod wanted to catch it. He dug into what reserves of hope he could find and also into his saddlebag to pull out a small bottle, not a quarter full. 'Here,' he said, reaching to pass it to Frank. 'You're a Trenholm. I imagine you were weaned on whiskey.'

Frank pulled the cork, took a mouthful and winced. 'Are you sure this is whiskey?'

'Ha. If you want to drink in this army, you'll take what you can get.'

Frank drank some more. Tod drank too. They crossed the island. The whiskey and the approaching shallow northern bank started to take the edge off the cold. The blackened homes of Florence, some no more than chimney stacks, rose up before them. At last the pontoon gained the northern trestle. Side by side, one bay and one gray, their horses hurried gratefully up the gentler grade. He had crossed the great Tennessee. As he'd told Frank, it was not a border of man: this was still Alabama. But it was Tod's side of the river. Tod's soil. Unless the Yankee army gathered itself in a hurry, there was nothing but marching yards and hoofprints between him and home.

Nashville, Tennessee – November, 1864

There was one passenger car behind the tender on the mail train, but Rice decided they should forego the comfort of the seats and stay with the first boxcar full of men. Shire didn't feel he or Tuck were in a position to argue, low as their stock was with their lieutenant. The cold sweat from their run back to catch the southbound train was yet to dry under Shire's shirt. By the time they'd arrived, panting into the night air, Rice had all the men aboard and was making his farewell salute to Beecham and Truesdail. The latter delivered a harsh look as Rice hurried over. 'Where in the name of all that's holy have you been? Truesdail was about to send his men after you.'

'Tuck left his fiddle at the lodgings,' Shire lied.

'And it's such a weighty instrument as takes two of you to carry it?' Rice glared at Tuck. 'Now get your skinny behinds aboard this damned train.'

Shire had been in cars – indeed on top of cars – a lot more crowded than this one. The men had plenty of room to sit on the floor in the dark, their backs to the rattling wood. Shire preferred to stand. Once again, his frame on the dim world was a small, barred window. This time he looked out to the west, where the dawn light was slow to reach over. He left the city a deal faster than he'd entered it, the driver no doubt trying to make up for the time he'd lost in starting.

Shire wasn't unhappy to leave. He felt hollowed out by the last few days and wondered what Nashville might have done to him if he'd stayed longer. Behind him, Tuck had already curled up on the floor. Shire wondered if he'd done the right thing, dragging his friend back to a war that wasn't particular over who it claimed. They'd done the same for all these men; back to the bullets and the blood. At least he had Tuck where he could watch over him.

They were down the line and pulling out of Franklin by the time the first patchy sunlight broke through. He pushed closer to the bars despite the cold breeze that picked up with the train. There was nothing to see as they ran through a cut. He was disappointed that he couldn't look out onto the town. Tod's town. Shire had spent his first spring in the army here, fired his first shots in anger after he'd forded the Harpeth River. He'd hoped to catch a glimpse of the Carter house and the cotton gin where he'd helped out Tod's brother. Perhaps it was as well not to think on that family. He was certain that Tod wouldn't have a fond thought left for him.

The train lifted out of the cut and onto the flatter plain south of town. He twisted his face to look forward. Through watering eyes, he could see the line of hills beyond. He picked out Winstead Hill. There were only sad memories of there too. He remembered racing out of the picket line, running to the top in the deep snow after Ocks had brought him news of Father's death. Exhausted in body and spirit, he'd found himself confronted by a great stag. Out of bitterness he'd wanted to shoot it, but failed. The memory laid a heavy weight on his heart, as if his father had died up on that hill and not alone back in England.

The train hit an incline and began to lose speed. It worked into a saddle in the hills and the whistle sounded, long and shrill. The saddle deepened to a ravine. There was no more to see and Shire stepped back from the window. The cold wind had provoked some tears and he wiped the sleeve of his greatcoat across his eyes.

There was a sudden squeal of metal on metal and Shire fell hard across Tuck. The train ground to a standstill with a last settling jolt that left it off-kilter. Tuck swore and shoved Shire off, who stood up slowly on the canted floor. He extended an arm for Tuck to heave himself up. The men who'd been sat facing sideways righted themselves. Rice unhitched the sliding door. Gunshots sounded outside. Rice drew his revolver and barked at the men. 'Load in here. Once done, follow me outside. Tuck, Shire. With me.'

Shire helped slide open the huge door and jumped down after Rice, landing hard on loose gravel. Dawn shadow filled the ravine but it was light compared to the boxcar. Beyond the passenger car and the tender, the engine was skewed and partly off the track, the black and bulbous smokestack canted at a precarious angle, sending up dark smoke into the triangle cut of sky ahead. There were maybe thirty armed men at the engine, some close, others up the slope and level with the engine cab. The driver stood with one hand in the air while his other kept him from falling from his tipped and derailed train. Like everyone else, his head was turned toward Shire, Tuck and Rice. The first shot wasn't slow in coming and rang off the car wheel next to Shire. Rice emptied his pistol in quick order. The ravine was dotted with infant trees and scrub bushes. Shire dived for what cover he could with Tuck. They set to loading.

'They ain't dressed like regular Rebs,' said Tuck.

Shire was shaking. 'Rebs or not, they're not very friendly.' There'd been no warning. Not like a battle where you knew a fight was coming and there was a chance to steel yourself.

Bullets rained in. Rice found his own cover close by. 'Irregulars,' he called over, reloading, 'figuring there's pickin's in the mail. They're headin' this way.'

Shire and Tuck got their shots away. Whoever the men were, they were creeping closer along the side of the train. Then the odds changed. The doors to the second and third boxcars slid open and a handful of men jumped out, a couple with pistols who fired up the track.

'This is a hazardous spot,' said Tuck, working his ramrod.

More men jumped from their own car and the firing from behind abated. Rice stood up. 'First six men form here and we'll give them a volley.' He was partly obeyed as the men stepped up but they didn't wait on his order to fire. Shire stood and shot again, taking a man down. The bushwhackers began retracing their steps to the engine. More recruits spilled from the train and Rice struggled to get them in order. Most ran past toward the enemy; one took a bullet in the shoulder. The Rebs, if that was who they were, scrambled up the loose rocky slope to get away. The driver and his stoker found their shotguns and took happy aim.

More and more men jumped from the train, hopelessly disordered but seemingly determined to get back in the war. Shire and Tuck raced up ahead to the engine and loaded again. Most of the Rebels had reached the safety of a tree-line high up the slope. Two were lagging, including a bigger man who turned and fired a long-barrelled pistol down at the engine cab then turned his attention to Shire and Tuck. His last bullet spat up the dirt between them, before he started away upward again.

'You pop the big fella,' said Tuck. 'I'll take his friend.'

They raised their rifles. Shire fired a fraction before Tuck. Both targets crumpled onto the scree. The last of their comrades disappeared into the trees. Shire and Tuck reloaded then began to climb. The shooting seemed to be over. The recruits whooped and hollered. A few headed up the slope as well to collect wounded Rebels. Shire and Tuck approached their hits warily, Tuck keeping his rifle on them while Shire edged in close. Tuck's man was struck high in the leg. He fought to sit up.

'Stay still now,' shouted Tuck, moving closer. 'Leave that rifle be.'

Shire moved over to the bigger man who lay on his back on the stony slope, arms flung wide, his eyes open and staring up into the morning sky, fighting for breath and bubbling blood. Shire had never stood over someone he'd shot before. This man's hair might have been red were it not so dirty. His tired and faded Confederate cape was cast half open, exposing a raw and pumping exit wound in his chest. A cavalry hat lay beside him, equally worn and with the remains of a feathered tassel attached. Shire toed the long-barreled pistol out of reach.

'He dead?' called the other Reb.

'Lung-shot,' said Shire. 'He needs to make his peace.'

The other Reb rested back on the slope and let Tuck take a look at his leg. 'Glory be,' the Reb said. 'That might take a while for Captain Bowman. He ain't well practiced at it.'

'Bowman?' Shire said.

'Who are you fighting with?' asked Tuck. 'Are you with Forrest's cavalry?'

'We never really fix to anyone,' Tuck's Reb said. He winced as Tuck tore his trousers to see the wound. 'Freelance you might say. We been encouraged up this way though. Didn't figure on half the Yankee Army bein' aboard the mail train.'

Bowman, speech beyond him, swiveled his eyes to meet Shire's.

Shire held his gaze while continuing the conversation with the other Reb. 'Were you with him in Ducktown in the summer? At the mines.'

'I was there alright. Wasted weeks. No profit in that business. What's it to you?'

Shire understood that lying below him was the very man who'd killed Clara's maid, Hany; the man who had left Clara for dead in the mines and burned Comrie to the ground. He'd be dead himself soon. No one lasted long from wounds like this. He should soothe the man's passing, say a prayer or at least leave him in peace to die, but what edges of pity he felt dissolved into the morning air. He heard himself say in a level voice, 'Bowman, your time is used up. I want you to know that Clara Ridgmont is alive and well. She has a new home only a short way from here.'

Rage and fear mixed evenly in the man's eyes.

Shire took a knee and leaned in close, tipped back his kepi. 'You know, when you burned Comrie, you also burned your friend Matlock. I could thank you for that at least. The best we can figure, you also burned some six thousand dollars he stole to pay you. It was there for the taking. Shame you were so set on violence. If you weren't queuing at death's door, I'd put you on your way for Cele's sake, the little girl you made an orphan. No need to trouble myself though. In but a moment, you will have to account to God for that.' He stood and left Bowman staring at the sky, heard the death rattle behind him but paid no mind. 'What about this one?' he asked Tuck.

Tuck didn't trouble to lower his voice. 'In the bone, I think. Won't bleed to death unless it's when they take his leg. I 'magine they'll hang him anyway, irregulars attackin' a train.'

'We had orders, of sorts.' The man appeared calm enough. The shock could do that sometimes. 'Best you finish me. I don't want them to saw off my leg just to hang the rest of me.'

'We ain't those kind of soldiers,' said Tuck. He called up some recruits to carry the man down the hill.

Rice told them both to take a dozen men and scout into the trees to see if the Rebels had truly gone. They found two good horses, one with a saddle stenciled *C.S.A.*, the other U.S. They left a picket inside the trees and led the horses back down the slope to Rice, who was standing with the driver. Rice said, 'Seems we'll need engineers to fix the track and a crane to lift the engine back on. We're gonna be here a while. The wire has been cut. The nearest place is Thompson's Station to the south or back north to Franklin. We need someone to get to a telegraph to start the engineers this way and it appears you boys have each found a mount.'

'Don't you need help with the men?'

'Some have provisions. I can walk out a forage party to visit the farms hereabouts.'

'I can't see us getting straight until tomorrow,' said the engine driver, surveying his stricken engine. 'Darndest thing though. There was just enough light for me to see ahead and brake. If we'd been running on time, the whole train might have come off. Different story then.'

Shire reassessed the value of his race across Nashville. 'Do we need to come back, Lieutenant?'

'What?'

'If we get the wire off? This wreck is going to block any more trains north or south so word will get out soon anyway. Only, if we go to Thompson's Station, there's someone further south I'd like to visit, above Spring Hill. Tuck and I can forage there for ourselves.'

Rice was exasperated. 'You've already gone roaming once today. I got two-hundred-fifty recruits here!'

'Not raw recruits, sir. They were up for the fight. We can be back at first light.'

Rice shook his head a while and then poked a finger into Shire's chest. 'If for any reason we miss each other, get the first train back toward the brigade. And keep an eye on Tuck's fiddle.'

Williamson County, Tennessee – November, 1864

'Is it you or your horse that's in such a fuzz of a rush?' Tuck shouted from behind.

Shire twitched the rein to stop his new mount and twisted in his saddle. 'We're not even trotting.'

Tuck and his horse caught up. 'I believe a slow trot would lose ground to your fast walk.'

'I don't know how long it'll take to find the place.'

'Just off the pike and north of Spring Hill, you said. Well, that's where we're at. Pick a farm and go ask. A new arrival in a place like this, 'specially a young Englishwoman alone, that ain't gonna pass unnoticed.'

Farms were set back from the road left and right, some grander than others but all smart enough. He'd sooner not ride up and ask. Two Union soldiers far from help might not be given the chance to get their question out. Tuck seemed to be in a good way, considering that before dawn he was only a hop onto a train away from desertion. Perhaps the fight had steadied him. What a strange thought that was, that a man could be set on an even keel by a skirmish at sunrise.

Earlier, after they had left the stricken train, they followed the rails south through a mix of forested hills and farmland in the vales. He'd not come this far south last year, when they were billeted in Franklin. He recalled there'd been a battle near Thompson's Station in March, soon after they'd arrived. The 125th wasn't involved. It was a big fiasco. More than a thousand Union captured. You wouldn't know there had been a fight to look at the country. This late into autumn the farms still appeared wealthy, well kept, unravaged. He didn't think he'd seen such rich country since arriving in America. They'd crossed over the Columbia Pike but stuck with the rail track as far as Thompson's Station so they could wave down any northbound trains. In the event, the first one they encountered was stopped at the depot and they rode up in time to prevent its departure. The telegraph was up and they stood over the stationmaster while he tappity-tapped out their message. After it was acknowledged and they were fancy free, they cut back to the pike and headed south on the white road. A low sun was out but it was bone cold and there was a bank of dark clouds edging down from the north.

Ignoring the farms, Shire started them forward again and they rode more slowly, side by side. 'Do you think we should mention Bowman?' Shire asked.

'You got a reason not to?'

'She's not long here. Her hope was to get away from all that. Make a new start. Then the man who tried to kill her pitches up a few miles away.'

'He's pitching up with Old Nick about now. I'd say after the peculiarity of it settles out, she'll be the better for knowing.'

Shire wasn't so sure. 'I don't want to upset her. We've only the one day.'

The determination he'd corralled over the last few weeks, that when next with Clara he should bring things to a head using the blunt instrument of a marriage proposal, began to waver. The opportunity had come sooner than expected. Telling her about Bowman didn't seem likely to put her in the right frame of mind for romantic overtures. And the closeness of Tod's hometown, passed by only minutes before the train derailed, had made him fearful of the new start Clara was hoping to make. The sun was swallowed up by the cloud bank, muting the reds and yellows of the trees. The white stone of the road faded to dirty gray. As so often before, he began to persuade himself that it wasn't the right time. He lifted his head and tried to block out his doubts. At least he was in a clean, lice-free uniform.

'I wanna say something,' Tuck said.

'Since when did you need my permission?'

Tuck looked pained. 'Well,' he said. 'You been looking out for me of late and I thought I'd return the favor.'

'If it's about Clara —'

'It ain't about Clara, but we can go there first if you like. You still of a mind to bend your knee?'

'It's a God-given opportunity, don't you think? The train derailed so close.'

'I can't deny that. Doesn't mean you can't row back against serendipity. Fate won't necessarily have your best interests at heart. Like you told me back in Nashville, we have a fight coming. Clara could be betrothed today but wandering a bloodied field to look for your earthly remains next week.'

'Thanks for that pretty picture.'

'You're welcome.'

They stopped to the side of the road to let a one-horse buggy pass that was headed north. Shire was unsure if they should be going on at all. It started to snow. Heavy flakes fell slowly through the still air. He reached out to catch one.

'What did you want to say?'

Tuck took off his kepi and punched it out before setting it back on. 'After the fight, when Bowman was dyin', I heard what you said.'

'And?'

'I'm not saying it weren't due him, an' all. And if I'd been over him, I might have said something meaner, but it weren't like the Shire I know. I guess I didn't realize you were that angry.'

'He killed Hany. Tried to kill Clara.'

'I know it, but he'll get his dues from the Almighty.'

'Do you think I should have put a coat under his head?'

They sat in silence awhile, side on to the pike, until Tuck said, 'I didn't figure we'd circle back to counties we've already fought for, backing up over old ground. We've been a long time at war, haven't we? I know I suffer it. Some days more than others. No one is untouched. Not even you.'

'Best we get it over with then,' was all Shire could think to say.

'Don't you feel kinda queasy watching a man die before breakfast and talking about marriage by lunchtime? We could always tell Rice we couldn't find the place.'

For an answer, Shire twitched his rein south. His horse started forward again. How could any trace of joy exist alongside this war if Tuck insisted on giving death the whip hand? He thought of Gideon and cobwebs. Change wasn't the problem, just the consequence. If he hadn't changed, this country would have killed him long before now. Regardless of what it might infer about the condition of his soul, he felt more satisfied than queasy over Bowman. In fact, he didn't feel queasy at all.

The snow grew heavier. Soon, they came level with a straight drive on their right that led to a farmhouse. Not grand, but smart in its way, pretty in the falling snow, an orange-tiled roof between two tall chimneys. It was as good a place as any to ask the way. There was a slate sign resting at the foot of the gatepost, its chalk letters washed by past rain but evidently reapplied several times.

'Eversholt,' Tuck read. 'Funny kinda name.'

Shire smiled and dismounted, picked up and then replaced the sign. Eversholt in the snow. 'This is the place,' he said, suddenly certain of his way.

*

Clara recognized Tuck before Shire. She was sitting at the table in her bedroom, working up lessons for Alice and Lena. She'd lost her thread of thought and was staring out of the window, hypnotized by the winter scene, when two men ghosted out of the white, leading their horses down the drive. There was the familiar jolt of fear at the sight of soldiers. For a moment it was hard to tell through the filter of snow if they were blue or gray. One was so tall that he surely must be Tuck. The second soldier looped his rein over the porch rail, and by no more than the way he gently stroked his horse's head, she knew that it was Shire.

She hurried down the stairs. It was hard to recall a recent arrival of Shire's when it hadn't been a surprise: in the slave hut above Comrie before Ocks killed Taylor; riding into Ducktown with Tod and a hundred mules. At least for once it wasn't at a time of extremity. She flung open the door and embraced him as he stepped up onto the porch, his snow-dappled cap in his hand.

'Hello, Clara,' he said. 'I thought I'd come and see your new home.'

She clung to him. He was broader across the shoulders, despite army rations. 'Why are you here? Are you on furlough?'

Mitilde and Moses bundled out onto the porch to share in

the welcome. Tuck shook Moses' hand before happily enduring a loud and wide hug from Mitilde.

'Just for one day,' said Shire. 'Our train derailed in the hills.'

Clara hadn't realized how lonely she'd been. Shire connected her to everything: a lightning rod to her childhood, to Ridgmont, even to Comrie. She stroked his day-old stubble, touched the heart-shaped scar high on his cheek. His dark eyes were smiling, but not perhaps as soft and unknowing as they once were. He was a soldier, after all. How much of *her* Shire, her boy from England, was left behind those brown eyes?

'Howdy, ma'am,' said Tuck, bending down for his own embrace.

'Come inside,' she said.

'Can we put the horses under cover?' Shire asked.

'I can do that,' said Moses. Tuck went with him.

Clara turned to go in. Cele looked out around the doorframe, but ran away when Shire stepped toward her.

'She's frightened of soldiers,' Clara said.

'Even ones she knows?'

'She'll work it out.' She led him into the parlor. There was no fire. She knelt and reached for kindling from the basket, but Shire told her there was no need.

'It's warm enough in here if you spend your life outside,' he said. He explained why they'd been in Nashville and that they were on their way back to Pulaski. He and Tuck could stay the night if there was room?

'Of course,' she said. 'It's not quite Comrie.'

'I like it. It fits better.'

What did he mean by that? 'It really is too cold. Let's go into the kitchen.'

Mitilde had coffee brewing and oatcakes on the table. Cele

sat on a stool in the corner squeezing a rag doll. Moses led Tuck in from outside, both dusting off the snow.

'Fine place, Miss Ridgmont,' said Tuck.

'Tuck, I don't even know your true name. Please call me Clara.'

'Alright.' He reached for a cake.

Mitilde slapped his hand. 'You wait till you's offered. This ain't no army tent.' She collected the plate and held it up to him, wide to tall.

'My apologies. Livin' with Shire has sunk my manners some.'

They swapped news. Shire and Tuck told of tracking Hood through Georgia and Alabama; Clara, helped along by Mitilde, spoke of the move to Spring Hill and how they'd settled in. She wouldn't mention the Carters for now. Maybe later. Tuck offered Cele half an oatcake. She came to sit on Moses' knee and said she wanted a whole one. When there was a lull in the talking, Moses pushed Cele from his lap and stood, brushed crumbs to the floor and said, 'I could use your help to check on the horses, Tuck?' He nodded his head at the door.

Mitilde, hands on hips, shot Moses a knowing look. 'Sure need a heap of attention, those horses. You figure they got lonely so soon?'

Tuck and Moses were already on their way out into the snow.

'Cele,' said Mitilde. 'You come with me and help light the parlor fire.'

Once they were gone, Clara said, 'We seem to have chased everyone out of the warm place.'

Shire looked ill at ease. His hand drummed the table. When she reached out and stilled it, he gave her a half-smile.

'Just the three of you?'

'And Cele.'

'Must be hard.'

She assumed he meant the farm and not Cele. 'We need more help but it's not easy to find with the war on. I'm starting to know people hereabouts. We'll get ourselves right by the spring.'

'I never quite saw you as a farmer.'

'What did you see me as?'

'Just as you.' He smiled more fully. 'Clara.'

'Yes.'

'We learned some things in Nashville. There aren't enough men to stop Hood, not before General Thomas gets reinforced from elsewhere. Even with the men we're taking south, we're only trying to slow the Rebels down.'

'But Hood's the other side of the Tennessee River, isn't he?'

'He was when we left Pulaski, but he'll get over sooner or later. Winter or not, I think he'll aim for Nashville.'

'And you think he'll get this far?'

'I don't know. Maybe. But it's likely my army will fall back toward help. And that means Nashville. I think you should leave if Hood starts this way.'

'I've not long arrived.'

'Moses and Mitilde. Cele. The Rebels will send them south and make them slaves again. You haven't ever seen an army on the move. They'll leave you nothing.'

'I know people who'll tell me if we need to leave but, in any case, where would we go?' Clara stood and moved to the window. 'This snow is thicker than ever. George and my other horses are out in pasture. I need to fetch them in.'

'You brought Old George?' Shire smiled. 'I'll come with you. It'll be like old times. You and I in the snow.'

That was bold of him. She laughed. 'Finish your coffee. I'll get the bridle.'

She slipped on the heavy, worn coat that she used about the farm and stepped out into the snow and the quiet. Across in the barn, she found the two army horses unattended, each working on a net of hay. They would be fine animals if they were fed. There were voices in the hayloft above her.

'Go easy.' Moses' baritone. 'My supplies are low.'

'That's hard news. It could be a long winter.'

'It's not like back in the hills at Comrie where every other farm had a still. That regulated the price some.'

Clara slipped in between the horses so she was directly below the conversation.

'You need to come to Kentucky,' Tuck enthused. 'We got the finest whiskey.'

'That so?'

'Plain fact. I grew up in Bourbon County.'

'Praise be. Master Taylor, as you helped kill, he used to keep a bottle or two from Kentucky. I never tried it.'

'If I'm passin' this way again, I'll procure you some.'

'Truly?'

'Only neighborly, seeing as you're sharing at a low ebb. When we're back in the house, get me to write down where my home is. That way I might get to return the favor.'

'Take another tug.'

Clara wanted to get back to Shire but was enjoying the conversation. With only their voices to go on, no one would suspect that Tuck and Moses were a soldier and a former slave. They might have been cut from the same cloth.

Tuck said, 'If I have much more of this brew, I won't make it back down the ladder.'

'It's safer up here, anyways. Those rungs wouldn't bear

Mitilde if ever she had a mind to climb up. 'Sides, I 'magine a man your height has scarce use for ladders.'

'That's not so far from the mark. When I was twelve, ma would have me clean the corner cobwebs from her kitchen to save her standing on a chair.'

'Gotta make use of your offspring. 'Specially when they're as sprung as you are.'

'Does Mitilde still give you a hard time over the whiskey?'

'More so since we married. If it was in the vows, I didn't hear it.'

'Hell, when did you get married? I thought you was just going to court her to your grave.'

'That was the plan, but Miss Clara said if we was headed out in the world perhaps it was a good time. Mitilde agreed. I was outgunned. But I got no complaints. We both have a new world of freedom to navigate. It's easier together.'

'Does Shire know?'

'I guess not. Not less Miss Clara wrote him. It was after he left to find you again.'

'Well, congratulations. How do we toast with one bottle?'

'In turn, I guess.'

'I'll take the lead.'

She should get back to Shire. She eased one horse to one side. The saddles rested on the stall wall. One was stenciled with *C.S.A.* Why would it have a Confederate saddle?

'You figure Shire and Miss Clara will ever marry?' asked Moses.

Clara froze.

'We might know by sundown. He's planning on askin' her today.'

Clara sucked in so much air she thought they must have heard her.

'Wait now. What you tellin' me?'

'He's gonna propose,' Tuck said. 'Got it into his head that if he don't, nothin's ever gonna change.'

All those weeks together in the summer, Clara thought. Why wait until now?

'He might not get the shape of change he's lookin' for,' said Moses.

'I know. I've tried tellin' him to leave it. Though the truth is he's been leaving it for a while now. Maybe he's right. Fine lady like Clara ain't gonna stay unattached overlong.'

Marry Shire? She'd never quite allowed herself to frame it that way; instead she'd simply assumed that he'd always be in her life. She had a sudden vivid image of them standing together at the altar in the estate church back at Ridgmont, her mother behind with an appalled look on her face.

'Thing is,' said Moses. 'I'm not sure how unattached she is.'

'Meaning what?'

'Well, every Thursday night she stays over in Franklin. She teaches some widower's children.'

She should say something. Make a noise. Anything to shut Moses up.

'What? Like they's walkin' out or somethin'?'

'I don't know the particulars. She stays with some other family, but Moscow, the widower, he's been down to help me plan out the crops. Fine man.'

'Moscow Carter?' Tuck's voice was high-pitched.

'You know him?'

'We were in Franklin for three months last year. We helped gin his cotton. I gotta warn Shire. He's walkin' off a cliff edge in the dark.'

'I don't rightly know if there's any romance involved.'

'Oh, there's romance on the menu alright, but not with Moscow. Let's get back to the kitchen.'

Clara considered kicking over the ladder.

'Now hold on, Tuck. Mitilde's there and he ain't gonna ask in front of her. There's two inches of whiskey left and a long inch of a story you's leavin' in the bottle along with it. If it ain't Moscow, who in the hell are we talkin' about?'

Clara stealthily collected the bridle and a leading rein and hurried back to the house. Shire was waiting at the door in his long army coat. She looked up at him, startled, as if seeing him afresh.

'What is it?' he said.

She didn't answer but turned and strode across the yard. Old George was two fields away. Shire would be right behind her. She knew that. That's how it had always been. She led, he followed.

*

It was Shire's turn to wonder what the rush was. The flakes fell thickly and had settled enough for Clara to leave hurried footprints in the snow. They might have been ten again and Clara leading him out into the Ridgmont woods, to the grand stables or the lake. With the moment upon him, he realized he had no idea how to broach the subject of marriage. He could wait all day for a natural spot in the conversation and still be left wanting. He'd have to catch up to her first. 'You know, you'd make a good drill sergeant. Can we slow down?'

'He's an old horse. There's no sense me bringing him all the way from Comrie and leaving him to freeze to death. My new wagon horses are out in this too.'

Shire tried to draw on the night they went caroling back

in England, a memory he visited often enough. The choir had met in Eversholt village and Clara had named this farm Eversholt. That had to mean something. He'd trailed in her wake that night too. She'd turned up unannounced at his home and he'd had no say in the matter. She'd talked happy nonsense about the stars as they made their way to the meeting place. There'd been a violin tuning up as they came down into the village. Later, the snow had driven them inside, to the fire… Set beside that memory and in the gray light of day, these white Tennessee fields didn't seem the same at all.

He spoke to her back. 'What kept you so long in the barn?'

'I couldn't find the leading rein. Tuck and Moses were at the whiskey.'

'No surprises there.'

'Would you rather be with them?'

He'd never got out of this habit, had he? He'd put her before everything else in his life and followed her to America when she needed him, survived battles to reach her, signed a parole so he could go and hunt for her in Ducktown and now, after she'd moved away to a new home, happenstance or not, he was following on again, when he could have taken Tuck's advice and ridden away. Well, he'd learned a thing or two about marching these last years. He moved to the double-quick to come up beside her, put his hand on her shoulder so she stopped and turned.

'I'm happy here,' he said.

She looked almost fearful. Or maybe hopeful. He couldn't tell, but she held his eyes so long. 'Clara…'

She stepped away. 'They're in the next field.' They moved on more slowly, up a gentle rise. After a few snowy steps, Clara moved the rein and bridle so she could take his hand.

'You're cold,' he said.

'America is cold, don't you think?'

'It's winter.'

'Yes, but I mean it's harder to get warm.'

Why did she appear so frustrated?

'England was lived in,' she said. 'Old stone rather than new wood. This country, it's raw. Sometimes, I just want to stay inside with a banked fire and drawn curtains.'

'That doesn't sound like you. The Clara I grew up with wanted to be up and away.'

It was steeper here. What he wanted to ask was who she imagined sharing the fire with, but that was a sideways approach to a proposal. He'd stood in line to take volleys of rifle fire, stormed ridges crowded with cannon, and yet he couldn't find the courage to ask her a straight question. 'I've spent so much of the last two years out in the air that I don't hardly feel the cold anymore, but it was good to be under a roof in Nashville.' He recalled some of the warmth he'd found there, then worked to banish the thought. If he'd known within a few days he'd be here with Clara, he'd never –

'One of your horses, why does it have a Confederate saddle?'

'Not much passes you by, does it?'

'I was married to a Confederate officer.'

Shire resented Taylor's introduction to the conversation. He'd been happy with the way it had been tending. 'The derailment wasn't an accident. They were Confederate irregulars hoping to find something of value on the mail train. They didn't expect it to be full of Union soldiers. The horses were theirs.'

'Fighting here? Just up the road?'

'Just up the rail. Only a few dozen of them. Not so many now.'

They let the gate to the next field swing open until it banked the snow and stopped. It took only one whistle from Clara and Old George walked over to them. The two younger horses followed. George was content to have his bridle slipped on, keen to get inside. Shire was pleased to see him and it appeared mutual. 'Hello my old friend.' George looked no good for anything but having his nose stroked and his ears gently pulled, but that was use enough. 'If you want,' Shire said to Clara, 'you can keep one Rebel horse. I'll tell my captain one went lame and we turned it over to the half-company guarding Thompson's Station. Tuck and I can take turns tomorrow on the other.'

'You won't get into trouble?'

'You need all the help you can get. I'd leave you both but I don't think the story would wear it.'

Clara smiled at him ruefully. 'What a fine pass I've come to when I have to rely on charity from Owen Stanton.'

Shire stepped closer. 'You don't think of me as Owen anymore, do you? Nobody else does except the army pay clerk.'

Clara dropped the rein and took both his hands, collected them up to his chest where their fingers interlocked. She looked up at him. 'I shall have words with your pay clerk. I don't mind sharing Shire with the world but Owen, well, he belongs to me.'

'I do,' Shire said. 'I always have. What if –'

'Shire!' Tuck strode across the first field toward them, making quick ground though some of it was a little sideways. Moses was a long way behind. Shire felt Clara's hands slip from his. What the hell did Tuck think he was doing? He was almost up to them, blowing steam. 'Lordy. This snow's getting deeper all the time.'

'Is something the matter, Tuck?' Shire said, tightly.

'Not so I know. You weren't in the kitchen and Moses was telling me about the farm.' He couldn't hold Shire's stare and instead turned on his heel and extended an arm to the view. 'So I thought I should take a look-see. It's easy to track a friendly couple in the snow.'

Moses caught up to them, out of breath and bent over. 'You gotta slow those legs when you have an old man in tow, son.'

Tuck patted him on his back. 'My, it's cold though, ain't it?'

'Whiskey not keeping you warm?' said Shire, pointedly.

'What whiskey would that be? Moses is a reformed man. He's sworn off the stuff. Say, did Clara tell you he's married? They pick off us bachelors one by one, don't they?' He made a show of looking out into the snow. 'You know, best not to dwell outside overlong. Bowman's boys are still out here somewhere.'

'Bowman?' said Clara. She looked sharply at Shire. 'You didn't say it was Bowman.' She collected up the rein.

'I know it's hard news.' Damn Tuck. He should have let him get on the train to Kentucky.

'Bowman's dead, ma'am,' said Tuck. 'Shire saw to that this mornin'.'

'You were going to gift me Bowman's horse? That man killed Hany and tried to kill me.'

Shire realized his rug was well and truly out from under him. The frustration lifted his voice. 'In case you missed it, I killed the man. And take which horse you like. We don't even know which one *was* Bowman's.'

Clara started off smartly, pulling Old George between the three men and back down the hill. Her new horses trailed behind. Shire kicked at the snow, given there was no wall to hand. He looked across at Tuck.

'Now don't give me those eyes, Shire. I'm right sorry I had to blow up your day. Did I keep your powder dry?'

'I was so close, Tuck.'

'I'm sorry, pard, but I don't think you were. She ain't done with your friend Captain Tod Carter.'

*

After Tuck resurrected Bowman, there was no way back for a proposal, nor did Clara want to hear one. The memory of evil had been set loose into the day. Moses and Mitilde were as shocked as she was that Bowman had been within a few miles of them. The slow-building safety of her new home, which she had come to believe would only grow stronger, was shot away. Though it wasn't yet midday, she drew the curtains across the parlor window. Shire reminded her more than once that Bowman was dead and gone, as if that should have settled her mind. But hosting Bowman's horse in her own barn felt like a subterfuge, as if in some way it harbored his newly born ghost. Orphaned Cele ran around the house taking advantage of a sudden surplus of hugs. It was as if poor Hany was only yesterday laid to rest.

Clara had no inclination to venture back outside. In any case, they were held in by the snow for a long afternoon. Shire sullenly asked if he might put his map in the box that he'd left with her at the end of the summer and which she'd faithfully moved with everything else. He followed her up the stairs and into the small bedroom that might have been a nursery in someone else's life. For her it was the room for the boxes she had no reason to unpack. She lifted one away to find Shire's and opened it up. The wooden soldier rested in there on top of Shire's only set of civilian clothes, bought when he was with her after Comrie burned. 'Here,' she said, kneeling, but when she turned it was to see that Shire had found his walking stick resting in the corner. He turned it over in his hands, looking at each darkly carved scene as if there was a message he might divine there, and not a happy one. 'Why do you keep it,' she asked, 'if it troubles you so much?'

'It's not easy to throw away a gift from a man I killed. See here. Waddell carved the word *Franklin* into the wood. I could never understand why he'd done that.'

'It was somewhere you had been. Somewhere you fought, like the other names on there.'

'Only a skirmish.'

Shire could make a riddle of it if he wanted to. She needed to see if any help was wanted with supper. 'Where's your map?'

He handed over a paper that looked like it had been folded and unfolded a thousand times. She felt much the same. She put it in the box, thinking as she closed the lid that it had been a map for Shire to find his way to her.

Even Mitilde's dinner failed to ease the tension. Shire hesitantly mentioned that Moses had shared something about her teaching in Franklin. It was dangerous ground, but she'd spoken about it, quite enthusiastically as concerned Lena and Alice, but left out the Carter name. Most likely Tuck had shared it already. She thought teaching might be a subject they could rally around, it being Shire's old profession after all, but he remained sullen. Well, there it was. He'd kept something back, so why shouldn't she?

After Cele was put to bed they all settled in the parlor, comfortable enough in body but with the conversation stilted.

Clara even thought to suggest that Moses dig out the last of his whiskey to ease the mood. She'd been staring into the fire so hadn't seen Tuck get out his fiddle. When he bowed an untuned chord it startled her, bit into the tension she'd carried through the afternoon, so much so she could have snapped at him. Instead, she closed her eyes and held back while he tuned. Mitilde said she'd beat him with the bow if he woke the child.

When he began to play it was as if he'd chased all her ill-feeling from the room. A rising and falling waltz that might have been the first melody born to the world, it was so perfect. She looked at Tuck anew, no longer an awkward gangle of limbs but magically transformed by the single centerpiece of his fiddle into a graceful angel; long working fingers, a flowing bow arm and soft eyes. It was a wonder that any soul could pass such a mixture of joy and melancholy through the air. It reached into her heart and melted the confused emotions of the day into whatever it is that makes up a tear.

'That tune deserves to be danced to,' said Moses, reaching for Mitilde on the sofa but plainly asking the question of Shire, who stood at the mantlepiece. For a second Shire looked as if he'd been asked to shoot his favorite dog, but he visibly rallied and extended a hand to Clara. She rose into his arms. Had they ever danced? The parlor was the biggest room in the house but hardly a ballroom. Tuck artfully slowed a phrase long enough for them to get set and Shire led her off perfectly. In a few steps they had escaped from the fire and the gathered chairs to the freer end of the room.

Shire was skilled enough that she relaxed into his gentle hold and fell deeper into the music. All manner of musicians had played in the grandeur of Ridgmont, and there was the delight that was George Barnes, the copper hauler who had played at her wedding. But it seemed to her that none of them had ever touched such sweet delight and sorrow at the same time. The pace was quick enough to excite but slow enough to sense the care in Shire's arms. Over the minutes, the music itself became the canvas for something more. Tuck might have begun again more than once, she didn't know. She was aware only that the man holding her loved her beyond any measure and that everything he said, or didn't say, was with her heart in mind. She'd been taught to arch her head away in a waltz, but instead she rested it against Shire's shoulder.

*

When Tuck had reached for his fiddle and started to tune, Shire had sunk lower still. In recent times that fiddle had been a medicinal device, used to soothe whatever flavor of inner-self Tuck had in residence. Frequently, that meant the melody was at odds with the real world surrounding him. Shire feared he might play a jig or a dirge, neither of which were likely to help. He turned away.

As today had worn on, he couldn't square why Clara insisted on remaining upset. He felt that it was reasonable enough, even considerate, that he'd not announced Bowman's death as soon as they'd arrived. And how was the horse implicated in the sins of the master? Moses had pleaded with her not to look it in the mouth and it seemed she might be persuaded. His own brooding mood, born of the knowledge that Clara had sought out Tod's home and family, colored every thought.

When it came, the unfamiliar melody snared him from its first tumbling phrase. It gathered up his not insubstantial competing collections of regret and hope into one intermingled whole. The totality of it made him glad he was facing away. When Moses suggested he should dance with Clara, he feared she would see him unmanned. But when he turned to look at her, he saw in her eyes the same apprehension mixed with longing that had wandered through his waking dreams for so many years. He straightened as if Ocks had barked an order. He reached out to her and tried to forget he'd not waltzed this side of the Atlantic and back home only at tented summer fetes. The easy, slightly quick rhythm of Tuck's waltz encouraged them. There was no time for doubt and it lifted them away together, through easy turns, to where there was a little more space.

Clara moved closer. Tuck played on and Shire marveled at the music. It wouldn't have resonated so well in England. There was a busy American quality to the pace. Hope lived in the climb to every high note. America was founded on hope, after all, but there was such sadness in the falling arpeggios. It spoke to him of all the loss he'd seen and the loss that had gone before. He'd never heard Tuck play this. He didn't doubt that his friend's grief was anchored deeply in the mix, and that Tuck was playing this for Shire, to heal the rift of the day, no matter the cost to himself.

Clara tucked her head into his shoulder and the melody finally slowed and drew toward a close. He supposed that if there was a time to propose it might be now. If ever there was a lovers' waltz, it was surely this one. Every ounce of their struggle, endurance, sacrifice and love was in the room. Tuck had drawn it there. The end phrase was a last slow tumble from the highest of notes to the lowest. It might have been contentment or peace, but also allowed for parting, a final farewell. Clara lifted her head after the last note and they held each other's eyes for a long while.

Shire had promised himself he wouldn't look back after Clara kissed him goodbye, but he'd already given in twice. She was standing by the pike, framed by bare trees and frosted snow. The kiss had been a surprise. Tentative as it was, it had felt more than sisterly. He wished he'd used the opportunity to convey something more himself. The gentle mood from last night had persisted when everyone rose early to see them leave. Moses and Mitilde had said goodbye at the porch with Cele. Clara had walked down the drive with him in silence, Tuck ahead and leading their solitary horse.

After that farewell kiss, they turned south rather than north. Understanding how close the station was, it seemed dumb to share one mount all the way back to the stricken train when they could simply wait for it to collect them in Spring Hill. Rice would see the sense in it.

'Well,' said Tuck, now they were out of earshot, 'I'd liken that to a tactical retreat. We lost half our cavalry but the infantry is intact with you fit to fight another day.'

Shire knew that Tuck was fishing for forgiveness, as if his tune of last night hadn't already achieved that. He was less subtle as he went on, explaining that, as he saw it, Clara could only be inserting herself with the Carters because she was hopeful of one day becoming part of the family. Shire was irked. He wanted to preserve the spirit of the dance as long as he could, but could see things pointed that way. It hurt that Clara still hadn't mentioned it was Tod's home she was teaching in; it hurt that she was having anything to do with Tod Carter. If he ran with Tuck's warlike metaphor, he'd missed a chance to get off the first shot, take the high ground, build a defensive position. Colorful thinking didn't help. He felt miserable. 'What if there isn't another day, Tuck? What if that was my last chance?' He turned again and this time Clara was gone.

They soon came up on the cluster of smart houses that comprised Spring Hill – barely more than a hamlet – and found the turn west to the station. A repair crew had gone north yesterday, they were told. The expectation was the line would open today. Just when, no one could say. They found a spot to wait and Shire lifted the saddle off the horse. No sense in her standing there carrying weight. 'We should have swapped the saddles,' he said. 'Clara has the one marked *C.S.A.* It wouldn't do for the Rebs to find it there. You think I should ride back and warn her?'

'Nah,' said Tuck. 'The ride would be quick enough, but I'm not sure we'd ever get you away again.'

Shire found the smallest of smiles.

'Anyhow,' continued Tuck, 'Moses is smart enough. He'll figure to cut out the letters or sew some leather over it.'

A corporal brought them coffee while they waited. Out of habit, Shire reached into his pack for his map before remembering he'd left it with his other treasures, such as they were, all stowed in Clara's home because he didn't have one.

'I'm cleaned out,' said Tuck. 'I spent my pay on deep-fried pickles, a good-time girl and a crooked bridge guard. They *were* good pickles though.' He sipped his coffee, his hands wrapped around the tin cup. 'Have we been good or poor friends on this jaunt? I can't quite figure it. Feels like we've got each other's interests front and center, but you've dragged me back toward Hood and I've stopped you proposing to your one true love. If we can't bear to be apart, maybe it's us as should be pickin' out curtains.'

Shire laughed. Perhaps Tuck had done the right thing by him. It was just that Shire's best intentions had got him precisely nowhere. Tuck's gear looked on the light side. There were no telltale ridges in his knapsack. 'Tuck! Your fiddle. Don't tell me you've really left it this time?'

'I asked Moses to look after it. It seems to me lately that sometimes the music found the sore spot right enough, but other times it just held me there.' Tuck looked down into his coffee. 'I sure miss my keepsake though.'

Shire dug into his own pack and pulled out the doorknob.

'What miracle is this?' Tuck reached out and took it, held it to his chest like it might fly away.

'No miracle,' said Shire, 'unless it's the fact I didn't tumble to my death in the ravine when I climbed down to find it.'

Shire didn't need any thanks; the look from Tuck was enough. ' I guess I need it a while yet,' Tuck said.

A whistle sounded to the north and two minutes later their train drew into the station, black smoke billowing into a cold blue sky. Rice hailed them before it stopped and they arranged for the horse to be taken aboard. Rice accepted their lie about the second horse with no more than, 'Huh. Is that so?'

It was stop and start to Pulaski, the line backed up as it was, but they made it before sundown. Rice reported to Opdycke but the colonel made a point of searching out Shire and Tuck in camp and thanking them. 'Two hundred and fifty men for the brigade is a windfall and then some.'

'And one horse, Colonel,' said Tuck. 'Don't forget your gift-horse.'

'I won't, boys. I won't.'

Florence, Alabama – November, 1864

Aboard Ashley, Frank was afforded a higher vantage point than most, but he looked away as General Hood was manhandled onto his horse. General Gist, mounted beside Frank, and many other officers from Cheatham's Corps had gathered on this auspicious morning outside the army's headquarters house in Florence. They watched on unabashed, so Frank forced himself to do the same. Maybe the sight of fifty men – lieutenants, captains, colonels and on up – all squirming in their saddles and picking at their horses' manes would be more painful for their commander than to have them watch. But to look on Hood was to look on the ruin of war.

It took three orderlies to get him mounted. One to take his crutch. A second to support his weight and push once Hood had his left and only foot in the stirrup. Then, while Hood used his good right arm to pull up into the saddle, a third orderly helped his wooden leg up and over the horse's rump at an utterly unnatural angle, before he hurried around to attend to it on the other side. There was a further minute of strapping and buckling the man to the horse before Hood's crutch was slotted home into an oversized rifle holster. At last, the orderlies backed away. Though Frank did his best to push the thought aside, it played out plainly in his mind that they were led by a man not personally fortunate in this war, unless you considered keeping a beating heart as your main objective.

Ashley lifted his nose into the icy wind that blew up off

the Tennessee River. Frank leaned forward and stroked his neck. The morning sky held the threat of winter. Florence, despite its charred bricks and desolate aspect, suddenly seemed more welcoming than the road ahead. He tightened his greatcoat and wished he could dismount to stamp the numb cold from his feet.

Hood circled his horse and, once mobile, looked for the most part like any other rider but for his pegleg hanging stiffly and a little outward. He was oddly graceful, considerably taller than most and up to Frank's eye-level. Everyone gathered sat up or stood straight as he looked them over. Frank had heard it said more than once that the general's energy was at odds with his infirmities. What remained of him still added up to a fine-looking man and his public romance with Sally Preston, conducted back in Richmond between campaigns, was common knowledge. Beautiful as she was said to be, Sally wasn't considered a lucky match given her earlier military paramours hadn't fared well either, many having resigned their commissions at the pearly gates. Her attachment to Hood was rumored to be less than wholehearted, but had nonetheless survived his partly crippled left arm from Gettysburg, the loss of his right leg – pretty much the full length of it – at Chickamauga, and the arguably even more painful amputation of Atlanta.

Gist, clean-shaven and with a boyish complexion, waited until Hood moved away then leaned from his saddle so he was fractionally closer to Frank. 'It makes you wonder, don't it, young Frank, how many orderlies might need to be on hand for him to conduct the finer details of his courtship with Miss Preston?'

The 'young Frank' label irritated him more than Gist's constant attempts to embarrass him. He'd yet to summon the courage to ask to be called Lieutenant Trenholm. Maybe that was something he'd have to earn.

Frank had met Hood on more than one occasion in Charleston and in Richmond, albeit from the cover of Father's shadow. But then most people were outshone by Father in public. Hood was an exception, his military reputation enough to rival Father's in business. Hood's mood was easy to read, his shovel beard flecked with gray despite his only thirty-three years. Today, he looked in fine spirits as he hailed the officers of Cheatham's Corps, who were gathered to finally start out north from Florence.

Frank was as excited as everyone else to get underway and follow S. D. Lee's Corps which had started north yesterday. They all knew the plan. Each corps had its own course. Lee was taking the middle route on a backwoods road. Stewart would move on the east flank up to Lewisburg, once he was across the river. Frank and Cheatham's Corps would take the most westerly course and Hood would go with them. Their objective today was Rawhide, up near the Tennessee border.

Frank had been up early to distribute Hood's proclamation to Gist's regiments. At the 24th South Carolina he was invited to read it himself. It took him by surprise. He stayed atop Ashley and a hundred or more weathered faces gathered to look up at him, their eyes tight in the winter wind. The army would, he said as loudly as he could without shouting, 'march today to redeem by your valor one of the fairest portions of the Confederacy.' Through Frank, Hood promised no more battles on the enemy's terms. For once, he implied, this army had the numbers to call the shots and to guarantee victory. The men appeared to wear it well, eager to get into Tennessee and take on the Yankees once again. If the sky was anything to go by, they'd have to take on the winter too. As the crowd broke up, he heard one wag mumble none too quietly, 'That speech might have carried more weight if delivered by someone whose balls had dropped.'

With Hood mounted, they finally set off. Frank at least had a warm horse below him but once he was outside of Florence, he decided to lead Ashley, so he could work some warmth back into his toes. He'd yet to write home as he'd told Tod he would, but a letter arrived from Father just yesterday. Irregularly for a private letter, it had been sent with the dispatches to the army command and Frank had sheepishly received it from an unamused member of Hood's staff. Being the Financial Secretary to the Treasury had its privileges, he supposed, but he wished Father would spare a thought to how it looked this end. It was dated two weeks ago.

East Clay Street,

Richmond,

Virginia,

7th November, 1864

Dear Francis,

I hope this letter finds you hale and hearty. I'm reasonably sure it will find you at least, since if the army doesn't know where you are, we are truly in trouble. It is the constant jabber of Richmond as to where Hood will go. We had recent news you were at Decatur and headed west to find a crossing, but Hood's intentions are kept even from Jefferson Davis so far as I can tell. The high command batters the President with telegrams complaining there is no news from Hood, that he is insubordinate and a law unto himself. I console myself with the thought that if we don't know Hood's intentions, General Thomas can hardly know them either.

The wolves close in, ever nearer to the city, but it's well defended and we are all well. I'd prefer to be in Charleston, of course, but duty has found me out at last and

A stiffer letter might have been less unsettling. Frank confessed to himself that he missed his family and he missed Charleston as Father did. Was anyone still at home in this war?

At the stop for the midday meal, Gist ordered Frank to scout out the cavalry brigade that was supposed to be covering their western flank. 'Just let them know where *we* are and tell me where *they* are. Go careful. Don't surprise anyone.'

Frank was glad of the excuse to get out of column and for once to do something that mattered. As soon as he was safely beyond their pickets, he gave Ashley his head and read the ground, keeping to paths if he found them and using the open land where he could. Breaking free of the forest on a low ridge he drew Ashely to a standstill. Outside the trees there were the first few particles of snow, barely heavy enough to fall to earth and dissolving in Ashley's snorted breath. They were at the high end of a sloping field of dead unharvested corn, brown and withered. The sun might be anywhere. Frank drew out his compass.

When he looked up to get his bearings, he saw movement below. On the far side of the field the dead corn had collapsed to the ground. Blacks walked the edge beyond, under cover of the forest. Not workers. A family. Frank swapped his compass for his field-glasses. The man wore a jacket barely fit for a cool summer's day and carried a bouncing girlchild at his hip, her head tucked in under his neck, the pink undersides of her feet showing. The woman had a baby strapped to her chest underneath her shawl. Her husband had a small pack, but they carried nothing more. He led on and encouraged his wife to keep up.

Frank knew he should round them up. There was a standing order. They'd be collected with others behind the lines; returned to their owners or sent south to be sold, unlikely to stay together, except the woman and the baby. He wondered what their chance was of moving faster than the army, what prospect they had of food. *We keep a good table*; Father's letter was in his jacket pocket. There was some hardtack in his saddlebag. He moved off the hill, but before he'd reached the corn he was spotted and the family vanished into the woods. No doubt he and Ashley could find them. Better to let them go and be about his business.

It was a long time before he found the cavalry. They were well spread out, as a screen should be, so it was longer still before he was successfully directed to the brigade's command and delivered his message. He figured that the way back would be easier. All he needed to do was intersect the road to Rawhide and go north or south depending on how much of the corps had passed by. But the light faded and the snow came on. He became ever more reliant on his compass. The picket saw him before he saw them and he had to shout his name and unit before they would put up their rifles. He was hungry. He wondered how hungry the fugitive black family was.

By late morning the next day, and the other side of Rawhide, the army was moving ponderously along. If this was a race to get to Columbia, then it was a slow race, despite generally high spirits. It was a strange thing that the prospect of a battle could heighten the mood, but Frank felt it himself, a quickening heartbeat if not a quickening of the pace. He asked Gist if he might ride up the column and report back. Gist said, 'You might. And give my compliments to Captain Carter.' Frank ignored the jibe. What else could he do? Besides, the fight would come soon enough: a chance to prove himself to Gist.

He trotted up the side of the road, overtaking the column, the snow several inches deep. It was an hour or more before he caught up to Bate's Division, then Benton Smith's Brigade and eventually Tod, who was busy directing the slowest wagons off the road and getting their mule teams swapped out.

'Once a quartermaster, always a quartermaster,' called Frank.

Tod looked up, unsmiling. 'Hello Frank. Climb down off that height and lend a hand? No wait. See that third wagon taking the bend? The one badly loaded and canted over like a drunk Yankee. Ride up there and get them off the road. Then get it loaded and balanced properly.'

'This isn't my division.'

'Do you want to help move this army or not? If they're so dumb they can't load a wagon, they ain't gonna gainsay you. 'Sides, you're a staff officer and a Trenholm. You should be topped up with assumed authority. Get to it, Lieutenant.'

Frank pitched in and it was as Tod had said. He enjoyed it. His own brigade might be miles behind but by moving things along here, he'd help them move along too. At least he'd have something to tell Gist. The logjam cleared, Tod took him further north, the army an endless line of alternating men, wagons and the occasional cannon. It was even colder than yesterday. The soldiers were stick-men in greatcoats, some shod, some barefoot and some with pretend shoes: wrapped cloth, boots without soles or soles without boots, held on by no more than frayed string and hope. And yet, for the most part, they were smiling.

Once in a while came the dull crack of rifles from the north. 'Yankee cavalry,' said Tod. 'They won't have enough to stop three corps. Forrest will push them.'

Cheering came from up ahead. A plank hanging from a bough over the road like an overly long store sign read, *Tennessee, A grave or a free home.* The soldiers passing beneath lifted their rifles and whooped. Tod took off his hat and Frank bit back something he wanted to talk over. It didn't seem the time. A minute later the line stopped dead. Tod swore and cantered forward beside the road. Frank chased behind, Ashley kicking up snow. They slewed to a halt when they saw the cause. A small semicircle of mounted officers, hats off, faced General Hood. Hood walked his horse forward and dropped his rein to receive a long-held handshake.

'Who's that?' Frank asked.

'Isham Harris. The Governor of Tennessee. He's on Hood's staff. Hood must have asked him to ride ahead to make a show.'

'A show of what?'

Tod turned to Frank. He seemed to have trouble getting

his words out. 'This is the border. He's welcoming the army to Tennessee.'

The Army of the Tennessee had stopped to watch. Harris made a short speech but Frank couldn't hear much from where he sat. Quite soon, the gathering broke up and the army started forward once more to the accompaniment of creaking wheels, stretched leather, and an endless line of men churning mud and snow.

'Welcome home, Tod.'

'It's colder this side of the border than it was in Alabama. Let's find some coffee.'

They stopped at the next roadside fire and took their turn with the men. Tod led them away to sit on a fallen trunk and they let the horses rest.

'Quite a day for you, I guess.' said Frank.

'Ah. I'm not at the garden gate yet. This was never how I pictured it. The war was supposed to be *for* home, not so close as this.'

'That sign. Kinda sets it on the line. All or nothing. Death or glory.'

'It's about what it's come down to.'

Frank moved to get more comfortable. 'Did you ever question it?'

'Why we're fighting, d'you mean?'

'Only it's been a long war for you. I'm only starting out. I just wondered.'

'It doesn't pay to overthink it. What choice did we truly have?'

'There's plenty in Tennessee on the other side.'

'Not so many.' Tod set down his tin cup in the snow. 'What are you chewing at?'

'Father's got slaves everywhere. At home, on his

plantations, on his ships. He doesn't trade them for profit like he does most everything else, but he buys and sells as it suits. He treats 'em better than most, I guess.' Tod said nothing and Frank had to search for solid ground. 'I always wanted to fight. And South Carolina ain't split like Tennessee.'

'Are you saying you might have fought against the South, 'cos this ain't a good time to be picking sides?'

'No. No… I ain't saying that. We were invaded. Can't have the Yankees tellin' us what to do. That much is plain.' A fife and drum band marched by, the drumbeats staccato and the pipe notes dying in the snow-muffled air. 'Only I saw this negro family yesterday, out in the woods. No coats. No coffee. No tent. They were running from *us*. I wonder what they might have written on that sign.' Tod looked aggravated, so much so that Frank wished he'd not brought this up, but who else could he talk to about these things?

Tod heaved a sigh and tilted his hat. 'You're in the thick of it, Frank. And soon these armies will tear into each other to the finish. After the war they might stop to think on the rights or wrongs of it, but I doubt that will change many minds. Second-guess yourself if you want, but not on the battlefield.' He lifted his coffee and tipped it out to stain the snow. 'You'd better start back down the road. General Gist will want his Trenholm back, so he can tuck you in.'

Wayne County, Tennessee – November, 1864

Tod rode away from the stress of helping to rescue Cheatham's wagon train. It was the third day out of Florence and the first time in a long while that he'd had a road to himself. He could choose between the morass of the pike or the thin strip beside it, both equally churned up by horses and soldiers. Either way, all he could do was walk Rosencrantz except for the occasions when the woods thinned and he could make better time keeping parallel with the road. It was late in the afternoon and still bright, but was every bit as cold as yesterday when they'd marched on until dark.

At first light this morning they'd started north again. Wagons were ordered to wait aside the road until the men passed. That allowed the soldiers to move on more quickly toward Waynesboro, but by early afternoon the wagon train following on was entirely stalled. Mules sunk up to their knees, wagons to their axles. Wheels broke, tempers frayed and whips cracked. Tod had been detailed with a number of other staff officers to ride back and sort out the mess. His throat was sore from three hours of yelling at wagoners in the cold. You'd think this far into the war people might know how to work a team through or around the mud. The wagons were moving forward again but wouldn't catch up with the army today. There'd be no tents tonight for the soldiers. He didn't relish delivering that news, but it was good to be free of the crowd and try to let the strain of the day subside. It was hard though. All the energy he'd expended today was to haul this army closer to home. That wasn't a restful thought.

He remembered a trip to Waynesboro with Moscow. They'd rarely had reason to travel below Columbia. They'd ridden down to purchase a prize bull and walk him home. It was a ten-day round-trip. After the money changed hands, they'd got drunk in Waynesboro with the seller and slept with their backs to the old well in the town square. You couldn't hurry a bull and this one was slower than most, distracted by anything and everything beside the road. Tod was seventeen. Moscow joked ever after that Tod was more trouble than the bull and had used the entire eighty-mile ride home to sober up.

He missed Moscow. He was a good colonel and a better brother.

He hadn't seen Frank at all today. That was no bad thing; the boy needed to be left to learn on his own sometimes or at least someone else could play nanny. If Tod was honest, he was still bubbling under after Frank's clumsy sortie into the ethics of the war. What made him think that Tod had all the answers? There'd been times enough when he'd his own doubts: after his escape from captivity and his time with the Amish; after he'd seen the might of Union industry in Pittsburgh; after nights spent making love to Clara on the Spirit of Kentucky as they steamed down the Ohio and the Mississippi. What man wouldn't dream of peace after years of war when God laid such things before him? But there was always duty. And that never stopped calling. Duty to his family, his home, his state. To his readers even; he'd be in a fine fix with them if he turned tail himself having penned so many entreaties to fight. But every mile closer to home bubbled opposing thoughts to the surface, like his blood was coming to the boil. And Frank had stirred the pot.

He ducked under a head-high branch at the last second and told himself to be mindful. Shire had cured him of his doubts once before; his friend as he'd thought, who turned out to be no more than an English Yankee who'd chosen to fight again despite having a free pass out of the war. He had no horse in this race. There was Clara of course, and the nagging doubt that she had been the true reason Shire had come after Tod and the copper outside of Ducktown. He felt again the hot blast after Shire exploded the charge, Tod and his horse cast to earth as if they were no more than dry wheat struck by a thunderbolt. But that wasn't the worst of it. As he'd got to his feet the mountain path that held his mule train had fallen away, down and down into the ravine. His men, his friend Waddell, the mules and the copper, all swallowed up and lost, all down to one Englishman.

He sensed his pulse starting to race but, as always, reason followed on: Shire was a soldier as he was, fighting for his side, for his own friends. He couldn't have known the hill would slide away. But on that long punishing ride out of the hills with what was left of his command, his heart had set hard. He had *his* own side to fight for. If Frank thought seeing one black family on the run was a hard scene, he hadn't kept his head up.

He should put this line of thought aside and focus on the way ahead with the light beginning to fade. But, unbidden, another time played out in his mind, one that had troubled him well before Frank's worries of yesterday.

Before Hood led them west into Alabama, the army had torn up the track toward Chattanooga, disrupting Sherman's supplies to try and tempt him back north from Atlanta to give battle. There were any number of Union blockhouses and small forts placed to defend the Western and Atlantic

Railroad. Hood had either gobbled them up or passed them by if they looked too hard a nut. They'd reached as far as Dalton and there was a small detachment – around seven hundred men – who hadn't got away in time or had been ordered to stay put. Hood was uncompromising in his terms. Give it up or we'll take no prisoners, he said. Only it was mostly black troops, the 44th U.S. Colored Infantry. The white Union officers made pleas for their men's safety, declaring every man should be treated the same. Delegations went back and forth under truce and Hood said he couldn't restrain his men if they had to attack. Tod had seen the pickets in Cleburne's Division take potshots despite the cessation, joking as they did. He hadn't seen any effort to stop them.

The Union commander, Colonel Johnson, had no choice and surrendered the fort. Tod's own division, under his fellow Tennessean, General Bate, had command of the prisoners. Tod had watched on as the shoes and clothes of the blacks were taken by Bate's order, had seen Bate himself disparage and insult Johnson and his officers at length and in terms unbecoming to any gentleman; unbecoming to any American, for that matter. The blacks were marched away including many from the hospital tent. Those that couldn't keep the pace were shot in the head, as if no better than spent mules. He'd been told those left were pushed to dismantle the track and that one man refused and dropped his crowbar, in no doubt as to what that would mean. He was shot too. The rest would be back south by now, enslaved again for having the effrontery to put on a Union uniform and fight for the freedom of their own kind. Whenever Tod had business at Division H.Q., he couldn't look at Bate as anything other than an evil man, but then they'd none of them done anything to stop him. He hadn't. Hood hadn't. So where did the evil stop?

He didn't know where Gist's Brigade had been, and Frank might have been a distance away, but it was common knowledge what had gone on.

It wrung Tod out today as it had at the time, but what was he to do? It was too late to unhitch his wagon even if he wanted to. It wasn't as if the Confederate Army had a monopoly on evil. There was that crazy Union lieutenant that Shire had killed. It was war. He shouldn't expect to resolve these things. He tried to find refuge in philosophy from his studies before the war. Aristotle had said something about practical wisdom. He couldn't recall the Greek, but it more or less amounted to horse sense.

Father had his own slaves, or at least he had before the war. He had no news of how things stood today. Tod had grown up with slave children. They'd swum in the Harpeth together, collected loose steers; small children with big sticks. When older, they'd ginned cotton, side by side, sun-up to sundown. He'd count their farm benign, but there *were* scenes that spoke to him now more loudly than they had in his childhood: a wagon rocking away down the pike with a wet black face, wailing from the slave cabins, dead eyes tilling the fields. In some way the hurt, the unconcealed inhumanity, was communally put aside, at least in the house. He doubted it was the same in the cabins. But it was how life was, even if looking back the shape of it was plainly cruel. Now he was fighting to preserve such things.

He realized that Rosencrantz was standing stock still in the forest. He may have been doing so for some time. In front of Tod's neck was a solid oak bough that would have more successfully stopped his internal argument had his horse not saved him. He smiled, thinking Aristotle might have considered that Rosencrantz had more horse sense than he did. He ducked under and edged them both back to the road. It was planked here and a little easier. He was alone, but the passing of the army was plain to see on either side. Boots beyond repair, empty flour bags, trickle-smoke fires.

You couldn't avoid the morals of the war for long. Someone would always provoke you if you let the argument sleep. Luther on his Amish farm, Shire, Frank. God. He imagined for a moment that the Confederacy prevailed and took its place among the modern nations of the world. They would be an outlier, an unwelcome guest at humanity's table so long as they preserved the institution of slavery.

Two white women and their brood of little ones, all barefoot, all filthy, were sorting through the detritus beside the road. At least that's what he thought in the failing light before he came abreast of them. They were butchering the leavings of a mule after the army had done the same, cutting flecks of flesh from the bones and collecting half-frozen offal into a basket. He looked away, tried not to measure their plight against Frank's blacks. That argument didn't stack up, but this was hardship brought on by the war just the same.

Dusk gave way to night as he passed along the road. He overtook the last of the exhausted stragglers limping into Waynesboro. Up ahead a thousand campfires did their best to match the stars that outgunned them. It was pleasant at first, to ride between the fires and listen to the men, to the singing, the swearing, the harmonicas and the fiddles. The ruin that had been Waynesboro was illuminated as he rode on. Not a house left standing, nothing but brick piles and chimney stacks. He looked for the church, but that was lost too. The brick well, where he'd drunkenly slept with Moscow, was the only structure left intact.

His soft heart ran and hid. War was a harsh thing. It might

have been Yankees that destroyed the town or it could have been Confederate cavalry. Maybe both. Wayne County had been split in its loyalties, but that wasn't the point. If the Yankee army had never come into Tennessee, this would never have happened, to this place or countless others. He cast his mind to Franklin and imagined his own town similarly laid waste, the gables on his home empty of the house in between, the cotton gin torn down, the fertile fields gone to seed. He wasn't fighting for slavery, even if this army was. It had never been that way for him. It was about Tennessee, about his family and his home. He couldn't cure all the ills of the world. It was time to gather himself for the fight. To hell with everything else.

Columbia, Tennessee – November, 1864

Shire hurried to the low-burning campfire like it was a lost child. He was so cold. He knelt and all but embraced the frugal flames. Away from him, Mason, Corry and Cleves quickly got into loose formation to stack arms. Cleves took the lead role, placing his rifle butt beside his left boot. Mason passed over his reversed rifle. Cleves cast the second butt away from himself then angled the two rifles together so the flats of their bayonets crossed. From behind, Corry threaded his rifle into the mix such that the bayonet angle supported the pair and there was the pyramid. Tuck simply leaned his rifle against the others. Without a word, Mason collected Shire's gun and did the same. Shire was grateful, not wanting to leave the fire. Five tall rifles, ends resting on the frozen earth and the cold blades crisscrossing to make an untidy steel crown. Around them the same scene played out beside every campfire, a sparse forest of rifle pyramids springing up as the company came in from picket.

'If you get any closer to that fire,' Mason said to Shire, 'your percussion caps will start to pop.'

'At least that might warm me up.'

Cleves placed a couple of hopeful logs across the fire. Shire forced himself away long enough to find his oilskin poncho, laid it as close as he could to his fifth of the fire and put his rolled and tied blanket there as a seat. The others did the same, except Corry who'd contrived to lose his poncho back in Pulaski. He found a fat log instead and clumsily dropped it into place so it nearly struck Shire. Barely two minutes after coming off the line, they were as five old tramps, collars up, fingerless gloves extended to the heat. Shire considered the only escape for the firelight was up, so tight were they huddled to each other.

They'd been on the south side of Columbia for two nights after their sudden and panicky departure from Pulaski. The lunette and the dam the regiment had helped to build were abandoned unused. The rumor coming down the column was they were in a race with Hood to reach Columbia and that he was trying to put himself between them and Nashville. That perilous prospect hurried them along, but in the event most of the army was safely together when they got here. The Rebels had arrived today and cuddled up a couple of miles south of the town, where the 125th was part of the line. The regiment was put on picket and Company B had just finished its four-hour stint which had straddled the winter sunset.

'You figure this is where the fight will be?' Corry asked no one in particular.

'Maybe,' said Mason. 'It's a strong position. Especially if we fall back over the Duck River.'

'Thing is,' said Tuck, 'Hood didn't come all this way to camp out under the winter stars. If he can't get ahead of us, he'll have to throw the dice somewhere. Is someone going to put the pot on?'

No one answered, reluctant to give up their place at the fire. They were still sitting there, enjoying the growing flames, when Ocks arrived.

'On your feet, Private Shire.'

Shire did as he was told. 'I'm only this moment off them, Sergeant.'

'It can't be helped. Captain Bates' horse has the glanders.

He's buying a new one from some major he knows in the 73rd Illinois. You're to get over there and collect it.'

'It's freezing, Sergeant. Can't it wait 'til morning?'

'You can shoot his old horse, if you'd rather? You'll be moving at least, and you can ride it back.'

Tuck stood up. 'I'll come along.'

'There you are,' said Ocks. 'Company as well. You'll be back to your fire before you know it.'

'In fact,' Tuck said. 'We should all go.'

'What?' said Cleves, his scarred face outraged in the firelight.

Shire caught the wide-eyed look Tuck shot Cleves, the tiny slant of his head. 'It's a dark night. The Rebs are close. You wouldn't want Shire out there alone.'

Cleves' expression failed to echo the sentiment.

To Shire's surprise, Ocks agreed they *could* all go. 'I dare say our Kentucky friend has something transactional in mind. I don't need to know. The 73rd is next in line to our east. Just come straight back.' He gave Shire a slip of paper with the major's name and left.

Tuck boiled some water and made thin coffee, fending off objections from the squad. 'Hear me out. There's a sutler that follows the 74th who's always well-provisioned and I got some items from Nashville he'd trade a loyal dog for.'

'Ocks said the 73rd,' said Cleves.

'I know it. Word is the 74th is the other side of them. I plan on making a killin' and need you fellas along as mules.'

'Why not use the horse?' asked Shire.

'Cos Bates' saddle don't have the glanders so I'd figure you'll be riding bareback. Drink up, boys, and get your packs. Stack that fire, Corry.'

'Don't I get a say?' asked Mason. 'You know, given I own

the only stripe an' all?'

'Corporal,' said Tuck, 'I bow to you on matters military, but this here's a commercial enterprise. I'd be obliged if you'd let me take the lead for the good of all concerned.'

Mason sighed and stretched his big bulk up from the fire. 'Let's get it over with,' he said. They collected their rifles, leaving a gap in the pyramid forest.

*

Standing outside his tent in the dark, roused from not more than ten minutes of sleep, Colonel Opdycke took a slow breath and found barely enough patience to acknowledge the order handed him by Wagner's staff officer. They were to move out at once. The officer saluted and turned to remount his horse.

Opdycke cursed Wagner under his breath then asked directly, 'Will it stick this time?'

'Sir?'

'The order. I got the brigade baggage sent away for the same order yesterday only to have it countermanded while we waited in the rain.' In the end, a citizen of Columbia had taken pity on Opdycke and offered him a bed for the night. If he ever *did* settle in these parts, he'd have no shortage of people to call on.

'I have no reason to believe the orders will change, sir.'

No. Why would he? The chances were that Wagner didn't know either. You could only hope that someone in the Army of the Ohio knew what the plan was. He let the man depart with half-hearted compliments to the general.

The brigade baggage had returned earlier in the night and he'd ordered it left packed. Wagner was solid enough. An ardent republican and one of the more experienced division commanders. He shouldn't think ill of him. It wasn't Wagner's fault that Opdycke hadn't got his promotion yet. Everyone was tired after the hurried march from Pulaski. He knew he was and Wagner probably was too. He summoned his own staff and gave orders to pull the regiments back. The 125th was out on picket so he sent his fastest rider to them. *Douse the fires, strike the tents.* The brigade had been allocated a crossing point below the town. He stepped back inside and rinsed his face.

Later, astride Ben on the south bank of the Duck River, he watched his units file in from the west and cross a fine stone bridge. Shame it would have to be destroyed once everyone was over. Such was war. It was an effort to sit up straight but it wouldn't do to let the brigade see him slouch. He wished they'd all get by so he could stop returning salutes. There was no panic. The Rebels weren't attacking and were probably as yet unaware that the Union was leaving. Largely static on the road from the south-east was a queue of civilian traffic, fearful faces looking to flee north and waiting their time to cross. They were being fed in piecemeal by a second lieutenant but Opdycke considered they'd be better kept together. That way they could support each other if a wagon broke down and not trouble the army. Best to hold them to the end. He waited for a gap between companies then eased Ben over the road to give the instruction. A man in the third wagon back hailed him. 'Colonel Opdycke!'

It was Mr Gordon from Pulaski. Opdycke smiled and moved alongside. Gordon's family, most as round as he was, were packed among and on top of the possessions he'd been able to bring. 'Why Mr Gordon, what of your home and our future investment?'

Gordon smiled despite his predicament. 'It wasn't looking

too friendly after you left, Colonel. I'd have been burned out if I'd stayed. This way my house might be standing when I go back. The better part of valor is discretion, an' all that.'

'I can't criticize, sir, not when we're making a tactical retreat ourselves. Is there anything I can do for you and your family?'

'We're anxious to get on the road to Nashville. My wife's people are in Sumner County. We plan to wait things out there.'

Opdycke considered it might be a long wait before a welcome back. You had to admire the man's confidence. He called over the lieutenant. 'After the next regiment has passed, let this whole line of civilians through.' Then to Gordon, 'I know it's hard, but keep moving as long as the horses hold out. You'll get moved off the road if you hold up the army. Hood will be after us once he knows we're gone.' He tilted his hat to Mrs Gordon and crossed the bridge to ensure its destruction was in hand.

*

Shire and the squad followed Tuck through the dark toward the glowing island of campfires that located the 73rd Illinois. Tuck insisted they could collect Captain Bates' new horse on the return trip, so they hadn't stopped except to ask the way to the 74th. That had been a deal further east through woods and over ditches. Mason was on the verge of forcibly resuming command when they at last reached the latter regiment and swiftly found the promised sutler wagon. To Shire's amazement, Tuck produced all manner of contraband from his pack. Small wonder he'd been cleaned out of his pay. Evidently, he'd been busy in Nashville, though Shire was hard pushed to recall when they'd been away from each other long enough. Tuck's stash included a bushel of steel pens, a half-dozen bottles of ink, two stoppered square tins of quinine and a small glass jar of blue mercury pills.

In response to Shire's dumb outrage, Tuck said. 'You'll recall, I was in distress and weak of mind. Besides, we was in an' out of hospitals and the biggest quartermaster store in Tennessee. That's prime temptation to a soul like me. None of it's stolen, as such. I just found the people with the keys and traded up. You remember Sister Agatha at the Female Academy Hospital? That lady could bargain the buck-teeth from the Devil hisself.'

The sutler said he needed to shut-up shop as the rumor was they'd be pulling out. Some rapid bartering eschewed and judging by Tuck's pained look, for once he came off second best. Nonetheless, a wide ham, two small paper sacks of potatoes and an assortment of liquor bottles had found new homes in the squad's backpacks when they started back. The extra weight added to a heavy rifle made jumping the ditches more hazardous. Things got worse when the campfires of the 73rd Illinois, where Shire was yet to collect Bates' horse, began to blink out in the near distance. The same was happening behind them in the 74th and soon there was nothing to light their way other than the stars, the moon having not yet risen. The 73rd was nowhere to be heard, let alone found. They struggled on semi-blind as best they could, but when they reached what they approximated to be where they had left the 125th, there was no sign of their own regiment. They cast around and found what had been their fire, kicked out but surrounded by their ponchos and blankets.

'What should we do?' Tuck asked Mason.

'Oh, I'm back making the decisions, am I? Bully for me.

Well, just about now, I'd say we're smack midway between the lines. I suggest we hightail it toward the north star before Johnny Reb comes to visit.'

Shire fell in beside Tuck, less concerned now about the cold than the dark. When he glanced behind, there was a glow on the southern horizon. Rebel fires no doubt. Rifle shots became frequent enough to quicken their step. Perhaps the Rebel pickets had discovered the army was pulling out. Ahead, the lights in Columbia didn't appear to be getting any closer. Mason led them on, his solid bulk outlined against the stars low on the horizon. He had them fix bayonets and detailed Shire and Tuck to act as the rearguard. Tuck asked if a five-man army really had a rear worth the guarding. Clouds began to eat up the stars and it became darker than the ink that Tuck had so recently exchanged. Corry looked behind so often that Shire told him sharply to face front and get a move on. They stumbled across a decent lane that appeared to head more directly toward Columbia and began to follow it. Approaching a corner, they heard voices. Easing themselves around the bend, they saw a nose-high fire and a group of civilians, fifteen or more, feeding the flames. They had a limp flag planted by the roadside, Confederate stars only partially hidden in the folds.

Someone else might have backed away, Shire thought, but Mason didn't let the squad break stride. 'Ease those bayonets lower, boys,' he said quietly and they marched steadily along the side of the road opposite the fire and flag. The crowd wasn't armed that Shire could see. Older men, some welcome party out to signal and greet the Confederates when they found the Union was gone and came forward. Five against fifteen weren't good odds. These men weren't soldiers though and the bayonets proved enough of a deterrent.

'You git yerselves out of Tennessee,' was all one of them managed to say, once Shire and Tuck had passed.

Cleves spun on his heels, walked backward and called, 'You jist wait a while. We'll be back for that rag.'

They hurried on toward town where Shire could see men and horses moving by scattered torchlight. A company defending the road allowed them to pass and soon they were within a mass of men all waiting their turn to use a pontoon bridge across the Duck River. It was a withdrawal, not a rout. Orderly enough. The 125th was nowhere to be seen, nor any units from their brigade. Unattached as they were, and with no officer of their own, it was hard to get a place in line for the bridge. They were held up a full hour or more before Tuck, at Mason's order, sacrificed one of his liquor bottles for the privilege of the squad getting into the line, only to be colorfully denigrated by the New Yorkers they'd cut in front of.

The clouds passed over and the moon was up at last. Shire never liked pontoon bridges. This one was no more than a hundred paces wide and anything but stable. Tuck was beside him. The torches were so few and the men so crowded, he could barely see to step ahead. If he wasn't careful, he'd pitch in. He felt the extra weight of his pack and imagined drowning on account of Tuck's potatoes. The river was up, high water streaming between the pontoon boats. The plank road rolled and swayed. He carried his rifle in front of him like a ropewalker. Tuck swore and told him to be careful with the bayonet. Some men concentrated in silence, others cursed and shouted. There was a skittish horse three ranks ahead of them that was having a worse time than Shire, sawing this way and that. The rider tried to soothe it. When that didn't work, he unwisely took to the whip. The horse backed up so suddenly it shoved two soldiers into the winter water. One grabbed the end of a pontoon boat and was heaved back aboard the bridge. The other was swept away, screaming when he could. Shire had given him up for drowned but then glimpsed a small boat tethered downstream, positioned to catch such hapless men, a single torch held high. They frantically worked to reach the man. Shire couldn't make out if he was saved. In any case he needed to pay attention that the same horse didn't back into him.

Once across, Mason led them away from the crowds around the pontoon. They asked an officer where Opdycke's Brigade might be. 'They crossed downstream, I think. Work your way north and a little east. Get onto a road toward Spring Hill if you can.'

Shire's stomach clenched at the mention of Spring Hill.

They pressed on in the dark up the high bluffs to the north of town. He felt better with a river between them and Hood's army but was anxious to get back to the safety of the regiment. They all were. The road was busy, full of brisk officers and angry sergeants. They were frequently stopped and held in place. None of them knew the hour. Out of frustration, Mason led them off the road altogether and into the woods and fields. A hard white frost emerged in the grass and on the branches. They found an abandoned barn partially collapsed at one end, but it was shelter at least. None of them had eaten since before going on picket. Tuck cut them each a thick slice of ham while Cleves made a fire. Shire closed his eyes and fell asleep as if he'd been given a direct order.

Franklin, Tennessee – November, 1864

Moscow and his father had spent the best part of the morning leaning on their front fence and watching the traffic on the Columbia Pike. Their easy repose was at odds with Moscow's racing mind. The flow both ways had been busy for several days but had reached a new high today. The speed of the constituent parts varied greatly, largely determined by whether you wore a Union uniform and the color of your skin. Lone dispatch riders or small squads of cavalry owned the right of way and generally moved south at a trot. Moscow would see them extend to a canter once they got clear and there was more room off the road.

Three of his sisters, Sarah, Annie and Frances, had carried a table around from one of the empty slave huts and set it with wooden beakers. Lena and Alice were in a constant relay to the well in the backyard to bring out pitchers of water. And Moscow had been to the root cellar and brought up a sack of apples which was almost empty.

Arriving from the south was a steady flow of heavily laden buggies and wagons, mostly white folk, moving at the quickest walk their tired mules or horses could manage. The road began to slope gently downhill past the Carter house and helped them along toward town. It was mostly older people with daughters and children, but there were young men aboard occasionally, avoiding eye contact, no doubt unenthusiastic at the prospect of being conscripted into Hood's army. Moscow had no issue with that. The drivers encouraged their teams on, eager to get through town. Slowest of all were the blacks, mostly on foot and exhausted. One approaching family had a low handcart with two infants soundly asleep among the sacks. Moscow waved them closer for some water. 'How far have you hauled your children?'

The man drank greedily. 'From Mount Pleasant, sir.'

Mount Pleasant was below Columbia. Forty miles at least. 'Your people let you go?'

'They's up the road somewhere, a day ahead. They was scared there'd be a fight, so we was left. We couldn't stay. Not with nobody to speak for us.'

No matter how scared they were, people shouldn't leave their people behind. That wasn't right. Moscow wondered how everyone was going to cross the Harpeth with the bridge washed away two weeks ago. That bridge itself had only been a shadow of the one burned down earlier in the war and wrecked several times by raiders since. The Harpeth wasn't the biggest of rivers and there was a flat-boat ferry running – the boat practically a third as wide as the crossing itself – but that could only take so many. The rail bridge was intact but in frequent use, the trains busier than ever up to Nashville and back. He was tempted to wander down and take a look but had heavier concerns in the other direction.

The wife woke her children so they could drink. Fountain passed her four apples and she hid them away beneath the blankets like they were silver. Moscow didn't need to ask these folks for more information. Any number of conversations this morning had told him Hood was advancing on Columbia. Tod would be somewhere with him. Earlier, the water had tempted in a dispatch rider moving north. Schofield had pulled back as far as the Duck River, he said. Cavalry scouts from both sides roamed across the country between here and there. The country to the south wasn't safe anymore.

'Father,' said Moscow. 'If I was going to warn Clara, I don't think I should leave it longer.'

'What are you waiting on then?'

'I'd be gone for the afternoon.'

'I can watch this road just as well with my daughters.'

'Are you thinking we should get the children up to Nashville?'

'You're the soldier. Where do you think the storm'll break?'

'Well, if I was for the Union, I'd want to fight at Nashville. The place is nothing but forts and guns. If I was Hood, I'd want to corner the Union Army way before there, or at least catch a part of it I could chew up. That could be most anywhere north or south on this road.'

'Maybe they'll settle it at Columbia.'

'Maybe.'

'We'd have a lot of children to move. And these refugees are slow. We might have a couple of nights in the open before we get to Nashville.'

'We're staying then?'

'My children are all grown up. One of them probably in the army headin' this way. I could stay and look after the farm and our people. You could get the children away.'

Moscow imagined starting down this road with his father left at the gate. Even if he could wear it, his sisters wouldn't. 'We'll all stay,' Moscow said, taking shelter in the decision, 'but it'll be too late to warn Clara if Hood gets past Columbia.' He left Father and went to saddle his horse.

Avoiding the pike, he instead edged out to the west across the Carter land, past the fancy Bostick house, and aimed straight up over Winstead Hill. At the summit he rested his horse and took in the view back over the cleared land to home, the noon light strong under patchy white clouds. The Columbia Pike was no less busy than it had been. Beyond it a train raced south. He counted twelve cars rising up out of the cutting, eight more than was usual. Men for Schofield's Army of the Ohio. Over to the west the Carter's Creek Pike was loaded too. He'd never seen the like. South Tennessee was emptying ahead of the storm.

He knew the best paths down the steep southern slopes of Winstead. He and his brothers used to hunt up here. Today, he might be the prey if he happened on a scout or a cavalry squad. He passed warily onto the farms and hills beyond, set a manageable pace for the hour and a half to Clara's land, coming into her yard across her fields rather than down the drive. He walked his horse around to the front as was proper when calling on a lady. He'd caught himself talking differently with her since he found out she was nobility back in the old country; shorter sentences, speaking when spoken to. He was annoyed with himself. What difference did it make? It was hard to get past it, all the same. He brushed himself down and stepped up to the door, thinking he wasn't here as a serf or a suitor, just a good neighbor in a time of crisis.

*

Clara opened the door and wasn't entirely surprised to see Moscow. Other than Shire and Tuck's random visit, there was rarely anyone else who called. And she'd seen the traffic on the road. Moscow looked a little awkward and she realized she was still wearing her frown from the argument in the kitchen. She softened. 'Moscow. Please come in.'

'Are you alright, Mrs Ridgmont? You look upset.'

'I'm fine. And please, we don't need to revert to Mrs Ridgmont simply because I let slip concerning my forebears. Clara will do fine.'

'My apologies.'

'You'd better join our debate in the kitchen. I imagine you're here on similar business.'

On the way down the hall he worked his way in front so he could open the kitchen door for her.

'Good,' said Mitilde, who had her back to the sink. Her hands went to her hips. 'Someone as'll talk some sense into you.'

Moses was where Clara had left him, sat at the table. He made to stand.

'Stay seated, Moses,' she said, exasperated. 'I've only been gone a minute.'

'I was standin' on account of there bein' a guest in the house.'

Clara drew a slow breath. 'Moscow, please sit too. I'll get you some coffee.' She wasn't sure that Moscow's presence was going to make this any easier.

He put his hat on the back of the chair and sat down. 'Where's the little girl?'

Clara brought coffee from the stove and poured. 'Cele's playing upstairs.'

'Thank you,' he said. 'Well, I promised I'd come and warn you if I thought the war might head this way. It appears it will. Most probably in just a few days.'

'Well, is that right?'

'Mitilde!' admonished Clara.

'I's sorry Mister Moscow, but it's the same road passes our drive as passes your place. We can see the folk runnin' north by lookin' out the front window.'

'It's what to do about it we can't fix on,' said Moses.

'Alright then,' said Moscow. He started again. 'We've asked ourselves the same question. Do we stay and hope the armies don't come or that they pass through, or do we run and hope to find everything is still standing when we come back? We're fixin' to stay, but I don't think that means you should.'

'I left my last home when I should have stayed,' Clara said. She felt surprisingly certain of her ground. 'It was nothing but ashes when I came back. I'm not leaving again.'

Mitilde came and sat down with them so they were all four at the table. 'You might've been ashes too if you'd stayed at Comrie. Tell her, Mister Moscow. It ain't safe to stay.'

'It's not so clear cut. I understand it was rabble that burned your last home. Much of Hood's army is from Tennessee. Soldiers from Williamson County, like Tod. They ain't about to set to burning and looting. The question is more where any fight might be.'

'And what about my livestock?'

'Livestock?' said Moses. 'We ain't but got the horses and a few chickens.'

'An army always has need of horses,' Moscow said. 'Likely they'll pay in Confederate dollars. New chickens ain't so hard to come by. And as to your people –'

'You roping us in with the livestock?' asked Mitilde.

'As to your people,' repeated Moscow, evenly, 'make clear they belong to you.'

'We're done with that,' Mitilde said angrily, 'I ain't ever gonna say I'm someone's property.'

'You wouldn't need to,' said Moscow. 'Being with Clara would be enough.'

Moses slid his hand to Mitilde's across the table. 'Would it be so bad,' he said, 'just this one time, if it meant we could all stay?'

Clara sat quietly, knowing she could end this by agreeing to go.

'Husband,' said Mitilde quietly. 'You wouldn't be at peace with it any more than I would. Someone thinkin' it, well, that's as bad as it being spoken. And what about Cele? What will we do for her if the fightin' breaks out?'

Moscow nodded. 'Sounds like you're decided.' He drained his coffee and stood. 'You'll stay together and make for Nashville. Best to get on the road today and plan for some nights spent in the cold.'

'Moscow,' said Clara.

'Ma'am?'

'I'll be staying. Can you tell Moses where best to go in Nashville?'

'Staying alone? Now that's another matter. I –'

'My mind is made up. Moses and Mitilde should go. And I spent good money on the wagon and team. I can't afford to lose them so it's best they use them to get away. I wouldn't insult my friends by asking them to pretend to be slaves. Above all, there's the child.'

'Come to Franklin. We can make room.'

'I've made up my mind.'

'I'd stay with you myself, Clara, but –'

'I know. You have your children. Perhaps the war will go elsewhere.'

Moscow looked pained. 'Truth is, I don't know where they might go in Nashville. They are thousands in the same scrape. Best I can think is to follow the pike right into the city and take help from the Union Army. I hear they're feeding people at least.'

Mitilde began to cry.

After Moscow left, Clara led the packing. It took them most of the afternoon. Moscow had told Moses to call at the Carter house. There was room out of the cold for one night. He'd promised to keep the fire burning in the cellar.

Old George would have to stay with her at Eversholt, as would the horse Shire had gifted her. That way she could ride away at need. It was easier when they were busy; making sure they had enough feed for the team, folding the thickest blankets, making a game out of Cele picking her favorite dress. Finally, Clara was walking down the drive beside the wagon. Mitilde's hand reached out and down from the seat so that Clara had to reach up to hold it. Her heart began to burst. Cele sat in the middle and complained she was cold. When they reached the pike, it was quiet for once. Moses halted the team. Clara had already given him money but pressed more dollars on Mitilde. 'You might need it. For lodging. If it gets too cold in the wagon.'

She'd told them to go as far as Cincinnati if they couldn't find somewhere nearer or if the weeks dragged on. Raht's home was there. He'd look after them. They'd have to sell the team and take the train. It was too far to drive.

'How will we tell when to come back?' Mitilde asked, suddenly angry again.

'I don't know,' Clara said gently. 'Write to me when things settle. Let me know where you are. It might all be over in a few days.'

Moses leaned forward and looked down at her. 'Miss Clara. It ain't too late. We can make Cele snug in the back and have you sat up here like old times. Please, Miss Clara.'

Clara looked up the road and then down at her Eversholt

sign. 'I can't, Moses. Somewhere has to be home. I'll be fine. You should get going. It'll be dark when you get to Franklin.'

Moses shook the reins and the two-horse team turned to the north. Cele stood on Mitilde's lap and waved around the side of the wagon. Clara waved back. How many more goodbyes was she going to say from this spot? But then, she thought, there was no one left to say goodbye to.

Maury County, Tennessee – November 28th, 1864

Shire was visited by a dream, the shape of which had become familiar in recent weeks. He watched his hand reach out, floating above a carpet of autumn leaves to his front-garden gate at home in England. He pressed the latch and heard it squeak and lift, the same exact note as in former dreams. And in that smallest sound lived everything he understood home to be: his father tapping out his pipe; the snap of the kitchen fire; the smooth run of the stair banister; the waking cool of a spring morning; the church bell. The gate was hung so well it needed only the lightest touch to swing open. The memory of its weight was perfect. It was always the same. He'd step into the narrow cottage garden but would never arrive at the door. He woke and had to wipe the tears from his eyes.

Through gaps in the torn end of the barn he could tell from the shade of the sky that it was well past dawn. All was quiet for a few precious minutes. Then Mason stirred and tended the fire which woke Cleves and Corry, who both sat up. Tuck's head was covered by his blanket, his legs below the knees suffering the deficit.

'It's late,' said Mason. 'We should be on our way. The army won't have stopped for the night.'

'There wasn't much night left to us,' said Cleves.

Corry plainly said what Shire was thinking, though it came out as if he were a child. 'I'm hungry.'

'We'll go quicker if we're well fed,' Shire argued.

Mason didn't need to be persuaded but asked that they

hurry. They got a small pan going and sliced some potatoes as thin as they could to boil all the quicker. Shire carved a heap of ham and, when the potatoes were done, they used the potato water to make some coffee. Poor dregs as they were, the aroma was enough to rouse Tuck who joined them for the feast, tipping a shot of whiskey into each coffee mug as was the squad tradition when they were in supply.

'Feels kinda like Christmas, don't it?' said Corry.

'You think?' replied Mason. 'You know, come Christmas, it'll be two years since the regiment mustered in. Not one of us has chosen to go home in that time.' Everyone took that on board, including Mason himself, who wistfully asked, 'Why do you suppose that is?'

'It ain't like it's been on the plate,' said Cleves. 'No one's offered me a furlough since last winter. 'Sides, if I had gone, I'd only have to bear up to returning to you people. I don't think I could enjoy my home time with that hanging over me.'

'Likely your mother would take a furlough herself if she got wind of you comin',' said Mason.

'Well, ain't that pleasant? I don't see you beating a path north except by the current necessity. You waiting on an invite?'

Mason lifted the heaped plate of ham to Cleves, which might have been an apology.

'Too far for me,' said Shire. 'Nothing there anyway.'

'There's your house,' said Tuck. 'Your father's house as was.'

It was as if the squad had shared Shire's dream. It clutched at his heart again. 'It'll be full of cobwebs and damp by now. Sound though. For someone else.'

Corry asked, 'Don't you ever plan to go back?'

It was the kind of straight-on question he was used to

from Corry. 'I try not to think beyond the war,' Shire said. 'I'm scared if I do, death will sneak up behind me. The last thing I'll hear is him laughing.'

'But it's there though, ain't it?' said Tuck. He looked at Shire directly, sharing a hurt the others might not see. 'The weight of it, I mean. Whether you choose to go or not, home is still there.'

'Perhaps,' said Shire. 'But the place isn't the whole sum. There's no family. My friends wouldn't know me. I might not know myself.'

'It's all in the future,' said Mason. He stood to look out around the half open barn door. 'Homes are built, not happened across. You need to find a wife to share a warm kitchen. You need to *make* a home.'

Tuck stood up, got busy with his pack then went outside.

'It's too long empty.' Shire said, back in England. His laced coffee had gone cold. He'd chased other dreams. He was still chasing other dreams.

'What about you, Mason?' said Corry.

Shire wondered if Mason had wanted his own question to be thrown back at him.

'I guess I'll go,' Mason said, 'but I doubt I'd stay. I'm not sure I've ever truly felt at home. Not in the way you all talk. Maybe as a small child. My grandmother's share in me, my Iroquois part, it was like Ohio was my home but at the same time it wasn't. That Indian had a thousand-year right to be there, but a seven-eighths welcome isn't a full one. To be home means being wholly at ease, not partly on edge.' He swilled his coffee. 'This is a particular kind of country we're fighting for, and not one where you're obliged to stay still. Everything is tending to the west. I think I'll head that way, if I'm spared.' He laughed. 'Perhaps I'll look back and think of this as home. A campfire, some coffee and five smelly soldiers.' He collected the pan and took it outside to clean in the damp grass. Corry went with him and Shire was left alone with Cleves, who was eking out his last piece of ham.

'How about you?' asked Shire.

Cleves stared at the ground. 'I got no want to go home,' he said. 'I was someone else there, before the war.' He chewed a while. 'It wasn't someone I liked and neither did no one else. They would think me the same man I was.'

'You could prove them wrong,' said Shire.

'Would be too easy to prove them right. Or I'm afeared it would. Maybe I'll stay. In the army, I mean. The country's gotta have an army. I'm a better soldier than I was, don't you think?' He looked up at Shire but didn't wait on an answer. 'After the war, the uniforms will be smarter, not stained with blood and dirt. I'll march into a town and some girl will look at the uniform and not at me.'

Shire stared back and took in the eyes rather than the scars, realized he couldn't see Cleves as wretched anymore and was no longer inclined to try. 'Do you want to wear a uniform your whole life?'

'I'm a better man inside it.'

'Then the better man must have been there all along.'

*

Well-fed for once, Shire stepped outside. The frost from the night was gone. A pall of white clouds flattened the light and it was warmer than it had been. It was even later than he'd thought. 'How long did we sleep?' he asked.

'Don't rightly know,' said Tuck, 'but if Ocks were here, he'd have our guts out.'

They argued which way was north and that maybe, if they could work their way west, they might hit a road that ran north. Without the sun showing, it was hard to tell which way was friendly. It wasn't at all clear to them how much of the army had pulled out of Columbia and how much was staying put. Shire guessed that the rumble of cannon that found its way to them through the trees and hills probably *was* Columbia, but there was a breeze up and the guns came and went. A loose consensus emerged and they headed out. It was a solid hour before they found so much as a path, which eventually spat them out onto what might have passed for a road. They followed it for a short while without encountering anybody. If anything, the guns were getting louder.

Suddenly, a rider rounded the next bend and cantered toward them. They unslung their rifles before spotting he was in blue. Mason waved his hands but the rider only slowed to a trot. 'Hey!' Mason shouted. 'Which way is north? Which way is the road to Nashville?'

'*I'm* headed north.'

Cleves hit at Corry's arm with the back of his hand. 'I done told you this was the wrong way.'

'If you head my way,' said the rider, 'in a mile or more there's a crossroads. Turn left there and you'll hit the Columbia Pike in another hour.' He moved to a canter again but called back. 'Take care though. I've not long since seen Rebel scouts.'

They turned about and quickened their pace, listening for other riders on the road, but seeing no one until the promised crossroads, which was guarded by twenty soldiers from a Kentucky regiment. Mason told their lieutenant they were lost Ohio boys trying to find their own command. He said he was happy to adopt them, as he didn't have enough men to hold this place as it was. There was nothing to be said and they were pushed out fifty paces along one lane in support of a squad much the size they were. After some back and forth, Tuck determined the Kentuckians were from Flemingsburg, not so far from his part of the state. Since they were all hungry again, he broke out the rest of the potatoes and ham and quizzed his new friends for news from home, or at least close to home. Shire and the others chafed at being stuck and no nearer to knowing where the 125th was. Mason went back to the crossroads to harangue the lieutenant but was turned around in short order. He reported back that they would pull out only when their host company received orders to do so.

Corry stood with a hand on a fencepost while Cleves knelt and sewed a new button onto his pants. Corry hadn't troubled to remove them. He angrily waved an arm back down the road. 'We ain't seen a soul since we was put here. We're defending a crossroads no one knows or cares about.'

Cleves paused in his work. 'You might pick up a flesh wound all the same, if you don't keep still.'

Corry looked morose. 'We ain't never gonna catch up to the regiment.'

The light began to go and it became apparent they would spend the night. With the ham and potatoes gone, there was only hardtack. The lieutenant wandered up to say, 'No fires,' then wandered away again. The conversation ran dry. Tuck's hospitality to his Kentucky neighbors plainly didn't extend to his whiskey. Each side of the road was bordered by a shallow ditch so, when Shire came off lookout, he made his earth bed ten paces into the trees. The clouds broke and the stars wheeled again between the bare boughs. He wrapped himself tight in his blanket and greatcoat and surrendered to the cold.

Columbia, Tennessee – November 28th, 1864

Tod took the slip of paper back and stared at it again. He was sat next to Frank on the tailboard of a stationary wagon. It was mid-afternoon in the supply park of Benton Smith's Brigade. Outside Columbia, this unit was as static as the rest of Hood's army.

'I can't figure you,' said Frank. 'It seems like a gift from heaven to me.'

A wagon-park was a good place to rest up and popular with staff officers, especially so if, as Tod, you were an ex-quartermaster and on friendly terms with your successor. They'd just finished a mug each of hominy stewed in what Tod guessed was pork broth. The unhitched wagons weren't going anywhere, parked up in rows while Hood decided what to do next after discovering that the Union had backed over the Duck River, their cannon occasionally dueling with him from the north bank.

Tod rested back on a box of horseshoes, the heavy load compensated by forage forward in the wagon. 'It'd be crazy to leave now. You'd think Benton Smith would want me on hand when we're so tight to the Yankees.'

'You can reason it that way, or you could roll your blanket tight and head for home.'

The scrap of paper under discussion was dated November 28th and read:

Tod hadn't requested it, though Smith knew well that Tod hadn't been home since he signed up at the start of the war. But then that was true of most of the local men, given the counties hereabouts had been occupied the majority of that time. His General had handed him the note when the brigade commanders' meeting broke up an hour ago.

Frank had found him and was playing Devil's advocate, or at least Benton Smith's advocate. 'What did Smith say?'

'That he didn't expect Hood to attack Columbia, but he might try to flank the Yankees to the east. Forrest is already over the river trying to set up a screen. He said if I was to come back with some intelligence on what the Union was doing that was all to the good, but not to take undue risks.'

Across the mud-furrowed track behind their wagon, a scarecrow squad stacked shell cases, struggling on the slippery ground to carry them by their rope handles. Tod resisted the urge to go and help.

'How far is it?' asked Frank.

'Straight, it's thirty miles, but the whole Union Army's in the way.'

Frank shuffled backwards in the covered wagon so he could lay on the forage. He spoke from back under the canvas. 'If the Yankees are planted in Columbia, you can get around and clear of them. If anyone can find a way, it's you. I can't figure what's stopping you? Hell, I've a mind to ask Gist if I can tag along.'

'I don't think your father would approve me leading you on an adventure behind enemy lines.' He folded the note only to open it again. 'I kinda hoped I was being useful here. Why do *I* deserve a home visit?'

'Is that what's bugging you? I heard the Maury County companies in the 1st Tennessee have been allowed two day's furlough. It's not judicious to do otherwise. Too much temptation when they've been away so long. Wives to kiss, children to measure. The same will happen when we get up into Williamson. You're just getting a head start, is all. It stands to reason General Smith wants a local man to scout at the same time. You know the ground.'

Just a few days ago he'd been annoyed at Frank for pricking his conscience, but here he was listening to him talking sense, though Tod was lacking in both wife and children. 'When did you get to be so wise?'

'I've seen Father reason his way out of any number of rabbit holes and leave people turned inside out. I can figure it from the other side of the fence if you want me to, but I don't think that's the side your heart will fall.'

'I told you. I'm not going. What if I missed the big dance, the battle to capture back Tennessee, and I was at home eating pear pie?' He thought back to ruined Waynesboro, to the women picking over the mule carcass. If ever there was a fight that was his, it would be the next one.

'Smith wouldn't send you if he thought things were about to kick off,' said Frank. 'He told you as much.'

'He don't know Hood's mind, and he sure as hell don't know Schofield's.' Tod picked up his mug in two hands and cuddled its dwindling warmth. It wasn't the way he'd imagined returning home. He'd thought the war would end in some far corner of America. Atlanta or Mobile. Or Lincoln would lose the election and peace would break out all over. Then he'd ride home any way he chose, up to the garden gate. The children would stream out. His sisters would embrace him and Moscow and Father would be there on the step. They'd all eat together and he'd tell his tales and sleep long and peacefully in his own bed. Win or lose, he'd have done his duty. Instead, armed with this piece of paper, he was expected to steal away and keep to the trees, travel through the country of his childhood by night and come to his house in the darkness like some criminal, some traitor to the Union. That felt nearer the truth of his disquiet; he wanted to go home, just not like this.

'Look at it this way,' said Frank, coming back to sit next to Tod. 'The fight might be here and you might do your bit, but say we lose or do no better than a draw and have to back up out of the state and lick our wounds. What chance will you have to go home then?' He lightly punched Tod's arm. 'None. And it might be another long year before one comes around again.' Then more somberly, 'If you're unlucky, it might *never* come around again.'

Tod was suddenly fearful of that. Maybe Columbia would be the high watermark of Hood's campaign and this was as close as they'd get to Franklin. 'That's a fair point, young Frank.' He could be back in three days, maybe with some intelligence his army could use.

'I only answer to Lieutenant Trenholm.' Frank lay back again. 'I'll hold the fort here, or at least I would if we had one. Go see your folks.'

As Frank had predicted, in the end Tod's heart staked its claim to the decision and all his earlier arguments were ridden down. He blew out a deep breath, slipped off the tailgate and wondered what he could forage from these supply wagons to take with him.

Williamson County, Tennessee – November 29th, 1864

Opdycke was anxious to move faster. It was late morning on a glorious fall day. He rode at the head of the long infantry column, nothing but a few outriders to the front and a thin screen of skirmishers working their way through the woods and fields parallel to the road. Wagner, commander of the 2nd Division, rode to his left, hat in hand, receding hairline on show and his usually well-trimmed shovel beard a touch ragged. Beyond him was Captain Bates in charge of Opdycke's old regiment, the 125th Ohio.

Uneasy as Opdyke was, it was good to be with the Tigers. They always gave him an extra fillip of pride. He was grateful he'd been able to keep them in his brigade. One of his regiments, the 73rd Illinois, was detached and some miles on ahead with the bulk of the Army of the Ohio's wagon train. All his other regiments were behind him on the road, his total brigade strength almost a tenth larger thanks to Rice's productive visit to the Nashville hospitals. It was an honor to be at the front of the main column, but if Wagner had given him his head, they could have been in Spring Hill by now.

'Should I pick up the pace, General?' he asked, not for the first time. 'We should catch up to the wagon train.' His own brigade had been ready to march at seven, but Wagner had delayed the order to move to eight-thirty.

'They'll be fine, Opdycke,' Wagner said. 'The 73rd is with them and Spring Hill isn't far ahead. If we did catch them up, you'd have to go slower still. The men needed to rest this morning.' He addressed Bates. 'I wager you're well practiced at the double-quick in the 125th, Captain. Am I right?'

'Colonel Opdycke ran a slick regiment when he was in charge. I like to do the same, sir.'

Good answer, thought Opdycke. Why not be a little pointed? The intelligence was Hood was trying to flank them again and that's why the decision was made to pull back from Columbia. So it would be as well to get some miles behind them. And there were hundreds of wagons exposed ahead. The army's main supplies: its shells, its bullets, its food. Everything. And here they were ambling along as if they were out for a Sunday picnic. They passed a fine and tall red brick mansion set back on the right. Its white columns and high windows faced west to overlook them as they passed along the road and between the rolling winter fields.

'That's a small mount you have there, Captain,' said Wagner, perhaps peeved at Bates' comment.

'It was the best I could get at short notice, General. My old horse got the glanders back in Columbia. I had to shoot her. I purchased a new one but the squad I sent to collect him got left behind when we pulled out. Lieutenant Rice found me this pony. Not that I'm ungrateful,' he called behind to where Rice marched at the head of Company B.

'Glad to hear it, sir,' called Rice. 'All horses look plenty tall enough from down here.'

Opdycke asked Bates, 'Did you find the squad?'

'There was no time to wait on them, sir. We kicked out their fire and left their blankets. Rice, did your lost squad catch up yet?'

'No, sir, but they're a resourceful enough bunch, Privates Shire and Tuck among them.'

Opdycke smiled despite the news. 'Hah,' he said. 'Better look out, gentlemen. That Englishman only goes missing in the thick of things. He's no bad penny, but I expect he'll roll back sooner or later.'

A rider at full gallop came up behind, racing down the side of the column. He slewed to a halt and saluted Wagner. 'General,' he said, his horse blowing steam. 'General Stanley sends his compliments. We have reports of Rebel cavalry beyond Rally Hill and proceeding toward Spring Hill. They are to the north-east of you, sir. The general requests you move to Spring Hill with all speed.'

To emphasize the point, there was a distant spatter of rifle fire.

'Damn it all to hell.' Wagner turned to Opdycke. 'Alright, Emerson. Here's that hurry-up you wanted.'

Bates didn't wait on Opdycke but gave the order for the men to move to the double-quick. Wagner, animated at last, began sending orders to his brigades back down the column. After they crested a low ridge, Opdycke, angrier than ever, hurried out ahead with Bates. He could see the village of Spring Hill on the next gentle rise. From the east came the rising sound of guns. Bates put Company B into a run for the last half-mile, and they both kept pace beside them. As they came into the village, Wagner caught up to them. Soldiers and civilians ran this way and that. Acres of wagons were tightly parked onto the commons on the road out to the rail depot. A teamster near to the road was fighting to nosebag his lead mule but the beast wouldn't have it; there was too much movement and excitement.

Reports from the small detachment of cavalry who'd been guarding the wagon train said there were also Rebels directly to the north. Freshly alarmed and freshly blasphemous,

Wagner ordered Opdycke to deploy in that direction to protect the wagons. He then stole the 36th Illinois from Opdycke's Brigade and left to see how he could help the fight that they'd been told was developing east of town.

Opdycke quickly threw out two regiments of skirmishers and put his remaining regiments into a battle line straddling the pike. They pushed north. There was desultory fire ahead and they drove a small number of Rebels who soon disappeared. But if there were Rebels already north of them, how were they to move on toward Nashville? Wagner should have got them here sooner. Opdycke withdrew his line to the strongest position and ensured that the rail depot and the wagon-park were both protected.

The day wore on, gunfire getting louder from the east. Orders arrived telling him to hold his sector, but all was secure here and he wanted to see what Wagner was doing with the 36th Illinois. He rode Ben back through the hubbub of the village, past a family sat on their porch steps: two children, a babe, mother and grandmother, the children eating cornbread as if they were in the bleachers and the fair had come to town.

He found the 36th held in reserve. Wagner, now under orders from the recently arrived General Stanley, was collecting artillery as it came down the pike and placing it in line atop the small ridge that ran east to west across the village.

'They're pressing Bradley hard from the west,' shouted the breathless Wagner. 'Mostly dismounted cavalry, I think.'

'It was the same north of town,' said Opdycke, though he couldn't be certain.

A shell burst high and short of the village, day-stars falling to earth, no more trouble than a dime firework.

'We have to secure the road to Nashville, Emerson,' said Wagner. 'The whole army's lost if we don't.' He raced off to gather in the next battery newly arrived from the south.

Rice came and stood below Opdycke.

'Have you abandoned your post too, Lieutenant Rice?'

'Captain Bates sent me, sir. An engine pulled into the station without its cars, sir. From the north. They say they were attacked up near Thompson's Station. Captain Bates wonders if you have any orders, sir?'

'I'll be right there.'

'Yes, sir.'

'And Rice.'

'Sir?'

'Get word to me when Shire and his squad show up. This is a tight spot and he's the nearest thing I've got to a rabbit's foot.'

'It's Corporal Mason's squad, sir.'

'You mean to say we haven't given that Englishman a stripe yet?'

'No, sir.'

'Remind me of that in quieter times. I'd say he's earned one. The army might be slow with its promotions, but it doesn't mean I have to be.'

Through the sunny mid-afternoon, Opdycke sat on his horse and watched Wagner's growing line of cannon firing shells to the east. A breeze picked up. Units arrived piecemeal, a company or a regiment at a time, some trailing wagons. Another battery of guns came into view. It wouldn't be enough if Hood had his infantry up. Not nearly enough.

Williamson County, Tennessee – November 29th, 1864

Shire and the squad were finally on the Columbia Pike, somewhere between that city and Spring Hill. It was into the afternoon. As best he could tell, the army seemed to be abandoning Columbia, but was moving north at the pace of its slowest mule.

They stopped again. Tuck stood sullenly beside Shire, supporting himself with his rifle. 'We was quicker by ourselves yesterday.'

'Quicker to get lost,' said Cleves, sat on the pale stony road with the others. 'At least we know where this pike goes.'

'That's no better than havin' a three-legged horse to lead you home.'

There was the occasional distant crack and echo of rifle shots from both sides of the road and even some up ahead, though the cannonade behind them in Columbia seemed to have stopped. That might mean the Rebels had hold of the place. At least they'd escaped that fight. Shire had come to believe they were much closer to the tail of the long snake of the Union Army than its head. Clara was ever-present in his thoughts.

The Kentucky lieutenant had eventually cut them loose at the crossroads mid-morning. They'd hurried west to intersect this pike only to find it crowded and fiercely governed by staff officers and company sergeants. Once they'd pushed themselves into the column, they were subject to the same stops and starts as everyone else. They could at least ask those near them for news of the 125th, which was rumored to be at the front of affairs with the rest of the 2nd Division. It was impossible to catch up when they weren't allowed to move along beside the column. He'd tried it more than once, stepping off the road he'd harangued the squad to follow, but each time, sooner rather than later, they'd be ordered or dragged back onto the pike. So many officers and dispatch-riders raced alongside that it was perilous to march there anyway.

If truth be told, the rest of the squad was as anxious to catch up to the regiment as Shire was. Though they were safely back with the army, they wanted to be with the 125th and in Company B. After the latest barrel-chested sergeant shouted at them to stand and be ready to move, Mason said, if someone had to do that, he'd prefer to be bawled out by Sergeant Ocks. But none of Shire's friends had the extra fear for Clara. Whether she remained at Spring Hill, he couldn't know. What could he do if she was? It might be that both armies would march right on past her home and leave it untouched. He tried to surrender his worry to fate, but it proved impossible. Love wasn't set up to work that way.

They started forward once more. The day wasn't uniformly slow and they got up some pace for a while, the column a noisy leather and steel chorus, tromping feet on the hard road. A soldier in front wavered, stumbled and fell. His friends broke ranks to drag him up. Others looked asleep on their feet. Soon the men concertinaed again, slowed and stopped. Everyone was bone-tired. Some of them risked a sergeant's wrath by falling out to sit or lie down. Shire tried once more to make up ground along the column, leading the squad on a weave through the men or walking parallel through the trees. The rifle fire built steadily, became less distant. No massed volleys, but enough to know the Rebels were out there. Cavalry most likely.

On one frustratingly long stop, Cleves gave voice to something Shire had been thinking these last few days. 'If we ever get going again, we'll come to Franklin soon enough. Tomorrow maybe. What do you think of that? The town where the regiment first went in to fight. Where we spent a cold spring. Two years later, we're back in the same place.'

As if to himself, Tuck said, 'All those roads and battles down to Chattanooga and Atlanta and Hood has chased us back here. We'll have to march those roads all over again.'

Tuck was back in a low mood. Shire wondered if it had been yesterday's breakfast discourse on home, but then they were all of them tired.

Mason tipped his canteen and wiped his mouth. 'Last I heard we still hold Chattanooga and Atlanta. Hood ain't won anything that matters yet. He's just out for a long walk.'

Shire looked up and down the road. This army might be tired but it wasn't beat. No one liked being on the run, but when the time came to fight, they'd square up readily enough. He remembered the day they'd hurried into Franklin and chased out a few Rebel cavalry. It had felt like such a big thing. They'd had to wade through the freezing Harpeth. He'd been so cold and frightened that he'd fumbled when he loaded and barely got off a shot. He liked Franklin, despite all that had happened to him there. He dragged up a smile. 'Do you remember stealing the beehives?'

Cleves laughed. 'Mason and you had to go serve dinner to Opdycke at the Carters' house as punishment.'

'Best punishment I ever had,' said Mason. 'New uniform and two slices of apple and cream pie.'

Shire found himself laughing too before the recollection triggered bittersweet memories of Tod, a friend gained and lost. Not that Tod was in Franklin back then or had likely been there since. He wondered where he was now; maybe with Hood back at Columbia. If he was alive. Clara might have moved all this way for a dead man. He pushed away such a shameful thought and reminded himself that Tod had saved his life.

By mid-afternoon the pace was more constant. Soldiers began to shed their goods in an effort to keep up. Beside the road were empty bottles and blanket rolls. Shire saw a Bible. Cleves suddenly bolted from the column and collected a shiny skillet, discarding his old one. Men fell out to remove their boots and to soothe bleeding feet on the cold ground.

There were two cannon shots. It was miles away, but it was ahead of them. Like every man in the column, Shire lifted his head and looked north, as if they might see the Devil himself unfold into the sky. It dawned on Shire that they weren't marching away from a battle; they were marching toward one.

Williamson County, Tennessee – November 29th, 1864

Atop a hill south-east of Spring Hill, his heart racing, Frank sat aboard Ashley and watched the infantry go in. Hood had done it. He'd left a whole corps of his army at Columbia to fool the Union, taken the rest beyond the eastern flank over the Duck River, and then won the race north. Now part of that army was going to sweep below the village and across the Columbia Pike. The sun was low in the sky, but there were some hours of light left: *surely* enough time to win the road.

His brigade – Gist's Brigade – was a mile behind, acting as trailing flankers. Frank had been sent ahead to Brown's Division H.Q. so he could go back and direct Gist when the time came to move up. Half of Brown's staff were on the hill with Frank to watch the advance below.

It wasn't as he'd imagined a battle in his mind's eye: an unencumbered view of row upon row of men, tightly packed, bayonets gleaming, flags waving as they raced under arcing shells toward mirrored lines in blue. Instead, he had to work hard to pick out the advance as it cut in and out of the trees and scattered fields. Entire brigades in the center had moved out of sight behind a low hill; a nearer regiment had disappeared into a wooded vale. The units were spaced over at least a half-mile. Where he could see them, they walked in measured stride. Officers repeatedly stopped them to dress the line. Totally absent was anything to advance *against*; no rows of blue waited for this walking charge.

The brigade nearest to him, below the hill, was well behind those to the north. Frank commented on it to one of Brown's staff. 'The line is in echelon,' the man patiently explained. 'The nearer units are set back in steps, so when they reach the road it's easier to wheel to face south and block the Union Army.'

Frank looked again. Sure enough, the units to the north were furthest ahead and nearest the village. The land was more open there. Flags were unfurled. Officers marched to the front with sabers pointing. There was nothing before them that he could see. Smaller lanes ran north toward Spring Hill but they were muddy tracks, not fit for a large army. Somewhere out of sight to the east would be the hardened Columbia Pike. Once the men below were astride that road, Hood's trap would be shut. He thought of Tod. Where might he be by now? When they parted outside Columbia, neither of them had thought that Hood could move this quickly.

The officer beside him struck his arm and offered up a plug of tobacco, talking around a bulging cheek, 'It takes the edge off.'

Frank declined, annoyed by the distraction, and looked back to the battle. He wished his brigade was part of the line. He wanted to be down there, bloodless as it was; to be a part of that trap. His duty was to get back and report to Gist, but until Brown had an order for him to deliver, he could only sit and watch.

Two stabs of smoke spurted diagonally out from Spring Hill. Ashley jumped beneath him when the delayed boom of the cannon reached them, strong enough to punch through Frank's chest even at this distance. The resulting explosions were well in front of the advancing men. He steadied Ashley. Nobody below so much as checked their stride. There was movement beyond the far end of the line. He raised his field glasses, a parting gift from Father. Union soldiers, several hundred, rose behind a rail fence and poured a firecracker volley into the right flank of the lead Rebel brigade. He saw men fall. A flag dipped, but was instantly up again. First the regiment taking the punishment, and then the rest of the brigade, wheeled to the right and faced up the hill toward the enemy. They put in volleys of their own. For a while, blue and gray traded blows. The cannon began to find its range and shells burst above the army, the smoke quick to clear in the winter breeze.

That brigade was part of Cleburne's Division, Frank thought: the best fighting unit Hood had. Those Union boys had flicked the ear of an angry Rebel bear and had better watch out. It played out slowly through his glasses. The second brigade, which had been a step behind, caught up and turned to face uphill as well. Then they all charged in. The ragged Rebel yell barely reached Frank, no more than an angry flock of geese high on the breeze. They easily overlapped the blue line which broke and ran to avoid being overwhelmed. Cleburne's third brigade also wheeled and realigned to point north toward the village. The units nearest to Frank, below his hill, stopped altogether.

'Aren't they supposed to cut the pike rather than take the village?' Frank asked his tobacco friend.

'Cleburne couldn't leave his flank exposed. What does it matter? The pike runs right through Spring Hill. When they take the village, we'll have the pike anyway.'

A shell screamed home into the trees not fifty yards to Frank's right. He had to wrestle Ashley and dropped his field glasses.

'We've been spotted,' said the officer, unperturbed. 'Nothing like a clump of mounted officers to temp the gunners.'

Frank settled Ashley better than he could his racing heart, dismounted and picked up the glasses. They'd survived the fall undamaged. He climbed back up, eager to see what was happening. The form seemed to be to show a touch of bravado, but when the next shot closed the range and showered Frank and Brown's officers with earth, to his relief they all steered their horses off the rear of the hill. He wondered where Hood was, and if he knew his Rebel bear had changed direction.

Williamson County, Tennessee – November 29th, 1864

The cannon fired again; two, three, four shots. In the barn, Old George pulled his head sharply up and pricked his ears. Clara's soothing noises had stopped working. She fought not to react to the detonations herself; it would only make him worse, but it was difficult. She didn't know how far away the cannon were. As best she could tell they were likely in or around the village, as much as a mile away, and they certainly weren't firing this way. Sometimes the guns sounded closer. Tremors rippled through George's shoulders again.

She'd lost count of how many times she'd put on his saddle and bridle and taken them off, but started at it again. It was something he was used to, even though she didn't ride him anymore. It calmed him to work with her and listen to her commands. She'd come to realize it did the same for her, up to a point. But there was still that shock to her core each time the cannon fired; that the war had caught up to her again. This time it wasn't a cruel husband, or a small band of evil men. This time, it was two wrestling armies.

Four more shots. She'd said goodbye to Moses and Matilde only two days ago. Thinking of them, she was watching the breeze move the scrub grass outside the barn door, when a single gray soldier ghosted through her yard. Memories of Bowman and his men pulsed through her. She dropped the bridle and it swung to tap the stall. The soldier looked across at her. She stood rooted next to George. The man simply lifted his slouch hat and moved on. She went warily outside but by then he was into the top field and fifty yards on with his back to her, a comrade ten paces to his right.

'It's not a time to be outside, ma'am.'

She spun. Another soldier was so close behind her that she took two steps back.

'Don't be afeared.' He looked around. 'You alone?'

Clara nodded, but then wished she'd lied. He had a sidearm.

'I have to drive my men, but you find a place to hunker down. Cellar's best. Take in a light and a blanket, it might be a long afternoon. Ma'am.' He stepped past her.

She hurried into the house, raced upstairs and out onto the covered veranda. Down to her right, south across the top field, was a widely spaced line of Rebel soldiers all walking in the direction of the village. They stretched to and over the pike and she watched until they disappeared into the oak brake that ran the far length of the field. She sat down in the rocker, its repose at odds with her heartbeat, thinking she should take Cincin – her newly named gift-mare from Shire – and ride away north to Franklin. She could trail Old George behind; he could manage it if she went slowly. How was it that Confederate soldiers had come from the north?

Before she could think further, rifle shots sounded away in the oak brake and she stood. Within a minute the same gray line reversed out of the trees, the men alternately moving or firing at targets she couldn't see. When the Rebels were halfway back across the field, a stronger line of blue, closer together and working in pairs, emerged from the woods. She backed into the doorway. Some of the Rebels took positions behind her fence on the south side of the drive. One fired right below her. She should get inside. They were calling at each other to hurry back and they hastened away north. A rogue bullet thwacked into a baluster on the veranda not four feet from her. She jumped back and fell to the floor. The shooting died away. It was several minutes before she was brave enough to creep to the bedroom window and look out. There was no one in the field. The Union soldiers must have gone back as well. She was left in-between. She cautiously returned to the veranda and picked at the new splinters in the baluster. There was a lead ball three-quarters buried in the wood.

Later, when the cannon had picked up to the accompaniment of what she took to be far-away massed musketry, she came out to check on the horses again, finding George standing where she'd left him with the saddle on but the girth untied. He was still shaking. She lifted off the saddle and decided to move him to the stall beside Cincin, who was calmness itself. It might help.

She came out into the yard and the bright winter afternoon sun. There was rifle fire and a train whistle from up toward Thompson's Station. It sounded again and again, plainly in distress. If she tried to get away, there was no direction she could go that was safe. It was too late now. Soon, to the north, a stream of white smoke rose up tilted by the breeze. The rail depot gone up perhaps.

She collected water, a blanket and a lantern and took herself down into the cellar. She pulled the angled doors closed above her and retreated through the sweet musk of past root crops to the driest corner. The cannon blasts were barely less noisy down here, just blurred and vibrating through the cellar walls. They stopped for a long minute and it was as if she was back in the mine at Ducktown. She could practically hear the drip, drip from the weight of imagined rock above. It was too much and she burst back up through the doors. They fell carelessly open either side of her. She had to steel herself to go back down and retrieve the lamp.

The light began to fade. She spent more time with the horses. Old George was better, Cincin occasionally reaching over the stall to nuzzle and nibble his neck. She remembered how Shire used to dote on Old George, to brush him and plait his tail. Shire must be nearby, somewhere among the cannon and the rifles. She said a small prayer. George was fine for now. She left them and took bread and some of Mitilde's cold chicken upstairs. It was nearly dark. She'd not heard a cannon for a while. She lit the lamp but turned the flame as low as she could, put it beside her bed and took a blanket to the rocker on the veranda. Loathe as she was to make use of anything that had belonged to Taylor, she took his revolver, loaded it and placed it on the floor beside her. Not overly hungry, she slowly ate her supper with her fingers while listening to the snap, snap of the rifles far away, and watched the dusky road fade into the night.

Williamson County, Tennessee – November 29th, 1864

Frank raced away south of Spring Hill on one of its lesser roads. The noise of battle, light as it had become, was wholly lost behind, snuffed out by the low hills, the woods and the breeze. The sun was almost down, the light starting to die. He'd been ordered to direct General Gist to quickly bring up his brigade and place it such that it would become the very right end of Brown's Division. That would make them the extreme right of the whole line when the just-now-planned dusk attack went in. But only if they got there in time. Brown had made it clear he wouldn't wait on Gist. Frank urged Ashley on. He didn't want to miss the second fight of the day.

He'd been there; right there in the clump of officers surrounding Brown, Cleburne and their corps commander, Cheatham. As he rode, Frank turned over Cheatham's summation in his mind so he'd be able to reiterate it to Gist. All the divisions Cheatham could bring to the field would attack together and take Spring Hill. As best they knew, there was only a couple of Union brigades facing them, though it appeared they had a hatful of artillery. That wouldn't be such a factor once the light went, but the poor light itself would make it harder to co-ordinate. Brown would start the assault and Cleburne and the other divisions to the left would go in when they heard Brown's guns. That way, the attack would sweep down the line and overwhelm the Yankees to take the village and the pike with it.

Frank barely slowed as he passed through the pickets, shouting out the watchword. Gist wasn't as far away as he'd expected. That was good. His general had held the men in column and they were on the march within minutes. Frank rode beside Gist and explained the afternoon's events as best he could. 'The attack aimed at the pike south of the village fizzled out when Cleburne was hit in the flank, despite him pushing the Union back. Now Cheatham's ordered an attack to take Spring Hill.'

'Was Hood there?'

'I haven't seen him all day.'

'That so. Only you usually move in such high circles, Lieutenant. Well, stay close and help me guide the boys in. I trust your pistol is loaded?'

They were barely in position in time. Brown started his division forward, but travelled hardly any distance before stopping. The light was all but gone. Frank rode in with Gist to find Brown and see what was going on. Otto Strahl's Brigade had reported a threat to his right and was afraid of being hit in the flank as Cleburne had been just a few hours before. Cheatham was nowhere to be found and Brown wouldn't go in without a new order. The scale of the threat was unclear. Gist calmly and reasonably suggested he take part of his brigade and sweep up to secure Strahl's flank, but Brown wouldn't allow it. He needed to find Cheatham, he said. To Frank, he had the look of a man who'd lost all volition beyond doing nothing. 'But without Brown attacking,' Frank said in Gist's ear, 'the attack won't be triggered down the line.'

'Welcome to the war, Lieutenant Trenholm,' said Gist. 'Some men fight and some men freeze.'

Despite the entreaties of several other commanders and the near insubordination of some of his own, Brown never restarted the attack. By the time Cheatham was found, it was too late and too dark. The cannon had fallen silent a while back and the rifles followed suit but for the occasional nervous picket. Frank helped Gist get their tired brigade into bivouac on the east side of town so as to be in position to attack in the morning. Frank knew he should feel tired himself, but with the trials and the frustrations of the afternoon he was still wide awake. The day somehow felt incomplete. Despite the darkness, he rode out with Gist to try and get the lay of the land. They walked their horses behind their division campfires then arced around to the south and east toward the pike.

'So many fires.' said Frank. 'They'll give away our position.'

'We have them just where we want them for sun-up. It'll more likely put the fear of God into them.'

Most people they spoke to appeared to think that the early afternoon coming together had been a small affair, but to Frank there seemed plenty of wounded, especially behind Cleburne's lines. Gist took a wide berth around a surgeons' tent. 'Nothing you'll want to see there.'

Bate's Division was next in line to the south, the Columbia Pike somewhere before its strung-out front as best they could figure. Frank wondered where Tod might be on his ride for home, and how he would find his way back to the army. They spoke to more officers and men, all weary from the long day's march but perplexed that the sun had set without them driving home their advantage. 'Wouldn't it be a simple thing to push on to the road?' Frank asked Gist.

'Maybe,' said Gist. 'Night attacks are the devil to pull off. Mostly you end up shooting your own men.' They steered their horses between the campfires and out to the picket line.

Gist whispered to a weary guard, 'How far ahead is the pike?'

The trees whispered too.

'I could throw a rock there with my sister's arm,' said the picket.

'You seen anything?'

'No. Not so much as a fox or an owl. And now the clouds are across the stars.'

Away to the right there was a rude burst and flash of six quick shots, then all fell silent again. 'Some officer got the jitters,' laughed the picket.

They stole away and Gist said, 'We'll bag them in the morning. That road's as good as closed.'

The night air swirled. For a second Frank thought he might have heard the roll and squeak of a poorly aligned wheel. Trees stirred in the breeze. They should get back to camp, Gist said. It was going to be an early start.

Williamson County, Tennessee – November 29th, 1864

Tod sat up, rolled his blanket as tightly as he could outside his coat and lay back down on the damp earth to try and sleep. It wasn't the cold; he was used to the cold. His mind wouldn't settle, even though he had rarely felt so dog-tired. Perhaps only when he'd jumped from the train in Pennsylvania, spent a wet night in the woods and stumbled like a tramp into the Amish farm the next morning. Back then he'd had a clear and sound purpose: to escape and get back into the war. Today, he had the best purpose of all. And at least this time he had a horse and it was country he knew. He craved rest, but it was so hard to sleep when he was finally heading for home.

After saying goodbye to Frank, he'd ridden practically due east, cutting off the necks of the larger meanders along the Duck River while looking for a place to cross. He'd bypassed Davis Ford where the tail end of Forrest's horsemen were busy getting over themselves, and decided against crossing at Huey's Mill since beyond there he could swing north anyway and head for Hardison's Mill. He was surprised to find that place crowded as well, but showed the guards at the ford his note from Benton Smith and was allowed to pass. The water had dropped a little, but he'd had to lift his legs across Rosencrantz's neck to keep them dry.

The road north was busy with Confederate cavalry. So many of them stopped him to check who he was and what he was about, that in the middle of the night he'd determined to get off the road altogether. He pushed further east still to avoid the trouble. It was galling to take the wide arc of a bow when all he wanted to do was follow his heartstring, arrow straight to Franklin. It had become slow-going in the dark woods and he'd decided to rest Rosencrantz and get some sleep. Only it wouldn't take hold.

He'd been three and a half years away from home and might step in under his own roof tomorrow. His mind spun at what he might learn. It had been so long since he'd had a letter from Moscow. He knew some of his sisters had moved back home but not how things stood now. He could have missed a marriage or a death. He might have lost another brother or added to his collection of nephews and nieces. He felt sure he'd have known if Father had passed. That sort of thing would have filtered through the lines, though perhaps not if it had been in recent months. He'd have to cope with the inevitable deluge of news, good or bad, only to ride away again within hours.

Sleep was as far away as ever. Giving up, he stood and spoke gently to Rosencrantz, started him forward again in the dark. Before dawn, he heard shots to the west and when he got up closer to Mount Carmel as the light came on, there was a sizeable engagement over that way. Cavalry most likely as the shots were scattered and random; no massed volleys. He swung east again but began to worry that if Forrest had made it this far north, Hood might be making his move sooner than Benton Smith had thought, and that he'd be absent when the battle was settled as he'd feared. His small army of relatives would remind him for evermore that he'd played the prodigal son on the day that Tennessee was rescued.

Wary though he was, he came near to being shot mid-morning. He had to race over an open field with three horses in pursuit. They gave up soon enough and wheeling to look back he was almost certain they were Confederate, but it wasn't worth the finding out.

Later in the day, as he came closer to Franklin, he went even more carefully. It would be better to arrive once most of the light had gone. There was a steady rumble of cannon fire from the direction of Spring Hill which gave him pause. It wasn't the higher note of horse-artillery but full-throated cannon, in good number. It must mean the infantry had come up while he was following his arc. It was excruciating. The closer he got to Franklin, the stronger the pull of home became, but at every creek crossing or at the edge of each field, he also felt the tug of duty to turn around and race back to his brigade. Rosencrantz was weary, so he dismounted and walked on. After sunset he crossed back over the Lewisburg Pike and came close by John McGavock's house. He thought about lodging Rosencrantz there. They'd help him, he knew they would, but it wasn't right to risk anyone else.

He waited for it to get darker and watered Rosencrantz at a wooded creek where he used to fish as a boy. His mood became even and contented, perhaps because he was so tired. When the light was three-quarters gone he stole out of the woods and across the railroad-cut and stealthily over toward the Columbia Pike, though it was hard to be stealthy with a gray horse. When he made out the shadow of the cotton gin, his heart skipped a beat. There were soldiers beside the pike, no doubt to challenge traffic on the road, though presently there was none. They might not be able to see his uniform, but a horseman crossing the road would arouse suspicion. A rider moved out past the guards and set his horse into a canter, passing not thirty yards away. Tod worked his way back south almost as far as the Neely house and risked crossing the road.

He found his way to a water trough he knew. There was no sign of the Neelys' pigs. In fact, there was no livestock he could see at all. He drew a cloth from his saddlebag. After soaking it he wiped it on the muddied ground and then on Rosencrantz, who complained at the indignity. He was a big horse to paint, and Tod should have taken more time, but it was better than nothing. He led his newly shaded friend around Privet Knob.

The darkness was almost complete as they walked back toward Franklin. Carter land. They reached the young grove of tightly clustered locust trees close to his home. Tomorrow would be the last day of November and a cold breeze rattled what leaves there were. It must have been his tired imagination, but he thought he could smell the honeyed scent of spring. Rosencrantz was unsettled, maybe picking up on Tod's own many-colored mood. He tied him to a cedar sapling rather than the thorny locusts and, conscious of each and every step, walked toward his home.

He laid his hands on the top rail of the back garden fence. There was a simple joy in just that. He stood there a full minute before he was ready to move on. Edging his way along, he reached the smokehouse, climbed over the fence and peered around the corner from the shadow of the low overhung roof. Across the yard stood his home, every bit as complete as the memory he'd kept these long years. Solid and warm. The long porch which ran across the back of the house and right-angled down the side of the ell was lit by a single lantern. An indulgence of Father's. He always said there should be a welcome put out after dusk for unexpected guests. No matter it was the back of the house. But here Tod was, and he'd be unexpected alright. There was light streaming through the ell window as well, and a lesser glow from a smaller window in one of the slave huts. The pooled luminescence meant that if he crossed the yard he would be easily seen, should anyone care to look outside. What did it matter? He'd been furtive all day but there was only his family here. He was suddenly aware he'd not washed in some time. He looked to his jacket and did up the top buttons then berated himself for being so foolish.

A Union officer appeared around the end of the ell. Tod pulled himself tight to the brickwork of the smokehouse, watching on. The Yankee crossed the yard, bold as brass, and half-ran up the porch steps as if they were his own handiwork. There were voices from the slave hut. The officer rapped on the door to Father's room. Why hadn't he gone to the front? A moment later, Father opened up and stepped out, closing the door behind. Tod ached to call out. Perhaps Father looked a pinch older, it was hard to tell. He leaned on the porch banister and offered the officer some tobacco which was declined. Father attended to his own pipe. It looked as if the two of them might have done this a hundred times before.

'You're still here, Captain.' Father's voice. 'They've not run you down to Spring Hill?'

'No, sir, they have not. From what I can gather, the likelihood is the army will fall back toward Nashville. I don't think they meant to fight at Spring Hill.'

'But now they've had to?'

The captain laughed. 'By rights, I shouldn't tell you the time of day, Fountain. You having sired any number of sons for the Rebels.'

Father drew on his pipe. 'That wasn't my intent at the time as I recall.'

Mother's old piano struck up inside the house and each tinny off-key middle C tugged at Tod's heart. Then the singing started. It made it harder to hear the conversation. Tod wanted to get closer to both the talking and the singing so backed up and crept to the gap the other side, between the smokehouse and the farm office.

'It's plain enough there's been fighting this afternoon,' Father said. 'The cannon and the people on the road tell me that, so you don't have to confirm it if it eases your conscience. But sons aside, I have a flock of women and children in here.' He stabbed his pipestem back at the house. 'Moscow only has them singing to distract them, otherwise people just start talking again on whether we should stay or go.'

'Truth is, I don't know more than you,' the captain said, 'but if we was fixing to stay for a fight, I think you'd see men marching south on the pike. Nashville's the hardest nut. If Schofield's army gets this far, I think we'll all skittle on for Nashville.'

'The road bridge is still out.'

Father's tobacco scent reached Tod.

'I heard they've asked for a pontoon to be sent. Anyway, Fountain, have you got somewhere you could go?'

A figure crossed the light in the bedroom window on the ell. Annie, Tod guessed.

'We know enough people in Nashville, but it's a hard point to come to, to leave your home to the wolves, whatever color their pelt.'

The men smoked in silence for a while. The piano stopped. The door opened and Moscow stepped out and joined them at the rail. 'Captain,' he said.

The scene grated with the homecoming Tod had imagined all day: Moscow, his brother and one time colonel, on friendly terms with the enemy. But then the Union had been here a while. He thought of Shire. It wasn't so difficult to get friendly, until the bullets started to fly.

'There's a request that you to lend your bass to the choir, Father,' said Moscow.

'You didn't pass muster?'

'Sarah tells me I lack conviction.'

'What you lack is a good ear.'

'I know it.'

Tod smiled.

'I'll leave you to it,' said the captain. 'But I have a request myself. I have two officers newly arrived this evening. They need a billet for the night.'

'Is it truly a request?' asked Moscow.

'I'd like it to be.'

'Well, it's not the first time. It'll be a parlor floor or a slave cabin. That's the best we can do, the beds are double-occupied as it is.'

'Thank you, gentleman. I'll find somewhere else tomorrow.' He eased down the porch steps. 'I'll fetch them right along.'

Father called after, 'Tell them they're expected to sing.'

Tod retreated around the smokehouse once more and faced south with his back to the wall. He was as uncertain as ever. He could run in before the soldiers arrived, but to what end? Later he'd have to skulk in a bedroom in his own house. He tried not to get angry; it wouldn't help. Maybe he should run over to Annie's window, rap on the pane, visit with her at least. All his hopes tumbled into nothing and he tightened his face against tears.

To the south there was a staccato series of flashes, seconds later the low rumble of guns. A battery of cannon taking a chance shot in the dark. That was the only certainty.

That he should be there with his army. He'd made the attempt for home, but it had failed. If there was still a fight at Spring Hill tomorrow, he wanted to be in it. And if that captain was right, the Union would retreat to Nashville anyway. If he made it back to his brigade, in a day or two he could knock on the front door as a conqueror.

He heard the captain return with his two officers, the singing momentarily louder as the door opened and closed. There it was then.

He dared not look at the house again. Instead, his heart aching, he climbed back over the fence and crept his way along to Rosencrantz. He felt more tired than ever; tired in body and tired in his soul. He could make his way to the Neely house or the McGavocks', but that would leave him a long way from Spring Hill when he woke. Better to go straight south. No arc this time. He mounted. There was another flash of cannon as he pointed weary Rosencrantz at the stuttering silhouette of Winstead Hill.

Spring Hill, Tennessee – November 29th, 1864

The ornately carved, dark-wood chair was set tightly against the papered parlor wall. Opdycke eyed it covetously. He wanted to make use of it. The seat was no more than a rush weave. Not the height of luxury, but if he could only take the weight off his legs. The Confederate officer they'd been interrogating was shown from the room and into the company of his guards, the door closed firmly behind him. General Schofield paced the floor, back and forth in front of the unemployed seat and the tightly drawn curtains.

Wagner evidently had no such qualms about resting in the presence of the Army of the Ohio's commander. He sat slumped at the table, hat off, rubbing his temple. Opdycke had walked with Wagner to this handsome brick residence on Main Street which was serving as Schofield's Headquarters in Spring Hill. Tired as Opdycke was, Wagner had struggled to keep pace. It was half-past seven by the case clock above the fireplace. The shooting had all but stopped outside. General Ruger stood alongside Opdycke and General Stanley leaned against the wall, his arms folded before him, seemingly at ease. As was so often the case, Opdycke found himself a colonel in the company of generals.

'Two corps!' said Schofield, twisting his fingers in his overlong beard.

A year younger than me, thought Opdycke. Thirty-three and already head of an army. The beard added fifteen years to Schofield. That and the dire straits they were in.

'Two damned corps,' Schofield said again.

'The man can't be trusted, sir,' said Ruger, younger in age and looks. 'He'd everything to gain by exaggerating.'

The Confederate, captured by Ruger's men as they came up the pike, had clearly enjoyed his cross-examination. He'd listed off any number of Rebel divisions and brigades.

Stanley spoke, no more animated than if commenting on the weather. 'If they truly have that many men up, they made a poor job of it this afternoon. They should have swept over us.'

Opdycke knew the there was no love lost between Stanley and Schofield. In the summer fighting around Atlanta, Schofield had been under Stanley. Then Stanley made the mistake of speaking his mind to Sherman – of all people – so was out of favor. Now he had to serve beneath Schofield. But there was little enmity in the room so far as Opdycke could tell. There was no time for it. They would sink or swim together.

Schofield dropped his hat onto Opdycke's fancied chair. Opdycke inwardly sighed and tried to match Ruger's ramrod stance.

'Even if he is exaggerating,' Schofield said, 'we know they're up in strength and close to the pike. I was fired on by their picket as I rode in. The army is strung out way back to Columbia. All Hood has to do is get across the road.'

Wagner rolled his neck. 'General, I think we should consider destroying the wagons. Hood could take his army on into Kentucky with a gift like that.'

'Sir,' said Opdycke, choosing to address Schofield rather than Wagner, his own division commander, 'we can't do that. There are eight hundred wagons and a good proportion of them carry ordnance. They're packed side by side on the commons. If we burned them, well, it would destroy Spring Hill.'

'The wellbeing of Spring Hill's not our prime concern, Colonel,' said Stanley, brushing at some mud on his jacket.

Schofield rubbed his eyes. 'We have to save the wagons somehow, but Opdycke, you make certain the teamsters know to destroy their horses in the last resort.'

There was a knock on the door and the smudge-faced engine driver Opdycke had sent for was shown in. 'I'd like you to hear this, General,' said Opdycke.

The man was timid. Opdycke told him to speak up and speak plainly. The driver said how he'd been coming down from Franklin when his train was attacked south of Thompson's Station by Rebel cavalry. 'There's a grade there, just past the blockhouse. So we was slow enough for them to ride alongside. We were certain to be captured. The whole train. I had no choice but to uncouple the engine, sir, so we could get away. The cars will have rolled back down the grade toward the station unless the guard got to the brake.'

'How many?' asked Schofield.

'How many cars?'

'How much cavalry?' It was said patiently enough, but Opdycke saw Schofield ball his hand.

'Hard to say. Hundreds, certainly.'

Wagner had his head in his hands so it was left to Opdycke to continue. 'I pushed dismounted cavalry back north of town early this afternoon, General. They were easy to move. We heard the train attack and saw smoke from that direction. Most likely the depot is destroyed.'

Schofield blew out his cheeks and leaned back on the table. 'Rebel infantry beside the road from the south and more attacking us from the east. Cavalry to the north. And no roads to get away west. Not many options, gentleman. Well, that makes it easier, doesn't it?'

'Sir?' said Stanley.

Schofield took a settling breath. 'We *must* own the road north. Ruger, take your division and clear the road to Franklin. Send word once the way is secure and we'll get the wagon train to follow.'

'Yes, sir.' Ruger looked up for the fight.

Wagner lifted his head.

'We *have* to make the attempt,' continued Schofield. 'Any other units that make it up from Columbia we'll march straight through. On your feet, Wagner, there's work to do.'

'General,' said Stanley, finally taking his weight from the wall, perhaps sensing the change of energy in the room. 'We'll need to disengage east of town. I suggest you let Wagner's Division form the rearguard. Opdycke's men are Wagner's freshest and Colonel Opdycke here his most experienced commander. He can be the last out.'

Wagner said nothing. Opdycke, gratified, stood taller still.

'Alright,' nodded Schofield. 'Go to it, gentlemen.'

Opdycke followed Wagner out into the hall. Stanley clapped him on the shoulder as he walked by. It was a clear set of orders at least.

Opdycke wanted a word with the engine driver. 'You did the right thing by protecting your engine, but it can't be saved now. Go blow the boiler. Then take a gun and find yourself a place on a wagon.' In the time it took him to say that, Wagner had left.

Opdycke had been in the vanguard this morning and would be in the rearguard tonight. The latter might require that God lay his hands on affairs to stop Hood getting across the road. God helps them who help themselves, he thought.

The lady of the house, Mrs McKissack, was remonstrating with a staff officer. She grabbed Opdycke's sleeve. 'Sir, please. I overheard this man say my home will be burned before dawn.'

'No, ma'am,' said the officer. 'You misunderstood. I only said there might be an unpleasant outcome.'

Far from placated, she begged, 'What does that mean?'

The officer looked abashed. 'That we might need to sign a surrender here.' He looked at Opdycke and then at the floor. 'I was just hypothesizing, sir.'

'Then I suggest you get busy forming a different hypothesis,' said Opdycke, stiffly.

Williamson County, Tennessee – November 29th, 1864

Clara found it hard to leave the dark upstairs veranda, preferring to shiver inside the quilt she'd brought out and laid across her rocker rather than go to her bed. At least here she might just see, or more likely hear, anyone coming down the drive. If she went inside, she'd only feel helpless again, trapped and waiting for a window to shatter or a door to burst in.

She lost track of time. On the other side of the pike a long line of campfires sprung up, building from the direction of Spring Hill and reaching ever further north. As best she could tell, they were well back from the road. The top branches of the trees, each lit from a hundred angles, turned to burnished copper, magical or devilish at her whim. She wondered whose army it was, but was thankful they'd not camped on her side of the pike.

A light breeze brushed through the three-quarter-grown poplar trees that the Tolivers had planted to protect the north side of the house. The gentle sound stretched out the seconds and the minutes. Slowly it soothed her and she slept, despite the cold air. When she woke the fires had dimmed. On occasion, when the breeze abated in the poplars, she could hear the squeak and crunch of wheels on the road. There were dark shapes, backlit by the lesser fires, moving up the pike toward Franklin.

The wind stilled again and there was a muffled whinny from her stable out the back. Old George unsettled no doubt, but there had been no shot to spook him. She'd look in on him and Cincin and then make herself go to bed. In standing, she trod on Taylor's pistol. She bent to pick it up. The cold weight made her more fearful than comforted, but she took it with her downstairs. She lit a lantern, set it low and hurried across the yard to the stable. The door was unbolted and she chastised herself. No doubt it had stirred in the wind and that had upset George.

She stepped inside. The weak shadows cast by the lantern tricked her. It looked as if all three stalls owned a horse. She lifted the light, took a half-step forward and slowly raised the gun. There truly was a third horse in the far stall. A gray. Her finger tightened on the trigger. She tried to sound bold, but it came out as little more than a whisper. 'Who's here?'

'Don't shoot, Clara. It's me. It's Tod.'

A figure ducked under the neck of the new horse and stood looking over the stall divide. It was hard to make out his features.

'You can lower that gun if you like?'

'Come out of the stall.'

'Can't you see it's me?'

'Most visitors ask before stabling their horse.'

'There's a lot going on at the front of the house. I thought you'd be asleep.'

The gun suddenly felt ridiculous in her hand and she lowered it. 'You mean to say you weren't going to come to the house?'

'I hadn't decided. Who else is here?'

'Nobody.'

'You're alone?' Tod stepped fully out of the stall. He looked a little shabby. 'What about your people?'

The aftershock of finding someone in her barn, and the

new shock of finding it was Tod, made her sound angry. 'I don't have any *people*. Only friends.' Maybe she *was* angry. 'And they've run away from your army so they don't become somebody else's *people*.'

'Alright, alright.'

'Tod, what are you doing here?'

'Turn down the light a little.'

He came closer. It had only been a few months, but he looked older. The lantern light, she supposed. He embraced her and she didn't resist. Something snapped inside. She leaned into him, let go of the stress of the day, and quietly wept. With her head still across his chest, she said. 'It isn't safe, Tod. I don't know what's happening across the road.'

'Neither do I. I'm trying to get back to my brigade, but I'm bone-tired, Clara. If I could just rest up in here.'

'With the horses?'

'If the Union found me, I could say I was hiding out and you didn't know.'

'Don't be foolish. I've seen both armies today and neither one has come into the house.' She stepped out of his arms and looked up at him again, amazed he was here. 'There are places to hide inside if you need to. I've some food and you can wash.' She turned to go but Tod stayed where he was.

'Clara, this horse. Is she yours?'

'Yes. Why?'

He touched the saddle resting on the stall divide. 'I recognize the type. It's Confederate.' He lifted up a saddle flap. In the dim lamplight it was just possible to read *C.S.A.* stenciled into the leather.

'Come inside.'

'It wouldn't do to be caught with an army horse.'

'It was Bowman's, or his lieutenant's. You remember who

Bowman was, don't you?'

'Sure I do. Trenholm told me what happened to your home, how you were coming here.'

'Burning Comrie wasn't the worst thing he did. Shire killed him. A week back in the hills up the road. He thought I could use an extra horse.'

'Shire was here?'

Her dance with Shire came to mind along with Tuck's melody, but she only said, 'You'd be surprised at the visitors I get.'

In the kitchen, Clara drew the curtains across and gave Tod the last of the chicken and some cold potatoes. In the better light she could see how worn he was. He told her he'd been given permission to ride home and that he'd come from there. 'I was so close, Clara. Close enough to smell Father's pipe tobacco, to hear my family singing at the piano.'

Clara stopped herself from suggesting it was likely Lena playing. Tod looked so lost. How would he take it to hear his family news from her?

'When I came away, I thought of you,' he said. 'How you'd told me last spring you owned New Farm.'

'I've given it a different name.' She saw he was too tired and wasn't listening.

'I should have gone back further east,' he said, 'but it was quicker to come over Winstead.' He shook his head and stretched his eyes.

'You need to sleep.'

'I have to get back to my brigade.'

'Do you know where they are?'

'I've not the first idea.'

She put him in Moses and Mitilde's room. It was the biggest bed. He made her promise to wake him well before dawn. By the time she'd brought water for him to wash, Tod was asleep. She sat on the bed and wished she could tell him about her time with his family. He'd come to know one day. If he found it strange, well, it *was* strange. She couldn't deny that. She remembered their parting in Ducktown, how he'd asked if he could come and find her after the war. Now here he was, though in truth, it was her that had gone looking. She felt the sudden weight of the secrets she held, secrets she'd expected to keep until the war was over. She was tired herself. More than tired, and afraid. Afraid that the Union might find Tod in her home. Afraid that Shire might not have survived the day.

A single rifle fired out in the night and startled her. It was closer than most. She thought about climbing in beside Tod. She doubted it would wake him.

Williamson County, Tennessee – November 30th, 1864

Shire did as he'd been told and strapped his canteen over the wrong shoulder so it wouldn't hang and clatter against his bayonet sheath. What came into his weary mind was playing hide-and-seek in the dusky Bedfordshire woods with Clara when they were young. That had been easy enough. Find a sand-hollow or a wide tree and stay still; gulp a breath and hold it if she got close. Quieting a column of men who carried packs and weapons, muting a thousand leather boots on a hard stone road, and all in the pitch dark; that was a good deal harder.

He was exhausted. It felt like an age that he'd been following the deeper dark of Mason's broad back. There'd been no rest since sunset, which was long hours ago. He'd eaten only hardtack all day. His head started to nod. Tuck, on his left, shook his arm and he found himself squinting at the dimly pale surface of the pike.

'Wake up, sleepyhead. You don't want to fall into Mason's feet. No getting' up from that.'

'Quiet,' came a whispered shout from the sergeant.

Tuck waited a while and then said under his breath, 'It's a thing of wonder to hear a sergeant try to whisper. It's not what God invented them for. Take some water.'

Shire did. The chill when it hit his empty stomach brought him fully upright. Evidently, the cold of the night had found its way through the felt of his canteen. 'Where do you figure we are?'

'Well, I'm right here. I'd have to send out a search party to find where *you* are. The dark has me all knotted as to time and distance. If you forced me to guess, I'd say it's long past midnight and we're somewhere short of Spring Hill.'

This army must be in a fix. There were plenty of occasions he'd been summoned to the roll before dawn in the last two years, usually to get a jump on the enemy. But marching into the dusk and on and on through the night; it could only mean they were in deep trouble.

A soft voice called a halt. Who'd have thought that by no more than stopping, men could make such a racket. They were told not to break out of column, but Shire and Tuck sunk to the cold stone like most everyone else. He could have laid down and slept right there. Orders were whispered down the line to prepare for absolute quiet when they were ready to start up again. Men wrapped pots and skillets in blankets then stuffed the blankets in their packs. Any old rags were tied around boots. Route march; stay out of step. As they stood again, Cleves, next to Mason, must have turned to face them as Shire could see the wide whites of his eyes. 'We're sneakin' past something for sure.'

'You think?' said Tuck. 'Maybe it's just General Schofield tucked up in his tent and needin' his shuteye.'

They moved off gently uphill and were anything but quiet to Shire's ear. It was impossible. Perhaps the dark heightened his senses, but above the communal shuffle of massed feet he could clearly hear the rumble of wagons ahead and behind. A horse whickered, no doubt spooked by the palpable tension. He sensed the land was open to his right. At least he couldn't hear any trees out in the dark, even though there was a night breeze cooling his cheek. They went on, still slowly climbing. Forward to their right he could see a yellow glow that, in the minutes that followed, resolved into an assembly of campfires. For a fleeting second, his tired mind thought they were at the end of the march, that soon he would rest, but the men around him trod ever more lightly. Not a single order was muttered, not a word spoken.

Coming abreast of what he'd quietly realized was a Rebel camp, he watched the silhouette of a man cross in front of a fire. It hinted at the distance. A couple of hundred yards at most. There was canvas, yellow in the firelight. How could the Rebels not see them walk by, this procession of sore-footed men and horses, their fatigued faces half-turned to their enemy? He sucked slowly at the night air, as if his every breath might give them away. He longed to reset his rifle's uncomfortable weight on his shoulder, but dared not risk it. Surely any moment they would be discovered, fired upon and swept from the pike. Their one avenue away north and to safety would be lost.

On they went, heartbeat by heartbeat, until they crested a rise and started downhill. The fires became no more than an amber glow on the undersides of the low clouds left behind. The column exhaled around him; laughter edged with nerves. Their step quickened toward houses with dim lights in the windows. More men, their own men, beside the road, not camping but standing at barricades or guarding cannon next to an occasional frugal fire. Mason asked was this Spring Hill. They were told it was, but that they were to march straight through and on to Franklin.

Shire couldn't believe they wouldn't be allowed some rest, some food.

'You're not done with your soft boots yet,' said a corporal who counted the men as they passed. 'There's another line of Rebel camps beside the road north of town.'

Shire's thoughts went to Clara but he asked, 'What brigade are you?'

'Opdycke's.'

'That's us,' said Cleves. 'We're in the 125th.'

'Welcome home then. The Tigers are along by the tollgate.'

They hurried on. Every space beside the road or between houses was crowded. There was no more attempt at silence. Officers and sergeants bearing lanterns managed the column and waved them forward. Beyond Tuck to the left, a wide jam of wagons reached back into the dark, waiting to be fed onto the road one at a time. Ahead, high torches set beside the road lit the walls of a tollhouse. Shire smelt coffee. There was a guard of maybe fifty men, every face familiar. It was Company B.

'Where the blithering hell have you lot been?' asked Ocks.

'It's nice to see you too, Sergeant,' said Mason.

'I had to enter you as missing on the morning report.'

The squad crowded around Ocks and Mason said, 'Sergeant, I'd like to request that corrected. We're no runaways. We've just been guarding the rear.'

'Alright then, but seeing as you didn't have the sense to walk on by, you can stay and guard the rear with us.'

'What's the commotion, Sergeant?' Colonel Opdycke loomed out of the dark on Ben, back straight, chin high. Shire and the squad stood to attention.

'It's Mason's squad, sir. Late up from Columbia.'

'Is my lucky Englishman with them?'

'I'm here, Colonel.'

'Thank the Lord. Maybe all will be well. Put them to work, Sergeant.'

Williamson County, Tennessee – November 30th, 1864

Tod started awake on the cusp of a scream. He stopped himself, panted through the fear in the darkness until his breathing slowed. He tried to remember where he was, to make sense of the wash of emotions born of a dream, only to have them slowly align themselves with yesterday: Father; Moscow and home; the night ride to Clara. The palest light showed behind a square of curtains. He moved under the blankets toward it, across the greater expanse of the bed. There was a memory of warmth and for a long moment he lay above it, his head in the dented pillow that owned a familiar sweetness.

He forced himself from the bed and opened the door. From somewhere, the faintest lamplight seeped into the bedroom, just enough for him to find the washbowl and jug and wipe the worst of two days riding from his body. He dressed. Carrying his jacket and hat, he went in search of the light and found it, barely alive, in an upstairs front room. Clara was outside on the veranda, looking into the dark. She turned and came inside, her hair loose about her face. 'It's a long way from dawn,' she said.

He edged closer. 'Have you seen anything?'

'The fires across the road have burned lower still. I think there's movement on the road, but it's hard to tell.'

'Aren't you afraid they'll see the light?'

'It's barely lit. And my driveway runs to the pike. If they want to find my farm, all they have to do is follow it. I'm not even certain there's anyone there.'

A hand on her shoulder, he moved past her and looked out through the half-open doors. He couldn't see anything. Maybe there was something living in the breeze, a bass rattle and shuffle that could have been nothing but a trick of his imagination. 'You said there were Yankees here yesterday. Did you see their regimental flags?'

'I saw Union flags. I wouldn't know one regiment from another.'

'Did they look like infantry or dismounted cavalry?'

'I don't know. The just looked like soldiers.'

Why was she angry? 'It matters, Clara. If I know the Union regiment, someone can work out the brigade, the division. It'd be useful.'

'What makes you think I want to be useful to your army, Tod Carter?'

He tried not to raise his voice. 'It's my home that's next up the road. My family.'

'And it's your army my friends are running from. A little girl, orphaned by one of *your* men, bundled into a wagon with stand-in grandparents in the cold. They had nowhere to call home but here. I'd sooner go to my grave than help an army that would put them back into slavery.'

'It's not about that.'

'It's *entirely* about that.'

'Not here, not right now. Not for me. You haven't seen places torn down by the war. Not just Atlanta, but in Tennessee. Florence and Waynesboro. I have to protect my family, Clara. What sort of son would I be otherwise?' There was a pause in the argument and he put on his jacket.

'I can close the door if you're cold,' Clara said more quietly.

'I'm going to see what's happening.'

'It's not safe.'

'Show me a war that is. For all I know it might be my brigade on the road.'

'And what if it's not?'

'Then I need to know whose men they are.'

'I don't want another dead soldier's horse in my stable.'

He put his hat on the seat. It wasn't needed.

'Please, Tod.'

'I'll be back for my horse.'

He let himself out the back and came around the south to the drive. Dark though it was, he didn't want to cross open ground so kept down the side of the field until he reached the oak brake. Then he worked his way east in the deeper dark beneath the edge of the trees and toward the road. There was no starlight, no moon, just a changeable breeze in the branches. He was almost sure he could see movement. The wind shifted and he was certain now. There was the creak of leather and harness, broken steps on the stone. He rubbed soil onto his face and got closer still and there they were, ghosts of wagons, creeping north. He got so near that he could hear whispered orders, a click-click from a waggoner to encourage his team. His vision became more accustomed. This was such a long train; it went on and on. They must be Union. If this was Hood's army, the wagons would be following behind, not escaping ahead.

There was a subtle switch from the low rumble of the wheels to the shuffle of hundreds of feet as the wagons ended and an infantry column began, four abreast and Union for sure. He could see the shadowy bills of their kepis. In his army at least half would be slouch hats. And they were well-shod, struggling to keep their boots quiet and out of rhythm. His countrymen would have less of a problem, what with many of them having no shoes at all.

On and on they went. Hundreds, thousands. His gut churned, or maybe it was a low burning fear that they were headed to his home. He'd heard Father say the road bridge was out across the Harpeth. This army might get bottled up and there would be a fight in Franklin for sure. He realized he was still angry that Clara wouldn't help, but then thought of the warm patch in the bed.

The campfires back in the forest across the road were barely alive. If they were Confederate, surely they wouldn't have left the road unwatched? There was sudden movement in the trees to his right, close at hand. He began to back away. Most likely a screen for the infantry was advancing through the trees. There was no way of telling how wide it was. He risked a diagonal run across the field all the way back to Clara's house, the darkness his friend as much as it was to the escaping Union Army. He crouched behind the fence lining the drive. He couldn't see but sensed men in the field coming on.

He hurried around the house to the kitchen door but paused and rested his head against the wood. He should go to the stable and wait until it was safe to ride away. Clara was never going to see things from his side. He turned but then heard a voice in the dark.

'Here's the farmhouse. You think there's some food, Joe?'

'It's dark as pitch. Maybe some chickens.'

'Shut up, you two. Keep moving.'

Tod opened the door as quietly as he could, slipped inside and closed it. It was dark in here too. He nearly died when Clara whispered from where she'd been waiting. He felt for her, held her and put a finger to her unseen lips. Footsteps outside came closer to the door. They stopped for a few heartbeats, before moving away. They breathed out together, then Tod followed Clara upstairs and into the faint bronzed light of the solitary lamp.

*

Clara had drawn the curtains closed upstairs but left the doors to the veranda wide open. The tension held her still, Tod beside her. She heard orders softly spoken out in the night for the infantry screen to press on. When all was silent, Tod gently closed the balcony doors. 'I have to get to my army.'

'What did you see?'

'Union wagons. Union men. Hundreds, thousands, marching north in the night. They must be desperate. The men coming through your yard were flanking the march, though I doubt they could on the other side of the road.'

'Stay until morning, until they've passed.'

When Tod had gone out to the road, Clara had found herself back on the veranda, hopelessly searching the dark, waiting for a cry or a shot. She understood about his home. How could she not? But she wouldn't betray her friends or Shire. She'd moved to the kitchen, thinking she'd hear the horses if Tod tried to slip away without seeing her again. 'I wasn't sure you'd come back.'

'I left my hat.'

She put a hand on his arm. 'You'll be caught.'

'I have to try.'

'But which way will you go?' It would be safe for him tomorrow if the Union Army was gone. She needed to keep him here. 'There's no way to get to your army if it's them across the road.'

'Maybe I can get away south, beyond the end of the column. Below Spring Hill. I'll find my way.'

'Hide here.' She was losing this argument.

'I don't want to hide, Clara. I had to do that outside my own home last night. Can you imagine what that felt like?' He grabbed his hat.

'I've been there.'

'Been where?'

'At your home. I've been teaching Lena and Alice.'

'You're not making sense.'

She was over the edge now. 'I met Moscow in Franklin… you'd asked me to deliver that letter in the spring so I knew the place. I haven't…'

'Why didn't you tell me last night?' Tod sat down, evidently bewildered. It was hard to read if it was hurt or hope beyond that.

'You were tired. It's not easy to explain. It's only two days a week. I overnight with the Lotz family.'

'Well.' Tod shook his head. 'How is everybody?'

Clara sat beside him. 'That's not a quick answer if you want the particulars. It's a big family.'

'You're right. I don't have the time. I'll see them myself soon. I just don't understand…'

'Lena and Alice are both well. Alice is in charge, of course.' She gently took away his hat.

He smiled and sat forward. 'She always was a spunky little thing.'

'Lena has a softer heart. She's built for music.'

'Who else is living there? I couldn't tell.'

Clara went through them one by one, not rushing. She told him how she took dinner there sometimes. She talked about his sisters: how Annie tried to boss Frances but how

Frances bit back and was a young lady with ideas of her own; how the women of the house seemed more hopeful for the South than did Fountain or Moscow. That his brother Francis was ill down in New Orleans last they'd heard. That the house was full of noise and life. How it was so different to any home she'd ever known.

'Our people,' he said. 'The blacks. Are some still there?'

'There's John and Susie, Jack and Calfurnia. But they might flee now.'

'Father and Moscow will look out for them.'

'Moscow has been helping here.'

'Has he now.'

'He's given us advice on next year's crops. He knows people who can help.'

'Does he have anyone on his arm?'

'I don't think so.'

Tod stood. 'It's taken the wind out of me, comfort as it is to hear all is well. It's so strange to have been so close, to have to come away and then to hear the news from you of all people.' He smiled at her and squeezed her hand.

Clara opened the veranda doors and ventured a look outside. The first light was above the trees beyond the pike. A mist had settled low in the field. She could make out the end of the drive and a hint of movement on the road. The Union Army was still passing by. 'Would you like to hear more?'

'I would.'

'Would you like some coffee?'

'Alright. I'll come with you. Only don't stop. Tell me everything.'

Spring Hill, Tennessee – November 30th, 1864

Shire built up the campfire with heavy logs, banked it so it would burn long and slow. Tuck was doing the same at the next fire, ten paces along the barricade. As the other units had pulled out of the Spring Hill defenses that faced south and east, Opdycke's Brigade had been sent back through the village and then further still, over a cold creek between the armies to replace the picket. A long and lonely hour later, they stealthily withdrew to the barricade and the fires. Everyone else had gone. They were a pretense only, hopelessly spaced should the Rebels belatedly decide on a night attack. There was nothing between Shire and Hood's army, its own slumbering campfires dotted out there in the fields and hollows.

He took what warmth the fire offered until Ocks stole down the line and quietly ordered them up and back to the road. They marched through the village for the third time. Spring Hill was empty of wagons and men. There was just the cold dark height of the houses, blotting out stars that had at last shown themselves on this longest of nights. As they marched past the tollgate, Shire looked behind over the shadowy heads of the few men that followed. There was no one else. Company B was the last company, in the final regiment, in the rearguard brigade. It was enough to keep him wide awake. He wished they could march a little faster, but they left Spring Hill much like they'd entered it: listening to whispered orders and in broken step. Rebels were in the woods to the right of the pike, they were told.

A low chill mist, no higher than his waist, bloomed out of patchy fields to the left. Feeble dawn light began to show in the east. They slowed where the pike narrowed to cross another creek. Though he was travelling the other way and it was mostly dark, Shire recognized the place from when they'd walked to the station from Clara's house. 'Swap positions,' Shire whispered.

'What?' said Tuck.

'I need to be on the left.'

They managed it, though Corry swore from behind, more loudly than he should have, as he was forced to break stride. It was still night to the west. Shire looked up at the stars, unfamiliar in their pre-dawn positions. There was Cassiopeia, Clara's favorite, low to the north-west, below the North Star rather than above and flung upside down by the night. Could the universe be upside down? Maybe it was this country that was flipped, and all was even with God in heaven who was watching over the spinning-top that was America. It brought to mind the old man they'd met beyond Chattanooga last year and his whirligig.

'Walk straight,' whispered Tuck. 'It's easier if you take your nose out of the sky.'

Shire looked for Clara's drive. It was so long in coming he thought he'd missed it. She would have fled, surely; taken Moses and Mitilde up to Nashville or on to Cincinnati to find Raht. Suddenly the drive was there, the wooden rails and the gatepost. He looked left above the blanket of mist. The silhouette of the roofline stood out sharply below the stars and between the two chimney ends. Did he imagine it, or was there the faintest glow from an upstairs window? He wanted to ask Tuck, but could do nothing but dumbly stare. There *was* a light. Clara hadn't left. He was nearly at the gate and was possessed by the insane desire to race down the drive. He didn't realize he'd broken out of line until a tight hand clutched his right arm.

'No time for a house call,' said Tuck.

'Let me be.'

The slate sign sat against the gatepost, its resident chalk script visible in the starlight. *Eversholt.* Shire ripped his arm free of Tuck and stepped out to dip down and collect it.

Ocks loomed out of the murk and shoved Shire back into line without a word.

'Well, that's smart,' breathed Tuck. 'What d'you plan to do with that?'

Shire had no answer. Instead, trying to march, he awkwardly unbuttoned his greatcoat and slipped the cold slate inside.

PART III

Franklin, Tennessee – November 30th, 1864

Moscow woke in fear. He reached back for a visiting nightmare. It might have been war or perhaps the loss of his wife Callie; both had frightened him awake in the past. There was insistent knocking and raised voices from the main house, loud enough for him to hear it from the ell. His newly woken hands stumbled to light a candle and he pulled on his shirt and pants, all the while trying not to wake his children. He crossed the porch and hurried in and through Father's room. Father was at the front door, seemingly afraid to open it, suddenly an old man. Sarah was a few steps up the stairs.

Thump, thump on the door. The case-clock showed it was gone four.

'Open up! United States Army. Open up!'

Moscow glanced up past Sarah and there was a line of fearful faces above the switch-back landing banister. 'Back in your rooms. All of you. Quick now.' He should have thought to bring his pistol. The Carter front door was flanked by thin lattice windows. He lifted his lamp and peered out: darker shadows, a hint of blue, a pale and dirty hand. He nodded at Father to open the door.

Father did. A bundle of officers looked in from the step, like undertakers out to collect. The nearest officer made way for a taller man with stars on his shoulders, young but tired eyes. He took off his hat and addressed Father. 'My apologies, sir, we have need of your home for our headquarters. I'm General Cox.'

Father didn't answer so Moscow spoke up, 'How many?'

'Eight.'

This conversation was only for form. They would take the space anyway. 'My Father has a full house. We can only offer you one room.'

'If it's a good size, one is all we'll need.'

Father stood aside and Moscow directed them into the front parlor, wondering if he used to smell this much when he was a soldier. Sword belts were unbuckled, cushions stolen from sofas and chairs. Someone carried in a saddle.

'Thank you,' said Cox. 'We'll sleep now.'

There was nothing more to say. Moscow left them to it and closed the parlor door, belatedly thinking he should have told them he had two of their officers in a slave cabin. No matter.

'They might sleep, but we won't,' Father said.

Sarah went to see that the children were settled. Moscow made coffee and brought it to Father's room in time for Sarah's return. She sat on Father's bed, lifted her cup to drink but instead said, 'This is the day then. Will we stay or run?'

'We already made that decision,' said Moscow. 'But I'll try to speak with Cox when he wakes, find out their intent.'

'If he'll tell you,' said Father.

'Sarah,' said Moscow, 'at first light everyone needs to pack one change of clothes. Then if we change our minds, all they need do is follow me.'

They sat and spoke until first light. The tired and broken step of columns along the pike barely stopped. Sunrise brought another general to the parlor. Schofield, head of the Army of the Ohio. Father wondered aloud if Lincoln himself might pay a visit after breakfast.

'You picked a soldier's spot when you built this house,'

said Moscow. 'On the crest of a rise, next to the road covering the run into town.'

After Schofield departed, Moscow waited by the door and put a hand on Cox's arm as he made to leave. 'General, I have nine children here and a squad of sisters. Should I stay? Will you make a fight?'

Cox turned while putting on his hat. 'I'm told you're a Confederate colonel.'

'Paroled, which makes me no more than a citizen and a widower looking out for his family.'

A moment's stare. 'I'll trust to that then, in return for your hospitality. I need to keep this room for the day.'

'We're used to Union soldiers in our town, General. I just need to know if today we should leave them to it.'

'As to that, I can't guarantee you'd find your home whole on your return.' He pulled on worn white leather gloves. 'We don't plan to stay another night, Colonel Carter, but we'll have to front up while we collect the whole army in. I don't know General Hood's mind on the matter, but if there's a fight, it'll be my fight. Schofield's put me in charge of the defenses. So, if you'll excuse me, I need to be about my business.'

The household was up and busy soon after, all noise and fret. Moscow scrambled some eggs then took himself down toward town. The pike was thick with wagons, many more already pulled aside and lined up twenty deep on the open ground immediately down from the Carter house. When he reached the first homes, he found most every family on their front porch surveying the deluge of blue soldiers. On the pike there wasn't room for a threadbare nosebag between the tailboard of one wagon and lead mules of the next. Wagons and teams parked between houses. Garden fences were pushed to the ground to make room.

He found Mary Larsson's mother, Elsa, eighty if she was a day, lost and fearful in the throng. He steered her gently back to her porch and held her by the hand until Mary came crying to the door.

In the town square he passed a squad of soldiers laid flat to the side of the courthouse steps, dead to the busy world around them. The square itself was full of still more wagons fronted by tired animals, heads down and eyes closed. Muleteers stretched limbs and arched backs then ambled toward the river as Moscow did to see the state of the bridges. There was any number of officer engineers, pointing and shouting, wading into the cold Harpeth where needed.

The road bridge had been destroyed earlier in the war and the 'make do' fixes washed away by high water only a couple of weeks ago. The small wooden piers that remained in place were being sawn down to the waterline. Evidently, there were hopes of repair but, unless Yankees were miracle workers, that was more than a day's work. The rail bridge was a better prospect: all they needed to do was plank over the rails. A blue swarm was busy destroying Widow Nolen's modest riverside home and carrying off her torn-apart walls to that purpose. She must have left. Otherwise, she'd have been out beating them off with the thick end of a garden hoe. He walked on to look over the ford. The river had fallen in the last day or two and was passable for a horse or a tall man, but the banks were too steep for wagons or artillery. He listened in to the engineers discussing the need for a scarp on each side. That would be quick work with enough men, and there was no shortage of those.

He'd stayed overlong. He walked away thinking that cavalry and infantry might get wetly across but they wouldn't abandon the artillery and this biblical exodus of wagons. Even if they had the rail bridge planked by noon, it would be well after dark before all the wagons could cross. The plain fact was, if Hood wanted a battle, he had the Union backed up against the river.

Moscow hurried back up the pike just short of a run, only slowing at Dr Cliffe's house, where there was a plethora of officers in and out. Schofield must be in there trying to work out an escape. Moscow needed to get back home. Below his house a major and captain stood nose to nose beside the pike, madly disputing who had rights to a half-acre of Father's open land. A sergeant pushed them apart. Above the noise of the mules and the men, he could hear hammer blows and wrenching wood. Maybe he should collect a traitorous spade himself and hurry back to help scarp the riverbank and get the Yankees the hell out of his town. He knew his side in this fight, and it wasn't that of either army.

*

'Sir.'

Frank looked down on a rag-tag soldier who might have been twice his age, blackened and missing teeth, squint eyes below a worn and stained slouch hat. The man placed a filthy hand on Ashley's neck and leaned into the horse like he was no more than a split rail-fence. 'Sir, are you expectin' us to march ag'in all day? Only we done caught the rabbit once.'

By rights, Frank should beat him away with his whip or ride him down. Other men were watching, wordlessly asking the same question. They deserved an answer from someone. 'I don't profess to know,' said Frank. 'The rabbit slipped the snare, didn't he? We're obliged to set another or run him to ground.'

The soldier placed his forehead onto Ashley's neck, then after a weary moment turned back to the road and got into column. This army was tired and it was angry. The men marched hunched over, like boys sent on a funless errand by their mother. A few of them looked Frank directly in the eye as if he personally had let the Yankees escape. His lowly rank didn't matter to them, he was an officer, and it was the officers and generals who were at fault. He was angry himself. The opportunity for his first fight had come and gone. Would he ever get his chance, or would Hood lead them to the gates of Nashville only to be chased home when the Union armies came together, bigger and stronger?

There'd been no orders in the night and no dawn attack. After first light, an hour passed, then another. A. P. Stewart's Corps had been given the lead. As part of Cheatham's Corps, Gist's Brigade had been obliged to wait. Finally, the order came to move into Spring Hill. They'd found the barricades unmanned and the campfires cold and untended. During the night, the Yankee army had dissolved like this morning's mist. Every man, Frank included, figured out the story for himself: that while they'd slept, Schofield's army had passed silently by. God had placed victory onto their palms, but they had failed to close their hands.

The officers were every bit as frustrated as the men. He'd seen the usually gregarious Gist riding alone, not a word for anyone. Others were more vocal. *Cheatham should have forced home the attack*, they said. *Why hadn't Hood been on the field?* Accounts filtered down that Hood was angrier than everyone else put together. The rumor was he'd torn into Cheatham and Brown, shouting that this army could only fight from behind the safety of breastworks.

As he rode out of Spring Hill beside the marching men,

Frank heard rifles to the north. Forrest's cavalry perhaps, harassing the escaping Yankees. Far away though. It had become a bright blue day, one that should have lifted his spirits, but there were thousands of men between Frank and the fighting. He was stuck in the middle of Cheatham's Corps, which, despite the fine day, marched under its own cloud of shame and recrimination.

The column bunched and slowed at a narrow bridge north of the village. Frank walked Ashley forward. This mood wouldn't do. They still had the Yankees on the run. Encouraged by the thought, he lifted his eyes and ahead stood Tod, his gray, Rosencrantz, somewhat ragged and dirty, cropping the grass. Beside Tod was a woman in a plain green dress, her dark hair shining in the sun. She was quietly collecting hat-lifts from almost every soldier that passed. Tod hailed him. Who was she? They shared a slow moment of recognition. No doubt he must have seemed as out of place to her as she did to him.

'Frank,' said Tod. 'I said, hello. There's no need to stare like the rank and file.'

Frank slid from Ashley and took off his hat. 'My apologies, Tod – Captain Carter. I was surprised at your company. It's a pleasure to see you again, Mrs Ridgmont.'

She looked surprised too, perhaps saddened as well. 'Clara will do, Frank, as we're old travelling companions. I had no idea you were with this army.'

'Would someone explain?' asked Tod. He led his horse a few steps down the drive to be further from the column. Clara and Frank followed on.

Clara managed a smile. 'I know Frank through his father, George, who gave me away at my wedding.'

'Trenholm. Of course,' said Tod, 'but I'd no idea the two

of you had met.'

'We visited Ducktown together when the war was barely begun,' Clara said. 'Frank was a boy then. Now look at you. Do you remember Ducktown, Frank?'

Frank did. The sulphur air, climbing the slagheaps. They'd both stood and listened to Father and Clara's husband trying to persuade the copper miners to join the war. 'That seems an age ago, doesn't it?' He recalled that Taylor was dead. 'I'm sorry for your loss.'

The smile withered and Clara looked away. 'That part of Tennessee wasn't good to any of us. And now the war has followed me, though I had you safely back in Charleston. George must worry over you.'

'Oh, I expect so. He delayed me joining the army long enough, but we haven't lost a Trenholm yet, so far as I know. And Charleston's not the safe place it was. Father's in Richmond.' He wanted to ask Tod how he came to be here but sensed something unsaid, or something waiting to be said.

A fife and drum band passed, loud in the cold air. The three of them waited for the music to move away. 'I should get back on the road,' said Frank.

'Hold on,' said Tod. 'I'll come with you. You can tell me where to find my division.'

'Bate is behind, but I'd like the company, if Clara can spare you?'

Clara looked for all the world like she couldn't. They returned to the road, the column marching by. Clara became oddly distracted, surveying the ground beside her gate as if something was missing.

'What is it?' asked Tod.

'The sign for my home. It's gone.'

'Sorry, Clara,' said Frank. 'These men are magpies for

anything and everything.'

'It doesn't matter,' she said, though Frank could see that plainly it did. 'Just something else I've lost.' She took Tod's hand and they seemed on the cliff edge of an embrace, but then Tod looked at Frank and at the marching men. He freed himself to pick up Rosencrantz's loose rein and pulled himself up into his saddle.

Frank lifted his hat and mounted too. 'My apologies I can't stay longer. Father would want me to pass on his compliments. I hope we'll meet again soon.'

Clara took a step backwards. 'You must take care. Both of you.' She covered her mouth with the back of her hand. Tod led on and they fell in at the pace of the column.

'I'm sorry,' said Frank, 'maybe I shouldn't have stopped.'

'How could you not?'

'I didn't like to ask, but how do you know Clara?'

'Same reason as everything else in our lives, Frank. The war.' Tod looked over his shoulder and slowed, as if he were being pulled in several directions at once. 'I need to get back to my brigade. What happened yesterday? I was stuck on Clara's farm most of the night with what seemed like the whole Union Army marching by outside.'

'We let them get away is what happened.' Frank told him the whole sorry story. 'Hood's furious. He's blamed Cheatham, Brown and Cleburne for not pressing the attack.'

'Cleburne? He's the best general Hood has.'

They passed other farms and the occasional roadside house. More often than not, people were outside, waving the soldiers on, handing out tobacco and any food they could muster. The bands struck up and the mood of the army lifted to the familiar melodies. The trudge became a march. The enemy's debris lay abandoned to the side of the road:

knapsacks, whole wagons tipped over, mules shot in their traces. Exhausted Union stragglers sat under guard in twos and threes. At Thompson's Station there was any number of burnt-out wagons and a destroyed depot. Ahead rose a high line of hills painted in late fall colors and bathed in sunshine.

To Frank's surprise, Tod stayed with him long into the morning. He was glad of it, but Tod was unsettled, governed by some anxious need. For a long time, Frank let him be. He watched Tod greet a whole family known to him, who were leaning on a fence-rail. They handed up some cornbread and it was Tod's first smile since Frank had collected him. As they rode on, Frank asked the question he'd held back on these last several miles. 'Did you make it home?'

That killed the new mood. 'I did, right into my backyard. Close enough to see my father and my brother and hear my sisters sing, but not to speak to anyone. Too many damn Yankees.'

'Well,' said Frank, wishing he'd not asked, 'you know this country and I don't, but if I understand alright from the maps Gist showed me, Franklin is the other side of these hills. We'll be there soon enough. This is good cornbread.'

'It is, isn't it.' Tod stared at his half-eaten chunk as if it were a family treasure. 'I'd best ride back down the line. Smith will be wondering where in the hell I am. So long, Frank.'

*

Emerson Opdycke had come to understand himself better in this war. It was a blessing of sorts. He'd always owned a temper stoked by a strong self-regard; he wasn't blind to that. War exposed people's frailties as well as their strengths. More than once this year he'd had to pen a letter of apology for an indiscreet outburst. That didn't make him wrong, just forthright, candid, outspoken. Now, here between Spring Hill and Franklin, Wagner had him ready to boil over. Keep busy, he told himself – as if he had any choice. Keep busy, Emerson, and stay in control of your worst self. If only he could talk to Lucy. She would patiently hear out his frustrations then gently turn him around to face the day.

His two hardworking cannon boomed again. Ben didn't so much as twitch below him. Lieutenant Stephenson knew his business. No need to intervene there. The section had reported to him not long after first light and were starting to pay dividends, keeping Rebel skirmishers pinned behind a low wall at the bottom of the slope. Halfway up these familiar hills south of Franklin, it was Opdycke's Brigade alone that held back the thrust of Hood's army.

Behind him, higher up, Wagner's two other brigades were resting and cooking breakfast, sending over nothing more than the occasional drift of meaty smoke. Opdycke's men hadn't had the chance to so much as brew a pot of coffee. Wagner should have rotated his brigades long before now. Opdycke's men shouldn't be left to do all the work.

He was operating a two-regiment battle line astride the pike, facing south with a good number of skirmishers out front. That had been the formation all the long morning. He'd build a second line with his other regiments a few hundred yards to the rear, wait until the Rebel dismounted cavalry deployed to attack, and then neatly withdraw the first line through the second. It required absolute vigilance. Two regiments didn't make a wide front, just enough to protect the road. He had to be mindful of the flanks. The Rebels constantly felt for a weakness. The men were as tired as he was and had the added burden of herding the plentiful stragglers from Schofield's whole army. He'd given orders to deal with them harshly, no matter how exhausted they were. His own men had endured a long march yesterday, been in line to defend Spring Hill through the night and now this rearguard action. They'd barely eaten the whole time. What was Wagner thinking?

Two white-tailed deer broke cover not fifty feet down the slope and sprung east. On another day they'd have been taken down in an instant, but no one was giving up a bullet today.

Opdycke understood that Lane and Conrad were utterly fresh to brigade command, promoted so recently that Wagner didn't want to test them on so difficult a task as this rearguard action. And his own brigade was the strongest in any case. But there was a limit. His men couldn't be worked into the ground. Wagner had fought well to defend Spring Hill, but when Opdycke had seen him this morning, he'd looked drained. That wasn't like Wagner. He was hardly an old soldier but appeared to be wearing the last two days worse than most. His wife was ill, of course; that was common knowledge, but there was nothing Wagner could do about that. They had the Union to defend. Opdycke impressed on Wagner that his men were tired and hungry, virtually spent, but nothing had come of it.

He rode out to his eastern flank, where the 125th Ohio were part of the current front, and told Bates to angle back the extreme left of the line. There was no sign of Rebels out that way, but they'd be there somewhere. An order arrived from Wagner that they were to pull out of the hills and into Franklin. Thank God. Rest at last. He'd have to keep up a front though. He gave the orders and cantered up the road to pick out the best spot for the next line. A half hour later they were nearly through the hills. He'd barely had his first glimpse of Franklin across the plain when Wagner's order was countermanded. They were to hold a line atop the hills, with no mention of Opdycke's Brigade being rotated. He closed his eyes and took a slow breath lest he explode at the fresh-faced staff officer.

Back they went into the hills, quickly, before the Rebels could claim the ground. He positioned his men astride the road again, collected Bates and rode to the top of Breezy Hill. 'Dear Lord,' said Bates. From their viewpoint they could see not only the Columbia Pike but the Lewisburg Pike as well, converging from the south-east: two wheel-spokes aiming at the hub of Franklin. A cold breeze rose up the hills. Each pike held a long and thick column of gray infantry as far as Opdycke's watery eyes could see. Thousands upon thousands of men. Fife and drum; crisp orders. This was an army with its head up. Opdycke couldn't hold both roads. He doubted he'd be able to hold this one for more than fifteen minutes.

'Bates, get over to our light artillery and order them to lay some fire down on the road. Then get back to your regiment. Quick now.' There wasn't time to find damn Wagner and tell him. There, his general had him swearing as well. He sent a rider instead. He needed to get busy again.

*

Shire changed his grip on his bayonet, the socket awkward in the palm of his right hand. He came at the soldier from behind. A strong kitchen knife with a decent handle would be better for this work. His target appeared to be young; it was hard to tell from the back. He was certainly fresh to the war, judging by the darker hue of the uniform and the oversized skillet that swung loosely below his bulging knapsack. He stumbled forward. Shire caught up and gripped his shoulder.

Before the boy could turn, Shire slid the bayonet in behind the blanket roll and sawed up through a shoulder strap. 'Stay still.' He spoke through clenched teeth, as if this boy was the single source of his woes. There was a certain grim pleasure in this work, a mild catharsis for his own two years of suffering. He stepped sideways and cut the second strap. The pack fell to the ground. Shire tossed it off the road.

Previous victims this morning had struggled more. They'd wanted to dig into their pack for letters from sweethearts, food or money. They had to be prodded with the bayonet or dragged on by their hair. Kind words didn't work as well as a kick to the rear. He'd lost count of how many times he'd had to march away from Clara on account of this war, so why should each deadweight, poor excuse for a soldier be allowed to linger? This boy should be thankful it wasn't Sergeant Ocks that was setting about him. The order to be harsh with the stragglers had come down from Opdycke, they were told. The boy twisted and walked unsteadily backward for a few paces, the hurt and pain in his eyes aimed at Shire, who growled, 'I can leave you for Hood, if you like? No? Get a shake on then!' This was army love, Shire thought. Keep this green boy moving or the Rebels would gobble him up in short order, and that might be the last of him; he'd be lost to the world, sick and starving in a prison stockade far from home. A scratch from a bayonet or a kick in the backside, either was a good exchange. It was hard to leave anger out of it. He'd lost track of when he'd last slept and had eaten only hardtack since the crossroads the evening before last, Tuck's potatoes and ham now only a wistful memory.

They hit the hills proper but were soon ordered off the road again, the stragglers left to stumble on without encouragement. Opdycke had the whole brigade dancing.

Two at a time the regiments turned to form a battle line facing south, letting the other regiments hurry north until it was their turn again. It was hard work forming the line only to dissolve it again ten minutes later and return to the road. A cannon fired from up the hill. The shell screamed overhead to explode somewhere out of sight. Rice and Ocks shouted at the company and they raced at the double-quick along the edge of a forest fronting a good-sized field. Tuck panted beside Shire. Corry and Cleves were ahead and Cleves had his hand in the small of Corry's back, helping him along, keeping him balanced. Something about that caught in Shire's throat. He was cast back to Kennesaw and the murder he'd done to save Corry from Wick. They all looked out for Corry, Cleves more than most. They all looked out for each other every God-given day. He was so tired. As the company halted and the two-man column turned to face south, he was tempted to close his eyes, if only for a few seconds.

Tuck was before him and the front-rank was told to take a knee. His friend had been quiet the whole morning. They'd been preoccupied of course, but that didn't usually stop Tuck from a running commentary. Maybe he was lost inside again. It wasn't the time for it, not when he should be sighting Rebels down the length of his barrel. Now he was fumbling in his cartridge box though they were all loaded from the last stop. Tuck fished out something bigger than a cartridge and slipped it into his jacket pocket. Shire caught the flash of red enamel and knew it was the doorknob. He felt a stab of guilt; he'd turned Tuck around in Nashville. From this distance that seemed in large part for himself, a selfish thing, born of need rather than care.

Across the open ground in front of them came the 24th Wisconsin. They'd been doing a do-si-do with them since sun-up, melting through each other's lines then making for the road behind, each time a measure more away from Clara. She'd be safe, he told himself. This was a Rebel county; they weren't about to hurt their own people. It didn't sit right though, abandoning her to the wrong side of the line, back with dead Taylor, back with Tod, back with the wicked side of America's argument where he could do nothing for her. He'd lived most of the war with that line between them. How long would it be this time?

The 24th seemed in a hurry. A smiling soldier stepped toward Shire and he recognized Corporal Cobb from Nashville, despite a growth of stubble. They'd traded nods from time to time. 'They's tight to us,' said Cobb as he stepped by. 'Keep your heads up.'

Mason called from his left. 'Everyone loaded?'

Corry fumbled his ramrod.

'Easy now. They ain't here yet.' Mason looked solid as always, as if he didn't need sleep or food. 'Take some water if you have any, boys.'

Shire had none.

Their own pickets fired and then fell back through the lines as well. Lonely gray soldiers appeared from the facing forest and came into the open.

'Steady,' said Ocks. 'They're too scattered and too far.'

Shire had fired one shot all morning. Bates would have them put up a front, force the Rebels to slow down and deploy, and then he'd order them to fall back. This time there were more of them emerging from the trees and coming forward. Another shell flew overhead and struck high in the branches beyond the Rebels. Captain Bates was to the front on his diminutive horse. 'Let's give them a taste, Rice.'

'With pleasure, sir.'

Bates rode back behind the line. A handful of shots from the Rebels flew high. They'd edged too close, testing the Union resolve. 'You've picked the wrong regiment,' said Shire.

'What's that?' asked Cleves.

'Aim!' shouted Ocks.

Shire lifted his rifle above the right of Tuck's head.

'Fire!'

The familiar rip of powder along the line.

'Reload!'

By the time the smoke cleared the Rebels had shrunk back into the trees, but for two still grey figures left on the cold grass.

They waited a few minutes before they fell back through the 24th, which was in place behind a straight ditch, another two hundred yards further from Clara. The land lifted into some higher hills and they were ordered onto the road. It must have been past midday and there was no sign of relief from another brigade, no chance to find water. Shire was out of hardtack but it would be impossible to eat without water anyway.

They marched hard on the pike, up and through the hills only to be sent right back and put into line again. 'Whose orders are these?' grumbled Cleves. 'I'd like to go one way or t'other, although right now I'd much prefer the t'other.'

Shire was on his knee in the battle line this time but even so, from this high in the hills, he could see clearly down the Columbia Pike. There was a snake down there, a gray snake lifting red flags into the blue Tennessee sky, twisting its way through the farmland and into the hills. He tried to swallow but his throat was raw and dry.

From behind Shire, Tuck spoke for the first time in hours, his voice distant and calm. 'They have a fine swagger about them, don't you think? Like they have a country dance to get to and a girl with loose hair waitin'.'

Mercifully, they were ordered to pull back once more. Tired as Shire was, tired as his regiment and brigade were, they marched smartly enough back through the hills a second time and down along the pike, down the northern facing grade to look out across the low plain toward Franklin. Memories crowded in on Shire. These were the slopes he'd seen from the train before Bowman had struck. This was Winstead Hill, that he'd raced up in the spring snow last year – his first desertion – after Ocks had told him that Father was dead. More than two miles away, on the edge of the town and across the looping Harpeth, sat Fort Granger, which he and the regiment had labored to build. And ahead of them, across empty autumn fields drinking in the rare and final sun of this November, at the end of the great white road, was Franklin: a handful of spires, neat and tidy houses of brick and wood, a barricade busy with blue soldiers. It wasn't his home, though it had been one of sorts for one cold spring. He'd been made to do some growing up in Franklin. Now it offered water and food, sleep and safety. That sounded like home.

*

The high, two-story Carter cotton gin was naked. Above its stubby brick corner pillars, almost every last weatherboard had been stripped away by eager Yankee hands. Only the poplar beam skeleton had been left to hold the shingled roof. The machinery and screw-press were bare for all to see. It seemed to Moscow that his father beside him, who surveyed the destruction as the mass of Union soldiers worked around them, was similarly diminished. The stoop in his back was more pronounced; there was a new weariness about his shoulders and neck.

'It's only boarding, Father. We'll reclaim it when they're gone, nail it back up. No more than a long day's work. You'll see.'

A soldier used the butt of his rifle to crash and splinter the last board free. He carried it to add into the barricade, a rough frame onto which a busy line of toiling soldiers heaped dirt, excavating a ditch and raising an earthwork parapet with the proceeds. A vocal captain organized men forward of the gin in the construction of an embrasure. There were two cannon waiting next to the gin to be slipped into their new home, four more already in place thirty paces away and immediately beside the pike. All of them would have a clear line of fire over the fields once every man in the Army of the Ohio was inside Franklin, though that work was not yet done. The pike carried a solid and endless column, but Moscow could no longer hear their march over the chorus of axe, pick and saw that surrounded him.

Father spoke while continuing to watch. 'Is it always like this?'

'Like what?'

'It's not the gin I mind the most, more that they set their spades into my land without so much as a how d'you do. Were you the same when you were soldiering?'

Moscow had not expected to have to defend himself. In truth this was on an utterly different scale to anything he'd seen early in the war. The line of works being built swept away toward the Lewisburg Pike, crowded the whole way with soldiers become busy blue ants. The Carter cotton gin was far from the only casualty. It gutted him as much as it did Father, but where did that get you?

'Being polite about our property ain't gonna save them

when the bullets start flying. I never had cause to, but I'd have done the same.'

'We should have left,' said Father. 'I wouldn't have had to see this.'

Moscow put a hand to Father's shoulder. 'Think of it this way. It might be our gin that saves us once they've finished. From Winstead Hill, Hood will see a strong set of works, cannon and infantry that can rake anything he sends forward. He'll take one look and have to work around the flanks.' He tried to sound convincing despite his own harbored doubts. 'Cox says the Union is pulling out in the night. Hood will chase him on up to Nashville and leave us to patch this up.'

There was a disbelieving look in Father's doleful eyes.

'Anyway,' said Moscow, 'we made our choice. Let's get back to the house.'

They angled back toward the road, but getting there was no easy matter. Every square yard was occupied by a soldier or a horse. Or both. No one made way. When they got there, they had to wait behind the four cannon while the latest batch of weary soldiers trudged in. Moscow picked his moment and hurried Father across. Their roadside fence was gone and the front garden had disappeared under two headquarters tents, one in busy use and the other just now having its canvas stretched taut.

He led Father around the side of the house only to find several squads of men fallen out and sat with their backs to his home. A company cook was giving out a whiskey ration in lieu of breakfast. The men drank it like medicine. No smiles, no thanks.

If he'd hoped that coming home would help Father feel better, he was wrong. On the back porch all of the family were huddled together, sisters and children watching on, variously sullen, tearful or angry, as still more soldiers wrecked their smaller sheds and outhouses. They were building a secondary barricade the other side of the farm office and the smokehouse, right along the line of the garden fence. The war couldn't get any closer. Frances came down the porch steps to hug Father; Moscow reached out to pull a weepy Lena to his chest. A tall officer emerged from the house, set his hat straight and spat a stream of tobacco juice out into the yard.

Sarah had such hate in her eyes that Moscow reached out and gripped her arm. 'It's alright, sister,' he said. 'We have to endure it. They'll be gone by the morning.'

*

Ben plodded along the pike, his head heavy and low to the cold white stone. Opdycke rode him at the head of the brigade, exhausted but proud. Proud of his men who'd formed the rearguard all the way from Spring Hill and proud of himself. He knew he'd handled his brigade skillfully and in response his regiments had fought well, despite Wagner affording them no relief. The 125th, the regiment he'd raised in Ohio and for so long his only care, marched behind him. He was leading them back toward Franklin through familiar farmland, back to a place where he'd molded them into a fighting regiment before their hot march to Chattanooga last year, before the hard slog down to Atlanta this spring and summer past. How strange to have fought full circle.

He struggled to sit up straight. In the distance he could see a formidable line of works which were still being improved. News reached him that Cox was in charge of the defenses. That was good. Cox would leave nothing to chance and would hear him out on Wagner. He couldn't let that pass.

Wagner might have a solid command record, but it had been self-evident that Opdycke's Brigade needed rest. Instead, there'd been no let-up whatsoever.

Close and to the left he recognized Privet Knob. He used to have his skirmishers push out to there and beyond when he was garrisoned in the town. Wagner had pulled Lane's Brigade off the road and placed them around the small hill's rocky base. At last Opdycke's men would get behind another brigade. A mile before town he'd be robbed of the honor of being the last unit in, but people would know what he had done. Cox would know. Opdycke would put it in his report: how Wagner had mishandled him all day, left his men tired, hungry and worn out.

He looked over his shoulder. Bates rode close behind and then came Lieutenant Rice on foot. They really should find Rice a horse, ex-cavalryman as he was. Sergeant Ocks was beside Rice; the buttoned-up, heavyset Englishman looked as if he'd just this moment emerged fresh and washed from his tent, rather than been up the long night and fighting a retreat since soon after dawn. Privates Tuck and Shire were behind Ocks, and then the long weary column of his brigade stretched halfway back to the hills. *His brigade.* Over two thousand men under his word. He was proud of all of them, but he reserved something more than pride for the 125th. His Tigers.

They passed beyond Privet Knob and Opdycke received a distant wave from Lane up the slope. It had about it the hint of an apology, as if Lane were admitting that he'd been let off lightly this morning and Opdycke had taken the brunt. It was as well he wasn't closer to the road. Opdycke might have barked out his frustration even if it wasn't Lane's doing. One more mile, Opdycke told himself. One more mile and we'll be safe inside those works.

Conrad's Brigade, the third of Wagner's Division, was in column ahead. Opdycke watched in puzzlement as a half-mile before Franklin they marched east off the road and deployed along a barely perceptible rise. It was one thing for Wagner to put Lane on Privet's Knob; what artillery Lane possessed could command the ground to his front and he could observe the Rebels if they came on. But what use was it to place Conrad in the open such a modest distance from the works?

Wagner trotted down the pike toward Opdycke, his staff officers and the brigade flag in his wake. Opdycke had been told Wagner had taken a fall earlier in the day and there was a crude walking stick across his pommel. He had no sympathy for the man but tried to suppress his ire; he'd hoped to get into Franklin without sight of him.

'Colonel Opdycke.' Wagner wheeled his horse to ride beside him.

'General Wagner.'

'When you come abreast with Conrad's men, I want you to wheel west off the road and extend his battle line to make a two-brigade front.'

Opdycke blew out a deep breath. 'General, my men have fought all morning with no support from your other brigades. They are exhausted, sir, and need to eat.'

'We're all tired, Emerson. Hood won't make allowances for that and neither will I.'

Whatever angry fuel had been smoldering inside Opdycke burst into flame. 'That's been plain enough. We've had no relief though it was entirely manageable.' He glared across at Wagner, saw his head lift, the whiskers of his shovel beard draw tight around the mouth. They were nearing Conrad's position.

'We all have our orders, Opdycke.' It was said in a

measured tone. 'Yours are to form line of battle alongside Conrad. Am I understood?'

Opdycke shortened Ben's rein and encouraged him to walk on. 'Sir, in the event that Hood attacks, that position is utterly untenable. There's no cover whatsoever.' He fought to keep his voice calm, but largely failed. 'My brigade could delay him in the hills, but on open ground your whole division would be instantly outflanked. And to what end? Our works are less than half a mile away. It's reckless. You are simply prolonging the torture of my men. I will not suffer it.'

A staff officer tried to intervene but Wagner cut him off. The battle of wills walked on in full view of the men and past the point where Opdycke should have led his men from the road. Conrad's nearest regiment watched on bemused as their sister brigade marched by, their division commander being dressed down by a mere colonel. 'This is insubordination,' Wagner spat. 'It will be the end of your career.'

'But not the end of my brigade. I'm telling you my men are unserviceable without rest. Will you not listen, man? If you prefer, we can continue this discussion in front of General Cox.'

'This is not a discussion,' said Wagner, angling his horse in a failed attempt to block Opdycke's path. 'It's an order.'

*

Shire squared his shoulders and stepped out along the pike. Tuck did the same beside him, as did the rest of Company B. They had no choice. Not if they were going to keep pace with Opdycke and in earshot of the running quarrel their colonel was conducting with General Wagner. In truth, Shire thought, the column marching briskly and in time worked somewhat against Opdycke's loud and repeated argument that they were on their last legs. But if their colonel was putting his military career on the line by going into battle with Wagner on their behalf, they were more than prepared to show their support by getting behind the defenses of Franklin as quickly as possible.

Shire had never seen the like. Opdycke walked Ben briskly forward while Wagner angrily sawed his horse back and forth alongside, spitting reprimands and threats in ever more colorful terms, at one particularly ill-tempered moment half-brandishing the walking stick he was riding with. Opdycke gave as good as he got. Conrad's Brigade was left behind, exposed out on the plain. Shire could see it was a blunder. Any soldier with a month's service could. Up ahead, Ocks glanced back, caught Shire's eye and rolled his own. It would be funny if it wasn't so desperate. Shire needed to rest as did everyone else, but he didn't want to lose his colonel. Opdycke was a cantankerous, stiff-limbed martinet, but he'd seen them through thick and thin. There was no one he'd rather fight for.

Wagner whipped his horse forward and positioned himself across the road. Opdycke blithely walked Ben around and Wagner was obliged to catch up again. He unbuttoned his holster but plainly thought better of it and instead restarted the argument. It seemed to Shire that the battle of wills had nowhere to go unless Wagner chose to have Opdycke arrested.

He looked beyond them to the steadily approaching town. To the right there was a long arc of earth and log entrenchments stretching and bending away toward the Harpeth, a wide ditch to the front. As he came closer, he recognized what had been the Carter cotton gin he'd worked at so long ago, a little way to the right of the road. It was no more than a square wooden skeleton, two cannon poking through the barricades to its front. He had a sudden thought of Kennesaw and the works they'd attacked there; the day he'd been saved and captured by Tod. Here he was back at Tod's home. Surely that must be some sort of cosmic clue: maybe nothing more than proof that God had a penchant for the preposterous. But they'd be inside the works this time. Thank the Lord for that. As Opdycke was presently reiterating to Wagner, Hood wasn't about to attack these defenses. The line was too strong. So why leave what amounted to several thousand pieces of blue bait out in plain view?

They marched in where the pike cut through the works and past four more cannon. It felt like coming inside from a hailstorm. Shire smiled across to Tuck but his friend didn't raise one in return. It wasn't only that Shire was behind the defenses that lifted his mood. A short way ahead was the red roof and smart brick of the Carter house, somewhere familiar in a world that had been anything but these last two years. Before the house was a second line of works, less formidable than the first and running along in front of the Carters' outbuildings and the smokehouse such that the main garden was between the two lines. It was thick with soldiers. Some busy on the works, others resting or cooking.

He heard a woman's voice, fierce and shrill, and found her among the toiling soldiers, tugging a girl-child away from under the swinging blades and picks and back toward the house. The Carters had not run, then.

The Opdycke-Wagner show finally ran out of steam. Both men stopped beside the road while the column marched on. Perhaps it had dawned on Wagner that Opdycke had successfully led him behind the lines. If he couldn't stop him before that point, he was hardly going to get him to about face and march back out. Opdycke looked no less angry than when the argument had started and prepared to continue the debate all the way to Nashville if Wagner had a mind to it.

As Shire marched by, he heard Wagner growl, 'Consider yourself in reserve,' as if trying to regain a half-ounce of his lost authority. 'If Hood attacks, you'll have to fight where you think best.'

Opdycke gave a lackluster salute and urged his horse on beside the men. For a moment, Shire was free to look over at the Carter house with its neat stepped gables. The roadside fence had disappeared and the front of the house was partly hidden by two large command tents. He could see between them to the door, of normal enough size and bracketed each side by a tall side window and a skinny Grecian column. There was a half-circle window above. He'd always considered the entrance a touch pretentious; it wasn't the biggest of houses. Yet somehow it managed to be homely and a little stylish at the same time. He thought again of Tod, his lifesaver and his friend for so short a time. The door opened and officers of rank emerged. It occurred to him that the house also served as Clara's school of sorts. He felt a stab of jealousy for all that implied: that Clara wasn't done with Tod Carter. Far from it. She'd moved halfway across Tennessee to be near his home and somehow inveigled her way inside it before Tod had even returned. If Shire's army pressed on to Nashville in the days ahead, there was nothing to stop them revisiting their romance beneath those gables. He was powerless to do anything about that. He'd had his chance when he and Clara had danced but, in the end, had said nothing.

Beside him, Tuck scratched the back of his neck and said, 'Well, here we are again.'

Bates led them on and the road fell slowly downhill

toward the town. After a couple of hundred yards, he took them off the road to the west and the 125th tucked into the open swale in the lee of the Carters' hill. With the rest of the Army of the Ohio already in town, Opdycke had to split the brigade's regiments on either side of the road to find room.

Shire and the squad collapsed to the cold but oddly comfortable grass, allowing weariness to claim them. The air was filled with the smell of fried pork and coffee. The whole regiment was low on rations and Captain Bates detailed twenty tired men to hurry and fetch some. Cleves found the energy to build a small fire. Shire wanted to sleep but was too hungry. At least they were inside the lines at Franklin, he thought; safe for the first time in many long days.

*

The grounds of the Harrison house were awash with majors, colonels, staff officers and lesser generals. Tod steered Rosencrantz through the crowd. Benton Smith had gone inside, though whether Tod's brigade commander was currently in Hood's presence, Tod didn't know. He'd seen Cleburne and Cheatham hurry on in, answering the summons, and here was Forrest arriving amid a dash of cavalry officers. That man never did anything slowly. Forrest swung down from his horse. The throng parted to give him a clear march to the white portico, as if he were old world royalty. He pulled off his gloves and took the steps two at a time.

Tod wondered where the Harrisons might be. On a normal day, in a normal year, he could have spent a happy hour with them. In point of fact, today seemed to have an abundance of hours, each one of them weighted and slow. It was getting on for mid-afternoon, but he'd slept so little last night and been up early before his long talk with Clara. That was still to settle out: how his Franklin world of nephews and nieces, the farm and the school, had collided with his Clara world of riverboats, lovemaking and some yet-to-be-defined future. Two universes of hope, until now held apart. It felt as if it was yesterday that he'd said goodbye to her, but that was only a few treacle hours ago and only a handful of miles back down the road. War could have that effect on time. Like a squeeze-box: squash it into an instant or draw it out like your last waking breath of the day. Fancy, the Harrisons' house, headquarters to Hood's army. How bizarre. He wondered where the Union command had pitched up.

Rosencrantz was tired. Tod dismounted and led him away. He nodded or saluted where he had to, not wanting to speak with anyone. He'd learned enough and no doubt would learn more when Smith came back out. He found a chestnut tree, took off Rosencrantz's saddle, bridle and bit, fed him a few handfuls of cool winter grass and let him rest. It was only yesterday at sunset that they were riding for home. Then they'd had to carefully pick their way, but now the country swarmed with troops. Hood had sent A. P. Stewart's Corps over to the east around the base of Breezy Hill to flank out the stubborn rearguard Union troops who'd been defending the Columbia Pike. Opdycke's Brigade, it was rumored. That meant Shire. Today, it was hard to feel anything much about that. Tod didn't want hate in his heart, not this near to home. What past hatred there had been had never stuck anyway. That Englishman had his own corner to fight. A part of him wished Shire well and hoped he was marching with his friends straight for Nashville.

It was the same with Clara. Of course, there was desire there, even love, but there was no space for it, not on this day when the hills of his childhood were crowded with guns, when this war had led him so close to his family, to home. He dug into a saddlebag for his oval horse brush, slipped his hand under the leather strap and gently worked away the dried mud from Rosencrantz. When he'd finished, he leaned into the warm, sweet smell of his horse and closed his eyes to make the assembled officers disappear. He wished the day was behind him, wished the war was already someplace else.

When he opened his eyes, Frank was walking toward him, leading Ashley and smiling. They'd not long parted. Tod hoped his jolt of annoyance hadn't shown. 'You found me again,' Tod said.

Frank's smile stayed firmly in place. 'I don't have to be an Indian tracker, not with Rosencrantz such a fine gray.'

Tod reminded himself he had a care for the boy, courtesy of Trenholm senior. No matter that he wanted to be alone.

'What do you think of the big pow-wow?' said Frank. He nodded toward the grand house. 'Perhaps we'll catch them today.'

'From what you and others tell me, we had them caught yesterday,' said Tod. Frank was still looking for the big fight, he thought. 'They should have invited me inside, lowly captain though I am. I know this country as well as any man in this army.'

'And what would you do,' asked Frank, 'if you were Hood?'

Tod had already thought about it. 'I'd show the Yankees a front alright. Keep them honest in Franklin while they're bottled up trying to get over the river. They've escaped these hills but there's better ones north of town where the road is tucked in tight. I'd send the cavalry round to block that, get some quick marching infantry up there as well and catch them on the road, then drive our main body through Franklin after they've left.'

'That's the same move we tried out of Columbia.'

'And it nearly worked. No sense attacking the town.'

Frank said nothing more.

'Let's find some food,' Tod said.

Before they could do that, the generals broke up. Forrest, having been last in, was first out. With a face like bubbling thunder, he cantered away. Cleburne emerged next, followed by Hood with his crutch. Off his horse he looked ten years older, unbalanced and angry. He barked at Cleburne from the top step of the portico while the Irishman mounted. The crowd of officers took a half-step closer but Tod and Frank were too far away to hear. Tod could see the grim set of Cleburne's face. Other division commanders looked similarly stricken. Lastly came Cheatham, his head bowed. He ordered the generals and officers from his corps collected to the side of the house so Tod and Frank hurried along, leaving their horses to graze.

Once Cheatham had them gathered in an arc, he told them, 'We will attack them in Franklin.' He looked from man to man. 'Cleburne's Division will advance down the Columbia Pike and to its right. Brown to the pike's left. Bate is to line up to the west of Brown.'

Tod sucked deeply at the winter air.

'Stewart's Corps will attack down the Lewisburg Pike, close into the river. As near as we can manage it, we all strike together. Schofield's had short time to prepare. One attack. You understand? Don't stop to fire, just charge the line and we'll sweep over them.'

Sweep over his home, his family.

'The marching order is Cleburne, Brown then Bate. We

spread out once we're through these hills. We need to get in position before we lose the day, so go to it.'

The next little while passed without a complete thought; not one could take root before the next blundered in. Frank said something about riding at the back of his division so they could stay together on the march. Tod ignored him and rode off the pike directly into the hills.

'Where are you going?'

He'd taken the same small path last night to come south to Clara's house. Now he took it north. He ducked and weaved through the trees. Frank kept pace behind, up and up until it brought them out onto a bald. He used to come here with his brothers. Back then it was rich with deer, but today the armies had scared them halfway to Arkansas. Below them and over the flat was Franklin, every acre known to him, every farm, every creek. There was a Union brigade at the base of Privet Knob, protecting the Columbia Pike as it ran toward town.

'Give me your glasses.' Frank's were better than his. He reached out for them without taking his gaze from the view. Rosencrantz was breathing heavily so he dismounted to steady his hand and to pick out the red roof of his home in the distance. Franklin wasn't as he'd left it last night. There were works both sides of the pike, long works with embrasures and cannon. Father's cotton gin was stripped to the frame and there were Union soldiers out before the lines, ready to cut down anything in their field of fire. The sight hollowed him out. Beyond the gin, works extended all the way to the river, Fort Granger on its far, high bank. Coming back to the west of his house he traced the same line of works for half a mile and more.

'What do you see?'

'I see a hard afternoon.' *Dear Lord, Moscow. I hope you've got everyone away.*

'Will they stand, or will they run for Nashville?'

'Those are strong works, and the bridge is out. They'll stay.'

As Tod handed the glasses back to Frank, he saw him for what he was: an over-tall boy, born to wealth and privilege, out to prove himself to the world. 'Frank.'

'Maybe today it should be Lieutenant Trenholm?'

'As you like, but I can't stay with you when we go in.' His care for the boy was suddenly no longer an obligation. He had to fight to keep his voice even. 'I have to be with my brigade, and you have to be with Gist.'

'I know it.'

'Don't do anything foolish.' He sounded like a parent. He supposed he *was* in absentia. 'It's going to be, well… busy.' Trenholm should have tried harder to keep Frank at home. 'Busy like you can't imagine. Stick close by Gist, keep your head low to your horse and hope for the best.' It was thin advice, but what else could he tell him.

'Father says only fools trust to hope, in business at least. He always told me to keep my stock in reality.'

'Your father's never been a soldier, has he?' *This would be the charge of the war.* 'Sell all your stock today, Lieutenant, then spend every last cent on hope.'

*

Moscow lifted the heavy cedar ladder from its cupped metal brackets. Father had always been proud of the ladder's home, neat and horizontal in front of the weatherboards below the back-porch balustrades. He'd nursed a line of diminutive juniper shrubs into a low neat hedge so close that it hid the ladder from end to end. Had Father not, some uniformed blue magpie would have taken it for the barricade. As it was, Moscow risked that outcome now. He struggled to be nonchalant while he maneuvered the ladder's balanced length around the corner of his home.

An hour ago, it would have been stolen from him for sure, but since then the buzz of the Union Army had abated. The local defenses built – to a large extent from repurposed Carter wood – the men cooked or rested. Variously spaced across his backyard, they were trying to bank as much sleep as possible before another anticipated night march, this time for Nashville. The headquarters tents had been struck from the front garden not ten minutes ago. Moscow had watched them efficiently packed into a wagon out front, ready to head north. Looking toward town, he'd seen a few wagons pulling onto the road. The Yankees must have made miraculous progress with the bridges. Good luck to them. Maybe the Union would get clean away after all. What then? What a scene if Hood's army, Moscow's own 20th Tennessee and perhaps his little brother, marched into town.

General Cox hadn't given up the front parlor yet. Not that he'd made much use of it in person except for a few minutes each time he passed along the edge of the defenses from west to east or east to west. Perhaps, like Moscow, he couldn't quite believe that the shape of the day was set; that it might yet be recast.

Manhandling the ladder was really a two-man job but he didn't want to draw Father back outside; seeing the place all torn up would only upset him again. Moscow's weighty field glasses, which had survived his army career, were hanging around his neck. An unshaven sergeant with his head on his pack, lying prone in the fall shade of the nearest cedar tree, cracked an eye. Moscow gave him a nod and a smile as if he were no more than a simpleton about his business, but the eye stayed fixed on him. There was nothing for it. He looked up to the roof. There were three chunky steps each side, climbing up to the chimney which sat there like the crown of some red-bricked Inca temple. He wrestled the ladder upright so that the top rung was level and left of the small second story window. He knew from past experience that if he was brave enough to get his foot on that top rung, he could pull himself up onto the lowest step of the gable. At least he could when he was younger. Tod used to hold the ladder. Today Moscow had to wedge a flat garden rock under one foot to take out the wobble. He took a breath and started up. Halfway to the top he felt anything but secure, but to come back down would have been a retreat. Besides, he had good reason to get up there. He needed to see the lay of the land but didn't want to leave home again, not with everyone so on edge. He climbed on, his feet three, then two rungs from the top. He steadied himself with his right hand on the frame of the window. His field glasses hung heavily from his neck. He noted as almost a comforting distraction that the frame could stand a lick of paint when spring arrived. He braced himself to make the final stretch. The ladder jolted suddenly, as if the rock had slipped. He gripped and froze, waited for the inevitable tilt and fall. He chanced a look down.

The scruffy sergeant, kepi tilted back, squinted up at him, hands firmly on the wood. 'Mister, personally I'd say there's enough hazard in the day without lookin' to add to the pile. But I can see what you're about. I'm content to hold tight to the low end, if you'll tell me what you can see from the other.'

'I'm obliged to you.' Moscow set himself once more and,

midway through a silent prayer, reached for the lowest step of the gable, numbing his mind to the danger. His field glasses swung and caught on the edge; he thought they'd be the death of him. A few anxious seconds later, he'd somehow managed to scramble up. After he calmed himself, he climbed up the two higher steps so he could stand leaning against the chimney and look out through and either side of the cedar trees that shielded the southern end of the house.

The first thing he noticed close down to his left was a Yankee general in the shadow of a parked wagon, pacing back and forth with a stick and talking to no one but himself as far as Moscow could see. That was the man who'd been shouting with Opdycke out the front earlier. Moscow had recognized Opdycke. He'd once been a dinner guest, but today hadn't been the time for reunions.

'What can you see?'

Moscow chose not to shout down to the sergeant that his nearest general was conversing with himself, so instead turned to face town and put up his field glasses. 'There's solid wagon traffic across the rail bridge and some people on horse braving the ford. Your supplies are underway for Nashville. The pike bridge isn't passable yet.' He carefully swiveled to look east. 'Plenty of metal pointing from Fort Granger, covering the Lewisburg Pike I imagine, and then your works run from the rail cut right past what was our cotton gin.'

'They built solid?'

'I'd say so. It was a solid cotton gin until today. Cannon there too. You got two brigades out beyond the works, 'bout half a mile. Can't see the sense in that. I imagine they ain't resting as easy as you are.'

The main line of works angled back from the gin to the Columbia Pike and the battery of four guns and then on to the west. Father's garden, visible through and to the right of the trees immediately in front of Moscow, was sandwiched between the main line and the lesser works down below – a retrenchment you might call it, he supposed – a second line if the first should break at the critical point were the pike ran into town.

'How does it look out west?' a new voice called up.

Moscow looked down at his enemy become friend by necessity and saw there were two privates with him, both taking an equal interest. 'Well, the line runs behind what was my father's locust grove, but your vandal army have cut that to shreds and left the branches and spikes in a tangle.'

'My apologies, sir,' said the sergeant, 'but we ain't lookin' to invite Hood in to visit.'

'Beyond that, the line runs all the way to the Carter's Creek Pike and on beyond that. There are men still working on it out there. It probably reaches back to the Harpeth again, one long line connecting the river as it flanks either side of town. You're tucked in alright.'

'I'm tempted to come up myself. Sounds like a fine view.'

'Too many Yankees in it for my liking.' There were thousands upon thousands in the open land behind the works and more again crowded in the town, resting in the side streets and the gardens. Every block in town was surrounded by wagons. Some edged forward, waiting their turn to cross the river. A breeze lifted up to the roof. His town smelled of sweaty horses and sweatier men, a tired army that had built itself a safe home for just one day.

A rider raced out and down the Columbia Pike to the lonely brigades out in the flat. Moscow followed him through his glasses and almost lost his balance. He caught himself on the chimney and took a breath. When he looked once more and searched for the rider, he overshot and found himself gazing far out instead to the gap between Winstead and Breezy two miles away, where the road cut down out of the hills.

Those hills were in motion. It was as if they were melting. He must still be dizzy. Maybe he should sit and gather himself, but he suddenly saw it for what it was, a flood of men and horses pouring sideways from the road or emerging from beneath the lowest trees, a sea of butternut and gray, flags of red and blue.

'What is it?'

A cold wave flushed right through him, head to toe. He took his glasses away, but forced himself to look again.

'What you seeing out there, mister? Is it Hood?'

'It's him alright,' he called down, 'coming out of the hills and setting up. Hold that ladder tight, I'll come down.' He swung his glasses behind him and slid his stomach over the lowest step to find the rung with his foot, the fall now a forgotten concern.

'How many? They gonna come at us?'

'Aw,' said Moscow, descending as quickly as he could. 'There's plenty of 'em alright. No doubt they'll form a line and come on, but the afternoon's wearing thin. Once they see your fine works, they'll pitch tents and put the coffee to boil.' He stepped to the ground. 'I'm grateful to you.' He backed away. 'I'd be obliged if you could put this ladder back behind the hedge under the porch. That's where it lives.'

'What did you see, mister?'

Moscow didn't answer. He hurried up the porch steps. It was too late to get away. He needed to find Father and get everybody into the cellar. Distant but clear in his mind's eye, he could see the quick step and direct purpose in those moving lines of men, the high hold of their flags, the urgency with which their officers moved them along. He'd seen it before. He'd been one of those officers. There wasn't a bone in his body that doubted that Hood's whole army was making ready to attack.

*

Frank wished Gist would give him something to do: deliver an order, check on the rearmost regiment. Anything to feel useful. With this extremity upon them, the free rein he'd enjoyed on Gist's staff didn't seem such a blessing. He'd sooner be in command of a company, busy like the officers either side of him; swords and voices raised, encouraging the men forward to their start position. Instead, he was left to tail his general, waxing between exhilaration and dread at what lay ahead.

Before they'd parted, Tod hadn't left him wondering as to what was coming. *Busy like you can't imagine.* Frank had offered his best salute but Tod had ridden in close and they'd silently shaken hands. Yesterday's action was nothing compared to what Hood was throwing in today. Gist had told him Hood's plan would make a two-mile front. Two miles! The Yankees were going to be swamped.

Now the army had spilled from the hills and the divisions were spreading out across the mostly flat farmland. Along with the rest of Brown's Division, Gist's Brigade was to go in to the west of the Columbia Pike. They advanced in several columns of four, moving untidily in parallel while they found their way across the fields, around hedges and through fences. Frank was behind Gist, near to the front of the most advanced column. The brigade band, close at hand, abandoned 'Dixie' one after another as they jumped a ditch and then reassembled the beat and the melody on the other side. Some of these players might be dead before the day was out, he thought, their orchestration never again quite so complete.

He looked down from Ashley to the men marching either side of him and was struck again by how different this army was to the one he'd so long imagined. Back in Charleston, when the war was younger and so was Frank, his brother William had organized the Trenholm Light Artillery Battery. Frank had gone along behind Father – who'd paid for every horse, uniform and gun – to the formal presentation of the cannon. There'd not been a stitch or a horsehair out of place. Boots were as polished as the metal. Of the men around him today, many had no boots to polish. Veterans though most of them were, under the slouch hats and behind the dirt and whiskers they were little older than he was. Many of them barely the other side of twenty. If he'd passed one of them on a country road, seen them barefoot and threadbare, he likely would have steered his horse to the other side. Alone they were vagabonds. Gathered as they were, tested through the hard years of the war and over the precious soils of the South, they were oddly magnificent.

Out front a sergeant major from the 46th Georgia guided the march. By some alchemy or unseen signal, he found their designated position and called the colors to him. Left and right of Frank the colors of the other regiments followed suit and magically the brigade had its line. Frank drew level with Gist and they both surveyed the panorama. From his height on Ashley, Frank could see to the east that an in and out line was in place all the way back to the road and beyond. That was Cleburne's Division. To the west, Maney's Brigade was coming up alongside Gist, but as yet there was nothing beyond Maney. Bate's Division would eventually stretch out that way, Tod with them, but they were last in the line of march and had the furthest to go.

'Take some rest. Water your horse,' said Gist. 'It'll be a short while yet.'

The brigade already appeared to know this. Men sat, or lay flat. They were mostly quiet.

'You've nothing for me, General? No orders, no errands?'

Gist looked at him so intently that Frank felt he and Gist might be there alone, rather than among twenty thousand men.

Gist sighed. 'If I could, Lieutenant Trenholm, I'd order you to pick another fight for your first test, somewhere the hell away from here.'

'I'd be ashamed to be anywhere else, sir.'

Gist ignored him so completely that he wondered if he'd said that out loud. Dismounting, his general said, 'Hood has to take his chance sometime, I suppose. Otherwise, we're simply herding them into Nashville. Snug as a bug in there. Trouble is, Hood's the kind of man who's eager to pick up the dice. And that'd be us. We're the dice. Tell you what, you look after Joe.' He handed up the reins. 'Water him too. I'll go visit with my men.'

Frank did as he was told, all the while watching the men himself. Over in the 16th Carolina there was a sizeable congregation surrounding the chaplain who was leading them in prayer. He watched one boy, who might have been no more than fifteen, fit and unfit his bayonet so many times that his corporal set about him and told him to quit it. Another soldier wrote in a pocket bible, ripped out the page and looked for a place on his person where he might safely stow his message. Finding none, he tore it up.

With the horses watered, Frank sank to the cold ground.

His boyish fantasies of war drained from him. His frailer half wished he was back hanging on Father's coattails, inspecting newly cast cannon guarded by men with just-stitched jackets.

*

Tod urged Rosencrantz forward on his way back from Bate's staff. Benton Smith had sent him over on a point of clarification. *Were they going in fully aligned or en echelon?* He'd got a curt answer but didn't much care. If all these unsmiling men would only get out of the way, he could get back to Benton Smith and ask his own question.

This was Bostick land, their neighbor's farm. The march of Smith's Brigade was flattening the winter grass so heavily it was certain to come up poorly in the spring. If Father had been here, he'd have had some choice words. The first company of the 2nd Tennessee dismantled a split-rail fence so the brigade could move on more quickly. He was pretty sure it was one that he'd help to build. They'd split the logs in the hills and carried the rails down and out onto the flatland, Francis one end and he the other. Easy work for young boys once you were strong enough to swing the hammer. You drove in the spikes and then wriggled the next one in along the split. They'd been known to build fifty yards of fence in a long morning if the trees were already down. Now those rails were cast aside in two minutes. He hastened over the discarded rails and tried to leave his childhood behind.

Hood's plan didn't suit him, but then Hood would have other concerns. For a moment he tuned out from the barked orders, the drums and the army's equine aroma, and imagined himself admitted into Hood's presence back at the Harrison house. Just the two of them, the army commander extending his working arm and a smile, not a bitter man after all. He'd ask Tod to come and stand beside him to see the map and the dispositions.

'See here, Captain Carter, I've marked out your home. It's the key, built on the low rise of Carter Hill as it is, where the pike starts down toward the town. Win your home and we win the day and the campaign. Maybe even the war.'

'But Bate's Division, General Hood. My division.' Tod picked up a pencil as a pointer. 'You have us attacking too far to the west. It means I won't be able to fight for my home.'

'It's all been arranged, Carter. You'll go in with Cheatham, front and center, not a man ahead of you. We'll follow you in.'

'Hey, look out there!'

Tod snapped out of his daydream as a whipped team pulled a cannon across his path.

A gunnery sergeant yelled at him, 'Are you fixin' to be first into the surgeon's tent?'

This battle would be on his very doorstep. He should at least be allowed to transfer across to Brown's Division and go in with Frank, straight for the red roof of home, but it wasn't worth the asking. Benton Smith would never allow it, so Tod had a lesser ask.

Way ahead in the west there was a line of dark clouds, but the sun was having the better of the fight, a golden goodbye to November. It didn't seem to fit: why fight, when both sides could stack arms and watch such a beautiful sunset? Perhaps the sun would hurry down today and the light would be lost before the signal could be made to attack. The Yankees would flee in the night and when the sun came around again tomorrow, he could trot on home for breakfast, the conquering hero.

He sensed his mind was breathless but he couldn't catch

it. He rode on through the files of men as if they were a ghost army, suspecting if he chose to put Rosencrantz into a canter, he'd breeze through the marching lines like they were no more than a cool mist, an end of day illusion and no threat to his home at all.

He found Benton Smith surrounded by the regimental commanders, up in his stirrups and pointing out the direction they would take. Tod hung back but followed his general's arm. It pointed to the Bostick house, an outlier from the town. Fine words filled the air: glory, victory, duty. Tod couldn't quite fix them together in any order that mattered. They seemed disconnected, dismantled like his split-rail fence. He waited until stiff salutes came down above twisting horses, until all but the staff officers had ridden away. Either side of him the regiments stood in line of battle, bayonets fixed, quiet, resigned. Every man, it appeared to Tod, wore a common sad frown.

'General.'

'Captain Carter. Lord only knows how you must be feeling.'

'I pray he does, sir. I can't seem to get a hold on it myself. General Bate says to go in as you see fit, sir, but to stay tight to Jackson on your right.'

'I suppose I could have guessed that much. But the Union line angles gently opposite where we will start. Do you see? If I stay glued to Jackson and don't swing left to hit it straight on, the Yankees will enfilade us.'

'That's all they told me, sir.'

Smith looked agitated. Tod waited as long as he could and then said, 'I have a request.'

'Go on.'

'I want to go in with the 20th Tennessee. The regiment was

raised here in Williamson County. My brothers and I, the three of us started with the 20th. Moscow, Colonel Moscow Carter that is, he used to command it, sir.'

'I know it.' Smith looked at Tod like he might an errant but favorite child.

Tod met his stare.

'Alright then,' Smith said. 'Request granted. Report to Colonel Shy, but you wait on Shy's command. Don't go screaming off into the fight before we're ready, you hear?'

'Yes, sir. Thank you.'

'After the attack goes in, come find me, tell me how things are with the 20th.' The general stiffened in his saddle, his eyes drifting somewhere above and behind Tod, who twisted to look. There was activity up on Winstead Hill. A high flag waved then dropped, the signal they had been waiting for. Smith cursed at not yet being in position but then said, 'God be with you, Captain Carter.'

Tod, conscious of his pounding heart, angled Rosencrantz away. He looked over the endless lines of men, thinking that on this day, even God might have trouble being with everyone and that some of them might get left to the Devil.

*

The rations for the whole 125th were laid out on a tarpaulin and surrounded by impatient men. Shire had to look over several sets of shoulders to glimpse that it was pork again, not that he cared. There didn't seem so much. They'd waited or slept – the veterans doing both at the same time – well into the afternoon. The smell of flapjacks and cooked meat had drifted over from other brigades on the soldier-strewn land downhill from the Carter house.

They were told the rations would be given out by company in reverse alphabetical order. Shire found it hard to bear. As they were suddenly at the back of an imaginary line –

except for the now truly morose Company A – they were at least each allowed a fistful of coffee beans doled out by a giant Irish sergeant, bless his bucket hands. Cleves had nursed a fire in expectation of frying rather than boiling, but they made the best of it. The coffee was a true consolation. They drank it as if it was consecrated wine, then tried again to sleep while waiting their turn. It was surprisingly warm. Shire rolled up his coat and lay his head down. But for the hunger, it should have been easy as breathing to drift away. He quickly realized that wasn't going to happen. So instead, he took his canteen and wandered back up the pike, thinking to see if Wagner's other brigades had been brought in behind the lines. Tuck would collect his ration if he wasn't there.

Endless numbers of soldiers lay either side of the road in the autumn haze. A young town boy was high in a tree, shielding his eyes from a sun that was low to the west. The cold would come on soon enough. As he drew closer to the Carter's house, Shire heard a commotion at odds with the restful army: raised women's voices, a child crying. The front door was half open. It couldn't be easy. He imagined his own lost and faraway home, his father's garden with soldiers laid out at all angles like overfed dogs. He'd like to have paid his respects and see if the Carters remembered him, their English waiter; he'd like to tell them their fine son had saved his life at Kennesaw. But as he came level with the gate, he had to step aside for officers breezing in like they owned the place. They pulled the front door shut behind them.

He passed by. There was no traffic remaining on the road. Wagner was there behind the secondary defenses, looking every bit as agitated as he had when they'd marched in. Preferring to keep his distance, Shire angled off the road to the left. He came up to the inner barricade which extended only a few paces on this side of the pike. The barricade itself was unmanned, most of its defenders sitting behind. He unplugged his canteen, took a pull and looked over toward the skeletal cotton gin. Several men had made pillows from the raw cotton. Gunners lounged with their backs to the cannon wheels.

It was hard to see out into the country beyond the outer defenses and a further slight rise of the land. To see better, he climbed half up on the inner barricade so his thighs were resting on the head log. What heat there was left in the day was enough to blur the air close to the distant ground, but he could make out the two brigades tight to each other a half-mile away. Several thousand men, their backs to him. Wagner must have pulled Lane back from Privet Knob and placed him to the west of the road, extending Conrad's line. It's where Shire would be had Opdycke not disobeyed Wagner's order. He fancied he could see flags beyond. He wished he'd kept Gideon's telescopic rifle sight from Chickamauga, rather than handed it in to the quartermaster like a good soldier. No doubt the Rebels would make a show. That was the form. They would have to be mad to attack these defenses, but the lonely brigades out there must look bite-sized. Wagner should have called them in. Shire looked over at Wagner who was pacing with a stick; his staff were keeping their distance.

Cannon sounded and Shire's head snapped back to the distant brigades. Two, three, four shots. He watched smoke billow into the still air. Around him men got to their feet, twisted on their kepis, collected rifles from stacks. The cannon out on the plain fired again toward the south. The gunners nearer at hand, at the outer barricade, stood to their weapons. Shire thought to get back to his regiment, but the fight wasn't here. There was no need.

Then a shell tore home to his right and exploded close behind the Carter's house. He jumped down from the barricade. The urgency doubled in the men around him. More officers ran to join Wagner at the road. A rider sped in through the outer line, his horse fighting the bit, and hurried on to the general. 'Hood's whole army is coming!' he shouted. 'Lane and Conrad will be flanked in short order. They should fall back, sir.'

Wagner brandished his stick. 'Get back and tell them to fight like hell!'

The messenger looked every bit as frightened of Wagner as was his horse, but wrestled his animal while he repeated the point. Wagner would have none of it. Without a salute, the man spun his horse and raced away. Immediately, a second rider arrived, no doubt from the alternate brigade but with the exact same plea. Wagner's own officers reminded him that his brigade wasn't expected to take on the whole Rebel Army. He should bring them in. A shell screamed in and hit the road outside the barricade, the ball bouncing high and off down the hill. Wagner beat his stick on the ground and broke it in two. 'Get back and fight!'

The second rider turned around as had the first, but on his way out was forced off the road by a retreating and panicked battery of cannon, the horses tossing heads, wheels shuddering and sliding. They slowed to twist in through the second line where it narrowed the road. 'All hell is let loose,' said their captain to Wagner and asked where to deploy his guns.

Shire looked back to the south. He imagined where he

would be if Opdycke had deployed his brigade out there as well, only to be abandoned by their general and now their artillery too. Those poor men. Soldiers took position either side of him. Horses were led to the rear; a caisson was dragged into place to support the four guns beside the road. All was noise and bluster. When on the march, he was surrounded by the creak of stretched leather and the scuffle of tired boots. Here, on the edge of a battle, the noise was of cold metal, urgent orders, shallow breath. Behind it all, he detected a slow distant thunder, as if Winstead Hill itself were advancing across the plain. A collective yell climbed toward a scream and crashed into the rip of a thousand rifles.

*

The explosion in the Carter backyard had a certain unifying effect. Until then, Moscow's attempts to move five sisters and nine young children to the safety of the cellar had, at best, been taken as something they should finish preparing for. No matter that he and Father had spent a long time yesterday clearing the space down there just in case, or that the bundles that Sarah had made each of them prepare were ready and waiting. The family were variously distributed upstairs, in the hall, in Father's room or in the ell. Discussions tended to arguments in each location. He'd lost his temper and yelled loudly enough to reach every room in the main house. 'This ain't a summer picnic. Get in the goddamned cellar!' That had set at least two children crying. Father thanked Moscow not to blaspheme under his roof. Moscow, his hand pressed to his temple, said pointedly that the roof might not be around to blaspheme under for much longer.

Then the shell tore in like a banshee.

It exploded outside and threw a shower of dirt in through Father's open back door, peppering Walter. Walter stood still and lifted his arms like he'd been drenched. There was a brief shocked silence before the wailing started up again, this time with an edge of true terror.

While panic took a grip among his family, the shell had a salutary effect on Moscow. After checking that Walter wasn't hurt, he told himself that this wasn't an everyday thing that he was trying to do: to pack his family into the cellar ahead of a looming battle. The crisis was upon them and the colonel in him stepped up. He was used to being scared under fire. This was just another and stronger flavor of fear. The trick had always been to accept it; give the orders, set the example.

A trio of riders cantered by the house, all yells and yips, almost past before he could look to the window.

He focused once more and decided he'd move the family a room at a time. They'd be exposed out on the back porch if another shell struck while they made for the cellar stairs, but there being no second shell, it seemed to have been a rogue shot. He placed his hands on Frances' shaking shoulders and asked her to listen. When he was sure he had her attention, he told her to take Walter, Annie and Hugh out and down to the cellar. As an afterthought he said she should take Father as well, who was gripping tightly to a chairback.

'Father,' Moscow said. 'Go on with Frances and set up camp below while I gather the others.' He supposed Father might be the one Carter man never to have come under cannon fire, not that any of them had suffered it in their own home before now. Father nodded and began to help Frances. Outside the open door, a company of Yankees ran across the yard through the last of the dissipating shell-smoke and on toward the barricade. He couldn't see any injured soldiers, but that wasn't his problem. John, Susie and little Oscar, the younger of the black families who'd chosen to stay on, were crouched in a tight huddle by the door to the hall. Moscow stood them up and asked if they knew where Jack and Calfurnia and their children were.

'In their cabin, last I saw,' said John. 'Should we run for town?'

'Too late for that.' There was no point in kicking himself. 'Susie, get Oscar into the cellar. John, collect Jack and Calfurnia and take them there too. Don't take no for an answer. And don't go back to your own cabin for anything, you hear? There's no time.'

With Father's room cleared, Moscow tackled a tearful Mary and her brood who were in the hall. She had Lannie in her arms and was failing to comfort Marcus who was near hysterical. Alice wasn't helping by telling him not to be such a sissy. Moscow bent a knee and asked eight-year-old Alice to lead her mother and siblings to the cellar and not pay any mind to Yankees that got in her way. Puffed up with this promotion, Alice collected her bundle and led Marcus by the hand. Her mother was left to follow on.

Moscow's next rushed thought was for his wife, followed by the sting that she'd been gone these several years. Alone in the hall he glanced in through the parlor door. At least four of Cox's staff were hurriedly debating over a large map, another looked out the window while loading his pistol. He had no call to talk to them. Before he could make his way upstairs, there was a knock at the front door, the politeness at odds with the recent shell-burst. He thought to ignore it but it quickly came again, less polite than before. He opened up, ready to give any Yankee officer a barrage, but looked instead on the strained face of Albert Lotz with his wife and three children. 'The army,' said Lotz, 'they have taken over my house. Soldiers everywhere.'

Despite the urgency of the moment, Moscow couldn't help but notice how well presented the Lotz family were. Albert looked like he might be headed for a night at the opera and Margaretha and the children to a church social. 'Not a thing I can do about that, Albert. You need to get into shelter.'

'I never dug a cellar,' he said.

It took Moscow a dumb moment to work it out. 'Of course, of course. You'll be fine with us.' He waved them in. 'I have business upstairs, but go straight through to the back porch and down. Quickly now.'

He left them to it and took the stairs two steps at a time, his need to yell at a Yankee unspent. He was angry at Cox for getting it wrong, angry at God for taking his wife, but most of all at Hood for shelling his home. None of it was of any use. Rounding the half-landing, he met the remaining fearful sisters and children coming down. He let them rush on by then followed them down the stairs and through the house. The brick kitchen cast a long shadow across the yard, almost to the porch. There was the once familiar smell of an exploded shell. The yard was largely clear of soldiers as they'd moved to the outer defenses. Barked orders sounded from over there. Nearer at hand there was a manned battery a little way beyond the smokehouse. Two artillerymen drew buckets from the well next to the kitchen and walked toward the cannon, bent sideways against the weight of the water. The children seemed to take an age to move down the steep steps. Moscow crowded behind his sisters on the porch. He looked up, saw that the shell had broken off a good piece of masonry from the roof on its way to earth. Dear Lord, that was closer than he'd thought. Cannon sounded far away. It was enough to hurry everyone along. Fort Granger opening up probably; it was hard to tell. Anyway, it wasn't aimed this way.

He was last down the steps and closed the cellar door, wishing it was sturdier. It would have to do. He let out a breath. They were all inside. He turned and everyone was looking at him, small to tall, lit only by the tiny ceiling window at the far end of the cellar dining room. The young were wide-eyed, his sisters a study of concern and care, and fear was etched deeply across his father's face.

'Where's Lena?' asked Alice.

Moscow didn't need to check, aware in a heartbeat that he'd not accounted for her. He wrenched open the door and raced back up. Two privates had come onto the porch. As he shoved them aside to get to his room on the ell, a shell shrieked past and clean through the ell's roof, detonating beyond the house. He didn't break stride and lunged for the door to his room, shouted inside for Lena but there was no answer. He ran back along the porch, through Father's room to the hall and upstairs to the bedrooms, calling all the way. He found Lena cowering behind the dolls' trunk and he swept her up.

'Daddy!'

He nearly fainted with relief. 'What would your mother think of me?'

Out on the landing he set her down and they hurried back to the cellar. Frances was waiting anxiously as they came down the steps. Alice was close beside her and tearfully embraced Lena.

'I couldn't find, Emmie,' Lena said, holding up her doll to show Frances.

'Alright. You're both with us now.'

As Moscow closed the door again, the battery beyond the

smokehouse fired four quick shots. The shock of the detonations sent his sisters and their cares to huddle at the very back of the room. Moscow looked up at the low wooden ceiling. Dust smoked down from the jolt of the cannon fire. He leaned back against the door and inwardly searched for a prayer.

*

There was a sudden shift of energy in the army. Around Frank, everyone stood. Rifles were collected, lines formed, bayonets fixed. He stood himself and looked back to the hills where, sure enough, the signal flag was waving. He struggled to swallow. His and Gist's horses were at hand. He gathered up their reins and tried to understand the new strange mood that surrounded him. Despite all the movement there was a certain serenity. He wasn't sure if something was missing or if something had been added. There were orders aplenty but no talk among the men, as if everyone here was alone, or stepping before a county judge to receive a verdict.

Gist hurried toward him and collected his horse. They both mounted. 'No wandering off today, Lieutenant Trenholm. You understand? If I look over my shoulder, I expect you to be there.'

'Yes, sir.'

They rode out before the regiments, Gist up in his stirrups to look east. Frank followed his line of sight to where Gordon's Brigade had just stepped off. Gist waved his sword. Commands sounded left and right. Their regiments started forward at a steady step on a wide front. Together they made up the largest brigade in Brown's Division. Cannon sounded from the east. Frank's heart beat with the step of the men.

Ashley picked up on the mood and fought his bit. The skirmishers out front disappeared over a low rise and soon after Frank and Gist followed on. The slight elevation afforded Frank a fuller view. The town spires were a good mile away but much nearer, out on the plain, a line of blue straddled the main pike, both flanks angled back but in the air. A battery of Yankee cannon fired from the road into the Rebel ranks to the east. Further east still, shells from a distant fort arced long and shrill, descending screams overlapping, bursting above a hundred flags held high.

Frank followed tight to Gist as he rode along the full front of the brigade. Gist waved his hat and shouted to the men over the cannon and the bands; how he knew they would fight this day; how proud he was to lead them. They roared back. To Frank, stirred by Gist and watching the brigade stride out, this tide of men appeared unstoppable. Gist spun his horse, pointed his sword at the blue line and quickened the pace. The Rebel yell rent the air, unholy, unearthly. Frank edged Ashley close in to Gist. Dozens of rabbits darted madly across each other out in the field ahead, driven wild by the high-pitched screams and the drumming march of the men. The color-bearer for the 24th South Carolina stumbled and fell but was up again quickly to find his place; he risked the flag to one hand in order to set his hat straight.

They caught up to their pickets and let them melt back through the line. The Union pickets began firing. Frank prayed not to be hit now, not before the battle was truly joined. On this alignment, Gist's men would strike the western end of the Yankees. The attack was already going in on the other side of the road where there was a sudden tearing rip of Union musketry. Frank looked over and watched what seemed like half the Rebel front line shudder and collapse, only to be stepped over. The momentum barely slowed. A sudden lunge and yell and the attack pressed home.

On Frank's side of the road, he stayed close to Gist while the men on foot caught up and then overtook them. The orders were to rush the Yankee line, no stopping to fire. Officers and sergeants made a last alignment, then pointed the men forward like hounds at a deer. The yell sounded louder than ever. Frank took a gulp of smoky air, screamed himself, waved his sword. Ashley reared. The men charged and the Union rifles exploded along their front. A buzz-whip of bullets sliced the air either side of him. He pushed forward, past and over screaming men who clutched at stomachs, held hands across bloodied faces. Gist urged them on. The smoke parted for a moment and Frank saw the Union line outflanked; it wavered and would soon be overwhelmed. The brigade hit home, bayonets and rifle butts, a chorus of pain and fury. All the world's words lost to anger and despair.

Ashley shied at the clamor and confusion as Frank tried to follow Gist into the melee. It was impossible to concentrate on any one detail, to pick out somewhere to help. He became lost in the all-consuming scene. He did nothing for a breathless time amid the carnage, his pistol held unused. No one came at him. The fight began to break up. The Yankees were pushed back; they were on the retreat. Then they simply turned and ran. The brigade saw the backs of the enemy and started after them. It quickly became a chase. Frank spotted Gist, moved toward him through the acrid smoke, through the sweet and sickly smell of blood. Ashley picked his way nervously among injured and dying men. A quartet of Union men held their hands up, not a mark on any of them, their jackets so uniformly blue they might have been dipped in paint just this morning. No doubt they were fresher into this war than he was. They turned to him, high on his horse, as if he might save them. He found his voice and ordered them to walk to the rear.

Gist, alight with excitement, rode over to Frank. Around them Yankees were captured or clubbed to the ground. Gist pulled up. 'You must be a lucky charm, Lieutenant Trenholm. Look at them run. You need to help me. Find the regimental commanders. Tell them we need to reform.'

Frank looked in all directions. Where in this hellish mess should he start?

*

Shire knew he should get back to the squad, find Bates or Opdycke and tell them what was happening, though surely they must both have heard the cannon. Fort Granger was in full fury. From the noise of the explosions and the telltale smoke, he guessed they were aiming somewhere well to the east of Wagner's brigades. That could only mean more Rebels, a wider attack. If he was going to report to Opdycke, he'd better find out the truth of it.

He hurried around the open end of the inner barricade then raced hand on hat over to the cotton gin. Skirting past it, he stopped behind the main line to the right of two cannon. The barricade was packed with men, all eyes to the front. 'Sweet Jesus,' one man said. Out on the flat Shire could hear rifle fire, heavy but not massed, screams and cries so distant and so many that they merged together into some greater animal. He searched for a space he might step up and squeeze into and see, but was spun around by a snarling sergeant. 'Where's your rifle?'

'This isn't my —'

'Corporal, get this man a rifle and fit him into the line. And you…' The sergeant's meaty index finger pressed Shire's chest in the exact spot where he'd been dented on Missionary Ridge. 'You report to me when this scare is over. Now get up there.'

Out of nowhere a rifle was thrust into Shire's hands and he was inserted up into the line. He loaded out of habit in what space he had. The rifle was much the same; the ramrod was a hair bent and the hammer was stiff to get to half-cock. The men either side of him stared forward; they hadn't spared him a glance. He'd have a look himself and then explain to someone that he needed to get back to the 125th.

The head log was low and he had to bob down to see beneath it. The sight dropped his jaw. There were no brigades out there anymore, at least not in any formation other than a fleeing mob. A quarter-mile away they were running back toward him and the barricades, every man for himself, a long and desperate race for safety. Those on the road had the lead, some with packs and rifles, others without even their hats. They sprinted for all they were worth. As Shire watched, men were shot down from behind. The battery to Shire's right shouted that they couldn't fire, that they'd hit their own men.

He must go, but couldn't look away. Many men were blown, unable to do more than walk or jog though their lives depended on it. Behind them rose an animated line of flags above an angry roar. The earth shook under the feet of the hunters and the hunted.

Shire's neighbor climbed the barricade and yelled at the distant men to 'Come on!' The cry was taken up. Shire shouted too and soon the whole line was screaming out at them, willing them home. The fleeing mass was drawn to the gap where the road cut through the barricade and it forced the rout to constrict into a wedge. The order came to aim and Shire, like everyone else, pushed his rifle under the head log. The mob was intermixed now, the Rebels fully among Wagner's men, shooting, clubbing, thrusting bayonets.

Shire glanced to his left and saw long lines of Rebels close in on the barricade. A look to his right showed that beyond the pike it was the same. How wide was this attack? To his front the exhausted men were no more than a few steps away. A handful, the strongest of them, made it through the ditch in front, climbed the barricade and were hauled over, but it was impossible to fire into the main mass. Shire watched a Rebel officer calmly empty his revolver, six shots into as many backs. He thought he could take the man, but a drift of smoke spirited him away.

'We gotta fire, damn it,' yelled the soldier next to him. More men clambered over. It was becoming a mess behind the barricade. Out in front Rebels shouted to each other, 'Follow them into the works!' Shire could see what was going to happen as plain as day. This line wasn't going to hold. The soldier next to him fired first, followed by random shots along the line. Only then did the order come. 'Fire!' Shire did his best to pick out a Rebel, but the yellow flare of rifles and the dense shock of smoke obliterated his result. When it cleared, the impact was horrific. Union and Rebels alike, felled to make a sudden low and bloody wall of gray and blue. A lucky few of Wagner's men had hidden in the ditch. In the breath that followed the volley, they scrambled over. Exhausted, terrified men. Shire looked out beyond the dead and the dying, beyond the Rebel mob. Line after line of ordered regiments were coming forward at the double-quick, bayonets leveled, yells rising in their throats, murder in their eyes.

There was no time to load before the wave would hit.

Shire didn't wait. He knew what it looked like, but Opdycke had to be told. He dropped his rifle, raced away from the roar, dodged the swinging arm of the sergeant and ran back toward the Carter house. A shell detonated to his left and he rode the blast for a half-second, fell, rolled and was up. He chanced one look. Back where he'd been at the gin, the line was holding and the two cannon finally fired, but the line was breached where the road passed through. The Rebels were over the barricade and through the gap, the four-gun battery had been abandoned and was being turned. Whole blue regiments ran as he did. There was nothing to stop Hood's army coming on. He was on the pike now, past Wagner who was struggling to mount his horse. Shire pelted down the road, pell-mell, arms flailing, shells falling. The tree-boy dropped down from the lowest branch and sprinted away. Other townspeople, come to look over the fields as he had, hurried for the river. Shire overtook them and ran on to his brigade, to his own regiment. Men were up and collecting their stacked guns. Opdycke stood right beside the road, looking south up the hill. Shire raced to him and his colonel caught him tight by the arm and helped him to stop.

'Private Shire.'

'Sir. Colonel.'

'What is it man? What's happening?'

'They are clean through, sir. Through the first line. A wide breach, mixed in with Wagner's men.'

'I told him. Damned fool.'

'Sir, it's a wide attack, their line stretches away on either side.'

'We can't protect the whole front. Our work is here.' He bellowed for his staff, all the while gripping Shire by the arm. 'Get the men in line!' He turned back to Shire, his eyes alight.

'Collect your gun, Private Shire.'

'Yes, sir. I will, sir. Just as soon as you let me go.'

*

Frank had to fight with Ashley to move across the charging men, force his way between them and through the gunfire and the carnage. He'd managed to speak with Lieutenant Colonel Watters in the 65th Georgia and Colonel Capers in the 24th South Carolina, but both had looked at him as if he were mad. How in the hell did he expect them to get the men under control when they were away chasing down Yankees? 'They've marched a thousand miles for this blessed scene,' Capers had said.

Frank reported back to Gist, who, with what cohesion he had left in his command, angled his brigade away from the pike, tending to the west. The bulk of the Union men were fleeing close to the road, but Frank could see there were a smaller number to the brigade's immediate front. They were escaping toward a grove of locust trees that had been hacked down to shoulder height, the branches snapped and sharpened and left in a tangled mass. All but spent, the getaways tried to claw their way through to the other side and on toward the barricade.

There was a lull in the firing as between claps of thunder. The smoke briefly cleared and the sky was red to the west. 'What now, sir?' asked Frank.

Gist stood in his stirrups to look at his gathered regiments, heedless of the lead that sliced the air between them. Frank tried to follow his example, but it was unnerving. He wished more than ever for a smaller horse.

A bullet split the rifle stock of a soldier not ten paces away who dropped it like an angry snake. Around them men knelt to reload or drank from their canteens.

'We have maybe half the brigade still with us,' said Gist. 'Our orders haven't changed. We will attack those works.'

Frank exhaled.

'No better time,' Gist said, then bellowed, 'Forward!' and urged his horse toward the grove. Frank stayed beside him. Their men yelled and took up the chase again, spurring the last of the routed Yankees to struggle ever more desperately to get through the evil branches. The brigade was halfway to the locust grove when a thousand rifles were leveled over and under the head log on the barricade, a single bright Union flag held high above. There was a weighty moment. Frank had time to remember to get his head behind Ashley's neck before the rifles fired, almost as one. The blast was instantly followed by a collective slap of lead on flesh or bone, impact grunts then cries of pain. Frank was staggered once by the blast and again to find he wasn't hit. Ahead of him Gist's horse reared. Gist jumped to the ground, his horse twisting in pain before going down on a front knee. Frank dismounted to see if his general was hurt. When he dropped his rein, Ashley turned and ran for Alabama.

'General?'

'I'm fine. We must keep on.' Gist started forward on foot and Frank followed, drawing his sword. As they reached the trees, a second volley struck. Men collapsed either side of Frank. There was no choice other than to press on into the tangle. He used his sword to hack a path. Gist made better ground to his left. Frank stopped to unhook a cursing soldier to his right whose thigh had been opened by the thorns, then hurried to catch up. Sooner than he expected they were clear through, the barricade no more than twenty paces before them, a ditch to its front. He could hear the Yankee orders to load, then to hold fire. He felt light-headed, as if his life-blood had already drained from him. Their own men bunched up; Rebel flags lifted over and through the cut trees. To stay was to die, so he pushed forward, his sword suddenly a child's toy. The Union rifles leveled again, as close as a firing squad. Frank had a sudden image of the spiral staircase at home, as if it led upward from here. He heard only the start of the order to fire before it was obliterated by the thunderous roar of rifles. He felt the heat of it, turned away as if that might save him. When he looked back, one eye open on death, Gist was down. Frank knelt beside him, protected him as the brigade struggled to recover. Incredibly, they did. And then as Frank watched on unbelieving, his countrymen charged the works.

Gist was hit in the thigh and in the chest; there was blood at his mouth. Frank caught a soldier running by, grappled him, threw away his rifle. 'Help me. Help me get the general away.'

'Frank,' said Gist. 'Take me home to my wife.'

*

Colonel Emerson Opdycke let go of Private Shire and bellowed for his horse. A mounted staff officer arrived from Cox and told Opdycke to get his brigade ready to support the front line. Once atop Ben he could see further up the road. A heaving mass of Union men were fleeing toward him down the pike. 'They don't need supporting,' he said. 'They need replacing.'

Careless of the fastest deserters, he pushed Ben fifty yards up the road. This terrified mob wasn't only Wagner's, he realized, but full of regiments from the barricade as well. Shire was right: the line was broken. Cresting Carter Hill came men in butternut and gray, triumphant men, wild men, their flags raised. Nearer at hand, a cannon ball bounced diagonally off the road and demolished a laden mule.

He had to get the brigade in order. He drew Ben around and hurried back to find his veteran men standing, coffee mugs thrown aside, skillets of half-cooked pork abandoned. They grabbed their rifles from the pyramid stacks. Lines formed without orders. There was so little time. If he could get the whole brigade to the east side of the road there would be more room. Perhaps he should let the worst of the Union deluge pass and then step back to hold the pike.

Without looking back up the road he could hear the roar behind him growing. He rode in among the 125th. Captain Bates was there on foot.

Opdycke yelled, 'Get the regiment over the road!'

Bates looked past him, stupefied. The din grew louder still.

'Bates!' Opdycke tried to point. Ben abruptly circled beneath him and he clutched at the reins. He heard someone yell, 'Forward!' from across the road and steadied Ben so he could look. Major Motherspaw was in front of his 73rd Illinois, one of Opdycke's regiments. They were drawn up in a ragged line. 'Forward!' Motherspaw shouted again and stepped off up the hill. His men stepped out behind him.

'No!' screamed Opdycke. Motherspaw had taken Opdycke's unbalanced pointing for the order to charge. Colonel Smith had started his regiment forward as well. It was too late to stop them. Dear Lord above. He'd lost control of his brigade.

Bates found his voice. 'Are we to charge, sir?'

Around him the men of the 125th looked to him, their grizzled faces contoured by the setting sun. His veterans demanded the order. There was no real choice anymore. They must all go in. They had to retake the barricade. He shouted as if he was Isiah come to Earth. 'First Brigade! Forward to the works.'

The 125th leveled their bayonets and ran past him up the right side of the road, the 24th Wisconsin beyond them. Opdycke rode inside the wave and headlong at the wild mass of fleeing men crowding down the hill. The brigade had little room and became squeezed together, a solid mass of regiments and companies, their weary limbs reanimated, maddened that they should have to fight again after their long efforts this day. But his men knew what they had to do.

Faced with bayonets, the mob fleeing down the hill tried to scatter, terrified of their army in front almost as much as by the Rebels behind. Those that didn't or couldn't veer away found no welcome, but were instead harshly thrown behind or trampled underfoot. A few, then more and more – men who'd had no chance out on the plain, or who'd been swept from the barricade by the rout – turned around to join Opdycke's gathering charge.

There was no further hope of issuing an order, not amid the wild cry of his brigade. None was needed. His tigers were set free and God help all before them. He bared his teeth at the gray traitors to his front and roared.

*

At the quick, Shire strode back up the road he'd so recently run down, tight to the right-hand side, his bayonet glinting and low. Tuck and the squad pressed in around him. Unlike his friends, he knew the scale of what was waiting; he'd seen the endless rows of Rebels, seen the barricade overrun. What good would it do to tell them? There wasn't a trace of fear or doubt in the men around him. They leaned into the slope, faces set in a collective snarl, screamed at the fleeing soldiers to get the hell out of the way.

A runaway team of horses dragged a caisson down the road, their eyes white, heads high, fighting their traces. Shire and Company B hurriedly veered off to the right to avoid being run over. The teamster swore and lost his hat. The lead horse's flank brushed and unbalanced Shire before the careering load clattered by. The gap created in the line closed so quickly after the caisson passed that Company B couldn't regain the road. They were left advancing off to the side. The smoke from up the road ghosted the setting orange sun. A single stray bullet clipped a tree above him. He lifted his bayonet away to grab at a panicked drummer-boy, threw him and his silent drum behind. They came to the solid head-high close-board fence that formed the southern boundary of the Carter yard, evidently so sturdy it had survived the earlier pillage for the barricades. Union fugitives escaped around its end. Shire could hear the smack, smack as lead balls struck the other side.

'Break it down!' came a shout, which might have been Ocks. His English accent was on the slide as was Shire's. What a time to wonder on accents. Along with the front line, Shire reversed his rifle and began to jab and beat at the wood, at first to little effect. A breach was made away to the squad's right. Men started to pour through just as a frustrated blow from Mason finally broke into their section. They tore at the boards like madmen, hurried through and then along the side of the Carter's ell to rush around between the corner and the well, only to stop cold.

Ocks yanked Shire and Tuck sideways by their collars and into line. Amid the smoky familiarity of the Carters' yard – the long back porch ahead to his left, the detached kitchen his right – were the last and bravest of the Union men who'd been pushed from the barricades. Facing them, and on this side of the inner barricade, before the farm office and the smokehouse, were any number of Rebels; some alone, some in clusters, not a few with rifles raised. Others dragged away or visited murder on the Union men that were left. Bodies were scattered across the yard. Wounded men tried to pull themselves away; others were the only silent, still characters in the scene. Seeing the 125th, the Rebels got into line; more men joined them from behind.

'Ready!' shouted Ocks, his pistol low to his side.

They'd all loaded them before they stacked.

'Aim!'

Shire's rifle was heavy and awkward with the bayonet fixed. He tried to steady the notched sight on the midriff of a bearded Rebel not twenty paces to his front, who was frantically ramming home a ball.

'Fire!'

Smoke blasted along the line of the company, made louder by the buildings that surrounded the Carter yard. 'Charge!' came the cry from all quarters. Shire leapt forward into the thin veil of smoke and the madness, his own wild scream escaping. Tuck was a long half-step ahead. Through the haze and his own zeal, Shire glimpsed a few Rebels get off a rushed volley. All was noise and chaos. He didn't see anyone go down. How could they miss? The enemy screamed the high-pitched berserker yell of the rebellion and charged, bolstered by fresh men, a solid line, bayonets leveled. To hesitate, to flinch or shrink, was to concede. Instead, Shire drew from a deep well of fury and rage; fury that he'd ever had to fight this war; rage that he'd lost everything; rage that these rabid men fought like devils for an ugly idea.

The collision when it came was like nothing on this earth, a dizzy frenzy of blows, shots and screams. His world shrunk to no more than the man to his front, who grimaced and lunged his rifle forward. Shire knocked it upwards with his own, recovered quickest and stabbed at the man, a half-thrust but enough to pierce him high in the stomach. Knocked in the back, Shire was propelled forward, his weight fully behind his rifle and his bayonet. The man fell backwards and screamed. Shire was over him, the bayonet in up to the socket. He could feel the hard earth of the yard on the blade and used it through the flesh to gain his balance. He twisted and pulled. The blade resisted but then came free so suddenly that he had to catch himself and stood there holding his rifle two-handed like a staff. His enemy rolled and curled on the ground below him.

Cleves was to his right, losing a rifle-wrestle to a bigger man. Shire jabbed his rifle butt hard into the Rebel's knee, heard the bone shatter despite the clamor. Cleves broke the hold, reversed his rifle and clubbed the side of the man's head.

Where was Tuck? The pressure built from behind: weight from the regiment. Shire was forced forward again. His every breath spanned a collection of scenes that played out before he drew the next. A Rebel backed off to raise an evil heavy pistol at him only to go down with a bullet through his neck. He found himself over by the Carter porch, close below a private fight on the steps, a Rebel with a hatchet hacking into a raised arm. Shire swallowed a breath thick and rancid with the taste of fear and blood. Hell had visited the Earth; wild hate, no quarter.

He backed into someone and spun to find it was Tuck. Tuck as a monster, high and crazed, screaming at the Rebels to come on. They did. Tuck was without his rifle, nothing but a naked bayonet in his hand. He flew at anyone that came in range. Shire raced at the Rebel busy with the hatchet on the steps; a low shoulder charge that took the man high beneath a raised arm between strokes, knocked him full over the banister to land down on the cellar steps, twisted and still. The victim of the hatchet was bleeding out, his eyes departing from the world. It was Corporal Cobb, his short stubble a measure of how long he'd survived his return to the army. Tuck reached into the scene, picked up the bloodied hatchet and ran madly at the nearest Rebel, a weapon in each hand. Shire turned to watch him and, elevated on the porch, looked out over a scene of insanity. A deep bellow of anger rose above the tumult and Shire watched Opdycke, on foot before his men, pistol flaming orange again and again as he emptied the chambers at the Rebels who came on. Opdycke reversed the weapon and clubbed them, striking over rifles and arms held up in defense, beyond fury, as if he could beat the Devil from the Earth. Sergeant Murdock took a bullet to the chest and was trampled under; Captain Bates shoved away friend and foe to haul him up and back. There was a chance to load if Shire was quick. He did it without taking his eyes from the scene. Ocks, his own revolver lost, was setting about the enemy with nothing more than his fists and his head, making ground until he reached a Rebel sergeant his own size and armed with a saber. Ocks dodged one slash but tripped and went down on one knee. Shire wasn't ready. The saber rose over Ocks as he tried to stand. Shire dropped his ramrod and fired from the waist, taking the Rebel high in the chest. Ocks drove the man back and collected the saber, raised it himself, but was lost to Shire as Company B surged forward.

The Rebels were forced back toward the smokehouse and the farm office, back to the inner barricade. Opdycke led his men on. There was Rice in the thick of it. Shire jumped down from the porch and added his weight alongside Tuck. Mason was there, blood streaming from the side of his head. He and Corry screamed in together with their bayonets side by side. It was chaos, no clear lines. The only prize that made sense was the inner barricade. Some of the Rebels raised their hands and were sent to the rear. Shire and Tuck joined with Corry and Mason and fought on until they came around the smokehouse, on to the inner barricade. Suddenly it was theirs. Along to their right a stand of Rebel colors fell. More Rebels surrendered and those that didn't retreated away in the smoke and the lessening noise, back toward the outer barricade. A ragged cheer went up as the stars and stripes were held aloft. There was a long empty moment. Everyone who still could caught their breath. Shire looked back over the small square of the Carter yard that they'd won. The smoke had settled into a low and level cloud not more than a few feet above the men left standing, a pale and sickly yellow shroud for the thick harvest of the dead and the dying.

*

The 20th Tennessee was close at hand. Tod was welcomed by Colonel Shy, but the nods from the men he knew, men he'd joined up with, meant more. This was their town too, their homes. It was impossible not to be drawn to the shellfire and the fury of rifles away to their right. Rosencrantz could have taken him there in a heartbeat; a quick canter. Who would say anything after today if he sidestepped in the line to fight on his own land? Whatever was passing over there was obscured by the bitter smoke that drifted through the ranks and lingered in the soon-to-be winter grass. Bate's Division was late; they'd had the furthest to go to get into position. The battle was already joined, and the join was Tod's home.

'Where do you want me, sir?' he asked Shy.

Shy looked him over and dug out a smile. 'I suppose it wouldn't do to ask you to report to the quartermaster in back of the line, see if he has everything in hand?'

'Maybe tomorrow.'

'Pick a company then, but go in on foot. A gray horse will draw their fire.'

'He's as good as a flag to the men. I'll stay aboard.'

'Alright.'

They passed through the tidy Bostick yard, a house much grander than his own. Everbright, they called it, for the candles Rebecca Bostick used to keep burning in the windows. Mother, Lord rest her, used to say how wasteful it was. Tod smiled and mumbled to himself, 'A thick slice of ham's a better welcome than a candle.' From behind them, a shell arced above the regiment and the house toward the town. A single long scream. He'd always liked Everbright, especially at this time of day when the light was fading. He spared a second to look for familiar faces but there were no candles today, only shuttered windows and a mute but somehow strident wish from the house that the army would pass on by and let it be. What would he do anyway, if he saw Rebecca's ashen face looking out? Tip his hat? Ride across and shout through the glass and above the battle-roar that he'd be back to help set straight her fences just as soon as he got a furlough?

Beyond the house the land fell away down to Carter's Creek. As they walked down, the town and the Union line became hidden by the low ridge on the other side. The tumult from the right was partly muted. After they crossed the creek, Shy had them dress the lines for the attack and Tod fretted on

Rosencrantz. The battle was raging. They should go in quick and hard, not trouble over alignment. When they started up the low ridge, Rosencrantz nervously sawed below him, back and forth between the guiding sergeants. Behind them the men came on with guns balanced against their left shoulders, some red of face, some pale as death; all stepped short to take the slope.

The crest broke slowly. When Rosencrantz gained the top, the battle was revealed anew and full-throated. Not two hundred paces away was a solid Union breastwork, bristling with rifles, a long line of them leveled below the head log, hundreds more angled at the sky, held ready. Down the easy slope to his right, the smoke cleared away. He could see his house plainly, the tiled roof an island in a raging sea of men. His home was swamped in anger. No neat and tidy lines, just a maddened and screaming throng. After all the long years and hard miles of the war, after having to turn away just yesterday, there were still Yankees between him and his home. Well, no more. Today, he'd sweep them away.

Closer below, halfway to his house, the locust grove was a scene of butchery. Father's trees had been hacked and shot to stubs. Bodies lay before and between the wood. Men forced their way through the bloodied and slain forest, stepping over and on the dead to reach the barricade. The thought of Frank somewhere in that mess… He could see Rebel flags beyond the defenses. The line must be taken then; his army across and into Father's garden. Hope wrestled with fear. He watched a Union shell sweep a clutch of charging Rebels from the world limb by limb. The scene found no lodgment in his mind and his gaze moved on. Union men crowded this side of his backyard, beside and along from the smokehouse. Union men defending *his* family ground, claiming it as their own, flags raised. Yankee dogs, every last one of them.

Around him the 20th Tennessee crowded forward so he had to nudge Rosencrantz on. He hauled his mind back to his front. Benton Smith needed to send them in, challenge the Yankee line directly ahead and widen the breach, force the enemy away. Why the wait? Shy was here. The regiment was all here. He took out his revolver and drew Rosencrantz around to face west. Beyond the 20th the other regiments of Smith's Brigade were only now cresting the hill, forcing the delay. As Smith had said, the Union line angled out here and Tod could see beyond the barricade. There was a battery of guns this side of the Carter's Creek Pike, all aimed his way. He watched the last gunner step back, saw a gunnery sergeant yank down his arm, saw the lanyard pulled. The shells arrived in the next heartbeat, exploding in and above the 20th, men dropping and dead before they had time to scream. Rosencrantz reared and twisted and Tod thought he must surely fall. He was still tucked into his horse's neck when the rifles opened from in front, a long sheet of yellow flame, their rippled blast barely ahead of the buzz and smack of lead. More men fell in the front rank. On this ridge the setting sun was half behind them; it made them easy targets for the Yankees.

'We must go in,' he screamed across to Shy. He might as well have screamed at the moon. Shy couldn't hear. Rosencrantz reared again. If he didn't give him his head, they would fall. The Yankees were loading, cannon and infantry both. Shy raised his sword but Tod could wait no longer and pushed Rosencrantz forward down the slope. He angled him to miss the locust grove, as near a path to home as he could find. He didn't see Shy give the order, but heard the Rebel yell and knew the men followed on. The ground was uneven. He had to look down, draw Rosencrantz to the left. He raised his pistol, looked up into a second sheet of flame and was struck hammer-hard. They fell together, Rosencrantz twisting so Tod was thrown down the slope. He heard his horse's winded grunt as the animal hit the ground and rolled, blurring legs and hooves so close. He needed to catch his breath but it hurt. Lay a moment. Where was he hit? He blinked to clear his vision but one eye stung fiercely. He lay facing back up the slope, away from his home, and the men ran on by, the roar of battle moving past him toward Franklin. He couldn't move. Rosencrantz thrashed and squealed beside him. The world blurred then cleared and still Tod couldn't rise. A sergeant – he didn't know the man – walked down the hill and shot Rosencrantz in the head. It pinched at Tod's heart but was then lost in a deeper lake of sadness. The sergeant walked on by without a word. Could he not see Tod? He wanted to call out but there were so many cries. He wanted to roll over and look at home. There was a spreading dampness under his back. He rested. When he looked out on the world again it was darker, redder. He could hear the battle but it was muffled. Men walked past and away from him but back up the hill, alone or supporting each other. One fellow – Tod couldn't tell if the man was laughing or crying – came within touching distance, a soldier on his back whose tattered leg was shot away below the knee. A flag, torn and low, moved away and over the hill. The battle grew quieter. It must be over.

*

Outside the day was dying. In the cellar they were yet to light a candle or a lamp. Moscow sat with his back to the cold whitewashed wall and felt the latest explosion resonate through the stone and down his spine. He'd never felt so sick with fear. He had one arm around Lena and the other around Walter. In turn, Walter held Hugh on his lap and Lena held tight to Annie, to whom she'd heroically donated her doll. Along the wall, as far away from the cellar door as they could collectively get, were similar studies of care in threes and fours. Only Father sat alone, his normally square beard become ragged. In the half-light he looked like an Old-Testament prophet who had, at the final day, come to doubt everything.

Earlier, while they could speak and still hope to hear each other, Moscow had asked the children to crowd in under the long wooden dining table. If a shell came through the ceiling it would be something at least. He'd had his own littlest ones, Hugh and Annie, go under first and it became a game, briefly distracting the children from the swell of musketry above ground. But when the cannon fired, when the first screams and wails found their way around the edges of the cellar door, followed by pitiful entreaties to God or to faraway mothers, the children had scrambled back out, preferring the more telling comfort of warm arms and kissed heads.

Persistent guilt gnawed at Moscow. A father should never gamble his family. If all his years in the army – in Mexico and then fighting for this concocted Confederacy – were ever to be of value, surely it should have been to get his family away from harm. Instead, he'd kept them at Franklin until it was too late.

The soundscape of battle was not new to him, it had been the necessary accompaniment to the butchering and the blood in his past. But back then, his eyes had suffered the lion's share of the horror. Here, clutching his children, his cold cheek against Lena's tied-back hair, sound ruled in their dim low-ceilinged world. Before the fight started, there had been urgent voices and strident orders from Father's room overhead: rushed footsteps, the heavy scrape of furniture. Then came the shattering of glass and rifles fired from the house. That was an experience rare to anyone, he thought, to hear your home torn and ruptured, pelted with lead, transformed into a poor man's fort. In time, there was the familiar thump of the hit, the solid fall of bodies.

Since then, there had been something of a let-up; less movement above and, as far as he could tell, out in the yard. Now there came cries anew. Battering outside, wood on wood, orders to present and aim. The burst and rip of rifles. Walter twitched so hard he struck his head on the wall. A roar and a yell. A collision overflowed with rage and agony. Father looked at Moscow in horror as if to say, *Is this war?* Something – *someone*, more likely – collided with the cellar door and his sisters cried out. A second later, a shell struck the house and left a long metallic note amid their cries and whimpers, as if they were huddled inside a bell. He couldn't sit still any longer. He jumped up, spilling children, and yelled to Father, 'Help me move the table!' Sarah was there first, but then Father too and they wrestled it tight up against the door. Somehow separate from the uproar outside, he heard a private killing up the steps. *Please. No!* Three strikes, two grunts.

'Into the storeroom,' Moscow shouted. No one moved. He grabbed Sarah and pointed. She nodded and hurried to the back wall and roused everyone. Moscow collected his pistol from where he'd left it beside the cold fireplace and returned to the door, prepared to shoot soldiers from either side if they tried to force the weight of the table. It was darker, the flare of rifles and the sudden brilliance of cannon flashing through the window grate, dotting time. His sisters, Albert Lotz and his family, all crowded toward the storeroom. They moved between the stab-light, as if the fabric of God's creation had begun to fray. Finally, came the two black families. He briefly caught Jack's fearful eyes, considered for a moment that it was their new and fragile freedom that was the grounds for the murder above and the danger to his children. He both resented them and chastised himself; they'd had no say in the matter. He followed on behind. Last into the storeroom, pistol in hand, he drew across the heavy curtain that served as a poor man's door, as if that might save them.

*

There was a respite. How long it might last Shire didn't know, but he began to spend it searching for himself, trying to recover his mortal soul that he'd lost in the frenzied and bloody fight across the Carter's yard. He stared dumbly at Cleves, at that ill-favored face he used to despise but that now, in its long acquaintance, seemed a safe anchorage. He didn't understand that Cleves was offering him water until the cold metal of the canteen touched his lips.

He thanked Cleves only with his eyes. The water garnered something in him and he looked about. They were all here: Corry was close behind Cleves; Tuck stared angrily out into the smoke to the south of the inner-barricade; Mason wiped the bloodied side of his head with a rag and Ocks stood wearily with his stolen saber, a hand against the smokehouse.

Tight around them Shire recognized more men of Company B, but just as many were not from their regiment. The Wagner rout and then the charge back up to the inner-barricade had jumbled them all. Captured Rebels were herded from the yard. Down the line stood a reassuring battery of six cannon, pointing south. He looked back to the front and the smoke briefly thinned. He could see across the large Carter garden, sixty paces of churned ground, bracketed north and south by the inner and outer barricades. The Union held the inner, but the Rebels were massing. Surely, they would not come on again?

He was wrong. First a volley had Shire and the squad duck their heads behind splintering defenses, then the Rebel flags rose. Over the far ramparts they came screaming. Shire desperately loaded in the thin space afforded him, thinking he should have done so before now. The cannon belched cannister out into the garden and men were variously knocked flat or swept into the air – some whole, some less so – and back into their comrades. Shire stood tall to aim. There was no command, just hundreds of men firing as they presented, felling the Rebels as they fought on, heads and hats lowered in the forlorn hope that might protect them from the pelting lead rain. They had no cover unless it was the flesh of the man in front.

Shire reached for a cartridge but his rifle was snatched away, another placed loaded into his hands. He faced front again. The Rebels were halfway over the garden. He fired. The smoke was bitter in his mouth. As he coughed the rifle was snatched again, a new one presented. Beside him Tuck played the same role: executioner. They fired and fired with every new rifle. It was happening right along the crowded line; the men at the back who couldn't fire loaded for those who could. He blinked and squeezed his eyes to clear the sulfur sting. The cannon fired once more. Endless Rebels emerged like wraiths from the smoke only to be struck and to fall.

It became a cycle. A brief lull, a Rebel volley and then they would charge again, across their own carpet of dead, sometimes reaching nearer, other times barely climbing over the outer-barricade before they slunk bag, chastised and bloodied. Shire became tired to his core of the shooting. Let someone else take a turn. He was no more than a servant to the Devil, helping death take control of this small patch of earth. There were shouts for more ammunition. He passed a rifle back but none came forward.

The Rebels crowded over their barricade yet again but this time paused to fire a massed volley at the cannon. Shire looked across and saw cannoneers down or clutching at wounds.

'Mason,' shouted Ocks. 'Your squad with me.'

Mason yanked Shire out of the line and he hurried after Cleves and Tuck across to the six cannon. Other men rushed over to man the guns as well. Out in the garden a thinner Union volley slowed the new Rebel charge. The squad stepped over or around dead or injured cannoneers to take over the first gun. There was only one man left: not an artilleryman but an infantry sergeant. He put his hand over the vent and directed them; yelled at Shire to get cannister from the ammunition chest. Ocks brought up a charge. Corry sponged out the barrel. Shire collected the gray cylinder and hurried to the muzzle. Tuck rammed home the charge and then the cannister and they rolled the gun forward, angled it toward the Rebel charge that raced at them. The sergeant set the primer and screamed at them to stand away, but Tuck was still at the muzzle. Shire shouted at him. Tuck held in his hand the burnt enamel doorknob from his home. He fed it into the barrel, screamed something unintelligible. A flock of bullets pinged off the metal. The cannoneer was struck in the hand and dropped the lanyard. Tuck collapsed as if his legs had been axed. Shire bent across him, reached down for the lanyard and looked up into the contorted faces of the Rebels who sprinted the last yards, their bayonets pointing right at him.

'Kill the bastards!' shouted Ocks.

Shire swallowed and tried to draw breath at the same time. Half-choking, he yanked the lanyard. It was as if he was part of the detonation. The cannon jolted back and caught him a glancing blow, enough to throw him to the ground beside Tuck and the dead crew. He scrambled up, unarmed, expecting the Rebels to charge home… but they were gone, shattered into remnants of men, strewn crimson across the garden, their flag tattered among the blood and gore. The cannon to their right fired one after another and the charge dissolved, the garden once more no more than a home for smoke and agony.

Shire knelt beside Tuck, who sat up. 'Did you see?' he said. He gripped Shire by the arm. 'I got Ma and Pa into the fight. Did you see?'

'I saw. Let me look at your leg.' Shire ripped away the bloodied cloth below the knee and Tuck winced. It was a mess, but not pumping blood. 'Corry. Help me lift him.'

'Let me be. It was worth it. Worth taking a bullet.'

A captain, his face black with powder, called for a Union charge. 'At them while they're reeling! Who's with me?'

A flag rose, not that of the 125th, but it didn't matter. A thin line of men quickly mustered. Mason handed Shire a rifle, the bayonet fixed. Shire looked to Tuck.

'Go,' said Tuck. 'Leave me with Corry. You go.'

Mason spun Shire to the front. The sun must be down, Shire thought; it seemed darker out in the garden though the smoke to the west was still tinged orange-red. Fistfuls of cartridges were shared, rifles loaded. The captain stood high on the barricade with the flag and called them on. Shire clambered over behind Cleves and they tarried briefly on the other side until most were across, around a hundred or more. They answered the captain's shout to charge with an angry bellow and sprung forward. It was no distance at all to the outer-barricade, but the ground was carpeted with men and slick with the blood Shire had spilled. At first it was hard to get up any pace, difficult to pick his way over the dead until he became careless of them, ran on and over them. He wished Tuck was at his side but outpaced Cleves, outpaced everyone but the flag-bearer. He surrendered to elation as the only way to go forward, breathless in the release. A tumbling crow, utterly out of place, tipped this way and that in the smoky orange light above the barricade. The volley struck, a breath of flame and hot lead from the Rebels massed behind the outer-barricade. Bullets smacked bone and flesh behind him but he didn't stop. The flag dropped but was picked up again only for a bullet to strike and splinter the staff. He was out in front now, almost there, the outer-barricade before him. There was no ditch this side. He looked sideways and was alone. He should go back. A Rebel leapt from the works; the butt of his rifle cracked down onto Shire's head. All was pain and light. He waited for the end, for the cold steel thrust of a bayonet.

'Take him.' He was dragged upright. Rough-hewn wood scraped his chest as he was pushed and pulled over the barricade to fall awkwardly the other side, only to be stood up again within a ditch full of screaming Rebels.

An angry and close face. 'Git to the rear! Git to the rear!'

He didn't know which way that was. He touched his head and his fingers came away wet with blood. Another man came at him with a knife and carelessly cut away his cartridge box. Rebels were packed inside this ditch. A volley out of nowhere struck down its length and felled Shire's captor. Men panicked, more jumping inside in the false hope the ditch might save them. They collided with Shire, trampled the injured men beneath. A second volley and more men fell, one clutched at him and held on tight, began to drag Shire down. Others tried to climb the barricade, preferring to charge again rather than face this new slaughter, but cannister swept them back into the ditch. A new corpse, the head torn away, landed on Shire like an axed bough and he crumbled, gasping for smoky air, screams above and below, writhing men, clutching hands that pinched and clawed. His mouth pressed hard into the bloodied earth. He couldn't breathe. He must already be at the gates of hell. Too much weight. No light.

*

As Clara rode Cincin nearer to the base of the hills, the guns became quieter. She didn't know if it was the battle diminishing or because of the tighter shelter of the ground. What if the battle was over and there was nothing to see, then she'd have wasted the day arguing the rights and wrongs of riding out. She was *still* arguing them.

The question of whether to come and see for herself had surprised her when it was prompted by the rising rumble of guns that had reached her new home from Franklin. She'd answered herself firmly enough at the time. She should stay on the farm as she had yesterday and let the war move on. After all, it wasn't her war. It never had been. It began after she arrived in America. She'd assumed, back then, like all the British wars she'd ever heard speak of, that it would be fought far removed from her. If she kept busy, she might pretend this battle was no more than distant thunder over the horizon of a pretend sea.

But as she rode on through the woods and up into the hills in the last of the light, the reply won out again. How could it not be her war when it had so long delayed her marriage, set wholly free the violence hidden in her husband, and robbed her of a home and people she cared for? But for this war, she would never have conceived and lost a child, or come to this new home where she was so utterly alone. It was self-evident that the life now granted her had been roughly hewn from her old one *by* this war.

The pike outside Eversholt had become busy in the late afternoon once the guns had started; less so with soldiers, more with the people of Williamson County, gawkers and voyeurs as she'd first considered them, as tempted by the prospect of a battle as they might be by a public hanging. Her thoughts had curved around to ask what right she had *not* to witness it herself? Beyond Shire and Tod there were the Carters, Lena and Alice, the Lotz family. What if they'd not managed to get away? And the surprise meeting with Frank Trenholm had unnerved her; a boy she'd briefly known who'd become a man who was off to fight. This war was old enough to grow up in.

The guns swelled once more and suddenly she was sure she didn't want it to be over. She needed to see it, witness the fight at its zenith. That seemed an evil thought, at odds with those that had drawn her from the safety of her balcony: that this war wasn't done with her or her loved ones. In a matter of days, she'd said goodbye to Shire, then Mitilde, Moses and Cele, and finally Tod. All at the end of her drive, in the exact same spot, as if God had put her on this earth to do no more than say farewell. At each goodbye she'd hoped the battle would be long delayed or happen far away, but here it was, just over this hill.

She crested the final rise and the sound of battle multiplied ten-fold. The trees were too thick and blocked any view, but she finally arrived at the sure truth of what had drawn her to the barn to saddle Cincin and hurry this way. It was something beyond voyeurism, beyond even the people she loved. It was the necessity that if this war was going to divert her life yet again and cull her possible futures, this time she wouldn't wait for the news to be brought to her door. She'd ride out and see it. Then at least in the years ahead, as the old and false dowager she may be destined to become, she'd have seen the brute force, born of this age, that turned the unsteady wheel of her world.

The argument settled in her mind at last, she rode out onto a bald that opened to the north. Cincin found her own place to stop. Clara couldn't have said how long she stared down across the plain to Franklin before she recovered enough of herself to begin to take in any detail. She'd come this way once before, in October, and looked out over the fall colors. That gentle landscape had been transformed to fire and ruin. The sun had set, and though there remained an orange-red sky to her left, it was Franklin that was aflame. The town was wreathed in dark drifts of smoke punctured by stabs of light: gunfire and cannon fire. Fort Granger to the north-east was almost claimed by the night but threw out a constant barrage of shells onto the plain. She watched them in awe as they arced toward her, only to fall far, far short and explode above or among the charcoal fields of men. She struggled to find the Carter house and had to retreat her view to the fading white of the Columbia Pike, then follow it forward through the mayhem to what appeared to her the very epicenter of the battle. Two miles away though she was, the anger and agony of the men carried to her, blended into the breeze like a howl not of this earth. Shire was likely down there. Tod and Frank certainly were. And for most of the day she'd been selfishly obsessed with what it meant to her. *Dear Lord, protect them.*

The twitch of a flag drew her eye to a scene lower down the bald. There was a clump of Confederate officers, all mounted, all with field glasses raised except the man out in front, an older man perhaps; it was hard to tell in this light. He sat tall but awkward, his right leg high and straight on the side of his horse. She watched for a while, but they were doing nothing but watching on themselves so she looked back to the battle. She tried to collect it all, gather in what was before her, but it was too vast, too much to carry in one moment. She searched for a sense of how the battle might be faring. The light was fading by the minute but she began to discern the drift of men back toward the hills, mostly in ones and twos, as if the weight of the fiery tide had turned. What flags they carried were held low. Wagons moved purposefully into the fields like they might to collect a harvest.

Below and near to her there was movement. A ragged soldier stepped out from the trees and climbed the slope. He was breathing hard but singing all the same. The officers were further down. If they'd heard him, they paid him no mind. He was coming straight toward her. Now he was well out in the open, she could see he carried two dead rabbits. Their back feet tied by a single cord, they swung as he climbed and sang. It wasn't a tune she knew but a happy melody. She could barely make out any words. Perhaps this man hadn't come from the battle at all. He had no gun and appeared insensible to the fields of destruction that served as his backdrop. He came within a few feet with no sign that he'd noticed Clara at all, content with his rabbits and his song. As he passed by, Clara twitched Cincin to turn so she could watch him go. By the sudden light of a distant shell, she saw the back of his head was crushed and open to the air, a wet and pulpy bloodied mass, like fresh turkey mince. Whatever functioned inside seemed to be working only to recall his song and the joy of taking supper home to his family, however distant they might be.

She looked over the undiminished battle for the last time. She couldn't know if her coming here might matter to her in the years ahead, only that she felt as desolate as the scene before her. She whispered a further prayer for those she loved. As she turned to go, she glanced down to the watching officers, but they were no longer there.

PART IV

Franklin, Tennessee – December 1ˢᵗ, 1864

Moscow Carter tapped his father's arm. Fountain dutifully moved his pocket-watch close to the lantern one more time. It was two in the morning. The single source of light left most of the storeroom and his collected family in the dark. To Moscow's right, on the loose pile of turnips and beets and under the few blankets they had, his children slept. Father kept vigil with him, arm-chaired in root vegetables as Moscow was.

How to tell when it was safe to venture out? There had been no gunfire for a good while. Above them their home was still; no footsteps on the boards, only the occasional moan mixed in with pleas for water or for the Lord's mercy. What use would it be to surface now anyhow? They could hardly put the children to bed as if nothing had happened. Two of his sisters were talking in the dark, soft whispers weaving in and out of tears.

Perhaps the worst was over. During the long evening the battle had died several times only to flare again, sometimes distant, sometimes closer at hand. In one of the longer interludes a lone voice outside, trembling to start with, had started to sing. *'We'll rally round the flag, boys.'* It was slowly picked up. *'Down with the traitors, and up with the stars.'* There was a somber edge to the melody, as if it were a requiem rather than a call to arms. He wearily imagined himself gathering his sisters to answer with 'The Bonnie Blue Flag', sung from under the earth, but if truth be told his heart wasn't in it any more than those Union boys.

Around midnight there had been movement in the house, a more purposeful rhythm to the footsteps, an excited tone to the muffled speech. From the pattern of the sounds, he judged many people had left the house. Minutes would pass without a gunshot and more than once he'd thought it was over, only for a sudden volley to crackle again and set back the minute hand of hope.

It was cold. Little wonder their stores kept so well. There was no fireplace outside of the dining room and he wouldn't have risked a fire in there anyway, but he couldn't endure the cold any longer. He struggled up, turnips shifting below him. Father extended an arm and he pulled him up too, leaving the sleeping children to settle out with the vegetables. Sisterly eyes watched him as he parted the curtain and stepped stealthily back into the dining room.

The bitter taste of smoke was stronger in here. He placed the lantern on the long table which remained pushed up against the door. Father stretched and took a chair. Moscow considered again what he might gain by going outside when several distant cannon boomed. Their ordnance shrieked high over the house and away to explode toward the center of town, as best he could tell. The firing went on. He counted by the dozen. The howls of woken children filled the gaps between screaming shells. He stopped counting after a hundred. Their own army shelling Franklin. Bombarding the patched-up bridges perhaps or the Union Army fleeing town. After ten minutes, the shells stopped. Inside the storeroom, his sisters had to soothe the children before the moans of the soldiers outside could be heard once more. He sat down with Father, who placed his watch next to the lantern and they got back to waiting.

It was near to four when they heard a few soldiers move

through the yard. Southern accents in low tones. Father took a deep breath. 'Lord be praised. He spared every one of us.'

Moscow pulled the table clear, lit a second lantern and lifted the latch. A weight against the door pushed it open and a body flopped from the cellar stair half in through the doorway, the neck canted at an unnatural angle. Moscow jumped back. He took a breath then came forward again and lifted the light over the body to look up the steps. His lantern illuminated a deposit of smoke which, heavy in the first December air, had pooled in the stairwell and now spilled in over the dead soldier. There was a gasp behind him. He turned and saw that Frances had come out from the storeroom. Moscow put down the lantern and dragged the body to the far wall.

'Shouldn't we carry him outside?' Father said. 'For the children.'

It was too late: small faces crowded behind Frances from her hip upwards.

'Wait until I say you can come up,' Moscow told her. Lantern in one hand and pistol in the other, he climbed slowly up and out onto the porch.

Around him on the white painted wood were many more bodies. The closest was fearfully hacked and disfigured, another sat with his back to the house, his chin resting on his chest. The night air stank of raw meat and open guts. He took a step sticky with blood and put the lantern on the porch-rail so he could turn up the light. Out across the yard, as far as the light dared go, bodies lay at all angles, dark islands of death in a settled shroud of smoke.

The sharper light provoked an anemic response. Fearful eyes shone back. Close-by, a soldier stretched his arm toward Moscow across the dirt. So many voices joined the calf-like bleat for water that it seemed as if the dead were pleading as well as the living. He heard a noise behind him, something between a weep and a gasp, and turned to see his father's face journey from relief to devastation. Sally and Frances had ignored his instruction, their second lantern widening the scene.

'At least keep the children down there until I check the house. Do what I say this time.' He picked his way to the door and entered, glass underfoot. The dead and the dying were everywhere. Father's room was shot to pieces. He avoided hands that clutched, ignored voices that begged. In the parlor it was no different. He stowed his pistol in a drawer; the fight was done. He lit what lamps weren't shattered and went upstairs. It was the same story in both rooms. His home was somewhere between an abandoned hospital and an untidy morgue. All Union, and not a single man left to tend them.

In the boys' room he found a stretched-out Union soldier too long for the bed, one trouser leg ripped to the knee, a bandage tight on the shin but soaked with blood. The fellow propped himself up on his elbows, eyes thin against the light.

'How long ago did they leave you?' Moscow asked.

'Some hours. Hard to say. The ambulances were long gone. Us as can't dance a reel was left.'

'That hurting you?' Moscow asked.

In answer the soldier held up a small whiskey bottle. 'My friends left me this comfort and I had someone to talk with in the dark for a while. A boy from Illinois.'

A still form beside the bed stared coldly at the ceiling.

'He's past talkin' now,' said Moscow.

'That's a sadness. He hadn't finished telling me about his home.'

'Listen, soldier. I have to have one cleared room for my

family and this is gonna be it. There's too many elsewhere and you're the only one with any anesthetic. My sisters will be along to help you move.'

'Well, that sounds almost pleasant, Colonel Carter.'

'How do you know me?'

'Hell, Mr Carter, half the 125th knows this place. We ginned your cotton a year last spring.'

Moscow left the soldier upstairs and found his way back to his sisters who'd ignored him again and come out to get water to the wounded. There were so many. Sally was working the well. He asked her to take someone with her and clear the boys' room of the soldier and the body, and then to get the smaller children moved up there before daylight arrived. Father said he'd do it and Albert Lotz went with him. The soldier would be disappointed. It was the smallest of starts. Other lights and torches moved out in the yard and beyond. Confederates coming to recover who they could. There was so much to do. He thought to move the dead to one side of the yard and the living to the other. The kitchen should be kept clear but the cellar could take wounded once the children were out. He'd get a fire lit in there.

'Is this the Carter home, sir? Are you the old colonel of the 20th Tennessee?'

Moscow turned. A scarecrow Southern soldier stood before him in the lamplight, tattered jacket and no shoes. He was wringing his cloth hat between his hands.

'Yes. I'm Colonel Carter.'

'I can't say truthfully as I recognize you, but I fought under you at Mill Springs, Colonel.'

Moscow's stomach took on a lead weight. 'Did the 20th fight right here?'

'I reckon I have some hard news, Colonel. Your brother,

Captain Carter, he's lying out in the dark a little way. He's all shot up.'

Moscow was across the yard and following before he thought to tell anyone. It was impossible to turn back; he would send the soldier again when they found Tod. *Pray God he's wrong.* They crossed into the garden. Despite his dire need to go forward, Moscow was forced to take a moment. *So many dead.* The yard behind him contained merely chaff to the death harvest that was gathered here.

'Go easy, Colonel. Some of our fallen friends have a tendency to take a hold.'

There was scarcely a place to set his feet down. The cries were pitiful, devoid of hope despite the handful of soldiers that moved among the slaughter in search of the living.

They reached the outer-barricade and had to scout in the dark for a place where they could pass over. Moscow passed up his lantern to the boy so he had both hands free to climb up the bodies and then down into the horror of the ditch on the other side, all the while fighting the urge to retch, numbing his mind to the touch of cold flesh or its give underfoot. The boy led him out further into the nightmare, across to what had once been the locust grove, but was now a felled forest for the dead. Moscow looked to each face for his brother's long-absent eyes, fearful they'd stare back cold and lifeless. They went on further beyond the grove.

'He was somewhere hereabouts. Should be easy to find. His gray horse is lying with him. Maybe he was more over this way.'

At a cry from below, Moscow swung the lantern to see a soldier trying to rise. He had a deep wound across the bridge of his nose and clean across his left eye. It was someone known to the boy, who knelt and wouldn't go on. Moscow was left to wander alone from body to body, sometimes bending to roll the dead, ignoring cries for water or succor. Other soldiers and townspeople were out in the carnage. He had no idea how long he searched. His hope started to gutter along with his lantern. When both gave out, he wept. He was lost on his own land, not a few hundred yards from home and amid a new rich topsoil of flesh and blood. Only in steering by the faintest line of light in the eastern sky did he find his way first to the pike, then on through the piles of dead heaped close to the bones of the cotton gin, and back to his house.

The front door was ajar. There was wailing within. Not soldiers this time but his sisters. Father sat on the stairs. The hands over his face parted and looked to Moscow. Brokenly, he said, 'We couldn't find you.'

'I had hard news.' Moscow's voice broke. 'I went out to find Tod.' He offered an arm as Father struggled to stand.

'His general came,' Father said. 'General Smith. He told us Tod was hurt and led us to him. He's lying in the parlor.' He wept. 'Your sisters are with him. He's come home.'

Spring Hill, Tennessee – December 1ˢᵗ, 1864

It had been a fitful night. Somewhere lost and out of depth, amid the distant rumble of cannon, Clara conceded she'd not done all she should have, and that this coming day she must put that right. Looking on from a distance wasn't going to help anyone. There were wounded in Spring Hill from the lesser battle. She should have gone there yesterday.

It was still dark when she rose from her bed and wondered if she'd truly slept at all. She fed Old George, left the stable door ajar and the gate to the pasture open, not knowing how long this day might be. Then she saddled Cincin. The warmth of yesterday was long gone and the light slowly crept into the east under a cloudy sky. She reached the end of her drive and found it impossible to turn south. There were people she loved at Franklin. Spring Hill would have to look after itself. She twisted Cincin to the north.

The road was busy and she had to move aside a number of times in favor of ambulances moving south. The light had grown flat and gray by the time she put in at the bustling Harrison house to offer her help. She was turned away by a lady in a bloodied apron. They had help enough. The need was at Franklin she was told. 'Try Carnton or the Bostick place,' the lady said. 'If half of what we've heard is true, every house north of the hills will become a hospital today.'

She pushed on through the ever-thicker traffic, the ambulances joined by lame and dazed soldiers. What water she had was soon given up. Every fresh image of blood and bone nourished the dread that swelled in her heart. When she came down out of the hills and the road evened out, she tried to steel herself to what lay ahead. So far, she'd only seen the living. Before yesterday, her only true frame of reference for war were the oil paintings that decorated the halls of Ridgmont. On occasion as a child, when sent from a room until she could *better demonstrate the demeanor befitting a young lady*, she'd stared up at those marshal scenes. The foreground was variously Wellington or Marlborough, calmly mastering a horse. The battle itself was always secondary, distant, hinted at only by a single bandaged soldier and a clutch of captured flags. It did nothing to prepare her for the ever-louder agonies of the horses and the braying of the mules, for the acrid stench of gunpowder, the stink of punctured bowels, the cloying, sickly, honeyed sweetness of blood.

Before she was within a half-mile of Franklin, she began to pass between the bodies; more and more of them in the fields as she went on. The road itself had been cleared such that it owned a curb of corpses on both sides. Cincin lifted her head, nostrils flared, aggrieved by the stink and the noise. Clara closed her eyes on the dead but Cincin shied beneath her and she had to open them again to regain control. She couldn't turn back now. She looked ahead to where the Carter house stood behind cedars that were reshaped and reduced by the battle. She should focus on that, not look to the side. If only she could shut her ears to the cries from the fields, the hundreds on hundreds of men, begging for God, for mothers, shouting out their name or regiment in the hope of rescue from the stunned soldiers and citizenry who walked the field, stupefied by the impossible scene they stepped through.

A hand clutched at Clara's arm and she looked down to a bandsman, a boy only. His fiddle was across his back like a knapsack but bloodied and shot to splinters, the catgut strings curled and sprung. He tried to form a word that might have been 'water' but couldn't get it said. In his attempt to spit it out he ducked his face to force the word free then heaved an unlikely amount of blood down Cincin's flanks. Cincin shied again and ripped Clara away and down the road where she twisted in the saddle and retched herself. The horse ran on toward what used to be the Carter's cotton gin. It was behind a barricade that might have been built from the dead so thick were they piled, and in front of that was a ditch full to the brim that stretched away both sides of the road. At last, she came to the Carter house and reined in. The cedar trunks were speckled a rude white where the bark had been shot away in a thousand dots and rents. The smokehouse, the office and the redbrick of the house were equally pock-marked. The roof was a mess of shattered tiles and half of the gable on the back side had fallen away. Two soldiers were at work in the front garden. They looked up at her, rested in the instant as if she were a timely excuse for them to stop and they'd been doing no more than digging a ditch or scything wheat. The moment passed; they got back to it, dragging bloated bodies next to the road where they stacked them like cordwood.

It was the Carters she should offer to help, but she baulked at the idea of dismounting, of stepping on the stained ground to share it with the dead. Down the road, on the slope into town, there was more industry. The people of Franklin crisscrossed the pike; wounded were helped downhill toward the houses. A single shot nearby made everyone jolt and look long enough to satisfy themselves it was no more than the dispatch of another mule. It freshly spooked Cincin, but she was steadied by someone who grabbed the bridle. It was Albert Lotz.

'Clara. Have you come to help?' Albert wore only a bloodied shirt despite the cold.

It was an effort to speak. 'Yes.'

'Good. I can use you.' He began to lead the horse down the road.

'I meant here, with the Carters. With the children.'

'There are hands enough in that house.' He looked back at her. 'And they are better by themselves today.'

Something in his voice made her heart sink. He seemed to notice.

'They all survived the night. I was with them.' He pulled them quickly on. 'They want houses for the Union wounded. Even in this wreckage the idiots want to stick to their blue and gray. No matter. I offered our home. Union or Rebel, they will stain the floors just the same.' He kicked at a dog with its nose in some offal. They came closer to the Lotz house. The near side second-floor bedroom at the back was half open to the winter. Formerly pristine white weatherboard was splintered and scattered on the ground. Albert didn't acknowledge it. The front porch was crowded with untended Union wounded. As they arrived, a further soldier was set down.

'They didn't ask for so many houses for the Union. Only a few they said. You must have seen the fields. How could anyone call that a victory?' He shook his head and helped Clara down. 'We can stable your horse and then help Margaretha roll the carpets.'

Margaretha, as Clara soon learned, was not built for this day. In truth, none of them were, but Margaretha couldn't stop crying, alternately lamenting in German and English that they had come to America to escape such things. While Albert was away trying to find more help, Clara gathered the three children and took them past the wreckage of the shell-struck bedroom and on up to the small attic room. She gave Paul, the eldest at nine, a sheet and sheers and told him to cut it into strips and get Matilda to roll them. They would have to manage two-year-old Augustus between them. The downstairs rooms were already partly populated with wounded. Albert was back, having found no one. They began to bring in those laid on the porch, helping who they could upstairs when the ground floor became full. The porch never emptied; newly arrived crippled or dumbstruck soldiers were waiting every time Clara stepped outside. Her dress became bloodied and she belatedly grabbed an apron from the kitchen. They needed a surgeon but none came. She washed and dressed what wounds she could, but some injuries didn't lend themselves to that: open stomachs or cleaved heads that she couldn't bear to place her hands on. It was a constant shock to find she could keep breathing, keep moving, in the middle of so much suffering. They learned not to take the worst wounded inside as they only had to drag them out the back once they'd died. She turned from a soldier who was fitting to find little Matilda, young eyes wide, offering up an armful of torn sheets she'd rolled tight and tied. Clara put a maternal hand to her shoulder to thank her, only to leave a bloodied stain. 'Let's find you more sheets.'

There was no time to comfort anyone. Foolishly, that's how she had thought the day might be: sat at a bedside, sharing a prayer or writing a last letter. The weeping and the cursing and the retching became no more than a backdrop to endless lifting and washing. She tore herself away to run upstairs to check on the children. Margaretha was with them, tearfully brushing Paul's hair. Clara bit down on sudden anger, but it made her curt with her weekly host. 'If you plan to stay here, then I'll need Paul to fetch and carry the water. Help

Matilda with the sheets.'

In the middle of the afternoon, an army surgeon finally arrived. He told them to get something to eat and drink while he and two orderlies inspected the rooms. She went out the back with Albert. She couldn't wipe the stain of blood from her hands so closed her eyes to put day-old bread to her mouth. The surgeon summoned her back inside, rushed her through the house and told her which patients were worth tending and which were 'at the gate.' He wanted amputations done in the air and told her to put a table outside with plenty of water set close. He'd be back when he was done elsewhere. Paul worked as hard as he could at the well, but there wasn't water enough as it was. A wagon brought barrels up from the river and left them just the one.

Once the surgeon had gone, Clara struggled to remember which patients he'd said to abandon. More blood, more stink, more death. She caught herself weeping and had no idea when she'd started. The light began to fade. She was in the parlor and there was a new soldier laid out tight to the piano. It was hard to tend to him from the one side. He stared at the ceiling, a pale sheen on his skin that she'd learned not to trust. The dressing on his shin needed changing.

'Missy.'

She stopped untying the dressing and looked up. 'Tuck?'

'Missy, do you have any water?'

'Tuck, it's Clara.'

'Saints be joyful, is that so?'

'Wait. I'll find some.'

'I ain't fixin' to run away.'

Paul had taken to filling all the canteens he could find and leaving them by the doorways. Clara collected one, put her hand under Tuck's head to help him drink. He came close to emptying it then asked anxiously after Moses and Mitilde.

'They got away before the battle,' she said. 'Most likely they're in Nashville.'

'Well, there's something to be thankful for,' he said. 'There's people in your heart rightly ahead o' me.'

It seemed a prompt to ask after Shire. She wanted to, but Tuck was suffering in front of her. 'I need to dress your leg.'

'Best tend to it then.' He winced at her touch. 'It's there to tend to at least.'

'Where did they find you? Were you out in the fields?'

'No. The Carter house. Been there all day. One room then another. My whiskey was gone and they wanted the Union boys taken out. They oughta let a man lay quiet and ration his breath. They brought me to you though. That's a comfort, but you need to go see.'

'The Carters? I should have gone there when I arrived.'

Tuck looked at her like he was weighing his next word.

'What is it?'

'They have sorrows. Sorrows surrounded by sorrow. Place is brim full of it.'

'Is someone hurt? Albert told me they all survived the night.'

'A son of the house was in the fight. Shire told me about him. That you know him. Tod Carter. He's lying in their parlor, I heard. And I'd say they was all empty of hope. The father, old Fountain, he was weepin' with a child as I was taken out.'

She let go of the bandage and the half-tied knot fell free. She tried again. 'I'll get this tight then I'll need to see to others. There are so many.'

'Didn't you hear me?'

'I heard.' *She'd said goodbye to Tod only yesterday.* 'There. I'm needed elsewhere.'

'Not yet.' He fought to lift his head. 'There's more.'

She desperately needed to get away, find somewhere to be alone, but Tuck held her there; weightless, helpless.

'After I was hit, the squad, they charged into the smoke. I was still there when they came back, not a minute later. A miracle really. The air had been so thick with lead. They all came back… all except Shire.' He reached for her arm and the words tumbled out of him. 'Mason came to find me in the Carter house before they pulled out for Nashville. They couldn't find him, Clara, but he must have been hit. Somewhere in the garden. He'll be there in the cold. You have to go look. We have to find him.'

She pictured the fields of dead, the stacked bodies, the filled ditches. Her heart, already broken, shattered. Paul was in the doorway and she knocked him so hard on her way out that he spun and dropped two canteens. 'Where are you goin', Miss Clara?' he called after her. She didn't answer, stepping over the living and the dead on the porch. The cold air was clean of smoke but rotten with death. She lifted her bloodied skirt and ran up the side of the road, between wagons and around the carcass of a bloated horse, past a pair of Rebel soldiers who were laughing and pulling on new boots, up to the Carter house and straight on, clear of the barricade and beyond the cotton gin. The wind pulled at her hair and tugged at her dress and she stopped, breathless. She wanted to scream out Shire's name like she used to in the Ridgmont woods when she'd grown tired of trying to find him. The fields were not as they'd been this morning. No cries, no wails, no crawling movement among the dead. Those left were still, pale and careless of the cold. Not ten paces from the road a long and shallow scrape stretched away, fifty Rebels laid side by side. The burial details were carrying in more. There was no ceremony, but they were set down easy, tucked in close, hands collected together across their breasts and a cloth or a strip of blanket placed over their faces.

She looked back toward the Carter house, but she could only think of Shire. *In the garden or beyond*, Tuck had said. The ditch before the barricade, full of dead Rebels this morning, belonged to the Union dead now. Some boys were still in blue, some with no more than bloodied shirts, some less than whole. They lay on and over each other. A final naked body was thrown in from the height of the works. It slapped down hard then slid with the weight of a bludgeoned fish to find an untidy home. Spades cut at the dirt and threw it over the horror. Soldiers walked along the bodies and from them raked down the soil so recently raised up as a barricade, dragged it to its old level or a shade higher. She watched and wept as the sun set, until rakes and spades were raised to shoulders, then she turned away and walked slowly back, past the lantern-light framing the shutters of Tod's home, back to her post and to her cares.

Franklin, Tennessee – December 2nd, 1864

There was nowhere to be alone. The house, the cellar, the slave huts; everywhere was full with the wounded. Moscow wanted a short while to breathe. Not to take stock, that would be too sad an accounting, just time away from the encircling and overwhelming weight of calamity. He ventured into the farm office but the south facing wall was shot through in a hundred places. He had no energy to begin sorting the mess inside. Instead, he moved on to hide behind the smokehouse but it was hardly a place of peace. He leaned against the cold red brick, chipped and peppered by the storm of lead, but at least able to support his weary weight. If he'd had a knife, he could have turned and prized out a hatful of balls lodged in the stone. Out in the fields, two days beyond the battle, the burials went on. The sickly-sweet stench followed him wherever he went, inside or out.

He felt no need to watch his brother die, and Tod wasn't short of an audience. There were never less than two sisters praying over him in Annie's room on the ell. And Lena and Alice had been there most of the night and this long morning, a brace of blessed virgin statues, burning candle after candle down to the wick. He thought Tod might prefer the curtains drawn wide and some winter light let inside. Moscow would himself, if it was him lying there senseless.

Shy, colonel to Moscow's old command, had visited yesterday and brought the 20th Tennessee's surgeon, Dr Roberts. Moscow had sent the children away while Roberts dug for the bullet above Tod's eye. Where was the sense in that? Even without the headwound, poor Tod had enough bullets in him to slay a squad. They should let him sleep until his time came. General Benton Smith had called again late yesterday and then, unaccountably, a clutch of young ladies from the Female Institute, friends of Frances' perhaps. How they had the time to pay visits with the whole town become one great hospital, drowning in patients, Moscow didn't know.

The bodies were gone from the garden; at least, there were none above ground. Most of those who had fallen there had been carried out to the graves in the fields. The garden-earth looked as if Moscow had cut across it several times with a coarse-chained harrow. It was leveled flat but for a row of raised bumps, a few marked by a crude cross. The barricade, its earth pulled over the massed grave of the ditch, was become no more than an untidy line of broken wood. In the garden, every last green stem or leaf had been ploughed under by shot or shell. He would have said it was fit for a fresh plan come the spring; he could rotate the squash plants from the corner they were in this summer past and set up the turnips and beets closer to the house. But he doubted he would ever again be able to bring himself to eat from this garden, or any of their land, bloodied and fed as it was with the crop of the South, his regiment, his brother.

He felt himself sinking. What was his prize for surviving the night? If Tod had walked in hale and hearty this morning after the battle, he wouldn't have found the home of his heart, but a place forever stained with the weight of death, Father grown old in a night, his nephews and nieces with memories harder to bury than even this heavy harvest of dead.

He made use of the hardened soldier in him to lessen the

pain: thousands had died here and Tod was only one more soul. Better to lose him than any one of the children who had no part in the war; his brother knew the risks when he took up the sword.

None of those thoughts helped when the wails went up from the ell and he knew that Tod was gone. Mercifully, he was left alone to weep. When he was done with that, he went to find and comfort his family.

*

Tod's death didn't change the need to nurse the wounded. Enough water was coming up from the river now, but food was a problem here and across the town. Hood's army provided only little as they prepared to march for Nashville. The Carters were provisioned better than most. Moscow and Fountain practically emptied their stores from the cellar, keeping back barely enough for the winter. He sent a barrowload of vegetables to the Lotz house, knowing they would be in need, and recovered hams from beneath the cellar floorboards where they'd been hidden for the extremity.

His brother's passing didn't stop the flow of visitors either. Moscow had to break the news many times over and beg apologies that he had those yet living to attend to. Albert arrived, thanked him for the food, said he'd heard of his loss and wanted to pay his respects if only on the doorstep. He let Moscow know Clara was helping him with the Union boys.

'Probably best you keep her there,' said Moscow. What a scene that might make. He wasn't sure his sisters would welcome her at present, and it would be better for Clara to remember Tod as she'd last seen him. He didn't know what had passed there anyway. 'I'm glad she's helping you.'

Behind Albert, a regiment marched on toward town. Their sergeant asked them to step out but was roundly ignored. Moscow hadn't had time to go and see, but doubtless the Yankees would have destroyed the bridges behind them and they'd have to be built yet again for the chase to be taken up to Nashville. The war had carelessly ridden Franklin down like an untended child and would leave them broken and bleeding. Albert turned to watch and said, 'They should stay and help clean up their mess.'

'That isn't how war works, Albert. They know the town will do the job for them. We have no choice.'

Albert was barely away and Moscow hadn't yet closed the door before a tall fresh-faced officer walked tentatively toward the house, his hat held to one side. Behind him, tied to the last remnant of the front fence, an impressive bay horse was nosing the ground in the hope of something to eat. Moscow, anger finally touching his bruised heart, girded himself to break the news once more and ask if they could just be left alone, but the soldier had a lost look that forestalled him. His jacket wore a stain but there'd been some attempt to wash it out. The right sleeve had a tear stitched and his buttons and boots had been polished. His face was freshly shaved. It came to Moscow that this boy was only a few years younger than Tod and at another time it might have been his own brother that needed some Christian kindness.

'Sir. I heard the news that Captain Carter is lost to us. I didn't know him long, only these last weeks, but I think I knew him well. He spoke so often of his home. I wanted to see it for myself.'

'His home is not as he might have described it to you, Lieutenant, but why don't you come inside?'

By rights, Frank shouldn't have been away from his command. There were so few officers left. All the brigade commanders in the division were gone. Of Gist's brigade staff, only Captain Garden was unhurt. After Gist was hit, Frank had helped to get him to the rear. He was barely alive when he left him with Dr Wright to return to the front. Half the brigade had wasted itself trying to hold the barricade they'd won. Frank had helped organize what resistance they could. He had a bullet-graze across his forearm for his trouble. Madly, he never felt the wound until the fight died down hours after dark and he'd tried to button his jacket against the cold.

By then Captain Gillis had the brigade. All those ranking above him were dead, wounded or lost. Frank couldn't find Ashley in the confusion, so it was a long night-walk back to the Harrison house where some of the brigade's wounded were being treated, most of them outside. Looking about him in the torchlight, he'd felt embarrassed to be tended to for his scratch, conscious he wouldn't have to suffer the hard time before you can pin an empty sleeve or patch an eye. Such sights.

In the morning, those that could rode out to a grand residence that had a family plot where Gist's servant, Wiley, weeping for his master, asked if they might bury the General. The woman of the house was gracious enough. Though it was nothing more than a cedar box that served as a coffin, it might have been the best burial a man could expect that day. All the junior officers left standing were there to honor him, but he was far from South Carolina; far from the wife he'd asked Frank to take him home to.

As they'd walked away, skirting the stink of the battlefield,

the talk was that Cleburne was dead as well: the South's
talisman. So many generals lost. The brigade was too beaten
up to help with the burials on the field so Frank was spared
that at least. He'd recovered Ashley and had gone looking for
Tod back of the lines only to be told by one of Benton Smith's
staff that Captain Carter had been found on the field at first
light. He'd been taken into his home, but wasn't expected to
survive.

Frank had ridden back to his brigade. Tod and Gist, the
two men he'd relied on the most, both gone, along with
countless others. He couldn't get his heart around it. What
was left of the brigade needed pulling together so Frank tried
to start with himself. He toured the regiments with Gillis and
collected the butcher's bills so they could report to division.
Each accounting was a fresh shock. Most half the men were
gone.

He and Gillis were with the assembled survivors of the
46th Georgia when a staff officer wearing an unblemished
uniform arrived and handed Gillis a note. Gillis read it without
a word then held it out to Frank. It was a proclamation from
Hood to be read to the men. Gillis wouldn't meet his eyes so
the duty fell to Frank, as it had at that more hopeful time in
Florence before the army came north.

It was impossible to find the right tone given the content;
in fact, it was hard to muster his speaking voice at all. 'The
commanding general congratulates the army upon the success
achieved yesterday over our enemy by their heroic and
determined courage.'

A corporal in the front rank spat out a stream of tobacco
juice.

'The enemy has been sent in disorder and confusion to
Nashville, and while we lament the fall of many gallant officers

and brave men, we have shown to our countrymen that we can carry any position occupied by our enemy.'

He lowered the note to see that the men were staring back at him as if he was Hood himself, come expecting to twist a lie into them. They well knew they'd been mishandled, their friends thrown uselessly against prepared works, their best leaders sacrificed in a reckless attack by a general not fit to lead. The Union hadn't left in disorder. They'd left knowing they had ripped the heart from the Army of the Tennessee and would by now be safely behind the guns of Nashville. First one or two, then all the men, turned and walked away without being dismissed.

Now he was standing outside the Carter house before a man that must be Tod's brother, Moscow, who looked like he'd already had one too many mourners visit today. Yet it felt like the one place Frank needed to go. Tod had spoken about his father's farm so often but now it took a feat of imagination for Frank to see it as it had been, or as it would be: patched up, the roof repaired, the bullet marks plastered over, the glass in the windows replaced, the perfume of death and decay faded away. He thought he was going to be turned around, but Moscow's face softened and he was invited in to be taken past the wounded and those caring for them. There was a room off the back of the house where Moscow paused at the door. 'Tod's laid out in here.'

Frank was unsure. He'd been all but suffocated by death these last two days. 'Sir, I'd sooner remember your brother as I last saw him, atop his gray and ready to fight for his family. It's just that he'd always promised to show me his home.' He hoped he hadn't caused offense.

Moscow simply said, 'Let's sit then,' and led him out onto a long wooden porch, newly washed down but with many bloody stories stained into the wood. There were two straight-backed woven chairs against the wall. Moscow dragged them over and they sat.

'Best I can figure,' said Frank, 'I was fighting not a stone's throw out that way.' He pointed out beyond some outbuildings to the south of the yard.

'From the cellar, it sounded like the whole army was fighting here or nearabouts,' said Moscow. 'I don't know that I'll ever sit on this porch again and not see the yard thick with bodies.'

A tide of sorrow rushed in on Frank. 'We made breastworks of the dead.' He looked down at his upturned palms. 'Like they were no more than freshly cut timber, we'd grip them and place them off-set, as you might bricks in a wall to keep it sturdy. I sighted a rifle above them, set my back against them while they collected the lead.'

Moscow placed a hand on his shoulder.

'I'm sorry,' Frank said. 'I should be the one bringing comfort. It was my first fight, Colonel Carter, and I don't know how to make my peace with it.' Frank felt the weight of a future that had veered wildly from his expectation. He wondered if he'd ever voice these memories again once he stepped off this porch.

'It's a fresh wound,' Moscow said. 'There's no peace to be found until it scabs over. You'll ride away, God willing, to your own home.'

'Today!' said Frank, incredulous and angry. 'We're to march away today. I can't square that either. We are supposed to just move on from the dead, leave our wounded behind.'

'If you stopped, well, Hood might never get you moving again. If he advances, he can at least claim it as a victory when he writes to Richmond.' Moscow sat forward, leaned in close.

'Lieutenant, this was no ordinary battle. You might come to see that if you fight again. I've never seen or heard the like. So many dead in so short a space of time.' He sat back, turned inward. 'All on my father's land. None of us thought this war would land here so hard. Not Tod, not me.'

Frank had come with some solace in his pockets, at least he'd thought he had. The Carters would want to know that Tod had made it home the night before the battle, that he'd stood in the yard and watched but couldn't come in. Looking at Moscow, busy with his own struggle, Frank thought what a trial it was going to be for him to stay here. Was there truly any consolation in knowing Tod had come so close the night before, that they could have seen him whole and well, that perhaps in some hidden way it might have led God to revise the list for the next day? He needed to think on it. Maybe he'd write in time. Perhaps it would be a comfort then. Instead, he said, 'Sir, I've had a change of heart. If you're willing, I would like to pay my respects to Tod?'

Moscow nodded and led Frank back to the closed door they'd visited earlier.

'It's the saddest story I've heard in this war,' said Frank, 'that Tod should fall so close to his home.'

Moscow appeared to rally. 'Oh no, Lieutenant. Broken as my heart is for Tod, I don't believe that. There are graves out in those fields unmarked. Union and Rebel both. Boys heaped together whose widows will never get so much as a letter, soldiers who'll dwell lost with us in Franklin until the Lord comes for them. Tod was found in his own fields by his father and his sisters, carried into the house where he was born, surrounded by family and love. We'll set him up a stone and visit him often. If a soldier's time has come, it's about as much as he could hope for.' Then he gently opened the door.

Nashville, Tennessee – December 2nd, 1864

Emerson Opdycke had set his headquarters in rear of the brigade, his personal tent opening with a view to the north. That was at odds with his war-long habit of facing the direction of threat, but it suited the ground and allowed him to look up from his desk and out toward Nashville when he chose to, which was often. Each time, as now, he drew a long and involuntary breath then pushed it slowly out.

The Capitol stood tall and white in the distance, kept company by any number of church spires that rose behind the daunting works. There were so many forts on the perimeter. He made a game of trying to recollect them all without reference to a map. Fort Casino, Fort Morton, Fort Houston; the others wouldn't come. It didn't matter; the Army of the Ohio was safe. Thomas had sent five thousand men out as far as Brentwood to meet them on the march from Franklin. There was also the city garrison and more men arriving all the time. If by some miracle Hood appeared, they could choose to simply retreat into Nashville. No army in America could take that city. Besides, if his fuzzy-minded math was correct, they now had more than enough men to defeat Hood, especially after the murder done to his army at Franklin. There might be another battle and he might yet come to harm, but he no longer worried for the outcome. It was sheer idiocy if the Rebels came north to challenge them again. You risked everything on that one charge, the whole campaign, Opdycke thought, and it was my brigade that turned you around.

He'd never been so tired in all his life. Two battles and two night-marches in the space of two days. And before Spring Hill there had been the march from Columbia. He was slowly getting his thoughts together for Lucy, ready to put them to paper. Schofield would get the credit. It was his army after all, and his bold decision to chance the road out of Spring Hill. What a miracle that was. But for the bigger battle, it was Opdycke they mentioned. He wrote. *'Everyone here says Colonel Opdycke saved the day at Franklin. Stanley, Wood and Wagner assert it.'* Even Wagner, who he'd disobeyed. Cox had praised him too. The revered General Thomas, head of the Army of the Cumberland – who Opdycke had fought alongside at Chickamauga – had pressed his hand and thanked him, promised a promotion that now *must* come. He wondered if that was another reason he felt so exhausted: the relief that he would be recognized and rewarded at last. He was certain of it.

Julia's gentle face peered around the canvas and into his view of Nashville. He smiled and waved her in. She set down a clean an ironed shirt. He'd no idea how she'd come up from Franklin and what adventures she might have suffered, but here she was, going calmly about her business, as reliable as his best officer.

It wasn't far from sunset and he put down his pen. Another war-long habit was walking the camp at this time of day. That had been easy when he only commanded a regiment, but his brigade was stretched out across well over a mile. And he was so weary. He would tour the 125th, he decided, convenient as they were no more than a stone's throw from the back of his tent. He declined the company of any staff, hoping instead to find Bates and see how things were with his old regiment, 'his boys' as he liked to think of them. Instead, it was Rice he met, sat alone in a camp chair at a low fire, flipping flat-cakes in bacon grease. Rice stood and began a tired salute, barked across at a couple of squads lounging outside their own tents to stand for their colonel.

'No need, Lieutenant, no need. I've brought no orders with me.' He waved at a second camp chair. 'May I sit?'

Rice looked surprised but pleased. Lieutenant though he was, thought Opdycke, Rice was one of those men who'd never seemed wholly at ease as an officer, but then this war had pushed most everyone beyond themselves. He was a fine soldier. They sat. Rice tended to the cakes.

'No one to eat with?' asked Opdycke. 'And you so popular with the rank and file.'

'Having been one of them, you mean?' Rice said it with a smile.

'We all started lower down the pecking order.'

'Some of us did our pecking lower than others.'

'2nd Ohio Cavalry, wasn't it?'

'That it was, sir. Trooper Rice.' His grin widened. 'I'm touched you recall.'

'Oh, I recall alright. The surgeon back in Cleveland advised that you shouldn't be allowed to muster with the 125th.'

'Ha. Lucky for me you've never been one to listen to surgeons.'

'You think so? You could have sat out the rest of the war in Ohio instead of tramping across half of America with me.'

'I'd have found another way into the fight, sir. Measles it was that got me discharged out in Kansas. But I bless the day I caught them, otherwise I'd never have fought with the Tigers.' He flipped the cakes.

'How's Company B?'

Rice looked about him. 'I'd report Company B as bone-tired for the most part. Proud, but grieving some, like the rest of the regiment. That was our hardest fight, wouldn't you say?'

'It was. And would have been harder still for the whole brigade but for the men you pulled out of Nashville.'

'Lots of good men gone,' Rice said. 'Lieutenant Blyston, he's wounded bad I'm told, and Captain Stewart of Company D, our Scot, is killed.'

Opdycke nodded, calling up faces. 'What about our Englishman?' he asked. 'Private Shire. I looked out for him on the way up from Franklin.' What a trudge that had been. They'd marched no more than fifteen minutes at a time and then had to rest, men dropping in the road, officers asleep on horseback.

Rice closed one eye and pointed with his spatula to a sullen clump of four men sat outside a tent at the end of the row, not an ounce of animation between them. 'That's Mason's squad,' said Rice. 'Diminished some, though I see my company sergeant is keeping up their numbers.'

Opdycke recognized solid Sergeant Ocks seated on the cold earth and leaning back on his arms, that skinny pit-faced private sat cross-legged next to him. They were nothing to look at; unshaven, unwashed. The younger boy – Corry, was it? – had his hands tucked into the opposite sleeves of his greatcoat. Every eye was downcast. There were only three rifles in their stack.

What made these men fight? He'd like to think it was himself, but knew better. He knew their pedigree. They were sons and grandsons of people who came into Ohio when it was no more than a wilderness, a hundred miles between each stockade. The fight was bred into them.

'That squad manned a cannon at the Carter house,'

continued Rice, 'just like you trained us to the first time we were in Franklin. Anyhow…' He prodded at the cakes and spoke more slowly. 'Private Tuck took a wound in the leg and we had to leave him to the tender mercies of the Rebels. Shire we lost in a charge to the outer-barricade. Someone saw him go down.' He waved his spatula toward the squad. 'Now I can't get a happy word from a single one of them. Shame. They were my best. Never out of the fight.'

The news took Opdycke in the gut. He'd liked that boy, but he didn't own the list; that was God's preserve. 'He and Tuck were quite a pair, weren't they? When I was colonel of this regiment, barely a month would pass without them in front of me for some misdemeanor or other.' Shire had always found his way back before. Perhaps not this time. 'You know they were once brought before me.' Despite himself he laughed. 'In Frankin it was, that first spring for the 125th, for stealing honey. Guilty as Adam they were. Caught sticky-fingered and with hive-slats scattered around their feet.'

Rice was laughing too. Heads lifted in the saddened squad.

Opdycke lowered his voice. 'I said to the offended party, no sir, my men don't steal. No matter what they'd done, I couldn't let the town folk get the upper hand.'

When their smiles had waned, Rice said, 'They was in the thick of it across the yard, both of 'em. True tigers. You too, sir. I ain't never seen the like from an officer.'

That was a raw memory; a sore place to visit from this short a distance in time. Opdycke fancied he'd lost his mind, standing tall above the Rebels and beating at their heads with his pistol butt until it fell apart. He'd collected a rifle and carried right on. Snarling faces, frightened faces; either way he'd beaten them to blood and bone-splinters. It appeared that to fight for God, you had to become the beast. How would he put that in a letter to Lucy?

'Are you cold, sir?'

'What? No, no I'm alright.'

'I got two cakes and, to tell the truth, I think I could only manage the one.'

'I can't steal your food, Lieutenant.'

'Sir, I'd be honored. Here, I'll eat from the skillet.' He passed his bowl to Opdycke and flipped in a cake. He fished in his haversack that was lying on the ground and pulled out a smile. 'It's not Franklin honey, but I do have some molasses.'

'Well then,' said Opdycke, sitting forward, 'let's eat to the Company B and the Tigers.'

Franklin, Tennessee – December 2nd, 1864

Clara woke and wasn't sure if the scream marked the end of her dream or the start of her day. She sat up too quickly, her back stiff from the floor, the thin blanket falling from her in the cold Lotz attic room. She guessed by the early light she'd slept only two or three hours. The scream died away only to be followed by loud quavering sobs, every bit as harrowing in their extremity. It wasn't from this sad house, but somewhere outside, away toward the town or in the surgeon's tent they'd set up a distance over the road yesterday. It wasn't her concern.

The Lotz children and Margaretha were huddled together close by. She rubbed her arms where they ached from yesterday's lifting. When Clara stood, Paul sat up and rose too. She took his hand and they went down together, back to the crusted blood and the pain. Shire came too. He'd stayed with her since yesterday, one time so palpably there that she found herself turning in the hope of finding him beside her.

In the hall, the grandfather clock was unwound and quiet. She entered the parlor with the thought that maybe she could earn Shire back: that if she only helped save enough of these men, he'd stumble in with nothing more than a scratch, or word would come that he'd been found in another hospital for the Union men. She'd sought them out yesterday evening. Albert had told her where to go in town. The houses were smaller but otherwise it had been the same. The same malodor, the same distant or frightened eyes. She'd hurried with fading hope from room to room. Out the back of the second house there had been a small untidy heap of bloodless limbs, as if the household had gathered firewood for the winter and were yet to stack it. Clara vomited before she could move away then walked slowly back up to the Lotz house, shaking all the way.

This morning there was only her and the soldiers in the room. Some were peacefully asleep; at least three had found a deeper peace. She closed eyes, lifted blankets over faces and thought to find Albert to tell him. The spot by the piano was empty. Albert was out on the porch. He looked like he hadn't slept at all. He tried to smile but it wouldn't take root.

'There's three dead in the parlor,' Clara said.

'I know. Two more in the study. I'm waiting for a collection wagon.'

'Where's Tuck?' she asked, fearing his answer.

'Who?'

'The tall soldier. He was by the piano?'

'They took him an hour back.' Albert waved vaguely. It might have been toward the surgeon's tent or toward the house where Clara had been sick. 'Him and another.'

Yesterday, ignoring near hysterical tears from Margaretha, they'd dragged the solid kitchen table out into the backyard as the surgeon had asked and placed precious water beside it, but the surgeon had never come. Instead, later, soldiers arrived intermittently to collect the badly wounded one or two at a time, taking mostly those whose wounds had corrupted. They were stretchered away, pale ghosts, some begging to be left here to die.

'I'm glad the surgeon hasn't chosen to work here,' Albert said. 'At least we were spared that.'

'I should have been awake for Tuck.'

'He went easy enough. His fever was worse. There was

nothing you could have done.'

Perhaps not, but Shire would have wanted her to go with his friend. Tuck was her friend too. The road was quiet. Perhaps it was earlier than she'd thought. The town didn't want to wake up. Who could blame it? A lone flat-bed wagon, with three soldiers perched shoulder to shoulder on the sprung driving bench, hauled up from town, but it wasn't for the dead. It was half full of fodder with a horse trailing behind on a short lead. Clara's own horse was alone and hungry in the stable out the back, the Lotz horses taken by the Union long ago. She gathered herself as best she could. Her dress hem stiff with blood and dirt, she stepped down from the porch to hail them and ask if she could take some hay.

'Surely.' They jumped down to help.

'I can manage.'

They said nothing but collected an armful each. Clara collected some more. Who knew when the chance would come again? Albert was gone from the porch. She led the soldiers down the side of the house to the stable.

'Out here is fine.'

One soldier put down the hay, but then undid the bolt. 'Might as well finish the job,' he said, collecting his hay again and following his comrade inside. When they failed to come back out, Clara went to see what they were up to. One was feeding Cincin and stroking her shoulders. 'Fine horse, ma'am. If you can't feed her, d'you want to sell her? We got army dollars.'

'She's not for sale.'

The second soldier had a hand in a saddlebag.

'You get out of there,' Clara ordered, reaching for and old authority she no longer possessed.

He ignored her. 'Fine saddle too.'

'Leave that.'

'What's this?' He'd lifted a saddle-flap and bent to look closer in the stable-light. '*C.S.A.* Now ain't that a find.'

'It was a gift.'

'A gift from a horse thief?'

'A soldier.' From a good man, she wanted to say. A man I loved all along and who deserved a better friend than me. She reached for the whip, raised it but was slapped across the face and fell hard against the stall.

'We'll not trouble with the dollars, seeming as this horse is the army's already.'

They unhurriedly saddled Cincin while she lay there crying, thinking they could have everything she owned if only she could have Shire back. She barely noticed them go.

*

All that long day tending to the wounded, her heart never rose an inch above where it had been on that stable floor. Mid-morning, she walked through a kitchen with a basket full of stinking bandages that were only fit for burning. Margaretha, a better cook than nurse, was boiling up soup with the vegetables that had come from the Carters. 'The Carter boy is dead,' she said in her blunt German way. 'He died yesterday.'

Clara stopped.

'Tod. His name was Tod,' Margaretha said. 'You wouldn't know him. That family is careless with its sons.'

Clara moved on dumbly and added the bandages to the pile outside. When she walked back in, Margaretha was still talking. 'You can't send them off to war and expect to collect them all back safely at the end.'

Clara took herself away and found the next soldier to work

on, the boy looking at the ceiling rather than her. She silently unwound the dressing from his stump. The folded-over skin fell loose and she had to tuck it back, even that harsh moment not enough to deflect her from her equally raw and bleeding heart. She tried to bring Tod to the forefront of her mind, her one true lover, see him as he was when she'd met him on the Ohio or the day that he'd ridden into Ducktown. Her memories wouldn't take shape. Instead, it was Shire she remembered, his eyes so close it was as if they'd just kissed. He was dead too. She knew he was. As if it was his name Margaretha had spoken. There wasn't room to grieve for everyone, for Tod, for Tuck, for all those she'd watched die in this house. She had only the one heart. Though the choice was now redundant, at last it was altogether made. She wished it had been made a long time ago. Perhaps it was and she'd just failed to listen.

At midday, Clara told Albert she needed to go home. There was no one at the farm to see to her animals, few as they were. It was a poor comparison to the necessity here. In truth it was as much down to the weight of grief she feared might overwhelm her if she didn't rest soon. Albert begged another hour while he tried to find more help. She needed to start back soon; it was a long walk if she was to make it in daylight. He did better than she might have hoped, returning to say Frances would come. Clara didn't wait on that; Frances would want to talk about Tod. She searched for her coat, said goodbye to Albert and Paul who were on hand and set off, long cold miles ahead of her.

At the Carter house she was surprised to see some of the broken windowpanes were already replaced. The door was ajar, but she didn't cross over to the Carter side or break stride. There would be time to come back, to visit and to mourn with

Moscow, to teach Alice and Lena again. A few more steps were all she needed before admitting that was a lie, something to tell herself while she walked by when she should have offered up her compassion, unearthed the deeper grief for Tod that she knew would surface sooner or later. The truth was it would have felt like a betrayal to Shire. She spared a final look at the red roof and hurried on, up past the wreck of the cotton gin and out onto the flat, newly populated sporadically with crude crosses, some alone, some clustered like infant plantations, leafless in the cold wind that whipped out of the east. She pulled over her shawl, recalling the sight from Winstead, the fire and the ruin centered here. The fire had passed so soon, but the floodtide of ruin might take forever to ebb. Did she dare go out onto the field itself, walk to the covered ditch she'd seen filled with Union dead two days ago, to say a prayer for Shire? She searched for the smallest vestige of hope inside but found nothing. She strode on, tears coming freely at last. They were still flowing a mile later and it was as if her last energy had flowed out with them. A dark bank of clouds blew in so it began to feel like evening rather than early afternoon. Ahead there was a house built close to the pike, a covered wagon drawn up outside and a black driver. As Clara passed by, a stretcher was brought out and placed in the rear and the canvas tied. The wagon drew out onto the road, quickly made ground on her and stopped.

'Where you headed, ma'am? It's a cold road.'

'Spring Hill.'

'That's a ways. There's room up here.'

There was no good reason to decline other than she'd have to swallow her grief. She climbed up, taking hold of the hard-skinned but warm hand that was offered. A sprung bench had never felt so comfortable.

'I got three wounded in the back you might care to water once in a while. It'll save me stoppin'.'

'Who are they?'

'Don't rightly know. Rebel off'cers most likely. I'm hoping to get them to Spring Hill before nightfall.'

They moved away and into the hills where the wind eased in the pass. For no reason other than the familiar rock and sway of the wagon and the comforting bounce of the seat, Clara recalled a long ride down into town from Comrie with Moses and Hany. It was a pleasant thought, followed by the shock that she yet possessed a happy memory. Hany had talked on and on; she'd met Cele for the first time in the square and they'd seen the Whirligig. But the day had turned sour. The war had arrived there and then, she realized, when the Whirligig was shattered. Now Hany was murdered and Cele and Moses were who knew where with Mitilde. It wasn't a happy memory after all and she doubted any such could survive more than a few moments in the swell of cold grief that swept through her once again. To spare the driver her tears, she moved back under the canvas, so tired it was hard to balance. It smelled like the Lotz house. One of the soldiers was moaning, the other two asleep.

'If they got any, they doses 'em up with laudanum for the trip,' called the driver from up front. That seemed to be the way of it. Two were amputees, the other bandaged around the head and across his eyes. There was nothing to redress a wound had she needed to. She was so tired that she thought to lay down but there was no room so she climbed back outside. She wrapped her coat and shawl tight and the driver shared his blanket so it was across both their laps. In that state she managed to doze between the larger jolts, in time leaning into the driver to balance the better, sleepily wondering what it must feel like to be a black man pressed to work for Hood's army, to carry away Southern heroes who'd fought to keep him in bondage. When they passed through Thompson's Station, she determined to stay awake from there lest she miss Eversholt altogether. At her gate she climbed wearily down from the wagon and thanked the driver, realizing she'd never troubled him for his name. He touched his hat and drove away, leaving her staring down for the chalk sign before she remembered it was stolen. That set her weeping again. Fearful she'd sleep for a night and a day, she didn't go inside but went straight to feed Old George who'd preferred the stalls to the pasture. The chickens escaped like a riot from their barn and hammered at the grain she scattered. She had to wait on them as the light of the day faded and they complained bitterly when she tried to chase them back inside. In the end, she tempted them in with more grain.

Only then did she find her way in through the kitchen and up the stairs in the near-darkness, not troubling to light a lantern. In her room she stripped and washed, glad of the poor light that hid the dirt and the blood. She could still smell the wounded over the soap, as if they'd followed her from Franklin. She sat naked on the bed in the cold, no tears left, and wondered what came next. No Shire, no Tod, no reason to stay in America.

Sleep would be a blessed escape. She slid into bed, asked her mind to quiet, but then sensed a still weight beside her. Unthinking, she reached out a hand which encountered another. She stifled a scream, jumped out and pulled her filthy dress up from the floor while backing away to the corner. She trod on a heap of clothes and kicked them away as if they might attack her. There was just enough light from the window to see a crumpled jacket that was butternut gray.

Franklin, Tennessee – December, 1864

Something shifted. It wasn't much. All was darkness and unbearable weight. There was no profit in trying to measure time. Better to drift away when he could; away from the treacle flow of blood that slowed across his face and then set, its dying spring somewhere above; away from the compost heat of bodies that held him tight while he sucked rationed and fetid air through grinding teeth; away from the claw grip of a hand that tightened and set rigid around the base of his neck. In one of his more lucid moments, moments he'd come to fear, he believed it might in the end be that hand that did for him. That would become his unknown end: to be strangled by a dead man, lost under all this dead weight.

Whatever had shifted somewhere above could not remotely be considered a relief, though it allowed his shallow pant to become a hair's breadth deeper, a fraction slower. Any number of ribs burned in response, burdened as they were. The shift also returned time back to his universe, horror as it was: it allowed for the possibility of change. Not hope, unless you hoped to die. Whenever he was conscious, a scream circled in his mind like a trapped animal, but there wasn't enough air to scream, and nowhere for a scream to go. His jaw was pressed tight into the warm and wet stink of the man packed in beside him. His head ached pitifully. There was the memory of the blow at the end of the charge. He'd been dragged over and into the ditch. Maybe his head hurt from the blow or maybe it was the crushing weight. His mouth was dry as August hay.

Another shift, more palpable this time. He could move his right hand enough to flex the knuckles. Despite that, he considered the possibility he was already dead, that above him the demons of hell were sorting the pile and the true torment lay ahead for all time. He felt his mind slip closer to the cliff edge of insanity and closed his eyes still tighter. He heard a dog whimper then realized it was himself. The weight above eased some more and this time he pushed up, moved the body above him a half inch. His would-be murderer's stiff fingers fell away from his neck and scratched him as a parting gift. The body atop was lifted away. Cold and beautiful air rushed into his lungs. His ribs burned in protest. When he raised his head, his neck unset like a stiff door-bolt. He fought to push up onto numb bloodless limbs, struggled to get his balance on the dead. At the shock of being released, he let himself fall freely from the cliff. The dead reached for him, grasping to drag him back. He flailed about to beat them off and his long-held scream escaped at last.

'Easy! I ain't takin' a wound with the battle done. I'd as soon throw you back in.'

A sharp slap made his aching head howl.

'I 'ppreciate your wits may have leached out in there, but such that are left, well, you'd better round 'em up.'

He gulped at the air and tried to hold himself steady, anchored himself in the man's eyes. Bloodshot but beautiful, they stared back.

'If you could let go of my arms, I could hand you some water. Would you like that?'

Too dry to speak, he nodded. It was an effort to let go of the man.

'Here. Let me do the tippin'. That's good. You got the

worst dose of the shakes I ever seen. Can't say I blame you. We've pulled out one alive so far but not from so deep down. I 'magine Lucifer had sight of you in the line.'

He gagged and the water ran down his chin. He looked about, only now conscious it was dark. There were torches near and far; shapes and shadows moved across a harvest of dead.

'What's your name?'

'Shire.' It came out as a whisper. He tried again. 'Shire.'

'Odd sort of name? Seein' as you just been reborn, I'm thinkin' you have a right to a new one if you care to change it. No? Well, I reckon there'll be a few around who'll use this day to start a second life.'

The joy of the cool air diminished. His shaking blurred to shivering and the soldier rubbed Shire's arms. 'It's cold alright. Your jacket's wet through and, well… no longer fit for service. Look here, this fella has no need.' He let Shire be.

A second man brought his torch closer into Shire. He didn't seem as friendly, but looked Shire over like he was a New World miracle. 'Lazarus.'

'What's that yer sayin'?'

'His new name. We should call him Lazarus.'

'I can see the sense in it.' Shire's own savior stripped a jacket from a corpse, fighting to yank it free from a stiff arm. He gave it to the torchbearer while he helped Shire out of his. 'Only who would that make me? Best not to get careless with the blasphemy. Not with all the soul-weighing that must be going on apace.'

There was no notice taken that the jacket eased from Shire was Union. Maybe they couldn't see in the torchlight, or perhaps they were used to Rebels wearing stolen Union jackets. It would go better for him if they thought he was Confederate.

'There. We gotta get on and empty out our boys from this ditch so we can bury 'em neater. I'm not expecting to find another keeper like you, but who knows. It's a time of wonders. Not all of 'em can be evil. You're proof of that. What's your regiment?'

Shire started to form 'one' with his lips but thought better of it.

'It not comin' to mind?'

'20th. The 20th Tennessee.' It was the first Rebel regiment he could think of.

'You must be close to home then. So that'd be Benton Smith's Brigade. Alright.' He took Shire by the arm and turned him. 'It's all a goddamn mess, but you walk slowly that way. The brigades, what's left of 'em, are lickin' their wounds 'bout a mile back.' He bent Shire over so he could look at the top of his head. 'I don't think that'll kill ya, but best get it seen to. They can't saw off your head, leastways, so that's a boon right there. Here, take on more water before you go. See that low light in the east? That's December. Keep that Christian month on your left and stay this side of the pike. Good luck.'

Shire staggered forward a few steps. Father had brought him up to thank people, so he turned and called out. The torch was stuck in the ground and the two men were already up to their shoulders in the ditch. They didn't acknowledge him. Busy as demons, they threw a body up from below. He looked along the length of the ditch and there were a squad or two at the same nightmarish task but nowhere near enough; his rescue truly *had* been a miracle. His head pounded. Where was Tuck? He'd been hit. Shire wanted to head into Franklin but supposed the battle must have been lost. It hadn't seemed to be heading that way. He turned full circle and in the patchy torchlight saw again the field of dead. Other soldiers went from body to body, stopping at some, leaving most. Close by, a procession moved slowly along headed and trailed by a lantern, three women weeping in rear of a body carried in the hammock of a greatcoat. If he wasn't in hell, then hell had surely visited Earth this night. He held his head as if he could wrestle the pain from it. His savior had said keep the dawn to his left. Maybe he should trust to that.

As he stumbled on, he began to sense men who stumbled alongside him, a wide and deep skirmish line of dazed souls who edged into the new day. Some went with a comrade, some alone. One was using a rifle as a crutch. All headed slowly away from the town, away from those wide acres of death. There was a light ahead, a lantern on the ground. Shire fought to avoid it, but in his stupor came closer than intended. A man, a civilian, was bent over a body, stripping at the uniform. Shire said nothing; he was wearing a gift from the dead himself. The man turned from the corpse to look at Shire, a sheathed saber in one hand, a knife in the other. The alarm in his eyes faded as he sized Shire up. 'You scat, now,' he said, regripping the knife. 'No business for you here.'

From the jacket, half on the body, Shire could see he'd been an officer. His belt was taken, his pockets turned out. There was a sack beside the thief, resting heavily on the ground.

'Don't you give me that sour look.'

Shire had no idea what look he was wearing. 'I…'

'You seen what you and your army did to my town? You think you can pitch up here and shell my home but I can't take a sword or a purse to make good on a burned-out barn and a child half-crazed with fear? Git, now. Git, before I stick you.'

The man lurched toward him, the knife raised. Shire backed off and fell, scrambled up and hurried away. He had to find his bearings again then went on, each step an achievement. In slow time, the bodies thinned out, like autumn leaves from a lonely tree. What smoke lingered from the battle-fires stirred in a chill mist. Shire blew into his hands. He might yet fall and die if he couldn't get warm. He found a body with a greatcoat and did his own share of robbing. Then he found a discarded kepi. It hurt to try and fix it on. He threw it away and looked for a slouch hat instead. There was no shortage. He bent down to collect one, swooned and had to take a knee. It was all he could do to get back up.

The light came on reluctantly. Lanterns and torches started to go out, giving way to flat gray. He walked through a busted battery, tripped over a cannon barrel on the ground and fell in among the splintered and broken wheels and the eviscerated gunners. He found a canteen and pulled himself to sit against a dead horse and drink. He was dizzy again when he stood. He looked out toward the hills. A quarter-mile away there were a few tents, figures hurrying this way and that. Surgeons' tents maybe. He reached his hand to his head, tipped some water up there. It shocked him sane for a short while. If he found his way to a surgeon's tent there would be questions and there would be a list. If he stuck to his line as being from the 20th Tennessee he'd go on *their* list and in time it would come back that he wasn't known there. He could give Tod's name, or Tod's friend Waddell. He'd liked Waddell, gloomy as he was. That man was a prophet. He'd seen this day coming and Shire had killed him in return, blown him up with the mule train and left him buried in some Appalachian gulch. Why had Shire been reborn rather than the men he'd killed that day? He felt himself tug the lanyard of the cannon again, this time not blinded by the blast but watching the men shredded by the cannister, their limbs and souls ripped and cast into the air.

He shouldn't go to the tents but, if Franklin was taken, there was no sense in turning back either. He angled off to the south-west with the vague idea he might arc out a long semicircle and ultimately head north beyond the Rebels and the town. But the camps were vast and, in the end, he was forced to wander right into them. Men were either laid out or tended an early fire. The slouch hat covered his wound and he tried as best he could to walk upright, but no one paid him any mind. Those awake had their heads down and their eyes inward. The coffee had a flat aroma and what food he saw cooking was meagre. He wasn't hungry. Not today. This Rebel army was at a low ebb. There were no picket lines going in or coming out. In time he found himself beyond the army and alone again, though he couldn't recall when he'd stepped beyond the last tent. He was at the foot of the hills. He eased his way in under the trees and out of the cold wind. Abandoning his idea to arc back north he started to climb, bitter memories of these hills and the snow two winters ago vying with the cruel present. His breath came faster as the climb steepened. He had to go from tree to tree to keep his balance. Somewhere in his light, giddy mind he found his old self, that careless, hopeful boy that had discarded everything to come and find – come and *rescue* – Clara. Had he succeeded one jot in that? Tuck should have let him ask her to marry him. At least then he would have known, and would be done with the long years of living inside faint hopes.

How had he managed to run up this hill two years ago? The parcel of energy that came with sudden grief, he supposed. There was no energy left to him now. He was suddenly back in the pit, in the darkness with the heat and the sweat and the gore pressed in around him. His legs buckled.

He tried to shake the memory from his mind only to ignite the pain in his head. He rose again and pressed on one tree at a time. He was still following that thin line of hope, he realized, some invisible cord that, just here, extended between tree-trunks. He should head east and north, back to his friends, back to find Tuck, but Clara was winning out again. The slope flattened out. What time was it? Bugles sounded behind and below. He found himself sat with his back to a fallen tree. Making a supreme effort he rolled to the sheltered side and, listening to the wind that stirred the trees, passed out.

His dreamscape was an unlikely dizzy compound of war and love, of people out of place and impossible geographies. He ran out of the stable of the Ridgmont estate farm and straight up and over the cannon-crested Missionary Ridge, took again the solid sting of the bullet to his chest, only this time it was Tod who fired the gun. The bullet spun him to Clara who stepped into the mine-cage at Ducktown and waved goodbye as she descended, looking beyond him as if at someone else. He spun again only to see Colonel Opdycke berserk in battle, his pistol reversed and raised. Shire ducked beneath him and was back in New York with the hung body burning and twisting above. He screamed and ran away along the meandering gray sheen of the Ohio River until he was in the winter tent with the squad. Lyman was there and Tom Muncie and Mason. All except Tuck aimed their laughter at Shire and his forlorn and lovesick hope. Tuck struck up a tune and Shire was in the snow again at Eversholt village, walking with Clara under the stars and she was waltzing alone, around and around, until he caught her and kissed her and the stars wheeled and turned, faster and faster...

It was dark when he woke. His head hurt so much. He drank the last of the water from the canteen, thinking how unusual it was to have only the one strap: no pack, no knapsack, no cartridge box, as if he was free of the army. In the patches of starlight that found their way in among the trees, he guessed his way over the crest of the hills and down the other side. More than once he heard movement and drunkenly reached for a gun he didn't have. He still wasn't hungry. He worried he'd come off the hills on the wrong side, sat and dozed again. Careless of the cold that reached inside his greatcoat, he waited for a second dawn. It duly arrived and he was surprised that it had come around so quickly. A squad of cavalry burst by just as he was ready to take to the open fields so he regrouped – alone. Either side would likely shoot him now. He plotted a careful course from hedge to oak brake to spinney, not able to face using the ditches.

When he found the rail track, he discovered himself unaccountably weeping for long minutes before he could go on. There were no trains, but rather than follow the track he crossed and kept it a few hundred yards to his right until he began to see what must surely be the houses of Spring Hill. They didn't look familiar, though it was only a few days since he'd left. He wasn't sure how many. With the end so near, he measured his strength by that expectation and found it had all but ebbed away. He couldn't hear much beyond his own breathing. He saw the busy pike ahead, blurry traffic passing both ways, and dared not go near. He couldn't tell if he was north or south of Clara's farm. Choosing the wrong way might be the death of him.

A shout from the road, possibly aimed at him, hurried his decision and he headed south only because there appeared more cover that way. He must have angled back toward the road because he hit her drive side on. He only recognized it once he'd managed to painfully bend and twist through the first fence. His head began to bleed again. The sign he'd stolen would be in his backpack in Franklin, lost forever. That felt unaccountably sad. He turned and saw the gray beams on the house and the simple, white porch. He staggered around the back, fearful he might yet be sighted from the road. Polite Englishman as he was, he knocked at the door. Though surely he was an American by now. No answer. The door was unlocked, the house cold. Maybe Clara was upstairs; the world wasn't keeping normal hours so why should she? He lifted himself up a step at a time on his backside while calling out. He stood at the top and might easily have fallen back down. He had nothing left to give. He stumbled into a bedroom and used his last strength to undress and let himself down into a cold, soft bed. He pulled a pillow under his filthy, scabbed head and sank deeply into a world without dreams.

Cockspur Island, Georgia – July, 1865

'No further than the south channel canal,' the commandant had said, before returning his attention to his paperwork.

A short while later, Frank Trenholm stood atop the diminutive quay that was the boundary of the granted parole. The air might have been salty but it was hard to tell over the pungent smell of the marsh. *Canal* was an overstatement; before him was nothing more than a broad ditch. He could see oysters down there, clinging to the red brick, and a blue crab blurred by the flow. Father had taken a weary seat down on the stone with his feet low to the slowly rising water. The tide was coming in, hurrying toward the moat that surrounded the fort, his father's prison.

'Thank you, Frank. You can't imagine what it's like to be in that cell day after day.'

Frank considered that he probably could. He'd been there not twenty minutes ago. It was a shock, certainly: to see Father, the worthy George Alfred Trenholm, businessman and empire builder, late Financial Secretary to the equally late Confederacy, brought so low. His grand parlor at Ashley Hall in Charleston, fit for fifty supplicants or petitioners, replaced by a damp six-by-six-foot cell where there was nothing to do but sit on the single cot and watch through the gaps in the planks as the moat beneath filled and emptied twice a day. Unsettled by his father's fall from grace as much as angered by his spartan confinement, Frank stupidly told Father to wait, before marching directly to the commandant's office. En route across the square he'd bypassed a company – their uniforms impossibly clean – drilling around a high Union flag pulled taut by the sea breeze. At the last moment, as he'd lifted his knuckles to rap the door, he'd caught himself and taken a long breath. His uniform had been put away many months ago, but he forced himself back into the demeanor of a staff officer. A straightforward request delivered in a military manner would have a better chance. He'd knocked politely and been summoned in. His more even temper had worked. He'd won an hour – on their honor – outside of the fort's walls to walk Cockspur Island.

Their honor was clearly riding low, as a brace of privates had lazily trailed them across the flat marsh. It was such a desolate place. The island was as good a prison as the fort unless they planned to swim the Savannah River, wide and choppy in its last briny mile before the open sea. He looked down onto Father's scalp. His hair was flat gray rather than its old shining silver, thinned out with any number of bloodied dots on his scalp from the mosquitos. 'We should walk,' said Frank.

'I'm not a marching man. Not like you.'

Father had gifted him Ashley, so Frank had never had to do much marching.

'The damp has got into my bones.'

'That's *why* we should walk.' He helped his father up. 'Let's head for the lighthouse.'

To reach it they had to go around the tidal marshes which meant heading back close to the fort and coming at the lighthouse from there. The soldiers breezed along behind, happy to stay out of earshot it seemed.

'The Cabinet will be jealous.'

'They're no longer a cabinet, Father, any more than Davis is a president.'

'What else should I call them? It's their common attribute. It's the reason we are all here.'

'You're here because we lost the war.'

Father stopped and arched his back, took a pull on the warm sea air. 'We're here because someone has to pay. And it might as well be me. I can bear it, if it helps. If making a few examples suffer excuses the populace.'

Frank looked over the marsh and across the channel. It was late in the day for Father to play the martyr. Mother had sent him armed with shirts and socks. It was what Father had asked for, but he'd begged her not to come. He wouldn't inflict that on her, he'd said. In the last month, the threat of the noose had receded. The accomplices to Lincoln's assassination had paid that price last week. For a while it had looked bleak for Father. Funds had been made over to the Confederate secret service in his name, funds that might have played a part in the plot. Frank could dismiss that easily enough. Father would never consciously be party to murder. To a *war* maybe, but not a murder. And now there were supporters aplenty petitioning President Johnson – Lincoln's replacement – for the worthy George Trenholm's release. Reverend Porter for one, though the Bishop of South Carolina might carry more weight, along with the worthy citizens of Georgia and the devastated business community of Charleston. All of them wanted Mr Trenholm back to help rebuild their communities. Even Union generals known to him before the war had written of his 'high sense of honor and duty.'

It was true. Father *was* honorable. Frank had seen it from his perch on Father's knee and later in his shadow. It's just that Frank had come to distrust the word. It appeared to excuse a great deal. He'd met lots of honorable men in the

Army of the Tennessee. Some of them had honorably sent other men across open fields to get slaughtered. No doubt Father was suffering in that cell, but there were images in Frank's mind that Father would never see; his war had been fought in smoke-filled rooms to the clink of brandy glasses, over lists of ships bought and lost, in profit margins entered in the last column of the ledger. Only toward the end had Father put all that down and truly served the defunct Confederate government. By then, it was too late.

There was nothing Frank could do to stop the scenes playing out again and again when he closed his eyes. Almost three months beyond the war's end, they still shocked him. Memories surfaced like the dead washed from shallow graves in a storm: a shell screamed past his head to decapitate men following on; a kneeling boy desperately tried to reach to a dropped canteen but needed both hands to hold onto his guts; two rivulets of blood, meandering across the stony road at Franklin, shining in the sunset, met and raced on as a new and stronger flow. This last one came often. Some he knew to be memories; others might have been inventions. There was no way to tell.

'How's your sister Helen? Still in love with our hero midshipman?'

'Should I take it you don't approve of the match?'

Father tugged at a stalk of marsh grass. 'You know Morgan's visited too, told me all about his plans to study law in Paris. Our fortunes won't rebuild themselves. He should stay.'

Even in a six-by-six cell, Father had a mind to the family empire. Sons, or prospective sons-in-law, were expected to pick up a spade. Father put a hand on Frank's shoulder. He had to reach upward these days. 'You too, Frank. Riches take to themselves and fly away. We have to gather what we have and build again.'

Perhaps Father should have been less careless with the empire he'd once had. And an in-law versed *in* law, albeit French, might not be such a bad thing. There was a resolute queue of lawsuits forming against Father's interests, no matter how much he tried to parcel them out among friends and family. Besides, Morgan deserved some credit. He'd protected Frank's sister's Helen and Eliza, along with the President's wife Varina and her family, as they'd escaped south from doomed Richmond. Father had fled separately on a train with the President and practically the entire cabinet, a story Frank had heard three times over but which Father started to tell again. 'Your mother was the only woman among thirty men.'

She'd brought me along some peach brandy.

'She'd brought me along some peach brandy. I wasn't well, but we shared it out. Dutch courage, I suppose.'

Frank wondered if Nero had peach brandy on hand while Rome was burning.

A few days later, as the Confederate executive fled south, Father resigned his office on grounds of ill health and let the President and the Cabinet go on without him. Mother and Father reunited with their daughters further south in Abbeville, a fugitive family looking for a place of safety. They might have headed for De Greffin, Father's grand bolt-hole purchased earlier in the war, but that had been sought out by the Federals and burnt to the ground. Frank joined the family in Abbeville. By then, Helen was besotted with Midshipman Morgan. Frank liked the man and couldn't reason why Father might not. Morgan had been there when Father had been arrested and had taken a heavy beating for his trouble. 'They're delaying their marriage. Until you're free.'

'That might be a long time. They shouldn't suffer my sentence with me.'

'You don't *have* a sentence.'

'I guess treason is a complicated concept. Maybe I deserve to be here. The country suffered so much. They looked so betrayed.'

'Who did?'

'The people. On the road south. Whenever they found out that the Financial Secretary to the Treasury was in our little procession, they pressed Confederate dollars on me and shouted for their gold. As if I was the Bank of England travelling in an open cart.'

Frank thought, but you did have gold, Father, when we had need of it. Twenty-five-dollar gold pieces that no one could change. Don't you remember?

They walked on and looked out over the Atlantic. 'That ocean made me a rich man. Blockade runners up and down this coast. Back and forth to England. Do you recall Clara, the Duke of Ridgmont's daughter? We rode up to Ducktown with her.'

'I met her in Middle Tennessee as well.'

Father turned, suddenly attentive. 'You never told me.'

'There was a lot that followed on. I didn't dwell on it. We were marching on Franklin. She was with Tod at her new farm.'

'Tod Carter? They were together?'

'So it seemed to me. She had a small farm. It looked like the war had beaten her down a little.'

'You could say that about anyone east of the Mississippi. Shame though.'

'What is?'

'There was someone else. Someone I always thought she'd settle on.'

'Well, Tod is no longer a suitor.'

'I guess not. Poor Tod. I'll write to Clara if you have the address. I've not heard from the Duke in a long while.' Father walked on.

They came near the rocky shore. The rising tide had made an island of the pile of low rocks that the stubby lighthouse called home, gray brick before a gray ocean. It had an odd door, simple and elegant, which was out of place: it might befit a townhouse were it not high in the stone, waiting for the tide to rise up so it might be used.

Frank thought of Tod, one penny only in the vast accounting in blood. His short spell in the army had taught Frank about fraternity, fighting spirit, the ties of heartstrings to a still young land. He could understand how that made men fight, how they would stand shoulder to shoulder. What if men like his father, men like Davis or the Cabinet – presently no more than an imprisoned collection of defeated ideas – perhaps even men like Lincoln, if they were made to count out the cost? A cup of blood or a rising soul at a time, until they truly felt the measure. How then would it tally against empires and self-interest, against principles and constitutions? He recalled the black family fleeing north through the woods of Tennessee. They owned nothing at all, not even a say in the argument that raged around and for them.

The path ended. Summer though it was, the breeze off the sea had turned chill. Frank nodded at the lighthouse. 'Can you see it from your cell? At night I mean, when it's lit up.' He shouldn't have mentioned the cell. That was clumsy.

Father pulled his coat tighter. 'It's not working, not manned as far as I know. It was hit in the fight for the island. Something else we broke. One more thing to fix.'

Bourbon County, Kentucky – July, 1865

'Don't scrub the flavor outta dat.'

'No, ma'am. I can leave the Kentucky dirt on it if that's the way you like your potatoes?'

'It'll all boil off. Won't hurt if Kentucky salts the pan.'

Clara smiled and worked the butter into the flour. Mitilde and Mason had been sparring ever since he'd arrived. The kitchen wasn't really big enough for the three of them. Clara wasn't the problem: Mitilde and the big Indian – that Shire said he was, in part – had commandeered the elbow room. If truth be told, they seemed to like leaning into each other; it allowed Mitilde to nudge him to reinforce any 'advice' she felt he deserved. Cele arrived from nowhere, rounded the table at pace and used Clara's dress to turn the corner then head out. That child was growing so fast you could make a reasoned case that she was taller when she left the room than when she came in.

It was a warm day, but the breeze blew through the kitchen almost as quickly as Cele did. The slow rhythm of a heavy hammer started up from the middle distance. Clara needed milk so she headed out to find Orville, who'd taken that on. She found him in the dark shade of the barn, seated on the stool and going at it so carefully that the donating udder might still be filling up. She encouraged Orville to greater efforts, but the milk was more than a few minutes away, so she came outside and shaded her eyes. She followed the knock of the hammer to where Shire and Tuck were looking to hang the crossbar gate they'd built together in the week. Rather than take the long curve of the dusty drive, she walked through the meadow grass, careless of launching any number of sparrow-sized butterflies. Shire was holding the high gatepost steady in a worked hole. Tuck was ready to swing the sledge. They hadn't seen her.

'How about you hold and I'll swing,' said Shire.

'It's my gate, ain't it?'

'And my head.'

'I'd like to think if anyone would trust my aim, it might be you.'

'It's not your aim that worries me. It's your balance.'

'Let me get set again.' Tuck angled his pegleg so it was well anchored on Kentucky and wound up into a wide swing, landing solid and straight on the gatepost.

Two more swings had it secure enough that Shire could step away. 'Do we have to do this today?'

'Well, tomorrow doesn't work so good for you, does it? And that would mean I'd have to press Orville into service.'

'He helped build the farm, didn't he?'

'He did, he did. Not such a hopeless cousin after all.' Tuck put down the sledge and finally spotted Clara. 'Hey, we've drawn an audience. I 'spect this young lady has brought us some lemonade.'

'No lemonade. I just came to see how you're getting on.'

'Don't fret. I'll have him back to you before lunch. He's all yours after that.'

Tuck was a wonder. It had been the end of January before Shire was able to travel and they could come north to Tuck's home in Bourbon County and find him. Shire's head had taken longer to heal than Tuck's stump, if either could ever be called healed. Tuck had written a letter from a hospital in

Nashville and told Clara he was heading back to Kentucky. There was nowhere else for him to go and no longer anywhere else he wanted to be. Even in that letter Tuck joked about his pegleg, writing that the surgeon had asked if he wouldn't mind having the good leg taken up so they could save on the wood. He hoped to find Moses and Mitilde at his farm, he told her. When at Eversholt he'd given Moses directions and a note to Orville telling him to take them in should they ever have to cut out of Tennessee, with or without Clara. The squad had brought him Shire's pack, he wrote, and he planned to take it home with him. He ended by telling her he felt lost without Shire. Clara had written to tell him Shire was alive and with her. She'd written to the 125th as well, but evidently the first letter went astray as, when they arrived on the farm, having led Old George from the station in Millersburg with Shire and Old George about even in the baggage stakes, Tuck had dropped an empty pail and then fallen flat in the dirt when he tried to sprint at Shire.

The boys wanted to get on with digging out the hole for a second gatepost so she planted a kiss on Shire's warm forehead. Before heading back to the farmhouse, she walked in under the edge of the forest to collect violets and anemones that grew under the hickories and the dogwoods, mindful of the lone white slatted beehive that Tuck had built there. Unaccountably, he claimed that the war had left him with a taste for honey. At least there *was* a farmhouse now, central in a gently domed and wide green pasture which was surrounded by the forest. When they'd arrived, Moses, Mitilde and Cele were living out of Clara's wagon with Orville and Tuck in the barn. Resurrecting that barn was as far as Orville had managed to get in the two years Tuck was away fighting. Tuck often berated him for not building a home first, but Orville had said that with no help on hand he preferred to make his mistakes on the barn. Shire and Clara had moved in alongside them and there had been nights when Clara lay awake fearing for the structure. When the harder storms threatened, they would push the wagon into the barn too, Moses once saying aside to her he'd feel safer outside under canvas than with Orville's swaying roof above. They'd survived. Shire had come on more quickly than he had back in Tennessee. And that was down to Tuck.

She took her time back through the meadow. It was a fine new farm they had built. Tuck didn't like to hear it called a rebuild, never having intended to settle here again after his parents' murder. 'It's a new build,' he'd said. He'd taken her to their grave not long after she'd arrived, told her how they were burned with the original farm for having the affrontery to set Adam free, their only slave. It was a hard story to hear and must have been harder to tell. Adam had plain disappeared not long after Tuck had left for the army. When she and Tuck had come away from the churchyard, for once Tuck had needed her steadying hand. He said he'd get them a better stone in time.

With the six of them – seven if you counted Cele – they made a better job of the house. Tuck had complicated things by insisting they build directly *across* the old base. He didn't want it orientated north to south, he said. East to west would encourage a healthier state of mind. No matter that it meant demolishing the in situ old chimney stack only to build it up again brick by brick. It mattered to him, so everyone got on with it and quietly made sure the blackened ends of the bricks were hidden. It was solid looking, the weatherboards yet to be painted. Tuck had stained them dark brown with some oily resin and a steep gray-tiled roof sat above. It was almost churchlike. They'd only moved in a few weeks ago. It was on the small side for them all, so Tuck and Shire were in the habit of taking to the wagon now it was summer. They seemed to have a lot to talk about.

She doubted she would ever return to Tennessee. Home had never truly taken root there. December and January were hard months at Eversholt with Shire slowly returning to himself a day at a time. There was still some of him to get back. She worried she'd never be able to convince him that he was hers by choice, realizing as she had that was the only way things could have gone, regardless of Tod's end. She would have to show him.

It was a hard day back at Eversholt when she decided to tell him Tod was dead. That had set him back. He'd almost stopped speaking altogether. He'd take that stick and himself over into the barn to sit with Old George and she'd have to go and fetch him in when the light got low. Most times he'd not hear her come in so lost was he in the shapes and shadows of the wood, like they might explain the whole war to him.

Raht had sold her land at Comrie for a poor price but it was something. As soon as peace broke out, he'd taken himself back to Ducktown to open up the mines again as quickly as he could, no doubt anxious to bring out all the hidden copper that Tod hadn't been able to carry away. Distant though he was, she'd asked him if he would sell the farm at Spring Hill for her and had given him Moscow Carter's name as someone who might help find a buyer. She'd no doubt that there *would* be buyers. That war had a way of moving people on. Hardly anybody was where they'd begun. Except Tuck. And he was at right-angles.

Orville and his broad grin came out of the barn as she was going in. He presented her with a half-full pail to carry along with her flowers. More than enough. He followed her inside and they caught the end of Mitilde's latest advice to Mason, who'd failed to wring out the washcloth to the last drop. Clara smiled. It probably made a pleasant change for Mitilde from putting Moses right, and Moses might be feeling the benefit as well. It was crowded but Clara called in Cele, stood her on a kitchen chair and got her to beat in the fresh milk, careless of the mess and enjoying the laughter.

*

Shire played second fiddle while Tuck fitted the hinges, then was sent to fetch Mason and Cleves to help mount the gate. As they all lifted, Mason giving the orders from long habit, Shire reflected it was the four of them who'd been together in Camp Cleveland when they were mustered into the 125th. Corry couldn't make it. He'd written that there was too much to do on his father's farm outside of Orwell.

Ocks was up in Warren, Ohio, where Colonel Opdycke had threatened to leave him in charge of a dry-goods store he'd established, Opdycke still for the most part away with the army. Cleves was on furlough, but wore a clean blue uniform courtesy of his new brigade, a corporal stripe on the arm. When Cleves arrived yesterday, Mason had said, 'I guess I don't outrank you anymore.' Cleves had smiled like a drunkard who'd found a lost dollar. It was good of them both to come.

After the gate was hung and tested – at least once by everyone present – they took the arc of the drive back toward the farm but diverted to the small spring house, a survivor of the fire. These days it had an additional essential purpose. Inside Moses tended to his still. As they all looked on, some through the open door, he drew what he claimed was the very first glass and passed it to Tuck. From the overacted enthusiasm with which both Tuck and Moses greeted their sips, Shire thought it unlikely to be the first sample for either of them, but he played along. It was better than army whiskey for sure.

'Now I can collect my whiskey with my water,' said Tuck, finishing the glass after it had done the round. 'Not too much for Shire, now.'

Mason ignored Tuck's advice and suggested a second round in honor of Layman, Tom Muncie and Hubbard.

Shire had considered whether Tuck's near constant bonhomie was feigned, and perhaps it was once in a while. It had to be a strange form of grief that came with the loss of a leg, but he'd been told by his good friend that he'd somehow gained, or at least rescued, more than most out of Franklin. One night, laid in the wagon with the canvas off and the universe above, he'd thanked Shire for not letting him desert from Nashville. 'I took Ma and Pa with me into my last fight,' he said. 'Sorry slaughter as it was, it was the full-stop to my war. If I'd run away, if I'd not been there, in my heart I might yet be fighting.'

Shire thought he understood what Tuck meant. It was an odd sort of peace to find, but everybody had to discover their own. He was still fighting to come to terms with his. Some nights he couldn't sleep for fear he'd wake up in the ditch, that he'd be passed over, soil shoveled on above to finally snuff out the last air, and he'd be quietly forgotten under the blood-soaked fields of Franklin like so many others. His memory of the walk to Clara's house was lost to him for a long time. To begin with, he couldn't talk to Clara concerning anything other than the day they were sharing. Slowly the memories returned, as if he were walking in reverse from her home, over the hills, back through the ravaged Rebel army and then to the ditch. When, sometime after Christmas, he'd spilled the full horror to Clara, he'd broken down and wept while she held him. They'd kept the lamp burning brightly the whole night. He worried she might never see him as a man after that, but that didn't seem the way of it.

Before Christmas, they'd watched for days from the bedroom window as Hood's Army of the Tennessee, utterly defeated after a further battle outside Nashville, trudged back down the Columbia Pike, piecemeal and dejected in the bitter cold and snow. At any time, a lone soldier or a company might have diverted down the drive in search of food. As it was, Clara used up her chickens one after another to give Shire some strength, dispatching them herself as if she were doing no more than twisting open a stiff jar. She'd excused the indulgence by saying she feared she'd lose them anyway. Shire kept on his Rebel jacket, though it was doubtful that would have saved him. The wound on his head was fresh back then, but scarred over now. Another for his collection. The last.

After the shambolic Rebel retreat down the pike, there followed a more purposeful rearguard then, at last, the gray cavalry turned to blue cavalry and Shire was in the Union again. Clara burned the jacket in the grate and buried the Confederate canteen. He couldn't recall when in the run of things Clara had told him Tod was dead. Though he was sure it was before they'd first made love. That hadn't been how he'd imagined it at all. The letter arrived from Tuck and that was a great happiness, but it had only been then that he'd truly felt the loss of Tod, as if he'd held off the pain until there was some joy to set against it. Somewhere in that bleakest of Januarys, amid the hurt and the hope and the night-fears, he came to understand that he really was loved, that Clara wanted him as much as he had always wanted her. And that changed everything. His strength returned. They made their plans. The trains were running again and they wasted no time. They booked Old George passage with them and didn't look back once as they led him down the drive. They walked to Thompson's Station, preferring the longer journey north than the shorter one south to Spring Hill.

It was wonderful when they all came together, no one with any plans beyond building the farm. The war played itself to an end, east and west. He missed sharing a bed with Clara though, and it was hard to find time alone, though not impossible.

Leaving the spring house, Shire discovered he needed a short while to process the whiskey before he ventured too near to Clara, so walked the squad and Moses around to the back of the farmhouse. The wagon canvas, and a second cleaner one from the new wagon that Clara had bought from her Comrie monies, had both been stretched over high wooden poles to provide a long, shaded area below which were two trestle tables, wiped clean but yet to be set. The poles were looped with ribbon like long candy sticks and there was a posy in the middle of each trestle. Shire smiled to think what Father would have made of this.

Two weeks ago, when Clara had travelled with Raht to New York to settle things with the Duke and Duchess, Shire had taken the train up alone to Medina to pull his sign-up money from the Phoenix Bank. A hundred and fifty dollars wasn't much to add to what Clara had, but it was something, and the army owed him some backpay. He'd looked up Dan who he'd sailed with from England. As luck would have it, Dan was at his parent's home, laid off from buying arms with the war over. Dan's mother had found the clothes Shire left there before he signed up, which were now a loose fit around the waist but tight across the shoulders. After a long night of drinking, Shire wasn't nearly done with his tales. So when Dan pointed to the paper and said that Shire's long-standing colonel and hero soldier Emerson Opdycke was home on leave of absence from the Fourth Corps, Dan travelled with Shire the extra distance over to Warren, Ohio, on the chance that Shire might get to shake Opdycke's hand and prove to him that once again his Englishman had returned from the dead. This last time that was truer than ever. He got his wish. Opdycke – promoted to a breveted major general of volunteers for his service at Franklin – exhibited Shire to his wife Lucy and young son, Tine. They got to visit Ocks too, quite a sight in his store clothes. Opdycke couldn't accept the wedding invite; he was ordered to return to duty in New Orleans, but congratulated Shire on his well-deserved good fortune. 'A private and a duchess,' he said. 'Only in America.'

Where *was* Dan? He was cutting it fine.

The others, all except Moses, had gone inside. 'Now aren't you glad you followed my advice?'

'Which advice is that? You dispense so much, I lose track.'

Moses didn't rise to it. 'To wait. To find the right time.'

'I think the right time found me,' said Shire.

'Still, it was you who proposed. A man should be allowed to get that right.'

Shire kept quiet. In point of fact, it was Tuck who'd proposed. He'd been stone cold sober as far as Shire could tell, but had gone down on the knee of his pegleg and asked them both 'for the love of God to get married.'

*

Soon after lunch, Cele called Clara outside and pointed at two men walking up the drive. One was dressed in a checked suit, carried a travelling valise and looked as if he had something to sell. The second, Clara recognized as Ocks. He appeared ill at ease in a tight jacket and what might be a new hat. He had a knapsack over his shoulder and a tied paper package under his arm. While Shire strode out to them, she waited in the dirt yard, considering that this house badly needed a porch if people were to be greeted properly.

Shire led them to her and introduced Dan.

'Well,' Dan said, 'now I can see why nothing as trivial as a great and fearful war could dissuade you.'

There was no need to introduce Ocks. He removed his hat and said, 'Miss Ridgmont,' as if he had once shoed a lame horse for her rather than saved her life. She embraced him and enjoyed his obvious embarrassment.

'You told me you wouldn't be able to make it,' Shire said to Ocks.

'Once Opdycke had gone back to the army in New Orleans, his wife, Lucy, insisted I take a furlough. She sends congratulations. I caught up to Dan on the walk from Millersburg, taught him how to stretch his stride once we worked out we were headed to the same place.'

'It's not a furlough outside the army, Sergeant,' said Tuck, who'd come out of the house on his crutch, Mason and Cleves trailing on. 'Least ways, I don't think it is.'

'My, my,' said Ocks. 'Almost the whole squad. I should ask you to shoulder arms.'

Tuck insisted the new arrivals should visit Moses in the spring house. Clara followed Mason back to the kitchen but was turned around by Mitilde, who said a bride wasn't allowed chores on her wedding day and that she wished Hany was here to help Clara into her dress. It was sad to hear Hany's name though she was pleased to have her inserted into the day. It was too early to get ready for the ceremony. Clara was at a loss until Ocks came out of the spring house ahead of the others, brighter-eyed than he went in. She walked him to the back garden so they could enjoy the shade under the wedding awning and apologized for not having a room for him.

'Not so many rooms as at Ridgmont,' he said, 'but I'm used to sleeping under the stars.'

It was direct of him to bring up Ridgmont. They'd barely begun to talk. She was off-guard and found herself recounting how she'd met up with her parents in New York, how she'd told them plainly that Ocks and Shire had saved her after they'd come to America.

'And Tuck,' Ocks said. 'You can't forget Tuck.'

'They don't know Tuck.'

'I guess not. How is he?'

'Better than he has a right to be. He's found his way to home, so perhaps he's doing better than most of us. Mitilde and Moses are going to stay on with Cele.'

'That's good. If he can make the women laugh as well as he does the men, he'll not be alone for long, even without the leg. There's a dearth of husbands just now.'

'What about you? A dry-goods store, I hear.'

Ocks smiled wryly. 'It doesn't sound like the place for me is what you mean.'

It was exactly what she meant.

'It'll do,' Ocks said. 'While I make up my mind.'

There was no need for a prompt. Ocks went on in time. 'There's the west, of course. Everybody's heading west. Cheap land. Or back to the army. It's busy shrinking. I could find a place right enough, but this old sergeant has got to stop fighting sometime.'

'You have thoughts of England,' she guessed.

'It's the strangest things you miss. A certain sea-scent in the air, even in Bedfordshire. A wren that lived in a hedgerow outside my door keeps coming to mind. Proper gravy. None of them a winning reason to make you sail back, but they pile up.'

'I could write a letter of recommendation for you. My name might yet count for something over there.'

'If it's your name I'm after using, we'd best be quick. You'll be a Stanton by supper time.'

She smiled at the thought.

'I'll see my way in time,' Ocks said. 'What's the rush? Anyway, we shouldn't talk of me when it's your wedding day.'

'I don't mind.' It felt right to talk about England. 'I'm very glad you've come.'

Despite everything that had happened in America, England had no such pull for her. Maybe for a moment at Spring Hill when she'd thought Shire was dead. And that was more of a push than a pull. She'd made her feelings clear to her parents. It didn't stop them begging her to return with them, even after she told them she was going to marry Shire; as if that was some passing fancy. Raht, there in case of paperwork and not for the family talk, had given them some space. At least her parents had come at last. For her, not for business or for themselves, but for *her*. She was surprised how much that mattered. There were hints of suitors, 'even though you're a widow.' She'd stopped them before they mentioned any names. The war was over. She'd lost a great deal, people, places, wealth, as so many had, but it was a clean slate now. A chance to see America at peace. It had been a harder goodbye for them than for her. They might have waved from the ship-rails, but she'd already turned from the Atlantic and gone to find Raht so she could start back to Shire.

It was a shame Raht couldn't make the wedding. He would have been the only person from her first false ceremony. She would have liked him to witness it put right. He'd apologized on the way back from seeing her parents, said there was too much to do at the mines. At least she knew he'd be happy at that. He'd been generous in taking the time to come all the way to New York.

Out across the fields she could see Tuck leading the squad in the shadow of the forest, putting Shire's walking stick to use. Dan looked out of place at the rear, still carrying his valise.

'That's an untidy column,' said Ocks, 'If you'll excuse me, I'll go and set them straight.'

With Mason out in the fields as well, Clara found she was tolerated back in the kitchen. The oven was being worked hard and it was hot despite the open windows. Mitilde said she had time to help Clara dress, if she'd like? It was only a Sunday dress Clara had found in Millersburg, but she wasn't going to deny Mitilde, not on their last day together. The dress was on in no time. Clara sat and looked out of the window so she could catch sight of Shire and his friends. Mitilde gently brushed out her hair, as if performing the last rites. 'He's happy here,' she said.

'He's marrying today. It would be a sad thing for me if he wasn't happy.'

'Tuck's here. Moses is here. It's a home.'

'It's Tuck's home and your home. It's not ours.'

'You certain he wants to go?' There had been talks like this all month, ever since Shire and Clara had announced they would leave after the wedding. 'Why d'you wanna go out into the wilds a'gin. You don't even know where you're goin'.'

Clara stood and hugged Mitilde, leaning her head into the wide warmth even though it untidied her hair. It didn't stop Mitilde laying every reason she had down on the table. 'Cele's warmed to you now, and Moses is an old man. What'll happen to the child when we're gone, heaven only knows. There's plenty of land near enough. You got the dollars. I know you have.'

'I'll write. And perhaps we'll be back. Maybe Kentucky is the best place on God's green earth. I just need to go and see. What about you?'

'What about me?'

'You can choose where you want to be.'

'Hah! We ain't used to choosin'. And we're too old to work our way.'

'But you're happy here, aren't you?'

'I would be if you were stayin'. I know, I know. You gotta go see… I don't think on happy too much. I got a whole collection of happy memories dotted through a life grounded in misery. D'you know what that's like?'

Clara didn't, but tried to imagine waking up for a whole lifetime in bondage. How that must color every thought, every action.

'Sometimes,' said Mitilde, 'I think if I gave up on those memories, I'd have to forget myself altogether. Best to gather my joy each day, in Cele and in Moses and in you. I don't need to go anywhere to do that.'

All of these debates had ended in tears and it was no different today. Clara was more than grateful that Tuck had given them a new home and they would support him and Orville on the farm. That might be enough for Mitilde and Moses, and everyone would look after Cele, try to ease the cruel hurt done to her. But not Clara. She would be gone.

She'd consider herself Cele's guardian, whatever happened. It was impossible to make Mitilde understand why she and Shire needed to leave. Or at least why she did. She wasn't sure she could explain it to herself. Why *not* knowing where they might go, or when they might settle, why that was where the joy was, so long as she was with Shire.

*

Ocks surprised Shire with the package barely an hour before the ceremony, and in front of the squad too. Even if only Ocks hadn't been there, it would have been hard to decline the honor. 'It was Opdycke's idea,' Ocks said. 'Really it was. He was going to send it. I knew your size or thereabouts. He had his quartermaster make it up and get it to Warren and, well, it was another reason for me to come.'

The string and paper held a full Union uniform. Deep blue pants and jacket; braces and a fine linen shirt; a smart new kepi with the cap badge of the old 21st Corps they'd fought under at Chickamauga, and where the 125th became the Tigers. Shire's first thought was that the last time he'd worn Union blue he'd been buried in the ditch at Franklin. From the quiet surprise in the group, he wasn't sure he'd hidden either the shock or the painful memory.

Ocks encouraged him to put it on. 'Opdycke told me to say that if you were still in the army, there'd have been a stripe included. No one deserves one more, he said.'

Shire wondered how Clara might feel about the uniform. He wasn't a soldier anymore. He had a new life. But as he threw the braces over his shoulders and slipped into the jacket, there were better thoughts. He was proud of the 125th; his friends were proud too. It was in a Union uniform that he'd

418

fought up and down America to find Clara again and again. Why not wear one to marry her? He walked into her room where she was letting Cele have a turn at her with the hairbrush. Clara said, 'There's my soldier,' which sounded condescending, but it came with a kiss so Shire felt he'd come out ahead.

The pastor arrived in an open trap behind a sweaty horse. Before so much as stepping down he said he had to be at a service back in Millersburg that evening, so if it was alright with everyone, could they get started? Shire marched him around the back and stood waiting with him in front of the rose arch. Moses had built and tended it from the first hint of spring. The yellow roses weren't quite across the arc, but it was pretty all the same. Once everyone assembled, Tuck struck up his slow waltz and Moses, father for the day, brought Clara from the house, Cele carrying a scaled-down posy behind. The walk was at odds with the waltz, but the tune was tender enough to alarm Shire to the fact that he was about to marry the love of his life, and that he might embarrass himself if he wasn't careful. He pretended he was on parade; squared his shoulders and lifted his head. It might have looked a little odd, but then Clara was so beautiful that no one would be looking at him.

The pastor was as good as his word and skedaddled as soon as the newlyweds' lips parted. Mitilde wasted no time, borrowing Mason to help bring out dish after dish. Tuck had hidden some wine in the spring house that was cool enough to make a toast; after that, Moses' whiskey replaced it as the drink of choice. Dan had brought some brandy along.

Shire, washed through with elation, sat hand in hand with Clara. Cele was before them carrying a square package. She thrust it at them with straight arms then ran away. Mitilde and

Moses stopped dancing to look over. Lost in his melody, Tuck played on. Clara let Shire unwrap it. Inside was a plain square frame around the chalk sign from Spring Hill, the faint edges of letters scrubbed over any number of times, but with Eversholt painted in white block capitals.

'I varnished it over,' said Moses. 'Figured you could hang it where you pitch.'

Clara cried and hugged him, eventually stepping back so Shire could shake his hand.

The bounty of food didn't appear to weigh on the dancers and, as the sun set, Tuck was still alternately slowing them down and speeding them up again. Mitilde was in the thick of it. Shire tried to remind anyone who'd listen, which was no one at all, that he and Clara were supposed to be leaving. Tuck begged a rest for his bow arm. Shire brought him over some water and sat next to him. A bat flitted in above them, about-turned and darted away. The scent of the summer grass began to win out over the food.

'I got to get so I can fiddle standing up,' Tuck said. 'Trouble is, I try to tap with my lost foot and it throws off my rhythm. Have you decided where you're headed yet?'

'Indiana, perhaps. Then maybe Illinois. I don't know. I got my map out yesterday, but Clara took it from me and folded it away again. I met a lot of good soldiers from Illinois though.'

'If that's how you're steering, you'd have to go to every state.'

'Clara would like that.'

'You sure you're right for it?'

'How do you mean?'

'After Franklin.' Tuck put down his water and turned to look at Shire. 'Clara told me how you was buried. I can't begin to imagine.'

He'd wanted to tell Tuck, but never had. Telling Clara had been hard enough. He was surprised she'd shared it. 'Don't try.'

'It's restful here. Clara says I have to build a porch. And I could use a smokehouse.'

'It's not me who's set on roaming. I'm just set on Clara.'

'Fair enough. You didn't answer though, about the ditch.'

Shire thought back to the lost boys in the hospitals at Nashville. He was better off than they were. And to Corporal Cobb, who often visited him in raw detail, bleeding out on the Carter's porch rather than living out the war as a hospital orderly but for Shire's persuasion. How could he square his hand in such things? He didn't want to go back to the ditch, not today, but tomorrow it would be too late. 'I can't undo it. And I can't replace the memory of it any more than you can your leg.' He reached to the end of the table, where Tuck had placed the walking stick that Waddell had fashioned. 'Will you keep this?'

'It was crafted for you, weren't it?'

'You've more need of it. You got up some speed using it in the field today. Almost the double-quick.' The cicadas were loud now the fiddle had stopped. 'Have you looked at it?'

'I have. Work of art is what it is. Don't go giving that away.'

'See here, these four soldiers around the stem, each one more ragged than the one before, the last one has no shoes at all, just bare feet stood on a mess of bones and skulls, and Franklin carved there along with battles we'd already fought, like he knew. Waddell *knew* what was waiting for me at Franklin.'

'Could be. People peek ahead in their dreams. What of it? You lived through it, didn't you? Lived to see this day.' He put a hand on Shire's shoulder.

'I have.' Shire turned the wood over in his hands. 'Sometimes I look at it and think how the war has whittled and carved me from who I was, how it's made us all into different people.'

'Life'll do that to you, war or no war. Besides, the fighting's over now. We don't need to be those people anymore.'

Shire wasn't sure it was that simple. He held out the stick to Tuck. 'I don't want it to come with me, but I can't let it go altogether.'

'Alright then, I'll mind your foreboding stick for you, but only 'til I grow back whole.'

Shire smiled and shook his head. 'I'm sorry. You got the worst of it.'

'You think?'

'How do you square it then, losing your leg?'

'Like I traded it for the Union and freedom, and that I got a good deal. You know me. I *always* get a good deal.'

Shire went to find Clara and at last they began their goodbyes. Their new wagon, which they'd been loading for weeks, was brought out from the barn. The canvas, having served its purpose for the wedding, was taken down by the drunken crowd and then drawn over the bows and tied. Moses put the two horses into the traces. The farewells took forever and more or less everyone told them to wait until morning. Shire looked at Clara to silently ask the question and she silently delivered the answer. They would leave now. The last embraces were made, they climbed aboard and moved off around the arc of the drive into the near-darkness. Behind them the cheers of the small throng died away and by the time they reached the gate they heard Tuck's distant fiddle strike up again, perhaps a shade more melancholy.

'Here will do,' said Clara.

'What?'

'I just wanted to make a start.'

'It's not much of a start, is it?'

Shire pulled the wagon over inside the gate so they hadn't even left the farm. He thought about staking the horses out, but they were so close that he reasoned he might as well lead them back to the barn. Everyone had returned behind the house so nobody saw him. When he returned to the wagon, Clara had unloaded a number of crates onto the grass. He asked, wouldn't it be easier if they slept under the stars as they'd done before.

'It's my wedding night,' Clara said. 'I'd rather the universe wasn't looking on.'

At first light they loaded the wagon again and Shire walked to the barn once more for the horses, stopping in the vegetable patch on the way for a carrot. He fed it to Old George, kissed him on the nose then led the other two horses away. Once they were in their traces again, Clara unlatched the gate and it swung slowly open, perfectly balanced. Shire drove on through. While Clara closed it, he took the Eversholt frame and, using the string from the package, tied it to the front bow of the wagon so it would be above and behind them as they travelled.

Clara climbed up, sat beside him on the sprung bench and took his hand. 'You would tell me, wouldn't you, Shire, if we were doing the wrong thing, leaving our friends behind, only for me?'

'Do you think I have the wherewithal to know what the right thing looks like?'

'Yes. I do.'

'Alright,' he said, taken aback. 'Then this feels like the right thing. Only I truly have no idea where you want to go.' He kissed her and handed over the reins, and they started away toward the velvet remains of the night.

Historical Note

When I was at school in Wales in the seventies and early eighties, it seemed to me that history was set in stone, a series of dates, facts and narratives that you could rely on, perhaps with the odd mystery or piece of intrigue thrown in. How naive I was to see it that way. In the thirty years or so that the American Civil War has held my interest, and indeed well before then, its particular history has been reinterpreted, revised and rediscovered. And almost constantly since the war's end, its 'story' has been spun to suit the political or cultural climate of a given decade including our current one.

I do little original research for my books. Rather I rely on accounts from the time, the official army histories, academic articles and respected historical works. The joy is weaving and inventing a narrative based on the historical accounts as they are presented. I try to remain faithful to generally accepted events, though key players and their motivations, are often in dispute. Historians love a good argument. It's clear to me now that history is not as reliable as I once imagined. Rather it is the ever-changing product of a long running and, for the most part, affable quarrel. Below I'll try to make clear what are my inventions, as well as my slant on a few of the arguments that may always remain opinions rather than facts.

My narrative backbone remains the 125th Ohio, Opdycke's Tigers. Where they go, I go. In fact, the trilogy began life as just one novel until, standing in the Carter House cellar come dining room for the first time, I understood how the Tigers' story circled back to this farm and to Franklin over two years of war. How the regiments natural story arc ended here.

Accounts from those in the regiment have found their way into all three books. Ralsa C. Rice's memoirs, *Yankee Tigers*, are particularly important for *Tigers in Blue*. Rice was a lieutenant leading Company B at this time. Later in the war he rose to the rank of captain. Hunting the spider's web was based on one of his encounters, although his version didn't result in the demise of the sharpshooter. It seemed slightly implausible, but I found many articles of the use of spider threads in sights and optical equipment, albeit later in the century, so I took Rice at his word. The squad getting lost during the retreat from Columbia, their encounter with the locals and crossing the pontoon on the Duck River, are all based on accounts from Rice, as is his march into Spring Hill with Opdycke and Wagner.

Rice also headed a mission to Nashville to recover 'lost' members of the brigade from the hospitals. It led me to read more around wartime Nashville. I became fascinated with this netherworld of the war, where so many soldiers had been laid low or forgotten. I tried to use the edgy mood of the city to further undermine Tuck's state of mind. Truesdail was the army officer in charge of policing the city. The raid on the mail train is also recounted by Rice, though Bowman, who survived *The Copper Road*, is fictitious.

Hood's army crossing the Tennessee River at Florence on a lightweight pontoon bridge is something I still find incredible. The river has been dammed in many places since, but at Florence it's only moderately wider than it was. You can still see the stone piers (all that survived the burning of the railway bridge) which Hood's engineers used to tether the pontoon to.

Hood's character and skill as a general is one of the more hotly contested points of the campaign. He had a very aggressive and successful war record before being given the Army of the Tennessee, and he certainly remained aggressive. If he had taken the Columbia Pike at Spring Hill, he would likely have captured or destroyed most of Schofield's army. Historians remain incredulous that Schofield escaped: in large part that was down to his brave decision to keep his army moving, but messy communications between Hood and his generals, as well as his absence from the field (which may have been due to his infirmities) was probably decisive. The rolling ground, the tiredness of the Confederate troops and even the wind direction, all played a part in what presented as a miracle to the Union. Hood's decision to throw the best units of his army against the strong positions of Franklin is less contested. It was reckless. But for Wagner's blunder, the results could have been even worse. As it was, it crippled his army which limped on to crumble outside Nashville. The only possible mitigation is the state of the war. The Confederacy had very few dice left to roll, certainly in the West. Hood knew if Schofield reached Nashville, the campaign was over.

Opdycke really did have a very high opinion of himself, but he was also an excellent regimental and brigade commander. He *was* pressed into engineering work at Pulaski and his host Mr Gordon did discuss post war options with him. He was not, as far as I know, at the key meeting in Spring Hill where Schofield decided to keep the army moving through the night, though his brigade did lead the column into Spring Hill and he skillfully managed the rearguard all the way to Franklin. The very public argument with Wagner is contested and relies mostly on post war accounts. What is certain is that it was a huge blunder by Wagner to leave his two brigades exposed and for so long. It almost led to disaster for the Union. In mitigation for Wagner, there were conflicting orders and the command structure didn't help. Schofield was in charge of the army but Cox in charge of the defenses as well as the 23rd Corps. Stanley, the 4th Corps commander, also had a hand in events. Any of these senior commanders could have insisted that Wagner pull his men back behind the lines, but failed to do so. Soon after the battle Wagner resigned his commission, citing his wife's poor health. Outside of Franklin he had an excellent war record. That Opdycke's brigade played a key role in restoring the line isn't in dispute, though to what extent he was in control of his brigade is up for debate. Either way, the fact he had developed such a strong and motivated brigade played a big part in saving the day and, despite the battle to come at Nashville, effectively ended any chances of success for Hood. Opdycke died tragically in New York City as the result of a gun accident in 1884.

The attack late in the day at Franklin, against largely veteran Union troops in a strong position, led to some of the bloodiest hours of the entire civil war. Possibly the fact that the Union retreated from Franklin, or that the Confederates still stumbled on to ultimately be turned around at Nashville, had, until more recently, led to the battles of Spring Hill and Franklin being underplayed in terms of their key roles in deciding the war in the West. Robert Hick's novel, *The Widow of the South*, and the determination of the Battle of Franklin Trust (BOFT) to reclaim parts of the battlefield and to put historical fact ahead of historical myth, have both illuminated and elevated the events of the 29th and 30th November 1864. Franklin is a wonderful place to visit, with the Carter House itself beautifully preserved as the epicenter of the battle. The

BOFT website at https://boft.org/ has a wealth of information.

George Trenholm was pardoned and released in October 1865. He fought a series of legal challenges against his businesses, many from the United States Government, and several of his ventures went under, but in general he re-established something of a commercial empire as well as entering the South Carolina legislature in 1874. He gained a reputation as a philanthropist. He died in 1876. Frank Trenholm actually married on June 1st 1865, not long after turning eighteen, to Mary Elizabeth Burroughs, but having no further details on this young romance I didn't include it. Frank died in Washington in 1885.

Moscow Carter remarried, twice more in fact, and was eventually the father to eleven children. Post war, Fountain Carter successfully extracted compensation from the United States Government for the damage done to his farm during the battle by preserving the evidence. Much of it can still be viewed today. Moscow often gave tours to visitors wanting to know about the battle, but he was scathing about war. 'Keep out! Keep out!' he wrote to his son Frank. 'Have nothing to do with war.' Moscow lived until 1913.

General Gist was eventually taken home to his wife. Janie Gist, his young widow, arranged for him to be disinterred and brought back to South Carolina in the spring of 1866. He was reburied at Trinity Episcopal Church in Columbia as Federal troops kept watch on the attending crowd.

Tod Carter's character is where I think I should hold up my hand and say that the character as portrayed by me is not a close fit for how he is perceived by those working at the BOFT. Newspaper articles, written by Tod from the field under his nom de plume of Mint Julep, are still being discovered as historical newspapers are digitized and made available. In fact, an article detailing his escape from captivity in February 1864 and his route back to the army, were only found by Kristi Farrow in, I believe, early 2020, well after I had imagined his probable route based on the lesser details available when I wrote *The Copper Road*. He did escape while being transferred between prisons by train as the family history had long said, but in Massillon, Ohio rather than in Pennsylvania. He travelled first to Pittsburgh and then overland as far as Cincinnati before boarding a boat for Memphis down the Ohio and the Mississippi Rivers, and then overland down into Mississippi. I'm pretty pleased with my guessed route; maybe six or seven out of ten for me. His relationship with Clara was entirely fictitious as, of course, is she. His newspaper articles present him as far more bullish about the war, somewhat fond of himself, and seemingly still gung-ho just months before Franklin. My Tod was more reserved, I think. I find it impossible to imagine anyone who experienced long years in that brutal war, not being changed, or having to ask themselves fundamental questions about the rights and wrongs of it all. I wanted to imagine how Tod would have felt as the armies inexorably approached Franklin. His pass to 'visit' home is real, although it read 'The.' rather than 'Theodrick'. It's not clear how close he got, though it's thought he spent the night at the Neely House just a couple of miles away. How he was feeling on that last afternoon right up to the moment he charged forward on Rosencrantz toward his home, is all conjecture.

The idea and power of 'home' was a recurring theme in the book. There were many far less noble causes for the Civil War than fighting for your home, but it was perhaps the most common motivation for the rank and file soldiers and is the same in wars still being fought as I'm writing this. America was already a country expanding westward at a rate of knots. The war caused a further enormous upheaval and displacement. I hope I have shown that none of the characters, real or fictional, were untouched by the war. They all carried their wounds whether psychological or physical, but I was glad to have Tuck to find a way home, for Clara to find the freedom to go and search for one, and for Shire to find his home in her.

Richard Buxton

Acknowledgements

Several sources used to support the historical context for *Tigers in Blue* are common across the entire Shire's Union trilogy. The letters of Emerson Opdycke, collected together by Glenn V. Longacre and John E. Haas in *The Battle for God and the Right,* is a wonderful resource, his letters written within a few days of the events, although it pays sometimes to check even Emerson's outspoken opinions against the official army record. The war time memoirs of Company B's Ralsa C. Rice in *Yankee Tigers*, written and serialized much later, were particularly useful for *Tigers in Blue.* Also, the collected letters in *Opdycke's Tigers* by Charles T. Clark and *Yankee Tigers II* edited by Richard A. Baumgartner. Other sources included Ethel T. S. Nepveux's *George A. Trenholm – Financial Genius of the Confederacy* and *Company Aytch* by Sam Watkins.

The principal studies needed specifically for *Tigers in Blue,* especially the battle sequences around Spring Hill and Franklin, were Wiley Sword's *The Confederacy's Last Hurrah* and Eric A. Jacobson's meticulously researched *For Cause & For Country: A Study of the Affair at Spring Hill and the Battle of Franklin.* In fact, I am indebted to many in Eric's team at The Battle of Franklin trust for their help and hospitality, in particular Kristi Farrow and Joseph Ricci for their enlightening tours of the Carter House and the battlefields, and also to Laurie McPeak for directing me to maps and photos of the period and for making me feel so welcome. Stanley F. Horns article "Nashville During the Civil

War." *Tennessee Historical Quarterly* 4, no. 1 (1945): 3-22, was extremely useful in understanding the mood of that city. Special thanks also to Joe Emert, formerly director of the Museum of East Tennessee History, for his repeated hospitality, kindness and infectious enthusiasm.

Thank you to the many other people who have helped or encouraged me. Certainly, my long-time friend and writing colleague, Phil Williams as my one stop copy editor, cover designer and book producer. Immense thanks to my M.A. colleagues Glen Brown and Jacqui Pack for such detailed feedback. They were effectively sub-editors and between them were an enormous influence on the book. Also, thanks to beta readers Bee Mitchell-Turner, Tracy Fells and Wendy Swarbrick for their expert feedback and to Ian Black who reviewed some of the early work. My gratitude to John Brinded for his encouragement and for sketching the rifle stack. As always, huge thanks to Major Jeff Houston for his constant support, for visiting the battlefields with me, and proving that distance is no obstacle to friendship. As always, my final thanks are reserved for Sally for countless coffees and enduring encouragement. I will take you too these places soon.

9 780995 769373